The Cover Girl Killer

Also by Richard A. Lupoff

Edgar Rice Burroughs: Master of Adventure (1965)
*The Case of the Doctor Who Had No Business, or
    The Adventure of the Second Anonymous Narrator* (1966)
One Million Centuries (1967)
Sacred Locomotive Flies (1971)
Into the Aether (1974)
Edgar Rice Burroughs and the Martian Vision (1976)
The Triune Man (1976)
Sandworld (1976)
Lisa Kane (1976)
The Crack in the Sky (1976)
Sword of the Demon (1977)
The Return of Skull-Face (with Robert E. Howard) (1977)
Space War Blues (1978)
Nebogipfel at the End of Time (1979)
The Ova Hamlet Papers (1979)
Stroka Prospekt (1982)
Circumpolar! (1984)
Sun's End (1984)
The Digital Wristwatch of Philip K. Dick (1985)
Lovecraft's Book (1985)
Countersolar! (1986)
Galaxy's End (1988)
The Forever City (1988)
The Black Tower (1988)
The Comic Book Killer (1988)
The Final Battle (1990)
The Classic Car Killer (1992)
Night of the Living Gator (1992)
The Bessie Blue Killer (1994)
Hyperprism (1994)
The Sepia Siren Killer (1994)
The Silver Chariot Killer (forthcoming)
Before 12:01 . . . and After (forthcoming)

RICHARD A. LUPOFF

The Cover Girl Killer

A Hobart Lindsey/Marvia Plum Mystery

ST. MARTIN'S PRESS ⨏ NEW YORK

n, who went to Spain to fight for Democracy,
anish soil;
ff, who went to Spain to fight for Democracy,
Silverstein Blanc, who went to Spain to nurse
those who fought for Democracy,
And returned to tell me their stories.

—RAL

Lyrics on page 55 are from "How Much Is That Doggie In the Window" Words and Music by Bob Merrill. Copyright © 1952 Golden Bell Songs. Copyright renewed 1980. Administered by All Nations Music. International Copyright Secured. All rights reserved. Reprinted by generous permission of the Hal Leonard Publishing Company.

Library of Congress Cataloging-in-Publication Data

Lupoff, Richard A.
    The cover girl killer / Richard A. Lupoff.
        p.   cm.
    ISBN 0-312-13455-X
        1. Lindsey, Hobart (Fictitious character)—Fiction.   2. Plum, Marvia (Fictitious character)—Fiction.   I. Title.
    PS3562.U6C63   1995   95-23245
    813'.54—dc20   CIP

First edition: October 1995

10   9   8   7   6   5   4   3   2   1

Introduction

by Bill Pronzini

RICHARD LUPOFF KNOWS.

He knows the past, its diverse forms of popular culture and the fascination these hold for many of us living in the present. He has the inquisitiveness of the historian, the passionate enthusiasm of the nostalgic, and the zeal of the true collector. His lifelong interest in comic art and the early days of comic-book publishing (a field in which he is an acknowledged expert) was the impetus for his first Hobart Lindsey/Marvia Plum mystery, *The Comic Book Killer* (1988). The second in the series, *The Classic Car Killer* (1992), grew out of his regard for the vintage automobiles and the era in which such finely engineered pieces of machinery as the Duesenberg were the ne plus ultra in personal transportation. *The Bessie Blue Killer* (1994) is a celebration of World War II aircraft and of the black fighter pilots known as the Tuskegee Airmen. *The Sepia Siren Killer* (1994) is a look at Hollywood filmmaking in the thirties and forties, in particular those features, barely remembered today, that were made by black producers for black audiences.

The fifth Lindsey and Plum adventure is a return to the world of publishing, specifically paperback publishing during the boom years of the early fifties—a boom created by the advent of the softcover original, in which popular novels and nonfiction works were written especially for sale to a mass-market audience in inexpensive pocket-size editions. Three aspects of the softcover original's heyday play important roles in the story. One is how they were published and who published them; a second is the type of books published and who wrote them; and third is their vivid, often gaudy cover art and the artists who created these covers.

Many small publishing companies were founded during those fifties glory years. Some flourished for a time and then floundered, while others floundered from the start—usually (though not always) those exploiters who bought inferior literary works, and used cheap paper and substandard artwork. Quite a few of the decade's paperback houses had short lives; so brief, in some cases, that virtually nothing is known about them and they are remembered only by the most ardent collectors. The Hanro Corporation, for instance, published fourteen digest-sized softcover original crime novels in 1951–52, some of which were written by established professionals and more than one of which is a cut above average; Hanro's Phantom Books line, however, was poorly packaged and distributed, and sold so few copies that individual titles are extremely difficult to find today. Another example is Peters Publishing, which brought out five obscure nonfiction titles in 1952–53 and then vanished without a trace.

The Chicago-based paperback line Dick Lupoff has invented here, Paige Publications, might well have existed in the early fifties. Those individuals who wrote the nine titles produced during Paige's two-year lifespan could have written for Hanro Corporation or Peters Publishing. (The anecdote Lupoff relates about the purchase of the Del Marston private-eye novel is based on a real incident involving a first novelist, a forties Chicago book and magazine publisher, and a well-known editor and writer.) The artist who painted the covers for *Buccaneer Blood, Cry Ruffian!,* and *Death in the Ditch* might have done similar work for Falcon or Lion or Zenith or any of the other small, independent, and now all-but-forgotten publishers. It is not only possible but probable that the nine Paige books would have such poor distribution and sales that very few copies survive to the present. It is also entirely feasible that Paige would have been forced out of business not only for financial reasons but for the political one which Lupoff postulates.

The paperback original's cover art was reflective (as were the books themselves) of the newfound sophistication of post–World War II society, and was a central selling point. Artists used the "peekaboo sex" approach to catching the reader's eye: beautiful women depicted either nude, as seen from the side or rear, or with a great deal of cleavage and/or leg showing, in a variety of provocative poses. One such cover on a Paige title, portraying one such beautiful woman in a typically sultry pose, is the springboard for the action in *The Cover Girl Killer*. It, too, might well have existed.

Today's paperback-collecting market also plays an important role in the narrative. Scotty Anderson could have been modeled on any of a dozen actual collectors, all of whom are as eccentric and benignly monomaniacal as Anderson. (I use the phrase "eccentric and benignly monomaniacal" advisedly, since my own collecting mania approaches this rather altered state. As does Lupoff's, I suspect.) Gary Lovisi, accorded almost mythical status in these pages, is a real person who does in fact publish a collectors' journal called *Paperback Parade*; he also publishes a magazine devoted to hard-boiled crime fiction, and is a noted fiction writer in his own right.

As enjoyable as are the publishing and collecting elements of *The Cover Girl Killer*, this and Lupoff's other mysteries are much more than nostalgia set pieces. He knows the social and political climates of the eras of which he writes, and sprinkles his stories with sometimes wry, sometimes angry, often insightful comments on the prejudices, excesses, misconceptions, and other prevailing attitudes of those bygone days. In his previous two "Killer" mysteries, the achievements of and problems faced by African-Americans in the early decades of this century are brought into sharp focus. In *The Cover Girl Killer*, a central plot component and theme is the Spanish Civil War of the midthirties, in particular the activities of the Abraham Lincoln Brigade—the several thousand Americans who fought on the side of the Loyalists, half of whom were killed in action or died from their wounds and disease.

Lupoff's interest in the Spanish Civil War stems from the fact that one of his cousins was a Lincoln Brigadier who gave his life to the struggle against Fascist tyranny in Spain. Thus Lupoff's description of the hardships faced by these American freedom fighters, both in Spain and on U.S. soil after the survivors' return, is deeply felt and justifiably bitter. As one of the characters, a former Brigadier, says to Hobart Lindsey, "I keep thinking, maybe somebody will care about the Lincolns someday. Dumb, eh? [People] didn't care then, they don't care now. Soon we'll all be gone, and no one will know." Lupoff cares passionately and wants others to care, so that thousands of men and women will not have died in vain.

Readers unfamiliar with the series may have gained an impression from the foregoing that the "Killer" novels are primarily time trips. This is not the case. Lupoff chronicles the present as effectively as he does the past; his mysteries are thoroughly modern in their depiction of the nineties in all of the decade's chaotic, harsh, farcical, frustrating, and fascinating complexity. Lindsey, in his capacity as insurance claims adjuster, and Marvia Plum, in hers as a Berkeley homicide cop, make expert use of the latest in technology and other contemporary investigative techniques. Their personal relationship is likewise modern, not only in its interracial aspect but in its spiritual and sexual contexts as well.

Just as change is the lifeblood of healthy human existence, growth and transition are the lifeblood of good series fiction. Few detective series, even when perpetrated by skilled writers, can last long without their principal characters undergoing a natural progression of changes, both positive and negative, in attitude, life-style, relationships. Neither Lindsey nor Marvia nor Lindsey's mother is quite the same person he or she was in *The Comic Book Killer*. More changes take place in this novel; one is major and will probably surprise fans, though it opens up all sorts of interesting possibilities for future entries. This, too, is the stuff of good series fiction. *The Cover Girl Killer* ensures that Lindseys' and Marvia's readers will come back for more—and that they'll likely bring a few friends along with them.

No question about it: Richard Lupoff knows.

Chapter One

ONE BOY'S SKIN was a chocolate brown; the other's, almost black. The lighter-skinned boy held a fishing rod in his left hand, a glittering Lake Tahoe salmon, easily a seven-pounder, in the right. The fish tried to flip out of the boy's control, but he held it tightly. "Come on, Jamie!"

The darker-skinned boy pointed a Sony Handycam, his eye pressed to its canted viewfinder. "Hold him still, I can't take your picture if you won't hold him still."

Jamie Wilkerson pressed *record*. The Handycam whirred. The late-afternoon sun glinted off the surface of Lake Tahoe. There was no wind; the surface was still. The boat, a 28-foot Bayliner, trolled toward the center of the lake, barely maintaining headway, following its Maxim/Marinetek fishfinder.

Over the purr of the Bayliner's Volvo Penta engine, a distant *whup-whup-whup* became audible. Jamie swung the Handycam away from his friend and the struggling salmon, swept it up the snow-covered slopes on the western shore of the lake. A black speck had appeared against the brilliant blue sky. The speck was approaching the lake.

"Hey!" Hakeem White complained. "You're supposed to be taking my picture. That's just some old heli—"

He stopped in the middle of the word. The helicopter seemed to wobble in midair. Its familiar *whup-whup-whup* sound developed a sickening syncopation. Hakeem dropped the lake salmon. It flexed the muscles of its silvery tail and launched itself over the stern of the Bayliner and splashed into the cold lake.

Jamie Wilkerson kept the Handycam focused on the helicopter.

Hobart Lindsey and Marvia Plum, relaxing in the Bayliner's half-open cabin, lowered their coffee cups and clambered onto the afterdeck to stand with Marvia's son and his friend. Even Captain MacKenzie, keeping one hand on the Bayliner's helm, shaded his eyes with the other as he watched the helicopter slow to a hover overhead.

The helicopter shuddered in midair, then rotated slowly on its vertical axis. It dropped toward the Bayliner.

MacKenzie yelped and shoved the tourist boat's throttle forward. Its 350-horsepower engine responded and the boat leaped ahead. Lindsey grabbed Hakeem and Marvia Plum grabbed Jamie to keep the boys from being flung into the lake. If they were, their orange life jackets would keep them afloat—but even a brief exposure to the frigid water could endanger their lives.

Somehow, through it all, Jamie kept the Handycam focused on the helicopter and the *record* button pressed.

The helicopter splashed down twenty yards behind the Bayliner, at the exact spot the boat had occupied when the copter began its plunge. Captain MacKenzie swung the Bayliner in a tight circle and headed back toward the foundering copter. He clicked the boat's Cybernet radio into life and called through to Lake Forest, on Tahoe's north shore.

He shoved the Bayliner's gear lever into neutral and the boat slowed as it approached the copter. "Bart," he yelled, "get on the blower—Coast Guard should be coming up. Tell 'em what happened—I have to handle this!" He barreled past the paying passengers and grabbed a downrigger. Jamie and Hakeem danced around him, trying to stay out of his path. Marvia Plum pulled the boys away from MacKenzie.

Lindsey had the Coast Guard station on the blower now. "A helicopter just crashed—it's in the middle of the lake. We're right next to it."

A voice from the radio said, "We got a distress call from them. We've got a cutter headed out there now."

"What do you want us to do?"

The voice said, "Don't go under with the chopper."

Beyond MacKenzie, Lindsey could see the helicopter foundering deeper into the lake. It looked like an old glass-bubble Bell copter, the kind popular with TV traffic reporters. He thought he could make out two figures inside the bubble. Only one of them was moving.

MacKenzie had swung a heavy cable out on the boat's downrigger. He climbed onto the stern gunwale and jumped toward the copter. Chilly water plumed around MacKenzie. Droplets hit Lindsey's face like icy pellets. Lindsey could see MacKenzie struggling to attach the cable to the copter. The aircraft's tail was pointing toward the Bayliner, and MacKenzie managed to clip the cable to the tail rotor mounting.

With a sucking noise, the helicopter disappeared into Lake Tahoe. MacKenzie disappeared, then reappeared, gasping for air, clambering hand-over-hand along the downrigger cable.

Marvia Plum shoved Jamie and Hakeem behind her, toward the Bayliner's cabin. Lindsey had dropped the ship-to-shore mike. He scrambled to the stern of the Bayliner. With Marvia at his side, he stretched his arms over the gunwale. MacKenzie had reached the Bayliner. Lindsey and Plum grabbed him by the hands, then moved their grasp to his arms. Even after his brief soaking in the icy lake, he was turning blue and his skin was frigid. They managed to haul him over the stern of the boat. He crashed to the deck and crawled toward the cabin.

Marvia Plum followed him.

Lindsey stood in the Bayliner's stern, watching the lake surface where the helicopter had disappeared. The downrigger was playing out cable slowly. The copter was bulky, and it displaced its volume in water, reducing its own weight by an equivalent amount. Bubbles rose from it, bursting when they reached the surface of the lake.

Then a hand appeared, then another. Lindsey shouted, "Someone's alive!"

Marvia Plum, still in her quilted jacket, and Captain MacKenzie, wrapped in a blanket, a knitted cap pulled over his dripping hair, tumbled back out of the cabin. MacKenzie yelled at the figure who was following his example, clambering hand-over-hand along the downrigger cable. The cable continued to play out, so the copter pilot's progress was slower than MacKenzie's had been.

When he was a few feet from the Bayliner, MacKenzie shoved a boat hook over the gunwale and the bedraggled figure released the downrigger cable and grabbed the boat hook. Lindsey helped MacKenzie haul the boat hook back while Marvia Plum grabbed the survivor's arm and pulled him over the gunwale. As he came over the gunwale, Lindsey saw that one of his legs stuck out from its socket at a crooked angle.

Now Marvia Plum tried to hustle the dripping man into the cabin. He screamed and collapsed. Lindsey realized that his leg wasn't really attached to his body wrong: it was broken, and in more places than one. Lindsey scrambled to help Marvia with the man, dragging him on his back into the cabin and wrapping him in a blanket.

Captain MacKenzie picked up the ship-to-shore microphone and shouted at the Coast Guard. Jamie pointed the Handycam at the Coast Guard cutter approaching from the north.

The injured man shook his head, shoving himself upright on his elbow. He tried to climb to his feet but fell back, screaming in pain. He yelled, "I've got to get him out of there! It's Mr. Vansittart!"

MacKenzie shoved past them. Lindsey could see him peering into the lake. He studied the downrigger. The cable had paid out to its end, revealing a polished metal reel. Lindsey could feel the Bayliner tilting. MacKenzie roared, "We're going to founder!" He pounded his fist on the Bayliner's gunwale, then tugged the heavy downrigger from its mounting.

It whipped into the air, missing MacKenzie by inches, then arched over the Bayliner's stern and splashed black water higher than the boat, disappearing beneath the surface after the helicopter.

The survivor lay on his back, a picture of despair. "It was Mr. Vansittart," he moaned. "I tried to get him out, but I couldn't."

The Coast Guard cutter hove to alongside the Bayliner. A guardsman called, "We're going to throw you a line, Bayliner. We'll tow you to safety."

Captain MacKenzie shook his head. "I don't need a tow. He does." He pointed at the lake, where the helicopter and its passenger had disappeared. "But I've got a badly injured man on board. I'm heading for port. He needs to get to the hospital."

HOBART LINDSEY, Marvia Plum, Jamie Wilkerson, and Hakeem White sat on the edge of the big bed. All had showered and changed into warm clothes. They were eating Chinese food and watching CNN with the sound muted, waiting for Jamie's videotape.

Hakeem was not very happy. "It was just 'cause I'm a better fisherman than you, Jamie. If you were a better fisherman, you would have caught the fish, and I would have had the camcorder, and *I'd* be famous."

"I'm going to be a TV newsman when I grow up. I've already got a start. And I've got a check coming, too."

Marvia Plum hushed the two boys. "Look." She hit the *mute* button a second time and the sound came back on. A talking head in the studio of CNN's Reno affiliate was jabbering at the camera. The image on the screen cut to Jamie's footage, starting with a flash of Hakeem's grinning face, Jamie holding the camera on Hakeem's lake salmon, then panning away to the tiny speck of the copter.

The studio announcer said, "These remarkable pictures were taken by a ten-year-old boy, Jamie Wilkerson, of Berkeley, California, vacationing at Lake Tahoe with his mother and best friend. The helicopter ran into trouble as it began to cross the lake en route from its passenger's Belmont, California home to a destination in Reno."

On the TV screen the helicopter hovered, the *whup-whup-whup* of its blades hesitated, and the copter shook, then began to whirl as it fell toward the lake. Almost miraculously, Jamie had kept the Handycam image steady and clear. Maybe the boy did have a future as a cameraman.

"The pilot, John Frederick O'Farrell of Mountain View, California, is a Vietnam veteran who operates a private air-taxi service. He was rushed to Doctors' Hospital in Truckee and is in Intensive Care, suffering from a compound fracture of the leg and internal injuries. A hospital spokesperson says that doctors are guardedly optimistic regarding O'Farrell's condition. Coast Guard authorities at Lake Tahoe said that only the quick action of Captain Kevin MacKenzie of the Bayliner *Tahoe Tailflipper* saved O'Farrell's life."

The screen showed O'Farrell climbing out of the lake, Marvia Plum hauling him by one dripping sleeve while O'Farrell clung to the boat hook that MacKenzie and Lindsey had passed to him. On the videotape, the injuries to O'Farrell's leg were horrifyingly obvious.

Then the image cut to a still picture of a white-haired, business-suited man. The surroundings were unquestionably an office. Letters running across the bottom of the screen read, *File Photo*. The announcer furnished a voice-over. "Albert Crocker Vansittart was the last scion of a pioneer California family. A lifelong bachelor, Vansittart inherited a fortune estimated at fifty million dollars and ran its worth up to ten times that amount. A lifelong resident of Belmont, Vansittart was traveling to Reno on holiday."

The scene cut back to Lake Tahoe. The news network must have hired a helicopter of its own and had it hover over the crash site. Now it was nighttime; the footage must have been shot within the past hour. A Coast Guard cutter had returned and its crew was working by floodlight, dropping lines into the black water. They hauled them back without results.

The announcer introduced a professor of marine geology from the University of Nevada at Reno. "Lake Tahoe is more than a quarter of a mile deep," the professor intoned. "Once you get past the surface layers, the temperature is a uniform 40 degrees Fahrenheit, year round. We don't really know what lies at the bottom of the lake—or who." The professor allowed himself a little laugh. "But you can be sure, if anybody rode that helicopter to the bottom of the lake, he isn't alive now."

"Haven't you tried this technique before, Professor, looking for Tahoe Tessie?"

"A lot of people laugh at Tessie, call her our own version of the Loch Ness Monster. But we've found some amazing species in recent decades. Why, no one believed that a live coelacanth could possibly be swimming around today, until—"

Lindsey jumped when the telephone rang at his elbow. As he picked up the handset, he glanced at his watch. It was 11:30 at night; it had been a long day and evening, but everyone—including the ten-year-olds—was too energized to sleep. "Stand by for Mr. Richelieu." Lindsey grimaced and mouthed his boss's name. Marvia mimed back in alarm.

Richelieu said, "Lindsey, I'm surprised you're still awake." He sounded like Jack Nicholson on Valium, Lindsey thought. "You're not watching CNN by any chance, are you, Lindsey?"

Amazing. Did the man have bugs everywhere? "As a matter of fact, I am."

"Do you know who died this afternoon?"

"You mean Albert Crocker Vansittart?"

"Go to the head of the class. That was you and your girlfriend in the, what was its name—"

"*Tahoe Tailflipper.*"

"God, you California people are so cute, I want to throw up. Yes, I thought that was you. Well, Hobart Lindsey, International Surety's hero du jour. I don't know how you always manage to land in hot water, but you're in it again."

Lindsey shook his head. Obviously, Richelieu had never dipped his toes into Lake Tahoe. Lindsey had carried the telephone as far away from the TV as he could, closed himself in the bathroom with the cord snaked under the door. Too bad the lodge didn't have cordless phones, but then guests would surely carry them away like souvenir towels.

"I don't understand, Mr. Richelieu. Why am I in this? What does this have to do with International Surety? What does it have to do with SPUDS?" And why, Lindsey wondered, had the director of the Special Projects Unit/Detached Service tracked him down to a lakeside lodge in Tahoe City long after business hours?

"Good thing Mrs. Blomquist and I were working late tonight and happened to turn on the set here in the office."

Lindsey didn't rise to that one.

"Vansittart has one of our flag policies. Had, I should say. I assume the coroner out there is going to certify that he's dead."

"Without a body, Mr. Richelieu?"

"Come on, Lindsey. Enough witnesses saw that copter crash. Including you of all people. And it's on tape. And the pilot—what's his name—"

"O'Farrell."

"—says it was Vansittart."

"Okay. Vansittart had an International Surety policy?"

"Four million dollars' worth."

"Four—four *million?*"

"That's right. Been paying in on it since 1951. Biggest life policy IS ever wrote."

"Well . . . well . . . I guess we'll just have to pay off, then. If they can recover the body. Or, ah, once the coroner certifies that he's dead. I don't suppose we can wait seven years? And no double indemnity?"

Richelieu's chuckle was oilier than Jack Nicholson's. "No seven years. And no double indemnity, either. I looked. Give thanks for small blessings."

Lindsey rubbed his eyes and looked at his watch again. It was quarter-to-twelve. Quarter-to-one in Denver. Sure, Mr. Richelieu and Mrs. Blomquist were working late. On a Friday night. Just like Nelson Rockefeller and his editor were when the Rock bought the farm.

"I don't see why you called me, Mr. Richelieu. I'm on vacation. Well, a weekend getaway, anyhow. That's a huge policy, and the death of the insured will have to be certified, but it still sounds like a job for the nearest branch office. Why don't they just enter the event through KlameNet and—"

"You aren't listening, Lindsey. This is a flag policy, understand? And there's something peculiar about it, aside from the circumstances of Vansittart's death."

He paused, waiting for Lindsey to ask what was peculiar about Vansittart's $4,000,000 policy.

Lindsey liked his job.

"What's peculiar about Vansittart's policy?"

"The beneficiary. Cripes, I'd never write a policy like this one. I don't care who the insured was; I don't care how much he was paying in premiums."

Lindsey did not ask who the beneficiary was. He didn't like his job that much.

Richelieu cleared his throat. "The beneficiary is the girl on the cover of *Death in the Ditch*."

"What?"

"The girl on the cover of *Death in the Ditch*."

"You're kidding."

"Lindsey, you know me. I handpicked you out of that crummy little office you were in. I gave you your big break in this company. You know I don't kid."

"Right. Okay. Who's the girl on the cover of *Death in the Ditch*?"

"I have not the foggiest. That's what International Surety is paying you to find out."

"Sounds like a book. I mean—the girl on the cover. Kind of like that porn star who posed for the baby-food label or the soap-flakes package or whatever it was. But *Death in the Ditch* wouldn't be baby food or soap. It sounds like a book."

"Find out, Lindsey. And find the girl. We owe her three million dollars."

"Whoa. I thought you said four million."

"Right. I told you this was a flag policy. If we find the girl and pay the benefits, International Surety gets a twenty-five percent finder's fee. That's a cool million smackers."

"And if we don't find her? I mean, this sounds like a long shot. When did you say the policy was written?"

"Nineteen fifty-one."

"After more than forty years, well, she may not even be alive. What happens if we can't find her? Or if she's deceased?"

"Then, Hobart, then . . . I told you this was a flag policy. If we can't find her, or if she's deceased, the money goes to something called the World Fund for Indigent Artists. Sounds like Vansittart was hung up on artists and models. Wouldn't be the first."

"And you want me to find the girl."

"Find the girl, right. *Cherchez la femme*."

"How long do we have to find her?"

"Policy doesn't specify. But we have to notify the artists'

fund, and once they smell four million bucks, they're going to start pressing us hard."

"And there's no finder's fee."

"That's right, Lindsey. I swear, young feller, you keep on showing your smarts like you been, you've got a bright future with this company."

"I'll get on it first thing Monday morning, Mr. Richelieu."

A moment later, Lindsey could have sworn that he felt a blast of heat come through the telephone line. Of course that was impossible, but . . . "You'll get on it first thing *tomorrow*, bucko. In fact suppose you get on it tonight. You've got your palmtop with you?"

"I have it."

"It's got a modem in it, right? Standard SPUDS issue, right? You do work for me, Lindsey, don't you?"

"Right."

"To work, then. You're not on an hourly wage, Lindsey. To work."

Lindsey opened the bathroom door. He could see Jamie and Hakeem silhouetted against the TV screen. They'd lost interest in CNN and switched channels to a Japanese monster movie. Something with two heads and lots of scales was breathing fire and flailing at a squadron of Korean War Era jet fighters.

After a couple of jets crashed into a mountainside sending up plumes of black, oily smoke, Lindsey quietly placed the telephone handset on its base. The boys did not budge. He pulled on his goose-down jacket and motioned to Marvia. She slipped into her own jacket and followed him onto the wooden walkway outside their room.

The lodge was separated from the lake by a broad lawn, covered now with drifted snow. The January moon reflected off the lake's smooth surface. The Coast Guard cutter had apparently returned to its pier and the news helicopter to its base. Across the lake, a torchlight ski party was visible as a cluster of tiny moving sparks.

Lindsey took Marvia's hands in his own.

She said, "We have to go back, don't we?"

He nodded.

"It was going so well. Like a real family."

"I know. But Richelieu—"

She looked angry. "How did he know where we were?"

Lindsey laughed without humor. "I guess he was watching CNN." He told Marvia about Richelieu and Mrs. Blomquist working late and just happening to turn on a TV in the office. "He must have had her calling every hotel and lodge at the lake, till she found us."

Marvia grinned bitterly. "We should have registered as the Smith family."

Lindsey looked down at Marvia's face. The moon reflected from her dark eyes like two bright disks. Her dark face and short hair were silhouetted against the snowfield that stretched from the lodge to the lake shore.

"Let's chase the boys into their own room. I can log onto the twenty-four-hour interlibrary net from my palmtop. Give me an hour or so, then we can turn in."

Plum pressed the palm of her hand to his face. Cold as the night air was, her hand felt warm on his cheek.

"You going to work until you fall asleep?"

Lindsey shook his head. She could always make him smile. He shook his head again to make sure she could see it in the moonlight.

Chapter Two

LINDSEY AND MARVIA Plum took Jamie and Hakeem to an old Tahoe restaurant for breakfast. It wasn't glitzy and it wasn't full of yuppies in the latest L. L. Bean and Eddie Bauer skiwear but the food was good and the portions were generous.

The boys were not pleased at missing their weekend in the snow, but Lindsey and Plum promised them another shot at it as soon as they could get away. Normally Lindsey was the one who worked Monday through Friday. Since he'd moved from International Surety's Walnut Creek office to SPUDS, he pretty well set his own days and hours.

Marvia Plum was the one who had to fight for the shifts she wanted. A homicide sergeant in the Berkeley Police Department had to be available when the department needed her. Murderers didn't knock off after six o'clock in the evening. In fact, they got busy after the sun went down, and peaked just about when most citizens were watching the evening news or crawling into their beds.

But this time it was Lindsey who had got the call, and this time it was Lindsey who clicked his heels, saluted smartly, and did as he was commanded: *Find the girl on the cover of* Death in the Ditch.

He dropped Marvia and both youngsters at her house. She would take care of them, get Hakeem White back to his parents and take her own son to her parents' house. They would spend the evening there. Marvia spent more time with her mother since her father's death. Not that Gloria Plum needed it. She had always been an island unto herself. But somehow, it seemed to Lindsey, Marvia drew strength from being in the house where she was raised, and where her father had lived almost until the end.

Lindsey left them at Oxford Street in Berkeley. Marvia would drive Jamie and Hakeem to Bonita Street in her classic Mustang. Once the boys talked things over on the ride back from Tahoe, they decided that their adventure would make better telling than an ordinary weekend excursion would have. They'd seen the helicopter crash—it almost crashed on them. They'd helped rescue the pilot, and Jamie Wilkerson was a real network cameraman.

Lindsey's computer search had turned up hundreds of books with *Death* in their titles, from *Death About Face* by Frank Kane, 1948, to *Death-Wish Green* by Frances Crane, 1960. Lots of *Death in*'s, too. There was *Death in the Devil's Acre* by Anne Perry, 1985, and there was *Death in the Diving Pool* by Carol Carnac, 1940. That was where *Death in the Ditch* belonged, right between *Death in the Devil's Acre* and *Death in the Diving Pool*. But it wasn't there.

Maybe it wasn't a book at all. Maybe it was—what? What would have a cover with a girl on it, with a title like *Death in the Ditch*, other than a book? A magazine? A record album? A pack of trading cards? They were making some pretty weird trading cards these days, everything from famous gangsters to friendly dictators. They weren't restricted to the athletes and movie stars that Lindsey remembered collecting in grammar school, but Vansittart's life policy had been issued in 1951. If the designated beneficiary hadn't been changed in later years, that would narrow the field.

He'd have to check on that, but first, after dropping Marvia and the youngsters, he headed for Walnut Creek. He pulled his rebuilt Volvo 544 into the driveway and parked beside the silvergray Oldsmobile that had been parked there increasingly often these past few months.

Inside the house he found Mother's new friend, Gordon Sloane, sitting in the living room with his shoes off and his feet on the ottoman. A CD was playing—it sounded like Mozart—and Sloane held a nearly full martini glass by its stem. He looked up, clearly surprised, when Lindsey came in.

"I thought you were up in Tahoe. Your mother said—"

"That was the plan. Had to come back."

"I hope nothing's wrong."

Before Lindsey could answer, Mother came into the room. She wore an apron over a pair of jeans and a warm blouse. Her hair had gone to gray—every time Lindsey noticed a change in her, it was a shock to him—and she carried a wooden salad bowl and a pair of hinged tongs. She looked like everybody's perfect mom—by Norman Rockwell out of June Cleaver. Lindsey embraced her and planted a kiss on her cheek. She smelled like flowers and cooking.

Lindsey said, "I guess you two were planning an evening at home. I can make myself scarce."

Mother smiled. "We wouldn't throw you out of your own home. There's plenty of food."

Lindsey looked past her, at Sloane. Sloane nodded. Lindsey said, "Okay. I'd better go wash up. I'm feeling kind of stale."

At dinner he told them about the events at Tahoe, about Jamie Wilkerson's debut as a network cameraman, and about Desmond Richelieu's telephone call.

Sloane said, "We caught part of the report on TV. It was in this morning's papers, too. They're going nuts over Vansittart. I didn't realize you were involved."

Lindsey reached for a slab of pot roast. "Only by accident. Of course, Jamie's beside himself."

"He's going to be Hobart's son," Mother offered. "When he marries Marvia. You know Marvia, Gordon. Such a lovely girl. No, woman—we don't say 'girl' anymore."

Lindsey couldn't suppress his grin. "That's all right, Mother. It's a small enough matter."

"Well, I try to do what's right. Don't I, Gordon?"

Sloane agreed. Mother tried to do what was right. And she did amazingly well. After decades in a twilight world, not knowing whether Ike was president or Ronald Reagan, forgetting half the time that her husband had died in the Korean War and forgetting half the time that the war had been over for decades and that her son was a grown man approaching middle age, Mother had come around.

Something had penetrated the fog. Something like a miracle. After dinner was over and the dishes cleaned and put away—six hands made quick work—Mother turned on the TV. It was getting late, they had lingered over coffee, and the evening news was just coming on.

There was a follow-up to the Vansittart story. The Coast Guard had dropped a plumb line, trying to find the helicopter. Nothing came up. The lake was too deep at that point; the line couldn't even reach the bottom.

There was a canned biography of Vansittart. The news people had turned up his high school and college yearbook photos, old newspaper shots and black-and-white footage of the millionaire. Toasting the mayor of San Francisco at some civic dinner, shaking hands with the governor of California at another.

Vansittart must have been quite a fellow. Apparently he'd been ambassador to several postage-stamp nations in the 1960s and 1970s, obviously the reward for generous campaign donations to the presidents of that era.

And newsreel footage of Vansittart escorting movie stars to premieres and rolling dice at the gaming tables in Reno and Las Vegas. Yes, quite a fellow. The reporter in Reno mentioned that Vansittart had been traveling by chartered helicopter to a planned seventy-fifth birthday party—his own—when the copter crashed and sank into Lake Tahoe, taking Vansittart with it.

In the morning the Oldsmobile was still in the driveway. Lindsey got into his round-back blue Volvo and headed downtown to the International Surety office. Now that he was assigned to SPUDS, he could have moved out, rented space for himself, hired a secretary. But he preferred to work out of the office where he'd worked for so many years.

Not that the atmosphere was perfect. Elmer Mueller, Lindsey's successor as area manager, was a loathsome bigot, and Mueller's handpicked office manager, Kari Fielding, was as vicious as her boss. But in a strange way Lindsey enjoyed seeing them once in a while. It was the way you enjoy having a really miserable day once in a while, he told himself: it makes you appreciate the rest of your life.

But it was Saturday and he was alone in the office. Agent claims would be filed directly through KlameNet. Anything else could wait until Monday morning.

Lindsey used the office computer to log onto the mainframe at National. He printed out the text of Vansittart's policy, checked the history file, verified that the peculiar description of the beneficiary had been there from the outset. The only changes over the years had come about when the alternate bennie had changed its name. Originally the Chicago Artists and Models Mutual Aid Society, it had become the National Welfare League for Graphic Creators, then the World Fund for Indigent Artists.

Each time the organization changed its name there was a new address and a new set of officers. Well, in forty-plus years, that wasn't especially surprising. The current address was 101 California Street, San Francisco. Lindsey knew the building well, a gleaming, modern high-rise full of high-profile law firms and corporate offices. A disgruntled ex-client of one of the law firms had burst in with an arsenal of assault weapons one day and reduced the California Bar Association membership sizably. Since then there was better security in the building.

The current president of WFIA was one Roger St. John Cooke. Vice president was Cynthia Cooke. The file showed that the Cookes had been running the fund for a decade. It sounded like a nice little mom'n'pop nonprofit foundation. The world was full of do-gooders, including those who did well by doing good.

Lindsey made a note to expect some input from the Cookes. (Brother and sister? Husband and wife? Mother and son?) There would be a polite phone call, then a lawyer letter. How handy! They probably wouldn't even get wet if they had to visit their attorneys on a rainy San Francisco day. But Lindsey wasn't going to worry too much about the contingent bennies today.

His job was . . . He must have been listening to too much music lately. His mind was setting his task to music. A silent orchestra played inside his head as he sang along.

Was the tune "Happy Birthday to You . . . "?

Find the girl on the book, Find the girl on the book, It's Death in the Di-itch. . . .

Or maybe it was Beethoven's Fifth . . .

Locate the girl! Locate the girl! Locatethegirllocatethegirllocate-thegirl. . . .

He found himself giggling into the monitor screen. Maybe this job was making him crazy. He shut down the computer, left the office, grabbed a snack downstairs, and walked to his car. Traffic in the Caldecott Tunnel was light.

It was a gray day in Berkeley. Lindsey was dressed casually, a heavy sweater over a woolen shirt. He parked in a city garage just off Telegraph Avenue and headed for Cody's, the town's premiere bookstore. A clerk at the center desk offered to help him. She had short hair and a spectacularly beautiful face. She wore a Dan Quayle for President T-shirt. Lindsey didn't know what to make of that, so he didn't comment.

He asked if she knew of a book called *Death in the Ditch*. No author, no publisher, but it was probably first issued in 1951 or so. The clerk smiled. "I doubt that it's still in print. Unless it was a classic of some kind."

"I don't know what kind of book it was, except there was a girl on the cover."

The clerk raised her eyebrows. "A little girl, you mean?"

"I don't know. I've never seen it."

"Or a woman. A grown-up woman."

"I don't know. I've never seen it."

The clerk turned away. Over her shoulder she said, "I'll look in *Books in Print*. On the CD-ROM." She punched some keys on a computer. Mysterious boxes and symbols raced across the monitor screen. Finally it settled down. The clerk turned back to Lindsey. "Sorry. Doesn't show anything like that. *Death in Venice? Death in the Bathroom? Death in a Warm, Dark Place?*"

Lindsey shook his head.

The clerk nodded. "I didn't think so. Tell you what." Lindsey had one hand on the counter, and the clerk put hers on top of his. "Maybe you could try Moe's next door. First floor—they have a lot of used paperbacks. That might be your best bet."

Lindsey thanked her and walked next door. It wasn't raining so he didn't get wet, even though he wasn't at 101 California Street.

The clerk was right, Moe's had thousands upon thousands of used paperbacks. Trouble was, they were arranged by author, not title. Finding *Death in the Ditch*—if Moe's had it at all—was about as likely as dropping a pebble from the Goodyear blimp and hoping to hit the right spectator in a stadium full of football fans.

But again a clerk came to the rescue. "You know the San Francisco Mystery Book Store? Twenty-fourth Street? If anybody can help you, they can."

Lindsey drove across the Bay Bridge, took Duboce Street to Market, and turned left on Castro. On a Saturday afternoon the city's gay community was out in force, but something struck Lindsey as odd. There were teenagers and twenty-somethings and there were gray heads and lined faces, but the thirty- and forty-somethings were missing from the scene. Those, he realized, were the population who'd been living it up fifteen years ago, when the HIV virus was spreading like a stealth disease.

At 24th Street he found a parking place and walked to the mystery specialty store. The place was crammed with books and book lovers. He squeezed through narrow aisles and reached the upstairs room. Hardcovers and paperbacks were intermixed. There must be thousands of them. If Lindsey had been a mystery fan—he was not—he would have been in paradise.

But again, the arrangement was alphabetical by author, not title. He squeezed back down the narrow staircase. A blonde woman with sharp, attractive features sat at a tiny battered desk. She had a Styrofoam cup of coffee wedged between stacks of books and papers. Maybe bookstores attracted good-looking women. Was that thought politically correct?

Lindsey asked the blonde woman if she knew a book called *Death in the Ditch*, published around 1951.

The woman frowned, shook her head, then said, "I never heard of it. You know anything about it?"

"Only that there was a girl on the cover."

The blonde said, "You sure of that? Cover, not jacket?"

"As far as I know. I've never seen it."

"Then it's probably a paperback. There weren't as many published back in the early fifties; that was just before the big explosion. You know, when Bantam got going, then Ballantine and Ace. But fifty-one—there were some pretty obscure outfits got started around then, and didn't last too long."

She took a sip from the Styrofoam cup. The cream in it—or whatever she used—had formed a thin scum on top of the coffee. The blonde grimaced and set the cup back down. "Maybe it'll get better as it ages." She looked up at Lindsey. "What you really ought to do is, you ought to talk to Scotty Anderson. You know Scotty Anderson?"

Lindsey shook his head.

"Great collector. Real scholar. If you need an old paperback, if anybody in the world has it, Scotty does."

Lindsey grinned. "Does he live here? I mean, nearby?"

"East Bay." The blonde shuddered. "You want his address, phone number?"

Lindsey did.

"Let's see." She moved a stack of publishers' catalogs onto the floor, uncovering a plastic Rolodex. She flipped the lid open and read an address and phone number aloud. Lindsey wondered if her tone was what they used to call a whiskey voice.

Lindsey flipped his pocket organizer open and jotted down the information. "He won't mind my calling?"

"Just tell Scotty I sent you." The blonde told Lindsey her name, and he added that to the organizer. He slipped his gold International Surety pencil and the organizer into his pocket, thanked the blonde, and headed for a pay phone.

Anderson was at home. Lindsey made an appointment for Sunday afternoon and hung up. Maybe he was getting somewhere.

He called Marvia's house and got her answering machine, then tried her mother's house. Gloria Plum answered. Marvia had taken her son, Jamie Wilkerson, and his friend, Hakeem White, to the mall to make up for their canceled snow weekend.

Somehow Gloria managed to blame Lindsey for the canceled weekend. Somehow Gloria managed to blame Lindsey for most things she was unhappy about.

This is really swell, Lindsey thought. I'm not even married, and I've got mother-in-law problems. He went home.

Mother had planned to go out for the evening with Gordon Sloane. They'd been dating—how can your *mother* be dating, Lindsey wondered—for almost a year now. They'd met when Mother got a job, her first real, out-of-the-home job, at Sloane's company, Consolidated Alpha. Whatever that meant.

Sloane worked in product development. Mother was a secretary, not a bad job for a woman entering the job market for the first time in her late fifties. She took to a computer as if she'd been born to use one, and she loved her work. But Sloane . . .

Lindsey had never been able to learn what products Sloane developed. Consolidated Alpha was one of those shadowy Bay Area corporations that seemed to have something to do with the University of California, or maybe with the Lawrence Labs, or with the Department of Energy, or maybe Defense.

Maybe they were building neutron bombs.

Maybe they had a crashed UFO with seventeen frozen aliens in a secret lab.

Lindsey fixed himself some dinner and tried to veg out in front of the TV. He couldn't get interested in anything. He went for a walk around the block. Mother had spoken of selling the house and buying a condo. Then she and Sloane had started talking about marriage. And Lindsey had asked Marvia to marry him enough times, and she seemed to be edging slowly, ever so slowly, toward doing it.

One way or another, Lindsey's comfortable life in the nest was coming to an end—that was for sure.

When he got home there was still no sign of Mother, no silver-gray Oldsmobile in the driveway. He showered and climbed into bed, but sleep would not come. He went downstairs and stared at the television set. It stared back at him with its single eye. He didn't even pick up the remote. He knew that he and the TV had nothing to say to each other.

He walked to the single, sparsely populated bookshelf in the living room and plucked a book that had stood there unopened for years. It was *The Buccaneers* by Edith Wharton. It was wonderful.

The next day, Sunday, he kept his appointment with Scotty Anderson. Finding Anderson's home in Castro Valley wasn't difficult. Anderson lived in an apartment in a standard, low-rise, 1970s development. The neighborhood was marked with strip malls and broad, treeless streets. The parking lot outside the apartment was full of ten-year-old Toyotas and deteriorating pickup trucks. A couple of motorcycles stood at the end of the lot. Even those showed signs of neglect.

Lindsey rang the bell beside Anderson's door. Anderson was a massive individual. He looked as if he'd combed his mouse-brown hair once, and had shopped with taste and care at Goodwill. His hair hung over his forehead, and he wore a denim work shirt and ragged, faded khaki work pants. He clenched an unlit match in his teeth. Well, at least the sulfur end was outside his mouth. When he greeted Lindsey, Lindsey felt as if his hand was being absorbed by a great, soft animal.

But the inside of Anderson's apartment was very different from its exterior. It was a combination library, museum, and shrine. The air outside might be cold and damp in winter and hot and dry in summer; inside Scotty Anderson's apartment, it was kept at a steady temperature and humidity. The Library of Congress had nothing on Scotty Anderson.

"So you're doing some research on paperbacks." Anderson put one bearlike hand on Lindsey's shoulder while he closed the outside door with the other. "Come on in. Let me show you around."

Lindsey had never seen a residence—at least he assumed it was Anderson's residence—so jammed with books. The walls were covered with shelving packed with books. The room was divided into narrow passageways, little more than tunnels, between rows of standing metal shelves. Books were everywhere. The ends of the rows were covered with posters advertising books, blowups of ads for books, reproductions of covers of books. Ninety-nine percent of them were paperbacks.

Anderson led Lindsey up one aisle and down the next, declaiming on cover artists, publishers, authors, points of distinction between first editions and later printings. Soon Lindsey's head was swimming.

Finally they reached a cramped room furnished as an office. Anderson gestured Lindsey to a battered wooden chair. He dropped his own bulk into another and leaned a massive arm on a desktop. There was a computer on the desk, a stack of reference books beside the computer, and a row of file cabinets beside the desk.

Anderson looked at Lindsey expectantly.

"*Death in the Ditch.*"

Anderson grinned. He had large teeth. "Lovisi sent you, right?"

Lindsey shook his head. "Who's Lovisi?"

"Come on, I know I'm a little late, but does he want it fast or does he want it right? This ain't easy. What did you say your name was? I know most of the collectors." He peered into Lindsey's face. His eyes were a pale blue. "I'm sorry, you don't look familiar."

"We've never met."

"The draft is done. I'm really sorry. He's been patient and I appreciate it. Another week. Two at the most."

"I'm afraid you misunderstand. I'm not a bill collector."

Anderson roared with laughter. "That wouldn't worry me."

"I'm with International Surety." Lindsey reached for his wallet. Anderson flinched, then relaxed. Lindsey handed him a business card. "You see, there's been a death. You may have heard about it."

Anderson offered a look of bland inquiry.

"Albert Crocker Vansittart."

Anderson waited.

"His helicopter crashed in Lake Tahoe. The pilot survived, but Mr. Vansittart was lost. They're going to try and find the wreckage, the University of Nevada is sending a team with fiberoptic equipment."

Anderson closed his lips around the unlit match. "Right." He nodded his massive head. "I heard something about that on the car radio."

Okay. At least the guy had some awareness of the outside world.

"My company—International Surety—had issued a policy on Mr. Vansittart's life. He hasn't been formally declared dead as yet—that's going to be a little problem. Who has jurisdiction:

Placer County, California, or Washoe County, Nevada? And of course there's no body as yet. If the fiber-optic scanner works, maybe we'll have proof."

Anderson frowned. "This is all fascinating stuff, I guess. But what does it have to do with me?" He tilted his head like a dog hearing an unfamiliar sound. "You sure Lovisi didn't send you to collect? Or to pressure me?"

Lindsey sighed. "I promise you, Mr. Anderson, I haven't an idea in the world who this Lovisi person is. And he certainly didn't send me to do anything to you."

"Okay." Anderson stood up. He must have weighed close to 300 pounds, and if he wasn't exactly in Muscle Beach shape, he was far from flabby. "Okay," he repeated, "if Lovisi didn't send you, how do you know about *Death in the Ditch?*"

"Vansittart. It was in Vansittart's life policy. He was killed in the copter crash—at least it seems he was killed—and his insurance policy names his beneficiary as the girl on the cover of *Death in the Ditch.*" Lindsey was going to say more, but the dawning light of comprehension had brightened Scotty Anderson's face like an interior sun.

"Poor Lovisi. I'm going to have to revise the article—I can see that."

This time Lindsey played the waiting game.

"Gary Lovisi runs *Paperback Parade.* It's a collector's journal."

"For people who collect paperbacks," Lindsey supplied.

"You got it. Interesting character. I remember when he started out; his stuff was so crude I couldn't believe it. Like he was the Ed Wood of publishing. But he kept at it and now he turns out beautiful stuff. Beautiful."

Good for him, Lindsey thought. But what does this have to do with me? He waited for Anderson to go on, and Anderson did.

"I promised Lovisi an article for *Paperback Parade* on the legendary Paige Publications. Everybody in the hobby claims he knows somebody who has some Paige books, even claims he's seen one, but none of them turn up at the shows; none of them turn up in dealers' catalogs."

"Do they really exist?"

Anderson's pale blue eyes lost their wide innocence. They narrowed and darkened and flashed. Anderson reached an oversized hand and clasped Lindsey by one wrist. He leaned forward so the unlit match clenched in his teeth nearly scraped Lindsey's cheek.

Scotty Anderson cast a suspicious look to the left, then to the right. The match head scraped Lindsey's face, but Anderson ignored the contact.

"I have one," he whispered.

Chapter Three

ANDERSON HEAVED HIS bulk out of his wooden chair and paced to the office door. He gestured to Lindsey, who followed him. They paraded through a warren of metal shelves until they came to a gunmetal door with a huge combination lock built into it. Anderson crouched, his bulk hiding the lock from Lindsey's view.

When Anderson straightened he swung the heavy door open to reveal a closet-sized safe. It was filled with metal boxes. He ran his finger across the rows of boxes; they were marked with index numbers that meant nothing to Lindsey, but were obviously plain as day to Anderson.

Finally he pulled down a box, opened it, and extracted a transparent envelope containing a paperback book. He held the book toward Lindsey. "Hold this." Lindsey did.

What kind of person would maintain this level of security on what was obviously a treasure, yet hand it so casually to a stranger? Lindsey couldn't figure it out, but he'd been working with collectors for years now, and nothing they did could surprise him anymore.

They made their way back to Anderson's office. Anderson poked his head inside the room, muttered something like "Too stuffy," and gestured Lindsey to follow him again. This must be the way Alice felt as she followed the White Rabbit.

They wound up in a living room, or what must pass for one in this bizarre apartment. There were actually a few square feet of wall space not covered with books. Instead, framed paintings had been hung. They were well executed, but they didn't have the feel of gallery paintings. There were scenes of gangsters blasting at uniformed police, spaceships silhouetted against blazing, multicolored suns and planets, gorgeous women in low-cut gowns lounging against pianos, cowpokes galloping straight out of the frame.

Anderson must have seen Lindsey's expression. He beamed. "You like them? Originals!"

"They look like movie posters. They're, ah, very vivid."

"They're paperback cover paintings. Look, that's a Mitchell Hooks. That's a Bob Maguire. And that beauty"—he pointed— "that's a Robert McGinnis. You won't see many of those. There's a Jim Avati. A Stanley Meltzoff. And that red one—the one with the spaceman and the bat-creatures—that's a Paul. Frank R. Paul. No, they don't paint 'em the way they used to."

"They must be valuable."

"You wouldn't believe it. Five or six figures. They used to throw them away back in the fifties. Listen, if I just had a time machine, what I couldn't do!"

Lindsey had to get the subject back to *Death in the Ditch*. "You said something about . . . " He gestured to the book in Anderson's hand.

Anderson slid the envelope across his desk. "Please don't open it. If you need to look at the book, I'll get it out for you. It must be done just right, or it can be damaged."

Lindsey leaned over the book. "Is it all right if I pick it up?"

"The way porcupines make love."

"How's that?"

"Very carefully."

Lindsey managed a polite laugh. He'd thought that joke was hilarious when he was ten.

The book was *Buccaneer Blades*. The author was Violet de la Yema. The cover illustration could have been straight out of a fifties pirate movie, maybe one starring Burt Lancaster and Maureen O'Hara, with Basil Rathbone as the evil Spanish governor of a Caribbean island and Akim Tamiroff as his comic aide.

He turned the book over carefully. "No price?"

"They were all a quarter. No need for a price back then. Did you catch the publisher's logo?"

"I see it there in the corner. Nice idea—the open book with all the pages, and the publisher's name, Paige. Was there a Mr. Paige?"

Anderson shrugged.

Lindsey turned the book over. The spine was printed in black with the title and byline dropped out, in white. The Paige Publications was reproduced at the base of the spine, along with a serial number, 101. Lindsey raised his eyebrows.

"Saw it, did you?" Anderson's matchstick bobbed up and down.

"You mean the serial number? Does 101 mean this was the very first Paige book?"

"Apparently it does. Nobody really knows much about Paige. When I turned this book up, I couldn't believe my eyes. Paiges are the holy grail of paperback collectors. Like the first ten Pocket Books. They printed 10,000 of each—you'd think there would be a lot of them left. Well, except for *Enough Rope* by Dorothy Parker; for some reason they only did 7,600. But they're scarcer than hens' teeth. People must have read 'em and threw 'em away. Or the L.A. Bantams. If you could get hold of *The Shadow and the Voice of Murder* or *Tarzan in the Forbidden City* . . . "

Lindsey shook his head. "I've worked on collectibles cases before, but this field is new to me."

"The first—oh, there's too much of this. You ought to read one of the books on the subject. Thom Bonn's, or Piet Schreuders's. Anyway, if you know anything about collectibles, you know that their intrinsic value doesn't really matter. What's the difference between two identical books, only one of them has a minor typo in it and the other doesn't, and we know that the typo was only in the true first edition and corrected after that?"

"I—" Lindsey tried to answer, but Anderson wasn't stopping.

"You wouldn't think there was a difference, but it makes all the difference in the world. It's the difference between a treasure and a reading copy. It's the difference between a book to kill for and one you can pick up at any lawn sale for a nickel."

Anderson's predatory grin returned. When he was relaxed, his eyes were a bland pale blue. Now they regained their deep intensity.

"Matter of fact, I got my Paige at a garage sale in Lafayette. Just cruising, stopped to see what they had. All the usual junk, last season's Robert Ludlum, fifteenth printing, couple of Agatha Christies and Ellery Queens, zillionth editions, and . . . and a Paige!"

Lindsey nodded. He understood collectors as well as anyone could who was not himself a collector.

"I asked where the book came from," Anderson continued. "After I'd bought it, of course. Nobody knew. Maybe Grandma read it when she was a girl. She always kept it, the old dear. But she'd gone to Valhalla now, and they were cleaning out her room, and nobody in the family really wanted Grandma's old paperbacks, so—out they went. For a nickel apiece." Anderson cackled gleefully at the thought of his great coup.

"One thing that I haven't been able to verify, though."

"What's that?"

"The book is autographed. That is, *somebody* wrote a message in it. No, don't open it up, please. I remember exactly what it says. *To my Comrade with thanks. Salud y suerte. Violeta.* That's health and luck in Spanish. *Salud y suerte.* But nobody knows what Violet de la Yema's handwriting looks like. And why 'Violeta' instead of 'Violet' or 'Vi'? So—is it an authentic inscription?" Anderson shrugged his massive shoulders. "I hope it is. I like to think it is. But nobody can tell me. Nobody."

Lindsey let his eye settle on the deep cleavage of the model on the front of *Buccaneer Blades*, then turned the book over. He could feel his heart shift into overdrive. The back cover of *Buccaneer Blades* was not devoted to a blurb extolling the virtues of the book, or a paragraph lifted from a particularly seamy scene, as he'd expected. Instead, it featured an ad for another Paige book. It was an ad for *Death in the Ditch*.

The copy read like a standard hard-boiled mystery—a struggling, penniless private eye ("he was down to his last sawbuck and he knew the check wasn't in the mail"), a one-armed bartender ("he'd left his grenade-hurling wing on the bloody coral of Tarawa"), a gorgeous babe ("smoldering eyes and gams like Grable's"), murderous mobsters ("the Big Guy was gone and they were ready to kill for a piece of his empire"), and corrupt cops ("they were there to enforce the law, but the law they enforced was written in dollars—and hot lead").

It sounded like something written in the late 1940s rather than the early 1950s. That one-armed bartender was the giveaway. By the early 1950s, Tarawa was yesterday's story, along with Iwo Jima and Saipan and Guadalcanal and the rest of the island-hopping battles of the Pacific campaign. The Cold War was under way, General MacArthur was commanding UN forces in Korea, and World War II was stale news.

Still, Michener and Jones and Mailer were writing their great novels. Why not—Lindsey had to squint to make out the byline on the miniature cover of *Death in the Ditch*—Del Marston?

Del Marston.

All right.

It looked as if finding Albert Crocker Vansittart's beneficiary was going to take some serious detecting. Maybe old Del Marston, the author of *Death in the Ditch*, would have had his hero solve the puzzle with a gat and a few slugs of bourbon, but Lindsey didn't work that way. The job could be laborious and time-consuming, but eventually Lindsey's patient, methodical efforts would bring him to his destination.

Unless somebody else had got there first and erased all the clues. Lindsey was a good investigator, but he was no magician.

He asked Scotty Anderson, "Would you take the book out of the envelope for me? I know you don't want me to—"

Anderson's huge hand took back the book. The big man's face took on a look of concentration, the unlighted match pointing straight down. He peeled back a strip of tape, opened a transparent flap, and slid the book gently from its reliquary. He held it toward Lindsey, but his expression made it clear that Lindsey was to look, not touch.

"Have you actually read *Buccaneer Blades*?"

Anderson shook his head, smiling again as if Lindsey had asked, "Have you ever taken tea on Mars?"

"No way. Much too fragile. Don't want to crack the binding. I did open it far enough to shoot the indicia and front matter, and the first couple of pages. It's routine Spanish Main stuff."

"I figured as much. Do you think you could open it for me? So I could copy down the publisher's address, and the like."

Anderson shook his head again, slowly. "Don't want to risk it. But you can have copies of my printouts. I'll get 'em for you before you leave." He slid the book back into its transparent envelope, sealed the envelope with tape once more, and laid it on a low table. He leaned back in his chair, his hands behind his head. He'd shown his treasure; his visitor had been clearly and suitably impressed. It was a good day for Scotty.

"The thing is, you see, I only found this Paige a couple of months ago. Nobody has one. I went to the Library of Congress to check on it, and they don't have any Paiges that they knew of."

That surprised Lindsey. "I thought—you know, for copyright registration, especially under the old law—wouldn't they have sent copies to the library?"

Anderson nodded. The matchstick was tilted at a jaunty angle, like FDR's cigarette holder back in the days when it was okay for a politician to be photographed smoking.

"The books were registered, okay. That's why I have a list of all the Paiges, or at least all the ones that they registered. The serial numbers jibe, though, so I think that's all. But they don't have any copies. A lot of old paperbacks and magazines just got shoved in a back room and they're still there. They'll shelve them when they get a chance, they say, but they never get around to it. But how's this—it looks as if some congressmen were pretty interested in the Paige books, and they leaned on the library staff to log 'em in so they could check 'em out. They were checked out by a HUAC staffer—you know about HUAC?"

"Uh—"

"House Un-American Activities Committee. Run by a couple of congressional lice named Martin Dies and J. Parnell Thomas. Tricky Dickie Nixon got his start with HUAC." Dies was the pioneer. He went way back. Thomas came along later, after the big war. A kind of bush-league Joe McCarthy.

Lindsey wasn't going to talk about Richard Nixon. Instead he asked, "Why would they want these particular books?"

"That's what I wondered. I think I have a good clue, although it might take some more digging in the *Congressional Record* to find out for sure."

"But if the books were in the Library of Congress, aren't they still there?"

Anderson grinned. "You'd be amazed how many books get checked out by members of Congress. They wouldn't lower themselves to deal with mere librarians, of course. They send staff people—generally low-level staff people. They check things out and they never give them back. I mean, what's going to happen? Somebody in the library calls up Senator Jones and says, *You have our first edition* Maltese Falcon, *you better return it or there's a nickel fine for every day it's late*—huh? Fat chance."

Lindsey was still puzzled. "You said you had a clue."

Anderson shoved himself upright. "You wait here." He picked up his precious copy of *Buccaneer Blood* and headed for the door. "Help yourself to refreshments."

Lindsey looked around for refreshments. He couldn't find any.

When Anderson returned, he had disposed of *Buccaneer Blood*, probably locked it away in its reliquary. He was carrying a few sheets of computer printout.

"This is my article for *Paperback Parade*. Just a draft—I have to work on it some more. Especially with this insurance story of yours."

He lowered himself into his chair. He selected one sheet of paper and handed it to Lindsey.

"This is a complete Paige Publications bibliography. At least, it's every book they registered with the Library of Congress. There might have been some that they didn't register, but I think that's unlikely."

He handed the sheet to Lindsey. The heading on the page gave Paige Publications' address. Paige Building, LaSalle at Kinzie Streets, Chicago, Illinois. There were three columns of type on the page. Lindsey scanned them carefully.

Buccaneer Blood	Violet de la Yema	1951
Cry Ruffian!	Salvatore Pescara	1951
Death in the Ditch	Del Marston	1951
Teen Gangs of Chicago		
aka *Al Capone's Heirs*	(anonymous)	1951
By Studebaker Across America	Walter Roberts	1952
Great Baseball Stars of 1952	J. B. Harkins	1952
I Was a Lincoln Brigadier	Bob Walters	1952
Prisoner!	("by the author of	
	Teen Gangs of Chicago")	1952

Lindsey looked up from the list. "That's all?"

"Far as I can tell."

"Why would a congressional committee care about these books? What difference does a pirate swashbuckler make, or a book about gangsters, or a Studebaker trip, for heaven's sake?"

Anderson extended a thick finger and tapped the paper in Lindsey's hands. "There's the one. That's the one I think got their backs up."

He pointed at the line for *I Was a Lincoln Brigadier*.

"You know about the Abraham Lincoln Brigade?"

Lindsey wasn't sure. "I think it rings a bell." He smiled. "Faintly."

"American volunteers, fought in the Spanish Civil War, nineteen hundred thirty-six. They went there to fight Fascism, to fight against Franco. They figured he was a front man for Hitler and they weren't too far from right."

"What's wrong with that?"

"Well, there was a lot of Communist influence in the Lincolns. Hell, there were a lot of Communists in there. But they went to Spain to fight the Fascists. At least that was their version. But once the Cold War got going, they were . . . how shall I put this?"

He removed the matchstick from between his teeth and studied it sadly. He broke it in half, dropped the pieces into a bowl, and located a fresh replacement in a pocket of his denim shirt. He smiled approvingly at the new matchstick, then clenched its nonbusiness end between his teeth.

"Once the Cold War got going, these guys were highly suspect. Highly suspect. So, when Bob Walters brought out his little memoir—I guess it was a memoir, I've never seen a copy—HUAC jumped up and down and started doing its war dance."

Lindsey studied the single sheet of computer paper once more. There was no more information there than there had been.

"Do you mind if I keep this?" Lindsey asked.

Anderson pushed himself out of his easy chair. The matchstick pointed straight ahead. "Feel free, I've got it all in my computer." With one sausage-like finger he pointed to his head. "You have to go now?"

Lindsey looked at his Seiko. He got to his feet. "You've been very helpful. If you want to bill us, International Surety will pay a modest honorarium."

Anderson waved that away. "Glad to be of help. Glad to have a chance to show off my collection a little bit. Better let me show you the way out. People have got lost in this place and starved to death."

As Lindsey started toward his Volvo, he heard Anderson's door open behind him. He heard Anderson's voice. "Mr. Lindsey?"

He stopped and turned around.

Scotty Anderson stood in the doorway, matchstick in mouth. "You're sure Lovisi didn't send you?"

Lindsey managed not to laugh. "I'm sure."

"Funny." Anderson frowned. "I had a note from Lovisi last week, said that somebody else was interested in the Paige stuff. Said he was a serious researcher, claimed that he was some kind of professor or something."

"Have you heard from this person?"

"Oh, no. No way. Lovisi wouldn't do that. Let the bozo do his own work. I don't mind helping you, Mr. Lindsey. You're not a competitor, you see? But this bozo . . . Well, never mind. Long as you're sure Lovisi didn't send you."

Lindsey waved his thanks and slid his key into the lock on his Volvo. Then he stopped and turned back to see Scotty Anderson disappear inside his apartment. "Mr. Anderson! Just a second!"

The big collector turned around. "Hmm?"

"Maybe—would you mind—do you have this Lovisi fellow's address? Maybe I should get in touch with him."

Anderson stood still for a few seconds, an abstracted look on his face. Then he said, "Oh, sure," and rattled off an address in Brooklyn. Lindsey pulled out his pocket organizer, jotted down the address, and thanked Anderson.

HOBART LINDSEY AND Marvia Plum planned dinner at an Italian restaurant in the Richmond Marina. Marvia had got hold of some old radio shows on tape and on the way to dinner, cruising up the freeway in her classic Mustang, the headlights of oncoming cars flashing by hypnotically, she slipped one into the tape deck. It was a fifty-year-old melodrama, complete with commercials. The Shadow in "The Little Man Who Wasn't There."

Between acts, a hearty-voiced announcer urged the audience to support the war effort by conserving coal. The war was obviously World War II. The Spanish Civil War was over by then, and the Lincoln Brigadiers were probably back in uniform, fighting Fascism again. This time they were heroes instead of traitors, but they needed only to wait a few years. They'd be traitors again.

At the restaurant, Lindsey and Marvia Plum settled into a comfortable spot in the lounge. It was a cold January night, and outside the lounge's windows, the running lights of sailboats sparkled on San Francisco Bay.

Marvia asked Lindsey if he was making any progress finding Albert Crocker Vansittart's beneficiary. Lindsey recounted his paper chase, from Cody's to Moe's to the San Francisco Mystery Book Store to Scotty Anderson's amazing apartment in Castro Valley.

"It's funny." Marvia put her hand on Lindsey's. "It looks as if I'm going to be involved in this case, too."

"How so?"

The cocktail waitress interrupted, ready to take their orders. Marvia asked for a hot toddy; Lindsey, for an Irish coffee. The waitress departed. It was a pleasure to be treated like any other couple, with no odd looks just because you and your companion weren't the same color.

"Jamie's videotape."

"Really?"

"My son the celebrity. CNN made dubs of his tape for editing, but Jamie got his original back. Then the Washoe County Sheriff's Department asked if they could get a look at the tape, and of course my good little citizen was happy to cooperate with law enforcement."

"I'll bet he was having the time of his life."

"You bet he was. Well, they got the Coast Guard into the act and studied some of the landmarks in the background of the tape, studied their precious maps, and decided that the helicopter crashed in Nevada."

The waitress was back with their drinks. The glass containing Lindsey's Irish coffee was hot. He wrapped his fingers around it, savoring the heat. He looked at Marvia Plum and smiled, then looked past her at the bay, remembering the time he'd gone overboard from a powerboat near the San Rafael Bridge, a bullet in his foot. That was the first time he'd worked with Marvia Plum, the first time he'd got to know her. It was just a few years ago, but he remembered himself as another man living in another world. There had been a series of experiences that had changed his life. It had ended with a young man dead in an alley in Berkeley, a young woman in a wheelchair in Richmond, a strange man named Francis Francis dead in San Francisco Bay, and an individual whose seething envy of those more talented than himself had led to those tragedies, in prison. That man, a former university professor named Nathan ben Zinowicz, still haunted Hobart Lindsey's dreams.

But that had been years ago. Lindsey looked at Marvia Plum and felt a warmth inside his chest. He reached across the table and touched her cheek lightly.

"Is Washoe County in charge of the case, then?"

Marvia smiled. "It's a can of worms. Turns out that initial jurisdiction is federal. Airspace is federal, especially on an interstate flight. NTSB is interested in the cause of the copter crash, but other than the safety kids, the feds are delighted to hand off to anybody else who'll take the case. So—it may wind up in California, it may wind up in Nevada. For the moment, Nevada has it."

Marvia sipped at her hot toddy, then lowered it to the tabletop. "They're trying to get that fiber-optic scanner down to the chopper. If they do, they're going to need a top computer-graphics analyst to help them with it. They've already called one in to try and sharpen up Jamie's tape. See if they can get an image inside the copter bubble before it hit the water. One guess who the designated genius is."

"Fabia Rabinowitz."

"Bingo! Your old friend from Cal, right here in town. And guess who's the designated liaison officer between all of these entities."

"That's great. It means we can talk about this project, feed each other information without having to sneak it out the back door."

"Yep."

"How did you fall into that job?"

Marvia laughed. "You know there are only nine people in the world, right? And all the rest are just holograms."

"I've had the feeling a few times."

"The phone rings at McKinley Avenue this morning and it's a sergeant from the Washoe County Sheriff's Department calling to set up liaison with BPD. I catch the squeal—"

"I love it when you talk cop."

"—and the voice I hear sounds strangely familiar. Turns out it's Willie Fergus."

"I wouldn't know."

"We were in the army together. We were MPs in Wiesbaden."

"Colleagues? Friends?"

"We dated a couple of times. Before I got mixed up with the wonderful Lieutenant Wilkerson. I wound up pregnant, then married, then discharged, then divorced, then back in school, then a cop."

"Ah yes, I remember it well."

"Willie joined up young, did his twenty and out, and now he's U.S. Army retired and a sergeant for the Washoe County Sheriff. And you know what?"

Lindsey didn't know what.

"Willie thinks there's something fishy about this whole case."

Chapter Four

LINDSEY WATCHED CHICAGO grow through the window of a 757. O'Hare would be a madhouse, O'Hare was always a mad-house, but it was all part of the job. He felt better about the Van-sittart case knowing that Marvia Plum was involved in it at the California end, and he felt good about leaving Mother in the ca-pable hands of Gordon Sloane.

Sloane was the best thing that could happen to Mother. She'd been robbed of her husband at the age of seventeen by a tragedy at sea off the coast of North Korea. She'd spent the better part of forty years in a mental fog, devoting what little sense of reality she'd retained to raising the son her husband never lived to see.

It was only when Lindsey started, ever so cautiously, to untie the apron strings and move away from her that Mother began to discover herself. She was not yet sixty. She was healthy, intelli-gent, even attractive. There was still time for her to have a life.

Lindsey recognized the Sears Tower, then Lake Michigan, the pale sun of a late winter's afternoon glinting from its surface. Lindsey shivered. January in Chicago might be no colder than it was in Tahoe, but somehow he knew it would *feel* colder.

Before leaving California, Lindsey had posted a message on International Surety's KlameNet/Plus system, addressed to his friend and onetime roommate Cletus Berry, now a SPUDS agent in New York. The message included a sketchy rundown on the Vansittart case and the information Lindsey had got from Scotty Anderson. He asked Berry to check on Lovisi in Brooklyn and see what light he could shed on the matter, especially regarding the inquiry Lovisi had received about Paige Publications.

The Boeing touched down and rolled to a stop. Lindsey

waited obediently for the captain to signal, then stood up and retrieved his heavy coat and hand luggage from the overhead rack. He was wearing his official cold-weather traveling suit, with a cloisonné potato pin in the lapel. He'd had enough of airline baggage checks.

He'd phoned the SPUDS rep in Chicago, Gina Rossellini. They'd never met, and he wondered what she was like. Her name conjured up the image of a glamorous Italian actress, surely a cross between Gina Lollobrigida and Sophia Loren. Yes, Lollobrigida as she'd appeared opposite Bogie in *Beat the Devil*. And Loren—well, there could be no question. *Boy on a Dolphin* opposite Alan Ladd. Lindsey's fantasies took a detour when he heard Rossellini speak. She sounded like a character out of *Death in the Ditch*.

Lindsey had Scotty Anderson's Paige Publications bibliography in his pocket. It was also in his computer and in the electronic case file he'd transmitted to SPUDS headquarters in Denver. Whatever happened to him on this case, the information was safe.

When Lindsey came through the gate he spotted a woman holding a placard with a picture of a potato on it, identical to the one on his lapel. That was the SPUDS logo. She looked like an Italian actress, all right, but not like Lollobrigida or Loren. She looked more like Anna Magnani, *Rose Tattoo* vintage. Definitely the earth-mother type, fleshy and muscular, with olive skin and deep, dark eyes. She wore a black suit, high-heeled shoes, and big hair.

Gina Rossellini's dark eyes must have been sharp; she caught sight of Lindsey's lapel pin and held out her arms like an ideal Mediterranean mother. She had rented a car in Lindsey's name, a white Ford LTD. It was waiting in the airport parking structure.

Lindsey tossed his carry-on luggage and palmtop computer in the Ford's trunk. He'd never been in Chicago before so Gina drove. Heading away from O'Hare, she told him that she'd heard from Denver. "You've got a great little job there. All you have to do is track down a model from a forty-year-old painting."

"Better than that," Lindsey replied. "I don't have a copy of the painting. Looks like nobody does." He told her about his visit to Scotty Anderson. "At least I wound up with Paige Publications' address. And a list of their books. It's a start."

"You bet. You busy for dinner?"

Lindsey looked at his watch. It was a little early, but the winter darkness had settled quickly over Chicago while he was still in the airport. He could use a good meal and a good rest.

He checked into the Drake Hotel on Lake Shore Drive. It was an elegant establishment; entering the lobby was like stepping into Chicago's past. He half-expected to see Elliot Ness conferring with an underling, Frank Nitti stubbing out a cigarette in a potted palm.

They gave him a high corner room with windows on two sides and a view of Lake Michigan. There was a lock-bar in one corner, a couple of easy chairs, and an elegant writing desk with a wooden chair. Gina Rossellini said she had some errands to run, she'd meet him in the Cape Cod Room at 8:00. She'd already made a reservation for them.

He showered, then sat with his feet up, looking out over the lake. Lights of freighters moved slowly across its black surface. He phoned Marvia at home, but he'd forgotten the difference in time zones and got only her machine. He told her that he loved her and would talk with her soon. He left his hotel number in case she felt like calling him back. He called his own home and left a similar message for Mother.

He turned on his palmtop computer, plugged it into the hotel's phone line, and tapped into KlameNet/Plus. The computer whizzes had enhanced KlameNet into a corporate information system. If you had the right passwords you could tap into International Surety's main data base, file reports, dredge up records. It was wonderful. Almost as good as talking to somebody who knew what was going on.

First things first: Lindsey and all the other SPUDS operatives in the company were told to stand by for a meeting in Denver. The alert contained a little information on the planned program. It looked like a combination pep talk/threat, standard Ducky Richelieu stuff, seasoned with elements of class reunion and corporate convention. Knowing International Surety and Desmond

Richelieu, Lindsey figured there would be precious little drunken ribaldry at the gathering, a good deal of maneuvering, some promotions announced, and some involuntary transfers posted.

At least Lindsey had been invited. In IS, when you heard about a meeting like this one from a colleague but you weren't invited, it was time to polish up your résumé. Sometimes it was already too late.

There was nothing new on the Vansittart case. Lindsey had keyed the Paige Publications bibliography into the computer, and even though he still had the paper copy that Scotty Anderson had given him, he called the document up on the screen instead and sat there, staring at the titles and bylines.

Baseball Stars of 1952. He wasn't much of a sports fan; he noticed the headlines when one of the local teams made it into the World Series or the Super Bowl but he wasn't really *involved*. He had no idea who the baseball stars of 1952 would be . . . well, maybe a little idea. Some of the names still popped up on the 10:00 news. Was Joe DiMaggio still playing in 1952? Stan Musial? And that pitcher—his rental car reminded him of the guy. Yeah, Whitey Ford.

Well, no matter. That wasn't likely to have any bearing on the case. And *By Studebaker Across America*—now that sounded like a hot one!

He checked his watch. He'd reset it for Chicago time, and it was nearly time to meet Gina Rossellini at the Cape Cod Room. He shut down the computer, pulled on his shoes, and slipped into his jacket. He was relieved that the Cape Cod Room was part of the Drake. He was weary and the temperature must be well below freezing. He could hear the wind whistling past his room, trying to make it around the corner from Lake Shore Drive onto Michigan Avenue.

As he was leaving his room the telephone rang. He turned back and picked it up. It was Marvia. She'd heard from Willie Fergus in Reno. The UNR prof had lowered his fiber-optic scanner into Lake Tahoe, looking for the wreckage of Albert Crocker Vansittart's helicopter. The scanner had located the wreck. At that depth, of course, there was no natural light, but the same fiber-optic cable that could bring back an image to the surface could carry light down to the lake bed. The image, Marvia told Lindsey, was dark and unclear, but there was an image. They were going to bring in a stronger light-source and a more sensitive probe and try to get a clearer picture of the crash.

Later, Fergus had told Marvia, they hoped to bring up the wreckage, with Albert Crocker Vansittart inside. If he was still there. If something—crabs, fish, or maybe Tahoe Tessie—hadn't eaten him by then.

Lindsey said there was no progress at his end, but he was going to work in the morning and he had his hopes.

Marvia said, "Bart, I miss you. I love you."

He said, "Me, too." It sounded stupid to him, but it was all he could think of to say.

Downstairs, the Cape Cod Room was jammed. What Cape Cod had to do with a Chicago hotel was baffling, but the place was attractive and comfortable. There was even a fireplace with a huge blaze in it, perfect for a night like this.

Gina Rossellini must live nearby. Either that or she kept a change of clothes handy wherever she went, like Clark Kent. She wore a scoop-necked blouse that displayed her chest to maximum advantage, and she'd put on makeup and earrings and a necklace. The earth-mother look was gone; she actually looked elegant.

Hey, Anna Magnani would have looked elegant, too, if she'd dressed like this.

The food was good and Lindsey and Gina Rossellini shared a bottle of Bardolino with it. A brandy afterward helped, too. Lindsey was asleep almost before his head hit the pillow.

In the morning Lindsey set out on his quest. The temperature had dropped overnight and a thin, frozen mist was falling. He had to stop and buy a hat and a pair of gloves. He surveyed himself in the haberdasher's mirror. He looked like Jim Dial on *Murphy Brown*. He wondered if Charles Kimbrough ever felt as desperately outmoded as the character he played. He wondered if he was becoming obsolete himself.

Maneuvering the white LTD through crowded, slush-choked streets, he found LaSalle and Kinzie, parked, and walked to the site of the Paige Building. He'd expected to find a modest, old-fashioned commercial structure, but instead he found himself gazing at a modern office building that managed to shimmer in the gray mist like the ghost of technology. Surely this was not the Paige Building, but he pushed through revolving doors into the lobby and looked for a building directory, just to be certain.

No, this was not the Paige Building.

A uniformed majordomo must have read Lindsey's distress. He asked if he could help and Lindsey asked if he had ever heard of the Paige Building or of Paige Publications. The man shook his head.

Lindsey was ready to give up. He started back toward the revolving door, then stopped. There was a lobby newsstand. The proprietor, sitting behind stacks of Chicago *Tribunes* and *Sun-Times*, looked old enough to remember the first Mayor Daley, if not the earlier lords of the city. Lindsey picked up both morning papers and dropped a bill on the counter.

"You remember the Paige Building?"

The man looked up at him. His hair would have been pure white if it hadn't been for some peculiar yellow patches. He hadn't shaved for a couple of days. Lindsey was amazed that the management of a building like this one would tolerate the man, but here he was.

"Sure, I worked there."

"What happened?"

The man shrugged heavy shoulders and grinned. His teeth were not nearly as white as his hair. "They tore it down. What do you think happened, the Russkies stole it and sent it back to Rooshia?"

"When? I mean, when was it torn down? The Paige Building."

"I know what you mean. That was in, let's see . . . " The man had taken Lindsey's bill but had not bothered to return any change. Lindsey waited.

"This building went up in eighty-eight. The place was a vacant lot in between, you know? Part of the time it was just boarded up; part of the time they let kids play ball here. For a while they had a parking lot here. I worked here all the time. I used to stand on the street hawking papers, you know, like the old-time newsboys. I guess you could say I'm the last of the old-time news-boys."

He picked up a heavy weight that held down a stack of news-papers. Lindsey didn't see why he needed it here in the lobby, but it must have been good outside when the wind blew.

"They tore down the old place in," a faraway look came into the old man's eyes, "in seventy-two. That's right. They tore it down in seventy-two and they were going to put up town houses but that fell through so it just stood here, I mean the lot just stood here, for sixteen years. This building now, it's all modern-like and they have air conditioning and fancy elevators, comput-ers every place."

Lindsey didn't know if he was called upon to comment. He said, "It must be a nice place to work."

The old man said, "It stinks. Gimme back the old place any day. People knew each other. They stopped and gave you the time of day. You could walk in the street and not get murdered. Gimme back the old times, any day."

Lindsey rubbed his lips with the back of one leather-gloved hand. "What happened to Paige Publications? Were they here until, when was it, seventy-two?"

The old man literally cackled. "Not on your life, mister, noth-ing like. Old Paige Publications went belly-up back in the fifties. Early fifties. Oh, they had government men around here then, people coming and going, you'd of thought Joe Staleen person-ally was running the place. Hell, no, Paige Publications been gone since Ike was president."

"Did you know any of the people who worked there?"

The old man reared back in his chair. "Of course I did. I told you, people had time to give you the time of day back then. They'd stop and talk about the Cubs and the White Sox, the Bears, what was going on in the world, what they was up to in Springfield. Oh, those were the days."

"Was there actually a Mr. Paige? Did you know him?"

"Of course I did. I told you, I just told you. I used to see him every day, Mr. Paige. He ran the company, had a sweet little wife, used to work there too. Had a couple of kids. Hey, it broke the old man's heart when he lost that company. He kept the building for a few years, just rented out commercial space, but then he lost that, too. I don't know what happened to him. Where'd he go? Where do they all go, I ask you. He's gotta be dead by now. Gotta be. Just like that other poor sap was takin' flying lessons."

Lindsey blinked. "I don't follow."

"You wouldn't want to." The old man cackled. "Not that kind of flying lessons, nosiree. I mean, flying lessons without no airplane."

The old man grinned at Lindsey. "You ain't tracking, are you, youngster? I mean, that poor fella took a header off the roof. I seen him with my own eyes. Was right around the time those gov'ment fellas come around, right around the time Mr. Paige decided to close up the company. One fella used to hang around here all the time, wrote one of them little books for Paige. Went right off the roof."

"You know that? You saw it?"

"Hell, yes, I seen it. Went across the street for a pack of cigs. I useta sell a lot of them, nobody smokes no more. Back then, ran through a couple cartons a day. But I run out and I wanted a pack for myself. Was a little candy store across LaSalle back then, Greek fella run it. I run across the street to buy a pack of cigs, and I turn around and start back, and this fella's on the edge of the roof. I seen him. Mr. Paige was up there, tryin' to get him to come back in, but he wouldn't come back in. Went off like a high diver. Wasn't but five stories, but that was enough. Kilt hisself."

Lindsey asked, "Are you sure about this?"

"Hundert percent, mister. I had to go testify at the inquest. Man, it was just like bein' on *Perry Mason*. They decided it was an accident, he was up there sunning himself, got dizzy from the sun, and fell over the edge. That was that. That was the end of him."

"What was the man's name?"

"I hardly knew the fella before he tried to fly, then I found his name. Never forget it, neither. Everybody was saying, *Poor Del, poor Del*. Like, he wrote things, said his name was Del Marston. But at the inquest they said that wasn't his name. I won't forget that, not as long's I live. His real name, they said, was Isidore Horvitz. Yep, I remember that. Isidore Horvitz. They said he got dizzy in the sun and fell off the roof, but I know he jumped."

Lindsey rubbed his chin. The old man seemed certain of himself, but Lindsey pressed him. "How can you be certain that he didn't get dizzy from the sun? It seems possible, doesn't it?"

"I told you, young fella, I remember that day as clear as I do yesterday. Clearer, clearer. I remember that day. It was springtime, it was right before Easter, and it was cold and raining. Cold and windy and it was raining cats and dogs. He wasn't up there for the sun, there wasn't no sun to be up there for. I remember, young fella, I remember."

Lindsey switched to another tack. "Did you know Mr. Paige's first name? Or his wife's or children's?"

The old man rubbed his eyes. His fingers had the yellowish-brown color of a longtime smoker's. "I think it was Wilbur, William, something like that. I never knew the wife's name, and the kids was just babies, they didn't have no names as far as I was concerned, they was just babies."

Lindsey leaned over the counter. "Do you know where the Paiges lived?"

"I don't know. I think somewhere on the North Side. Maybe out of town. Where the heck. I think they lived up in Evanston or Skokie. Plain people could live there back then. You didn't have to be a millionaire to live anyplace. I tell you, mister, I tell you about the modern world."

Lindsey waited.

"The modern world, mister. It stinks."

LINDSEY TOOK A light meal, then returned to the Drake. There was an IS office in Chicago, and a separate SPUDS operation run by Gina Rossellini, but Lindsey set up a base of operations in his hotel room.

He started with a stack of Chicago-area telephone books. There must be hundreds of Paiges in the greater Chicago area, but the last of the old-time newsboys had mentioned Evanston and Skokie, and that was a logical place to start.

Paige, Wilbur.

Or Paige, William.

Or something like that.

He's gotta be dead by now. Gotta be.

But maybe not.

And even if Paige, Wilbur, or Paige, William, was dead—maybe there was a Wilbur or William Paige, Jr., living in the old house, or at least in the old neighborhood. In the old town. Living in the old hometown.

And if that didn't work—if there was no Wilbur Paige or William Paige, or if there was, and it turned out to be the wrong Wilbur or William Paige—Lindsey had the Paige Publications bibliography. God bless Scotty Anderson, and God bless Lovisi, the publisher, for getting Anderson to do the research.

If he couldn't find Paige, he could look for Violet de la Yema or Salvatore Pescara or Del Marston or Walter Roberts or J. B. Harkins or Bob Walters.

Somebody still had to be alive.

Lindsey would find the survivor.

An hour after starting, Lindsey realized that it was mid-afternoon and he hadn't eaten any lunch. He ordered a sandwich and a pot of coffee from room service and went back to work.

After another hour, he rolled the room-service cart back into the hall, yawned and stretched, and stood at his window looking out over Lake Michigan. The frozen mist had stopped falling, but the sky was still filled with fat clouds. They looked full of moisture, ready to let it go any time the mood overtook them. The lake itself looked cold and black and ugly.

Lindsey went back to work. He'd already tracked down two William Paiges in Skokie as well as three in Evanston, plus three Wilbur Paiges in Skokie and none in Evanston. Why was that? Had Evanston banned Wilburs?

Not likely.

Worse, none of the Williams or Wilburs or their spouses or children had anything to do with Paige Publications, or had even heard of Paige Publications. An Eleanor Paige in Evanston ("I live with my son William since my husband died") remembered the Paige Building in Chicago. It had been a family joke between her husband and herself. ("There's our building. Isn't it nice being landlords? I wonder how the tenants are doing.") But in fact her husband had been a wholesale butcher with a shop near the stockyards, and her son was regional manager for the Piggly-Wiggly supermarket chain. They really had nothing to do with the Paige Building or with Paige Publications.

Lindsey straightened his tie, slipped into his suit coat, and took the elevator downstairs. He walked into the bar and ordered a whiskey. There was a TV set above the back bar, tuned to CNN. Of course there was a set in Lindsey's room, but he hadn't turned it on. The picture looked murky, and for a moment Lindsey thought the satellite was acting up; but the bartender leaned his elbows on the wood and pointed at the set with one thumb.

"What do you think of that?"

Lindsey tried to figure out what he was looking at. This might be one of those wonderful medical shows featuring super blowups of some poor soul's intestinal parasites.

The announcer intoned, "These are the photographs that have the world of ichthyology in an uproar. Have scientists from the University of Nevada really found Tahoe Tessie, the mountain lake's cousin of Scotland's famous Loch Ness Monster, or is it merely a sunken log, or perhaps an overgrown Mackinaw trout?"

The image cut to a perfect co-anchor team seated behind a news desk. They weren't Dan Rather and Connie Chung but they could have passed for clones. The Connie had been speaking. Now the Dan took over. "In the Kremlin today, forces loyal to former leader . . . "

The bartender used the remote control to cut the volume on the set. "Lake Tahoe, hey? That's a little puddle. Those professors ought to take a look at the bottom of Lake Michigan. Then they'd see what a real monster looks like. Whadda ya think?"

Lindsey said, "You're absolutely right." He paid for his whiskey, left most of it in its glass, and headed back to his room. Once there he looked out the window again at the now black sky and black lake. He sighed and went back to work.

He could go in either of two directions. He could spread his net wider—look for Wilbur or William Paiges in Chicago proper, or in other suburbs—or he could keep trying Paiges in Evanston and Skokie, but not limit himself to William or Wilbur.

He decided on the latter course.

Another hour's work, and he hit pay dirt. He'd had to go a little past Evanston, but not very far. A Paul Paige on Willow Road in Winnetka announced that he'd just got home from work at the Chicago Museum of Science and Industry, where he was a senior curator. Yes, he knew about Paige Publications and the Paige Building. No, he didn't know any William or Wilbur Paige, but his father had been Walter Paige, founder and president of Paige Publications. No, he was no longer alive. Nor was his wife, alas.

But Paul was alive and well, thank you very much, and what was it that Mr. Lindsey wanted?

Lindsey explained that he was with International Surety and was trying to find the beneficiary of a life-insurance policy.

Mr. Paige said, "I've heard 'em all, brother, and believe me, that one's the oldest in the book."

Lindsey dialed Winnetka again. This time a woman answered. Lindsey asked, "Is this Mrs. Paige?"

Her voice was smooth, but not particularly friendly. "No, Mrs. Paige died many years ago. Who is calling?"

Lindsey said, "I'm sorry. I meant, Mrs. Paul Paige. I'm trying to—"

"Are you the insurance man?" she cut him off.

"Yes, but I'm not a salesman. I give you my word of honor."

"Then just what do you want?"

Lindsey tried to explain the Vansittart situation in twenty-five words or less. He must have done pretty well, because the woman who was not Mrs. Paige finally said, "All right, you may come to the house. Tonight. It's"—he could almost hear her look at her watch —"almost six-thirty now. We should finish our dinner by eight o'clock. You may join us then for coffee. Paul and I will try to assist you."

Lindsey thanked her.

"But I warn you," she added, "if you even try to sell me anything, I will go in the other room and get my gun and come back and kill you. I'm not joking."

She hung up.

Lindsey vowed silently not to try to sell her anything.

The phone rang. It was Gina Rossellini. How was Lindsey doing, did he need any help with the case, and was he all at loose ends in a strange city and looking for company for dinner?

He thanked her for the offer but begged off. He thought about phoning Marvia or Mother at home, then remembered the difference in time zones. He dialed Marvia at Berkeley police headquarters.

He got through to her and told her that he'd located the Paige family and was going out to their house in an hour. She said that Willie Fergus had called and told her that the fiber-optic probe at Lake Tahoe was getting good results. Lindsey told her about his conversation with the bartender. They promised to keep each other informed.

That was the end of the call.

He thought, Maybe if we were married I could get her to quit the police force. Then she could travel with me. This would be one heck of a lot pleasanter if I weren't alone in this city. I wouldn't have to fend off Gina Rossellini.

Then he thought, Do I *want* to fend her off?

Then he thought, Yes, I really do.

Then he thought, What if she looked more like Sophia Loren and less like Anna Magnani? Would you still fend her off?

Then he thought, *Yes*.

He ate another room-service sandwich for dinner, put on his Jim Dial topcoat and fedora, and picked up his white Ford LTD. The drive to Winnetka wasn't as bad as he'd feared; they kept the roads pretty clear in Chicago and the northern suburbs.

The Paige home on Willow Road was a tall Tudor set behind a broad lawn. A gravel drive led to the front door. Lindsey's prospective hosts had left a light burning—that was a good sign. The house sported a three-car garage, but there was already a new-looking Chevy Caprice in the driveway. Maybe there was more company tonight, or maybe the Paiges were a four-car family.

Lindsey had left his palmtop computer in his room at the

Drake. The only equipment he brought with him to Willow Road was his pocket organizer and his gold International Surety pencil.

The woman who answered the door wore a black maid's uniform complete with white apron and cap. Lindsey hadn't seen anything like her since AMC reran *My Man Godfrey* with William Powell and Carole Lombard. She took his fedora and topcoat and his card away and came back and ushered him into the living room.

Yes indeed, the family was assembled for their after-dinner coffee, and Lindsey was invited to join the fun.

The ceiling was high enough for a few small clouds to form among the heavy wooden beams. The floor was blue slate. The furniture was late Curt Siodmak hunting lodge. Lindsey half-expected C. Aubrey Smith to stride through a doorway, shotgun over his arm, a couple of newly killed partridges in his hand.

The woman who rose to greet him wore her white hair in a graceful upsweep that might not have been current but was definitely fashionable. She wore a dark green woolen dress and a simple golden chain that reached halfway down her chest. A tiny golden crucifix hung from the chain. Jesus looked happy and contented between the woman's breasts. She had received Lindsey's card and glanced at it as he approached.

She shook his hand. He noticed long fingernails, a first-rate professional manicure, a wedding band, and a large glittering rock.

"I am Patti Paige Hanson. Please do not make any jokes about the doggie in the window, I was tired of them thirty years ago. You are Mr. Lindsey. Please sit down. Doreen will bring you a cup of coffee. Is that satisfactory or would you prefer tea?"

She steered him to a sofa. He managed to get in a few words. "Coffee would be just fine."

Doreen poured the coffee. The silver was polished and the china, Lindsey would have bet, did not come from Japan. Tiny cubes of sugar were served with tiny silver tongs formed into tiny birds' claws. The creamer had a round belly and four little birds' feet.

There were three more people in the room. The older man—

his features faintly resembled Patti Paige Hanson's—sat quietly observing. His hair was not pure white, like Patti Paige Hanson's; it was silvery gray. His face was seamed and leathered, with the look of an outdoorsman's. He wore a blue pinstripe suit, a white shirt and a quiet tie. He was perfect.

He nodded to Lindsey. He said, "I'm Paul Paige. We spoke on the phone."

Patti Paige Hanson asked if Lindsey's coffee was all right. He tasted it. It was superb.

A boy who might be a youthful twenty or a regular sixteen sat on the edge of an easy chair. He wore a hounds-tooth jacket, a button-down shirt, striped tie, flannel slacks.

A girl who might be a year or two younger sat sideways in another easy chair. Her hair was cropped boyishly short and dyed jet-black. She wore death-white makeup, black eyeliner, and black lipstick. Her clothing was black and ripped in three or four places. She wore one fingerless glove.

Paul Paige said, "Ah, my nephew, Theo, and my niece, Selena. Hanson. Theo and Selena Hanson. They're my sister's children by her late husband, Gelett. Gelett Burgess Hanson, a nephew of the original Gelett Burgess. You've heard of Gelett Burgess, the famous author?"

Theo Hanson stood up and advanced to Lindsey. Lindsey stood. The boy said, "A pleasure to meet you, sir." He shook hands with Lindsey, then returned to his seat.

Selena Hanson sneered at Lindsey.

Lindsey confessed that he had never heard of Gelett Burgess, the famous author.

Patti Paige Hanson said, "A pity. His books are worthy of attention. I suggest that you investigate them when you return to your home." She paused to preen briefly, then went on. "Now, Mr. Lindsey, just what was it about this alleged insurance policy? My father—Paul's and mine—was indeed in the publishing business in the early nineteen-fifties. But you were not very clear on the telephone about this insurance policy."

Lindsey went over the case again. Mrs. Hanson seemed to listen intently. Lindsey couldn't be sure about the rest of the family. "What I was hoping, then, was to find any kind of records of

Paige Publications. Personnel files, financial records, anything that could help me find the girl on the cover of *Death in the Ditch*."

Mrs. Hanson shook her head. "Father seldom spoke of the publishing business. That all ended so long ago; then he concentrated on real estate. He had hard going for several years, but eventually he did very well, as you can see." Her gesture included the room, but it seemed to indicate the whole house, maybe all of Winnetka.

"There's a new building on the old Paige site at LaSalle and Kinzie," Lindsey said.

"Yes."

"I was there today and spoke with the man who runs the news kiosk in the lobby. He says he knew your father and mother. Knew both of you when you were small children."

Mrs. Hanson shot a look at her brother. "I wouldn't remember any of that. I was just a baby. So was Paul."

"The thing is, he mentioned some government agents visiting your father. Said that they came around repeatedly."

"Probably about taxes. Or some bureaucratic matter. You know how the government can be. They're a pack of self-serving Socialists in Washington. If not worse. Let me tell you something, the Soviet Union was never a threat to this country. The Communist menace comes from Washington, not from Russia. From Washington and Boston and Jew York. Decent people are going to have to build walls around themselves soon to keep the other kind out."

That's what Lindsey thought she said. He didn't ask her to repeat it. He said, "I do have a list of books that Paige Publications issued."

He unfolded Scotty Anderson's printout and spread it on the coffee table. Theo Hanson came over and looked at it. Selena Hanson sneered. Patti Paige Hanson said, "I'm sure I am not interested. What I would really like to know, Mr. Lindsey, is whether this insurance settlement involved the Paige family. If this money was left to an employee, perhaps the company is entitled to the money. I mean, some casual model, not even an employee, really. I never met Mr. Vansittart, but of course I knew of him. I was shocked to hear of his death. I'd think that the money should come to the company, you know, under the law of agency."

Lindsey shook his head. "I doubt that, frankly. It's really a question for Legal, of course, but I really don't think so."

Mrs. Hanson reached into a purse that appeared miraculously and extracted a jeweled eyeglass case. She unfolded a small pair of glasses and perched them on her nose. Lindsey almost expected her to use a lorgnette. She peered at the Anderson bibliography and sniffed. She shook her head. "No. No." She shoved the paper back toward Lindsey.

"Do you think your father might have left any personal notes on the company? Correspondence? If I could just get a lead on this girl . . . "

"Nothing." Mrs. Hanson stood up. Her brother and son followed suit. Selena swung one leg over the end of her chair, up and down and up and down.

Doreen reappeared with Lindsey's hat and coat. She must have been summoned telepathically. She helped Lindsey into the coat and handed him the hat. He turned to Mrs. Hanson and the others. "If you do think of anything, I'll be at the Drake for a little longer. Or you could try me at International Surety in Chicago after that; they'll get the message to me. If you do think of anything."

Paul Paige and Theo Hanson shook his hand. Patti Paige Hanson sniffed, touched her fingertips to his, and turned back into the house. Paul Paige wished Lindsey a safe drive back to Chicago.

Lindsey walked to the LTD and turned on the engine. He left the radio off during his drive back to Chicago, listening to the purr of the Ford's engine, the hum of its heater, the hiss of its tires on the slick black streets. There had been some snow here, but all that remained were low icy berms along the sidewalk and small patches on the broad lawns.

Somehow the car's sounds and its rhythms and counterpoints turned into a melody. By the time he pulled the LTD under the Drake's canopy and handed the keys to the parking valet, he was actually whistling.

All the way up in the elevator, walking along the corridor to his room, crossing the room and staring out again into the black winter night, he whistled, and wondered what the familiar tune could be. At last he remembered what it was. He actually sang a couple of lines.

> *How much is that doggie in the window*
> *The one with the waggily tail?*

He'd been stymied by Mrs. Hanson and her subservient brother, but somehow, as he fell into bed, he was grinning.

> *How much is that doggie in the window*
> *I do hope that doggie's for sale.*

Then the phone rang.

Chapter Five

OH, PLEASE, DON'T let it be Gina Rossellini. Lindsey looked at the digital clock on the night-table and calculated the time in California. Only nine o'clock. Maybe it was Marvia. Maybe—

"This is Sarah Kleinhoffer." The voice was low, almost a whisper.

"I'm sorry, I can hardly hear you, Miss—"

"Then listen harder, stupid. I have to keep my voice down. I don't want her to hear me."

"Listen here," Lindsey was annoyed, "I think you have the wrong room. Who was it—"

"You're Lindsey the insurance man, aren't you?"

"Yes."

"You were just at my house."

"I was at—"

"In Winnetka."

"Yes, but—"

"What's your room number? I have to see you, dig? I'm going to sneak out of here. Just don't leave, all right? Just stay put. What's your room number?"

He told her.

She hung up.

Dig.

Lindsey turned on the TV and channel-surfed. He finally settled on a rerun of a black-and-white episode of *Bewitched*. Samantha's evil look-alike cousin Serena was trying out her wiles on poor stupid Darrin, who couldn't keep his eyes in his head when she flaunted herself in front of him. The show was fun but

Lindsey preferred the earlier movie version with Veronica Lake and Cecil Kellaway.

The episode ended and another, featuring the visiting Dr. Bombay, began. They didn't even run a commercial in between. It looked like they were running a *Bewitched* marathon in Chicago.

Lindsey must have dozed, because he was awakened by a soft tapping at his door. He stumbled across the room in his suit trousers, shirt, and socks. He opened the door and confronted a witch—black hair, pale skin, black lips, tattered black clothes. She was clutching a shapeless sack that might contain anything from a jack-o'-lantern to a flock of vampire bats.

"That thug in the comic-opera uniform didn't want to let me in," she snarled. "Good thing Theo was along. My goody-goody brother."

Lindsey's head was beginning to clear. The witch was Selena Hanson. Selena, not Serena, but close enough. Her tweed-jacketed brother Theo stood behind her, grinning uncertainly.

"Uh—come in. I, ah—does your mother know you're here? Why did you—I thought your name was Paige; why did you say you were Sarah Kleinhoffer?"

The two young people moved past Lindsey, Sarah/Selena brusquely, Theo diffidently. As if he'd never left Winnetka, Theo perched carefully on the edge of a chair. His sister flung herself on the bed. She plopped her witch's sack beside her hip. Lindsey was relieved that he'd only lain down on top of the bedspread, and not pulled the covers back.

"My real name is Kleinhoffer." She looked around. "Swell pad. You got any dope?"

Lindsey gawked.

"Never mind. The bitch's real name is Kleinhoffer, too. Was. I guess she came by the Hanson honestly; she did marry the guy. But I wouldn't want the same name as her, so I went back to Kleinhoffer."

Lindsey shook his head. What was this all about? He decided to take it bit by bit. As the computer people would say, byte by byte. "You're talking about your mother, of course."

"Duhhh, no kidding. What was your first clue?"

"Her maiden name was Paige. Her father was Walter Paige, of Paige Publications. Her brother is Paul Paige, right? And your mother was Patti Paige? Like the singer?"

"I wouldn't know."

"She was very popular at one time. Patti Page, I mean. Uh, Patti Page the singer, not your mother. She spelled it differently but it sounds the same."

"I wouldn't know."

Sarah/Selena pushed herself upright on the bed. She reached for the remote, turned on the TV, hit the *mute* button, and surfed until she came to a shopping channel. "Look," she said, "I don't know what this business is all about, but I hate that bitch with her social climbing and her fancy airs. She's an uptight, materialistic bigot. She's a racist and an anti-Semite. That's why I took back Grandpa's name. Kleinhoffer."

"You—" Lindsey looked from Sarah to Theo. Theo nodded silently. Lindsey looked back at Sarah. "Walter Paige wasn't his real name?"

She smiled condescendingly. Lindsey must have the mind of a retard, based on Sarah's expression.

"Grandpa changed his name for business. Assimilation, that was what they all wanted to do back then. In his personal life he was still Kleinhoffer. And his first name wasn't Walter, it was Werner. He was a German Jew who got out of Europe just in the nick of time. Hitler and all that, you know."

"Yes, I do." Lindsey nodded.

"He came to America and assimilated. That was the name of the game. I don't think it was right but I can't blame him either. Not after what he'd seen in Europe."

"Aren't you awfully young to know all this?" Lindsey asked.

"I'm fifteen."

"Is that why your brother came along?" He nodded to Theo. The young man had allowed himself to slide back into his chair, maybe a fraction of an inch.

"Theo drove the Caprice. I would have driven myself, but the last time I got busted driving without a license, they kept me overnight in jail and the bitch threatened to send me to boarding school if I got busted again."

Lindsey looked at Theo. "Is this all true? I mean, do you agree with your sister?"

Theo nodded. "Every word, sir."

Sir.

Sarah—Lindsey had to accept her as Sarah, at least for the time being—Sarah laughed. "Theo's the radical in the family. I'm just a mild case compared to him. The straight clothes and the polite manners are just protective coloration. I guess he's right, but I couldn't make myself wear those stupid clothes and go to her stupid luncheons and mix with her stupid, shallow, bitchy friends. But hey, Theo puts me in the shade."

"Is that true, Theo?" Lindsey asked.

"Yes, sir," the young man said. "Every word, sir."

Sarah burst into laughter. "If you don't have any dope, a shot of booze would do."

"Uh, I don't know. I mean, that would be illegal."

"Right. Go take a piss while I open that little lock-bar. What's the combination? Don't tell me, just hold up your fingers."

Lindsey told her the combination.

She opened the lock-bar, tossed a miniature Scotch to her brother, and took one for herself. "Nothing for you, Mr. Lindsey?"

"Uh, I don't think so."

Sarah shrugged her shoulders, twisted the top off the bottle, and raised it high. "Here's looking at you, kid." She drained the miniature in one swig. At least she had good taste in movies.

Lindsey leaned on the writing desk and lowered himself onto the wooden chair. "You know that I'm looking for a model, right? You heard me explain things to your mother and your uncle? His name is really Paul Paige, isn't it?"

"Paul Paige or Paul Kleinhoffer—take your pick."

"Well, I mean, how do you know all of this? You're—you said, fifteen? And Theo, you're—?"

"Eighteen."

"And how old were you when your grandfather died? Had he

told you all this, about escaping Hitler and changing his name, I mean?"

"I was thirteen and Sarah was ten." Theo took over the narrative. "Dad had already died, and Mother refused to go to Granddad's funeral. The Jewish Sacred Society did the burying. The Jewish community honored him. The funeral procession passed the Mishna Ugmoro Synagogue on the way to the cemetery, and they opened the doors of the temple. I don't know if you understand that, Mr. Lindsey. Somebody not Jewish might not understand. We don't bring the dead into the synagogue. But to open the doors as the procession passes means a great deal."

Theo paused to gather his thoughts, then he continued.

"He was buried at the Shalom Memorial Park out in Palatine. He'd left instructions in his will, he'd talked with his lawyer about it, and if Mother changed his instructions, she would have lost her inheritance. She was furious. She said she might have gone to the service if it hadn't been Orthodox. She just couldn't put up with people tearing their clothes in grief, not washing, covering mirrors. She called it all absurd, throwback superstition. She couldn't see how her father would do such a thing to her."

Sarah interrupted with a giggle; then Theo resumed his narration.

"She left town. She wanted us all to leave town and boycott the funeral—can you believe that? But Uncle Paul insisted on staying, and Sarah and I stayed with him. Mother didn't get over it for months. She still beats us up with it when we get her riled."

"And he was buried as Kleinhoffer?" Lindsey asked. "Werner Kleinhoffer?"

"That's right. Of course, Sarah and I were baffled by the whole thing. We thought he was Walter Paige. We thought Mother was Patti Paige Hanson, not Patti Kleinhoffer Hanson. So after the funeral, Uncle Paul took us out for dinner at Charlie Trotter's over by Halsted. He let us order cocktails. The waiter was pretty pissed, but Uncle Paul was a regular there, and he got away with it. And he told us everything."

Lindsey stood up and walked to the window. Housekeeping had closed the drapes, but he pulled them open and looked out at Lake Michigan. After a minute he turned around again and looked at Sarah and Theo.

"Why are you telling me this? Why did you come here?"

Sarah rummaged in her witch's pack and emerged with a hand mirror and lipstick. She proceeded to replenish the blackness of her lips. Around the lipstick, she answered Lindsey's question.

"To burn the bitch. That's all, just to burn the bitch."

"Theo," Lindsey nodded, "you feel the same way? But you seem to be going along with your mother's game plan, her whole life-style."

Theo grinned. "This will get me into any college I want. This is my junior year at prep school, and I've already been accepted at Northwestern, University of Chicago, Oberlin, Harvard, Brown, Princeton, and Yale. I might have preferred McGill or Cambridge, or maybe the Sorbonne, but Mom thinks that any college outside the U.S. would just fill my head with bad thoughts." He laughed.

"Which one will you go to?"

"Which would you pick, Mr. Lindsey? Where did you go?"

Lindsey turned toward the lake again. "Hayward State." It sounded like an admission. He returned to the wooden desk chair. "You say your uncle told you all this family history."

"Right."

"What's his role in the household? If your mother is as bad as you say, why does he live with you? Is he a widower? Divorced? Or what?"

"He was never married." Theo had held onto his miniature Scotch bottle since taking it from the lock-bar. He got a glass from the bathroom, some ice cubes from the bar, and built himself a Scotch on the rocks. "Some story about a grand love, tragedy, heartbreak. Amazing melodramatic stuff, Aaron Spelling kind of stuff, Danielle Steel kind of stuff. He's lived with us as long as I can remember."

He took a careful sip of his Scotch on the rocks.

Sarah climbed off the bed and took another bottle from the lock-bar.

Theo crossed his legs and leaned back in his chair. "Uncle Paul is a goodhearted wuss. He hangs out with Sarah and me, he knows Mom is a total shit, but he won't confront her. You'd think he was pussy-whipped."

Sarah sat on the edge of the bed. "He is. Paul is the only man I've ever known who could get pussy-whipped without at least getting laid. Poor son of a bitch." She lifted her miniature bottle of Scotch. "Here's mud in yer eye!"

"Do you think you'll really find this model?" Theo asked.

Lindsey shook his head slowly. "I really don't know. The name 'Werner Kleinhoffer' might be of help. It would have helped a lot more if he were still alive. Are there any other sur-viving relatives? Other than your mom and your uncle, I mean."

"Nobody." Sarah took careful aim and tossed an empty mini-ature into the wastebasket beside the desk. She held the second empty over her mouth, stuck out her tongue, and managed to coax a drop of Scotch from the bottle. "Adolf got 'em all. Every last one of 'em. He really didn't like us Jews, you know."

Lindsey caught an exchange between Sarah and Theo. A look, a nod. Sarah got off the bed and carried her witch's pack to Lind-sey's desk.

"Grandpa kept a lot of records, you know. All his life. When the Paige Building was gone, he brought them home. He wouldn't throw anything away. Uncle Paul says that Grandpa always felt that Paige Publications should have been a success, that it was ruined by those Fascist bastards from Washington. Uncle Paul says that Grandpa wanted to keep an archive, that the family would see someday that he was doing something fine with Paige Publications."

Lindsey nodded.

Sarah resumed. "Then when Grandpa died, Uncle Paul says, the bitch burned everything."

Lindsey waited.

"But Uncle Paul saved something."

She opened her witch's pack and reached inside. Carefully, one by one, she removed the nine objects it contained and laid them out in neat formation on Lindsey's desk. They were a com-plete mint set of Paige Publications books, including both the *Teen Gangs of Chicago* and the *Al Capone's Heirs* versions of Paige serial number 104/105.

Theo Hanson—he still used that name—stood next to his sister. He put his tweed-coated arm around her shoulders, and she slid her slim arm in its ragged black sleeve around his waist. Theo laid his free hand on Lindsey's shoulder.

"We want you to take the books, Mr. Lindsey. We even talked this over with Uncle Paul. He was afraid to come with us. He was afraid that Mom might wake up and think the house was too quiet and start looking for us, and then the *merde* would really hit the fan. So he stayed home in Winnetka to calm her down if she starts to make a fuss. But he wants you to take the books, too. He's afraid that Mom will find them in his room and take them out and burn them, and that will be the end of Grandpa's dream."

Lindsey could have sworn that there were tears in Theo's eyes. "We want you to take them, Mr. Lindsey, and see to it that they're safe. Maybe they should be donated to a library or something, but we were afraid that Mother would find a way to get them back and destroy them. Don't let her do that, Mr. Lindsey. Promise you'll take care of the books."

Lindsey promised. Then he asked, "Do either of you know anything about Del Marston?"

Theo pointed to the books. "I know his novel. That's all."

"About his death?" Lindsey asked.

Theo shook his head, no. Lindsey looked at Sarah. No.

"Or Isidore Horvitz?"

"*Nada.* Blank. Sorry. Who's Isidore Horvitz?"

"I think he was Del Marston," Lindsey replied. "I think he killed himself sometime in the early nineteen-fifties. Long before your time. I just thought that your uncle might have said something about him."

"Sorry." Then, "About the books . . ."

Lindsey promised to guard them, to make sure they found a good home.

Theo and Sarah seemed satisfied. Theo said, "Thanks, Mr. Lindsey. You do what you can. I don't think you should try to contact us. Just take the books and find that girl. I think Grandpa would be pleased."

The two youngsters headed for the door. Before they left, Theo said, "Thanks again, Mr. Lindsey."

Sarah said, "Thanks for the booze. Some dope would have been better, but the booze was okay."

Lindsey blinked. The youngsters were already in the hallway but he stepped out and called them back. "I'm sorry. I just— what about this Burgess fellow your mother mentioned? He'd be, I guess, some kind of second or third cousin of yours. Your parents seem to think he was important. Do you—?"

"We have his books at home," Theo supplied. "Mother keeps them in a place of honor. I guess she didn't think you warranted a look at them. I'm sorry."

Lindsey said, "That's okay. I was just curious."

"They were murder mysteries. Of course, Mother refers to them as criminological studies. They're just whodunits. They're in a glass bookcase behind lock and key."

Theo and Sarah started toward the elevator, then Sarah stopped her brother again. "Nobody reads old Cousin Gelett's books anymore. They're dead as doornails. But I'll bet you've heard his magnum opus."

"I have?"

"*I've never seen a Purple Cow,*" Sarah quoted.

"*I never hope to see one,*" Theo continued.

"*But I can tell you, anyhow,*" they changed in unison, "*I'd rather see than be one.*"

"That was his great contribution?" Lindsey said.

"Yes, sir, it was." Theo took his sister by the hand and they left.

Lindsey sat on the edge of his bed. He tried to figure out Patti Kleinhoffer Paige Hanson and her hatred of her father. Maybe . . . Lindsey had a faint suggestion of an idea . . . maybe there had been something between Werner Kleinhoffer/Walter Paige and the model. Maybe young Patti found out about it. What happened to Patti's mother, Werner/Walter's wife? Had Kleinhoffer thrown her over in favor of the model? Was that the reason for Patti's cold rage?

He returned to the desk and laid out the Paige Publications books again. Typical paperbacks of their era, with garish colors and lurid blurbs. But for all that, they looked like brand-new books. Out of curiosity he picked up the beautiful copy of *Buccaneer Blades* and opened it, ever so carefully, to the title page. In blue-black ink that had not faded with the years, someone had written, *Salud y Suerte, Violeta*. He had never seen the inscription in Scotty Anderson's *Buccaneer Blades* so he could not tell if the handwriting was the same.

Lindsey got into his pajamas and climbed into bed. He left the drapes pulled back, the room lights off, and watched the first large snowflakes of a new storm drift by his window, illuminated by the lurid colors of an advertising sign.

THE MORNING SUN warmed Lindsey's face; its brightness wakened him. The odd visit of Sarah Kleinhoffer and her brother Theo Hanson had left him staring at the ceiling until sheer fatigue, and maybe a belated attack of jet lag, took effect.

He ordered breakfast from room service, then set up his palmtop and logged into KlameNet/Plus while he waited for the cart to arrive. There was a message from SPUDS/Denver. The World Fund for Indigent Artists had filed for Albert Crocker Vansittart's death benefits. The claim had reached Desmond Richelieu, and he had personally started the Standard Corporate Delay Hourglass running. Lindsey was to contact the Cookes in San Francisco ASAP.

It was too early to phone anyone in California, including Marvia Plum, so he turned to his meal. Both Chicago morning papers, the *Trib* and the *Sun-Times*, were included with Lindsey's order from room service. He browsed through the newspapers while he ate his scrambled eggs and sweet rolls. The events of the world kept rolling along on their usual disastrous course.

He turned to the sports section. There was the standard hype that preceded the Super Bowl each January; but with the Bears out of the running, as usual, the local sheets were more interested in the ongoing exploits of the Chicago Bulls. There were even a couple of early articles speculating about the scheduled opening of baseball spring training. Would the Cubs do any better this year? Would the White Sox do any better this year?

Would there even be a baseball season this year, or would labor disputes wipe out the entire schedule?

Lindsey put down the newspapers and picked up his coffee. It was amazing, a hotel that actually served hot, fresh, strong coffee to its room-service customers. He sipped from the china cup and gazed out the window. Something was tickling inside his skull. He squeezed his eyes shut and tried a mental exercise he'd once heard of, softly humming an ancient James P. Johnson tune he'd heard on a CD at Marvia Plum's apartment.

Put your mind right on it . . . put your mind right on it. . . . Don't you hesitate . . . put your mind right on it . . . let it percolate. . . .

Lindsey knew it was silly but strangely enough it worked. An image appeared in his mind, something that had happened only a few hours ago. Sarah Kleinhoffer in her stark black outfit, emptying her witch's pack onto his desk, spreading the nine books that Paige Publications had issued during its brief career in 1951 and 1952.

He opened his eyes. The books were still there. He picked up *Baseball Stars of 1952* by J. B. Harkins. Werner Kleinhoffer—and after Kleinhoffer's death, Paul Paige—must have kept the nine books in a safe place for all those years because the covers were just as bright and glossy as they would be on brand-new books. Lindsey picked up the baseball book and turned it over.

There was no author photo or biography on the back, but then there seldom were on paperbacks. Paperback publishers usually devoted that precious display space to harder-sell material, either for the book at hand or for others in their line. That was what Paige Publications did. The back cover of *Baseball Stars of 1952* featured a miniature reproduction of the cover of *I Was a Lincoln Brigadier* by Bob Walters.

That seemed odd to Lindsey. You'd expect a cross-promotion to be devoted to a book with a similar theme, a western on a western, he thought, or a mystery on a mystery. Of course Paige had turned out so few books, that might have been impossible.

Hmm.

Lindsey laid the book back down, then turned over the other eight titles. Now an interesting difference revealed itself. On the

1951 titles, the cross-promotion principle was carried out.

He'd already seen one Paige book, Scotty Anderson's copy of *Buccaneer Blades*, with promotion material for *Death in the Ditch* on the back cover. Now he held a copy of *Death in the Ditch*, and its back cover ad space was given over to *Cry Ruffian!* by Salvatore Pescara. Okay, he mused, that one made sense. *Cry Ruffian!* was blurbed as "A rough, tough, angry novel of a poor kid who vowed to make society pay for his father's death—and kept his word!"

There were a great many exclamation points on the back covers of Paige Publications books.

The 1951 books worked like a round-robin. *Buccaneer Blades* promoted *Death in the Ditch*, which promoted *Cry Ruffian!*, which promoted *Teen Gangs of Chicago*, which promoted *Buccaneer Blades*. The books were numbered 101 through 104.

But *Al Capone's Heirs* was something different. It was the same book as *Teen Gangs of Chicago*. Lindsey checked the contents of the two books, opening them carefully only as far as he needed to, so the dried glue that held the pages to the cover wouldn't crack. No question about it. Only the cover and the title pages were different.

But *Al Capone's Heirs*, Paige number 105, must have come out after the 1952 Paige line was in progress, because its back cover was given over to promoting *I Was a Lincoln Brigadier*. And *all* of the 1952 Paiges had the same back cover: a miniature reproduction of the *Lincoln Brigadier* cover and an almost-poetic paean to the Spanish War volunteers, with a long quotation from Ernest Hemingway, of all people.

More to the point, though, was the copy of the Del Marston book. He returned to *Death in the Ditch*, studying the gang moll on the cover. *Schweetheart*, he whispered to himself in his best Bogie imitation, *you've got one big pile of money coming to you.* And then added, *If you're still alive. And if I can find you.*

Lindsey shook his head, stacked the nine Paige books carefully, and packed them away in his airplane luggage. He carried the Chicago papers back to the desk and leafed through them again. Then he opened his luggage and extracted *Baseball Stars of 1952*. On the front cover, beneath J. B. Harkins's byline, was the tag, *Ace Chicago Sports Reporter!* Lindsey couldn't figure out why that rated an exclamation point, but who was he to judge?

He checked the Chicago telephone directory for J. B. Harkins. No such listing. Rather than repeat the search that had led him to Paul Paige and Patti Paige Kleinhoffer Hanson in Winnetka, he looked up the Chicago *Sun-Times*, punched in a number, and asked for the sports desk.

Two minutes later, he was talking with Maude Markham.

He'd found her picture at the head of a column called "Fifty Years Ago in Chicagoland Sports." From the looks of the photo, she was more likely to write from memory than she was from the newspaper's doubtlessly extensive morgue.

Lindsey could have asked his questions on the phone, but he'd found in the past that personal contacts often yielded better results than telephone inquiries. He cut an unprepossessing figure—he knew that—and he was the master of a ploy that he called the *I'm-just-a-poor-working-stiff-doing-my-job-ma'am-won't-you-please-help-me-out* approach.

Maude Markham sounded like an amalgam of Marjorie Main and Jane Darwell—strong, gruff, with just a touch of the old heart-of-gold. She'd just shivered in from covering a Polar Bear Club meeting and swim in Lake Michigan, she announced, and she was freezing her bunions off. If Lindsey wanted to come to the office and ask her a few questions about old-time Chicago sports, she could give him a few minutes. He said he'd be right over.

An hour later he presented himself at the sports desk of the *Sun-Times*. Leaving the Drake, he'd been presented with a spectacular sight: downtown Chicago glistening in bright sunlight under a coat of fresh, sparkling snow. He knew better than to think it would stay that way. Even though he wasn't accustomed to seeing big-city snow, he had no illusions that this urban wonderland would last. Chicago, Illinois, was not Tahoe City, California. But for a little while, at least, until the salt of a thousand snow-clearing machines turned it to slush and the soot of a hundred thousand chimneys turned it to filth, the overnight fall had turned Chicago into a living greeting card.

Now he walked through the lobby of the *Sun-Times*, confirmed that he really had an appointment with Maude Markham, and rode up in the elevator to present himself. He had his pocket organizer and his International Surety gold pencil with him, his shield and his lance. And in another pocket, carefully protected by a Hotel Drake envelope, *Baseball Stars of 1952*.

Maude Markham was a perfect match for her voice and for the picture that headed her column in the *Sun-Times*. She had an electric space heater beside her desk, sending orange-red warmth toward her knees.

Her first words to Lindsey were, "You'd think that five columns a week would be enough for the sonsabitches, but I have to take spot assignments to boot. Fucking Polar Bears, they ought to freeze their dicks off in that freezing lake. Then I could sleep in every January." She nodded toward the space heater. "Illegal as hell. Nobody better try and take it away from me, or I'll skin 'em alive."

Then she looked at Lindsey and said, "What can I do for you, sweetums? I don't have as many swains as I used to." She was wearing a sweater. No, Lindsey realized, she was wearing a series of sweaters. There might be a shape under all that wool, or then, again, there might not.

"I was wondering if you ever knew J. B. Harkins."

Maude Markham's eyes popped. "Jeb Harkins? Of course. Everybody knew Jeb."

Lindsey started to say something, but she cut him off.

"What are you after, bubby? You must be the first person to ask about Jeb in fifteen years. Maybe twenty."

Lindsey didn't want to go into the whole Vansittart–Paige Publications–*Death in the Ditch* story, so he said, "Harkins wrote a book called *Baseball Stars of 1952*, right?"

Maude Markham nodded. "I even did a column on it."

"You did?"

"I write about fiftieth anniversaries, so I did a piece on Jeb's book when spring training opened in ninety-two. Filed from Florida. I hope they have a baseball season this year; I could sure use a little Florida sunshine."

Lindsey wrinkled his brow. "Wait a minute. Nineteen ninety-two minus fifty doesn't give us nineteen fifty-two, it gives forty-two."

Maude Markham grinned. "You ain't so dumb, sweetie. Smarter than my editor is, he didn't catch on. I figure, by the real fiftieth anniversary, Jeb might not be around anymore to enjoy the piece I wrote. Hades, I might not be around to write it. So what the heck, I went ahead and you know how many letters I had about it, not one, would you believe that? Not one. The world is full of morons. Nobody can add two and two without a damned Univac anymore."

Lindsey nodded encouragingly.

"I sent Jeb a copy of the piece, and he wrote me back a letter, like to break my heart. Poor old bastard, we used to have some great fights, but he didn't deserve what happened to him."

She shook her head. She turned away from Lindsey and punched up a file on the monitor screen on her desk. Lindsey read the headline. *Polar Bears Brave Snowstorm and Icy Lake for Big Swim.* Maude Markham said, "They try to rotate that assignment, send somebody else out every year to cover the Polar Bear swim. Doesn't matter. They always come back with the same story. Change a few names to cover the old bears dying off and the young ones joining the club, you could recycle last year's copy."

She blanked the screen and swung around in her swivel chair.

"You have a copy of Jeb's book?"

"Yes."

"Real nice. So do I. So what?"

"Well, I'm actually trying to track down a woman who modeled for another book published by the same company. The same company that published *Baseball Stars of 1952*, you see, and I thought if Mr. Harkins is still alive, and I could talk with him, he might be able to help me. So if you could help me get in touch with Mr. Harkins, don't you see . . . "

Maude Markham looked up at Lindsey. "You really have a copy of that book? 'Cause I haven't seen a copy in eons, ducks, except the one on my shelf at home."

"Here it is." Lindsey laid his copy of *Baseball Stars of 1952* on Maude Markham's desk. He grinned.

Maude Markham opened the Drake Hotel envelope gingerly. She must know something about old books, then, or maybe she was just naturally cautious. She slipped the book out of the envelope and laid it on her desk. She smiled wistfully.

"Look at those ballparks."

The cover of *Baseball Stars of 1952* featured a montage of faces of ball players in their colorful caps, and around them, like a giant wreath, a circle of pictures of stadiums. The players' portraits looked like miniature paintings; the ballparks were pen-and-ink sketches. All of this on the cover of a book no bigger than four inches wide and six inches tall. Lindsey recognized some of the ball players' caps, if not the men wearing them. Others might have belonged to the Beijing Ducks, for all he could tell.

Tersely, Maude Markham identified the teams for him. "Boston Braves, Brooklyn Dodgers, Philadelphia Athletics, St. Louis Browns, Washington Senators. You ain't a baseball fan, are you, sweetcakes? No, I didn't think so."

"And Mr. Harkins himself?"

"What about him? Great old-time news hound. Went way back. Way back. Used to work at the old *Daily News*. Got his jock-journalist start on the *Inter-Ocean*. Bet you never heard of the *Inter-Ocean*, did you?"

Lindsey admitted he had not.

"Terrible paper. Don't know how it lasted as long as it did. But an old news hound could always get a gig there. More alcoholics than a drunk tank on New Year's Morning. But it was a lot of fun. Oh, yes. Old Jeb, he worked with Vincent Starrett, Ben Hecht. He knew everybody, told stories you wouldn't believe."

She shook her head as if she didn't believe it either.

"Killed me when he retired. I always felt young when the old coot was around. Nowadays, everybody thinks *I'm* old. Even *I* think I'm old. Heck, who am I kidding, I *am* old. What am I going to do, sit in a rocker and crochet? Hades, I don't know *how* to crochet and I'm too damned old to learn, so I better keep on working. What were you asking me, darling?"

"About J. B. Jeb Harkins. What happened to him? Where he is now. He's still alive, isn't he?"

"Far as I know."

"Then—?" Lindsey left the opening, waiting for Maude Markham to fill it.

She did.

"Die young, sweetie, that's my advice. I should have took it myself, but it's too late, I'm old already." She heaved a sigh. "You've been standing there all this time. Pull up a chair. Hey, steal one—nobody cares."

Lindsey complied.

"Jeb was one of those poor souls who keeps falling in love with the wrong woman and getting thrown over, you know what I mean? Got married three or four times, I don't know how many. Had a son with one wife, boy was in the air force, got shot down over Russia, never heard of again. Whole thing was hushed up, just one more Cold War casualty. Had a daughter, she got married, had some kids, they went off to God-knows-where. Jeb's daughter and her husband moved to San Francisco. Then he died—Jeb's daughter's husband—and she couldn't take it being alone, so she talked Jeb into coming to live with her."

She stopped talking, opened a desk drawer and reached into it for something, then pulled her hand back empty, shook her head, and slid the drawer closed. Lindsey recognized the series of actions. Another involuntarily reformed smoker.

"Jeb was living in a little apartment out on Trumbull Avenue near Garfield Park," she resumed. "You know Garfield Park? No? Well, no matter. He had his pension then, so he kept puttering. He'd write a piece now and then for the weekly shopper or sell something to the Sunday magazine—more for the fun of it than for the money."

She shook her head, looking past Lindsey, seeing something that he might see someday.

"So like I said, Jeb's daughter talked him into coming to live with her. Bad move. He lost his place, you know what I mean?

New surroundings, new people, he wasn't independent anymore, poor old coot. Then his daughter got sick and she couldn't take care of him anymore, and she put him in a home. Then she died. And there he is. I don't know what the hell he does with himself. Probably sits around waiting for the undertaker, poor old coot."

Lindsey felt for his pocket organizer, slipped it unobtrusively out of his jacket, revved up his gold pencil.

"Ms. Markham—"

"Call me Maudie, sweetheart, just Maudie. When I start to lose it, I know exactly what I'm going to do, believe me. I'm going home, swallow a handful of pills, and climb into a nice hot bath with a full bottle of brandy. I'll have five Sinatra CDs started on the player. I'll drink up that brandy and I'll listen to Frankie. I think the last thing I'll hear in this shithole of a world is Frankie singing 'I Did It My Way.' Or maybe 'Come Fly with Me.' Just not 'Chicago.' This town does *not* toddle. Not anymore it doesn't. I don't want to check out with that damn thing in my ears." She blew out a breath that made her lips vibrate. "Now, I've got work to do. Anything else I can help you with before you run along?"

Lindsey nodded. "Did you know anybody else connected with Paige Publications?"

She shook her head. "Nope. Just Jeb, and only because we worked for the same paper."

"Are you still in touch with him? Do you have an address for the nursing home, or a phone number? What kind of shape is he in? Do you think he could answer some questions about Paige?"

Maude Markham laughed. Threw back her head and laughed. Lindsey noticed that she had excellent teeth, especially for a woman of her age.

She flipped open an industrial-grade Rolodex and pulled a card. She laid it on the desk in front of Lindsey. He jotted down the information and put away his pocket organizer and gold pencil.

"One other thing," Lindsey said.

Maude raised her eyebrows inquisitively.

"Did you ever meet Del Marston? Or Isidore Horvitz?"

A new expression came across Maude's face. "Of course I did. Everybody knew about him."

"What really happened? How did he die?"

"Got dizzy. what a tragedy. Only man I ever heard of, dying of dizziness. Went up on the roof of the Paige Building to sunbathe, and got dizzy from the sun and fell over the parapet. I think he must have been drinking a little, too. Booze will do that to you, booze and strong sunlight."

Lindsey tilted his head. "But I thought he died on a rainy day. Cold and rainy."

Maude said, "It was the sun. Sun and booze. Look, I'm really a busy person, I have to do my job. If you don't mind." She pulled her outermost sweater up until her face was half-concealed, then turned away.

Lindsey said, "Thank you, Ms. Markham, you've been a lot of help," and left the *Sun-Times* building. At least he'd got another lead. He had J. B. Harkins's address. Harkins lived at the Shady Oaks Retirement Villas in Livermore, California.

Lindsey had done about all he could do in Chicago. He retrieved his Ford LTD and drove carefully back to the Drake on Lake Shore. Once upstairs in his room, he packed his belongings and called the desk to have his bill prepared. Before putting his palmtop in its case he plugged it into a phone line for one more check of KlameNet/Plus.

There was a message waiting for him. From Cletus Berry.

Berry had located Lovisi at the Brooklyn address Scotty Anderson had given Lindsey. Lovisi had been open and cooperative. He told Berry that the inquiry he'd received shortly before arranging to run Anderson's piece in *Paperback Parade* had surprised him because *Death in the Ditch* and all the Paige books were so very obscure. Even many serious collectors had never heard of Paige Publications. And most of the serious collectors knew each other, either in person or at least by reputation.

Lovisi had never heard of the person looking for information on the Marston book. It was an unusual name, too. Lovisi hadn't written it down—he hadn't needed to. He had an eidetic memory. The caller's name was Nathan ben Zinowicz. The only address ben Zinowicz had given was an electronic-mail number. As far as Lovisi—or Cletus Berry—knew, the e-mail could be picked up from anywhere. Just as Lindsey had picked up Berry's message here in Chicago.

Lindsey felt a cold hand grab his insides and squeeze. Nathan ben Zinowicz was the man behind the theft of the rare comic books that had started Lindsey on his career as a de facto detective. Ben Zinowicz might not have killed the poor kid who operated the comic-book store, but he was the man who beat a young woman and put her in a wheelchair for life, and he was the man who had put a bullet through Lindsey's foot and left him to drown—very nearly—in San Francisco Bay.

And he was the man who—the local police said they had no jurisdiction, and the United States Navy didn't want to hear about it—but he was the man, Lindsey was morally certain, who had caused Lindsey's father's death aboard the destroyer *Lewiston* in the Sea of Japan, a few months before Lindsey himself was born.

Lindsey sent a brief thanks to Berry. Then he opened the Vansittart file and updated it before logging off. He phoned the airline and reserved a flight back to Oakland. Fortunately, the snowfall had ended and O'Hare was open.

Lindsey passed up the food on the 757. By the time it touched down at Oakland International, he had a first-rate appetite. He'd splurged International Surety's money to place an in-flight telephone call to Marvia Plum and another to his mother. He told Mother he was on his way home and he'd see her either late tonight or else tomorrow. She was pleased. He thought he heard Gordon Sloane's voice in the background.

Marvia agreed to meet him at The Fat Lady in downtown Oakland. She had some things to tell him, but they could wait for an hour. There was nothing he could do in a Boeing six miles over Colorado.

Chapter Six

IT WAS RAINING in Oakland and the air was cold and damp, but the blue Volvo 544 started without hesitation. Lindsey paid the parking fee and hopped onto the freeway. As he passed the Oakland Coliseum he switched on the radio and punched the preset for KJAZ. Marvia had helped him cultivate a taste for both classical music and jazz, just two of the many reasons he had to be grateful to her.

Instead of the piano of McCoy Tyner or the horn of Sonny Rollins or the voice of Billie Holiday, Lindsey's ears were assaulted by the last notes of a wild salsa tune followed by a commercial in rapid-fire Spanish. He didn't understand the language but he recognized the brand of tires every time it was mentioned.

He hit the preset for a classical station. Maybe some Mozart or Haydn would get him through the traffic. A nasal tenor voice was ranting about the latest disagreement between the President and the Senate Majority Leader over the best way to deal with the soaring budget deficit and the soaring crime rate and the soaring. . .

Lindsey turned off the radio.

Nothing good seemed to last.

He parked on Washington Street and pushed open the cut-glass front door of The Fat Lady. Marvia was sitting at the bar. She must have had one eye on the street entrance because she swung around as Lindsey came through the door. In an instant she was off her bar stool and in his arms. She felt warm against him. He was home.

On a chilly night Lindsey savored the double warmth of an Irish coffee. Marvia was nursing something in a tall glass. To the bartender, she said, "Don't take it personally, Jim. We have to talk." She dropped a bill on the bar and took Lindsey's hand. They sat at a table in a half-concealed booth. The place was decorated with antique advertising signs from San Francisco and with romantic nineteenth-century nudes; the bar was jammed with dress-for-success types unwinding after their days' work.

Just looking at Marvia made Lindsey grin, but she did not look happy. She held both his hands in hers. He said, "Marvia, something's the matter."

She didn't pull any punches. "Ben Zinowicz is out."

"Out of prison?"

She nodded.

He said, "That's no surprise. I've already crossed trails with him."

Now Marvia was surprised. She asked how Lindsey had encountered ben Zinowicz, and he told her about Cletus Berry and his conversation with Lovisi.

Marvia's comment was a grunt of annoyance.

Lindsey said, "But I thought he was in San Quentin for the long haul. I'll admit that I was startled when Berry told me he was back on the street. How could they let somebody like that out?"

"They're cleaning house again, dumping prisoners to make room for more prisoners. Three strikes and all that."

"But—"

"I know."

"But he killed—"

"I know."

"He—" Lindsey pulled one hand free from Marvia's, squeezed tighter with the other. He held his temples between thumb and forefinger of his free hand, staring into the hot golden-brown liquid in his glass.

"He killed that poor kid in Berkeley. He killed my fucking father! He crippled that poor girl, that radio announcer, Sojourner Strength. He put her in a wheelchair. He shot me and he was going after Mother when you guys finally caught him."

She squeezed his fingers with hers and touched his cheek with her free hand. "You knew about his plea bargain."

Lindsey half-moaned, "Sure."

"The navy wouldn't prosecute him for what happened in Korea. Even though there's no statute on murder, it was just too many years, the evidence was too flimsy, the whole thing was conjecture."

Lindsey looked into her eyes. "How can you say that?"

She looked straight back. No avoidance. "You know he did it and I know he did it, but the navy just didn't want to get involved in a case that was almost forty years old. And that took place halfway around the world. And that their records looked clean on. They just didn't want to get involved."

"Anchors away." The words sounded as ugly to Lindsey's ears as they tasted bitter in his mouth.

"And you know he had an alibi for killing that boy behind the comic-book store. His weird friend with the weird name—"

"I know. Francis Francis. I had a nasty encounter with that one, too."

"Well, he's dead. And Nathan ben Zinowicz wasn't above pinning everything he could on Francis."

Lindsey took a deep breath. "So the long and the short of it is, he's a free man. Three people are dead—at least three that we know about—because of him, and that poor girl is crippled for life, and ben Zinowicz is free as a bird. And back here, too, I suppose."

"They had to parole him back here. That's the law. But he's not quite as free as a bird. He didn't insist on serving his time to the last tick of the clock and then walk away, give us the finger, like that fellow who brained his faculty adviser down at Stanford. Ben Zinowicz is on parole, and I know his parole officer. So that's something, anyway."

"Yes, I suppose." He pulled his hand free of Marvia's and sat up straight in the booth. The warmth of the room and the pleasure of being with her and surrounded by dark wood and old paintings had evaporated. "Can I find out this parole officer's name? Is that public information, or do we have to protect the privacy rights of the good professor? I mean, he only goes around killing people he doesn't like. It isn't as if he forgot to put a nickel in the parking meter or something heinous like that."

"I'll give you his name. You can go talk to him. He's a good man, an ex-cop. You'll get along."

"But?"

"What?"

"Isn't there a *but* to this?"

"No. Let's get out of here. Let's go home and go to bed."

"No." Lindsey shook his head. "You haven't told me everything. I know I'm not the world's most perceptive guy, Marvia, but I know you haven't told me everything."

"He has a job."

"Sure. They probably made him Dean of Students at Cal. Nothing like helping an ex-con rehabilitate himself. I'll bet he has a federal grant to write his memoirs: *History Will Vindicate Me.*"

"No."

"What is it, then?"

"He's the executive secretary of the World Fund for Indigent Artists."

THEY STOPPED FOR take-out on the way to Marvia's flat in Berkeley. The turret in the Victorian on Oxford Street had become Lindsey's favorite refuge. When he was there with Marvia, Lindsey felt safe, insulated from the violence and madness of the world.

Lindsey didn't have much appetite tonight. The format changes of the two radio stations were just annoyances; they had nothing to do with him anyhow, but they'd seemed like omens.

The news about Nathan ben Zinowicz was not just an annoyance. Maybe the man would have kept away from Lindsey and Mother; that was Lindsey's thought when Marvia first told him that ben Zinowicz had been released from San Quentin. But that job—

Lindsey had to talk with Roger St. John Cooke or with Cynthia Cooke, maybe with both of them. They had a material interest in Albert Crocker Vansittart's death benefits, and Lindsey fully expected them to play hardball in their efforts to collect four million dollars.

That was bad enough. Anticipating that had given him plenty of bad moments. But the knowledge that Nathan ben Zinowicz was now associated with the Cookes was like a hot dagger in the side of Lindsey's skull.

Marvia put the take-out food in the refrigerator in the common kitchen. Lindsey said he wanted to take a walk. He couldn't sit in the downstairs living room of the Oxford Street Victorian with Marvia's friends hanging around, arguing about politics and recipes and sex and Joe Montana versus Steve Young and brands of beer. Nor did he want to go upstairs to Marvia's flat. Normally it felt cozy to him, a happy nest in the center of a tempestuous world. Tonight he knew it would just seem claustrophobic.

They walked up to the Berkeley rose garden, watched skateboarders and roller bladers honing their technique, then stopped and looked at the view. From the rose garden they could see across Berkeley to the Bay and to San Francisco across the water, the lights of the bridges and of the city's buildings glittering like special effects.

Marvia Plum told Lindsey about the Tahoe and Berkeley end of the Vansittart investigation. It had taken a series of attempts, but finally the UNR people had gotten a usable fiber-optic probe to the wrecked helicopter. The feds were involved, and that helped ease the costs of the project. The chopper was lying upside-down on the silty bottom of the lake. Getting the probe to the helicopter had been only the first hurdle. Getting a clear view through the Plexiglas bubble came next; even once that was achieved, the results were ambiguous.

Fabia Rabinowitz had tapes from the probe and she was working to clear them up. She also had Jamie Wilkerson's Handycam tape and had started sharpening the definition of that as well.

Marvia Plum had seen the tapes and described them to Lindsey. The crabs had got to Albert Crocker Vansittart, and the flesh was coming off him in strips. It was a horrifying sight, but in a way it was helpful, because the probe caught a picture of his skull. It was badly bashed in.

"But that doesn't prove anything," Marvia Plum said. "That might have happened in the crash. John O'Farrell, the pilot, came out of the crash with a broken leg. The same impact that snapped his leg bones could just as well have broken Vansittart's skull."

"Or maybe not."

"No?"

Lindsey was getting interested. Sherlock Holmes had found puzzles more interesting than cocaine. Hobart Lindsey found them more appealing than depression.

"What if O'Farrell killed Vansittart?"

"What makes you think that?"

"I didn't say that I thought it. I just asked a question."

"Okay. Why would he do that? And how?"

They were walking down Summer Street, past Arch, back toward Oxford. Marvia asked if Lindsey wanted to stop for a cup of coffee, but he said no. He returned to her previous question.

"Let's take the how part first, okay? Vansittart was an old man. He would have been strapped into the chopper. O'Farrell was half his age, a strong, agile guy. You saw how he came up that cable, freezing water, broken leg, and all. In the helicopter he was on his own turf; he knew exactly what he was doing. He could have whacked Vansittart on the bean with a wrench or a crowbar. That would account for the broken skull just as well as an injury when the chopper crashed. Better, I think."

Marvia nodded. "Okay. Possible."

"Or," Lindsey went on, "he could have shot him. Maybe shot him in the head. That would account for the broken skull, too. Or—look, maybe he didn't shoot him in the head. Maybe he shot him in the heart or in the belly."

"Then what broke Vansittart's skull?"

"The crash. The bullet killed him, the crash and the broken skull were gratuitous."

"Hah. Some gratuity. Why did the helicopter crash?"

Lindsey chewed on that one for a while. Finally he said, "Two possibilities. If O'Farrell shot Vansittart, the bullet might have gone right through him and wrecked the controls, cut a cable or whatever. You saw how the copter shuddered before it started to fall; you saw that on Jamie's tape, right?"

Marvia conceded as much.

"Okay, that's possibility number one. Possibility number two: the crash was no accident. It was staged to look like an accident. If O'Farrell murdered Vansittart somewhere up there a few thousand feet over the Sierras, what the heck was he going to do with the body? Throw it out of the chopper? That might be embarrassing. Even if nobody found Vansittart—and up in those mountains he might have gone undiscovered for a long time—there would have been questions, hey? Things like appointment books, hotel reservations, flight manifests. You don't just take off with two people in a helicopter and land with only one and nobody's going to think that's odd."

Lindsey was gesturing with both hands. Marvia Plum was watching him the way a streetwise kid might watch a People's Park crazy babble about aliens shooting him with rays.

"Or, look," Lindsey went on. "If O'Farrell hadn't dumped Vansittart's body, if he touched down smoothly in Reno, how in the world could he explain this fresh corpse? No way. He had to find a way to land the copter, have everybody know about Vansittart's death, and yet look clean. How? Answer: crash the chopper into the lake. O'Farrell gets out safely, Vansittart's body is disposed of, everything on the up-and-up. Just a tragic accident."

He took Marvia Plum's hand and resumed walking.

"I don't think O'Farrell figured on coming out of it with a broken leg, but once it happened, all the better. If they give you a lemon, make lemonade. Instead of looking like an incompetent copter-jockey, O'Farrell comes out looking like a hero."

They had reached Marvia's house again. Her Mustang and Lindsey's restored Volvo 544 were parked nose-and-tail at the curb.

Marvia said, "There's only one problem with your theory, Bart. There's no evidence that O'Farrell killed Vansittart. Why would he have any reason to kill him?"

Lindsey grinned wryly. "Just a theory."

They were standing face-to-face. Marvia Plum took Lindsey's hand. "You want to go upstairs?"

He shook his head. "Not yet. I'm feeling better, but I'm not ready to go inside."

"Okay. What do you want to do?"

"Let's take a ride."

They climbed into the Mustang and cruised up the freeway to the Richmond Marina and parked and necked like a pair of hormone-drunk teens. Finally they drove back to Oxford Street and climbed the stairs to Marvia's flat.

She put on a CD of Ellington indigos and they got undressed and climbed under the Raggedy Ann comforter on Marvia Plum's bed. A few hours later, Lindsey woke up. His stomach was growling. They never had eaten the take-out food. He told his stomach to be patient and put his arms around Marvia and went back to sleep.

They shared early-morning coffee at a bistro on Shattuck Avenue. Lindsey said, "I want to talk to Nathan ben Zinowicz's parole officer."

Marvia Plum took a calling card from her wallet and turned it over and wrote the information on the back. The parole officer was called Dave Jones and his office was in downtown Oakland. Lindsey could call him up for a quarter. If he played his cards right, he might even find a way to charge the call to International Surety.

DAVID M. JONES was his full name, and he was dark and muscular, but he spoke very softly. He told Lindsey that he'd cultivated the soft tone deliberately. It made his charges listen carefully to what he had to tell them, and that was the first step toward getting them to understand and comply.

"We can't follow them around like watchdogs," Jones said. "There are too many of them and too few of us. We have to rely on voluntary compliance mostly, and spot checks, and make them report in regularly. But it's all pretty much a crapshoot; I won't try and kid you."

Lindsey grunted.

"Well, just what was your concern?"

"Nathan ben Zinowicz."

David Jones nodded. "Recent parolee. We had a meeting just last week."

Lindsey clenched his fists involuntarily. He felt his fingernails cutting into his palms. "I thought the victims had rights. Don't they hold hearings, give people a chance to have their say?"

Jones nodded again. "That's the procedure. What was your connection with this case?"

Lindsey told him, struggling to hold himself in check when he described his father's death on the deck of U.S.S. *Lewiston* in the Sea of Japan, and his own encounters with Nathan ben Zinowicz so many years later.

Jones did not interrupt. He wore a tan shirt and a broad tie with a brown and yellow print. He sat with his elbows on the arms of his swivel chair, his chin in his hands, a forefinger laid against each cheekbone.

When Lindsey finished speaking Jones walked to a file cabinet and extracted a manila folder. He laid it on the desk between them. "I can't show you this material. Mr. ben Zinowicz has privacy rights even though he is still technically under control of the Department of Corrections."

Lindsey chewed his lower lip. "What does that mean?"

"It means I probably shouldn't be talking with you at all, but Marvia Plum is a very old, very dear friend. She's mentioned you many times. You going to marry her?"

Lindsey hesitated. Then he said, "Yes."

"Good luck. She's a wonderful person. Her son Jamie is a cute kid, too."

"I know that. I want to talk about ben Zinowicz."

Jones opened the folder and scanned its contents, turning the pages slowly. Finally he said, "What do you want to tell me?"

"That he belongs behind bars."

Jones burst into laughter. "Mr. Lindsey, even if I wanted to put him away again, I need to have cause. I'll bet you've been watching old movies about nasty parole officers harassing their clients, snooping into their private lives, threatening to revoke their parole if they drop a chewing-gum wrapper on the street."

Lindsey said nothing.

"What did you see? *This Gun for Hire? I Died a Thousand Times? The Big Shot?* Bet you didn't know about that one. Bogie. Great flick, I don't know why nobody pays attention to it." He slapped the folder. A ring on his hand glinted in the light that fought its way through a dirty window. "Don't believe it. We're mainly a combination bureaucrat and social worker. Trying to keep these guys straight. Trying to keep them out of the slammer, not send 'em back there, Mr. Lindsey."

"So they can get away with anything? Do anything?"

"I didn't say that, did I? Look." He leaned across his desk and pointed a finger emphatically. If Lindsey hadn't been sitting back in his chair their heads would have collided. "Most of my parolees are minorities and most of 'em are pretty young. They're the victims of hyperactive gonads, among other things. Gotta prove themselves to their buddies and to themselves. Most of 'em are blacks or Latinos with not much education, no work skills, no prospects. They have to have a job to get out, they sign on to flip burgers at the Golden Arches. They show up for work once, then disappear."

He leaned back. "I violate 'em, we issue a pickup order, they wind up disappearing into the Mission or they split for the L.A. *barrio*. The blacks head for Richmond or the Fillmore or the Western Addition or Watts or Compton. Try and find 'em. There are tens of thousands of parole violators out there—the system is completely out of control."

He stood up and walked around the room. He was too big for this little room. He must feel like a prisoner himself. Maybe that was how he developed empathy for his charges.

"See, Mr. Lindsey, once in a while I get a good one. I certainly understand your feelings about Nathan ben Zinowicz, but let me tell you, first of all, with his plea bargain, I'm kind of surprised that he did any time at all. Second"—he held up his hands and began ticking off points on his fingers—"he was an exemplary prisoner in Q. Worked in the personnel office, taught literacy classes, kept his nose clean, and stayed out of trouble. Didn't mess with the gangs, and that's not easy, believe me. Not one beef in forty-two months. I'm surprised he didn't get out sooner."

Lindsey suppressed a groan.

"Third"—Jones ignored Lindsey's display—"he has a first-rate job now. He reports for work every day, his employer gives him an A-plus rating. He comes in here for his little progress meetings, he dresses neatly, he combs his hair, he wears these tweedy outfits and those thick glasses and that little gray beard of his, he looks like a college professor."

"He ought to. He was one until he—" Lindsey paused.

Dave Jones pointed a blunt-tipped finger. "I wish my caseload was full of Nathan ben Zinowiczes."

Lindsey pulled a handkerchief out of his trousers pocket and rubbed his hands and face. Jones's office was stuffy and the sun coming through the window heated the air inside. Lindsey was sweating.

Dave Jones said, "Is there anything else you want?" He looked at his wristwatch. "I've got a meeting."

Lindsey gave it one more try. "Don't you think it's odd? I mean, we know this man's history, both in Korea and here."

Jones said, "I don't know anything about Korea. Personally I know what you told me"—he held up a thick hand, classic traffic-cop fashion—"but officially I know only what's in the folder, and the only thing the folder says about Korea is lieutenant commander, USN, Navy Cross, Purple Heart, honorable discharge. The rest, I don't know."

Lindsey wanted to scream. This was why people bought Uzis and went berserk. "This killer is out of prison, he goes to work for the WFIA, suddenly Albert Crocker Vansittart is killed under suspicious circumstances, and WFIA is mentioned in his insurance policy for four million bucks. Don't you see anything peculiar about that? Don't you smell something rotten about that?"

"No, sir, I don't. I think maybe you're being paranoid. I have to warn you, Mr. Lindsey, not to harass Mr. ben Zinowicz. I mean, Dr. ben Zinowicz. He has rights. Leave him alone."

Chapter Seven

SURE, LEAVE HIM alone.

Lindsey wanted to spend another evening and another night with Marvia Plum, but he'd promised Mother. He phoned Marvia instead, and promised to call her again tomorrow. Then he set about planning the next phase of his investigation.

He'd left David Jones's office depressed, and returning to the International Surety office in Walnut Creek had not raised his spirits. Just for a moment he tried to believe that he'd walk in and find Mathilde Wilbur, his old friend and mentor, still running the office, playing mother hen to him, keeping him posted on corporate scuttlebutt that nobody else lower than a regional vice president could have known.

Alas, Ms. Wilbur was retired. International Surety's outer office was presided over by the blonde and spiteful Kari Fielding; the inner office, by the loathsome Elmer Mueller.

Lindsey made his way to the desk that was reserved for him, even though his transfer to SPUDS had technically removed him from the branch office and the normal corporate pecking order. He filed a brief report on his meeting with Jones through KlameNet/Plus. Then he took a deep breath and prepared to do what he had to do.

He needed to talk with Roger St. John Cooke or Cynthia Cooke at the World Fund for Indigent Artists. They had initiated the contact; International Surety would have been happier to avoid dealing with them altogether, or at least to delay the exchange until the late Albert Crocker Vansittart's primary beneficiary had been located. But now it couldn't be helped.

And he needed to talk with J. B. Harkins, late of the Chicago

Inter-Ocean, Daily News, and *Sun-Times,* late of the weekly neighborhood shopper, and author of *Baseball Stars of 1952.*

Which one to call first? Mother had always made him eat his spinach before he got his ice cream, and the habit had stuck. He looked up the World Fund and punched the number into his telephone. At least the voice that answered was not that of Nathan ben Zinowicz. He hadn't heard that arrogant, supercilious tone in the years since ben Zinowicz's trial. He wasn't sure he'd recognize it if he did, but he was sure that this wasn't it.

He identified himself and asked to speak with Mr. Cooke.

At least that worked out easily enough. Cooke took the call and suggested that they meet the following day. "No need to come up to the office. This is just an informal chat, is it not?"

Lindsey was far from convinced that such was the case, but if that was how Cooke wanted to play it, the decision was up to him. At least, at the outset.

"What about one o'clock? I've a busy morning calendar, but I can break away by then, I hope. And I'll see if my darling is available. Shall we say Liberté—you know it?—on Sutter Street? Oh, of course, in San Francisco." He laughed warmly. "I assumed that a company like—oh, well, never mind. See you then. Just ask for my table, Marthe holds one for me every day."

Lindsey laid down the telephone and made a note in his pocket organizer. Then he looked up another number and punched it into the phone.

The woman who answered managed to get more good cheer into the words "Shady Oaks" than a department-store Santa could get into "Merry Christmas to all." And now that it was January, where had all the department store Santas gone?

Lindsey asked if could speak with J. B. Harkins.

The cheery voice asked him to wait just a tiny moment, please.

It seemed like a lot more than a tiny moment, but eventually the cheery voice came back on the line. "Mr. Harkins is in the little game room. He hates to have his poker game interrupted. Could I tell him who's calling? Is this a relative?"

"No, I'm not a relative. I'm—" Lindsey contemplated explaining the situation to the cheery voice. It would take too long, and once he got the message across, who knows what her reaction would be? He had to get past this saccharine dragon and talk with Harkins.

"Sir?" She was still smiling, he could tell that even without a picture phone. "Are you still there, sir?"

Lindsey cleared his throat. "Ah, would you tell Mr. Harkins that this is a friend of Maude Markham's, from Chicago."

"Oh, of course. You're calling all the way from Chicago? Mr. Harkins will be so pleased. Please hold the line. I'll try to be just as quick as I can, but you know Mr. Harkins is quite elderly and our seniors don't always move as quickly as they once did. We have to be patient with them. Think of the future, you know; that's what our director always says. If you start to feel impatient with one of our seniors, just think of your own future and you'll be more forbearing. I think that's a very wise attitude. Don't you think that's a wise attitude? But there you are all the way in big Chicago, I mustn't run up your phone bill, must I? Please hold."

Harkins sounded old enough. His voice was dry and rasping. But he sounded as if he still had all his marbles. He said, "You calling from Chicago, are you?"

"No, I—"

"Nurse Ratchet there says I have a call from Chicago. You a friend of Maude Markham's?"

"Yes, I—"

"Well, any friend of Maude Markham's can go take a good flying splat as far as I'm concerned!"

Lindsey heard the receiver crash into its cradle at the Shady Oaks Retirement Villas in Livermore. He moaned. Kari Fielding shot him a hostile glance. He grinned back at her. If his encounter with J. B. Harkins had resulted in his annoying La Fielding, at least it had done something good.

He hit *redial* and got the cheery voice again. He asked if she would get Mr. Harkins on the phone once more, but first explain to him that he wasn't really a *friend* of Maude Markham, he'd just got Harkins's location from Maude Markham, who was a crusty unpleasant individual, but that Lindsey was eager to talk with the author of *Baseball Stars of 1952*.

Nurse Ratchet said, "Now, we mustn't rile up our seniors. If I fetch Mr. Harkins a second time, you must promise me faithfully not to get him upset. He really turned quite red when he spoke with you before. I stood there and watched."

Lindsey promised to be very soothing.

Nurse Ratchet fetched Mr. Harkins. Lindsey could hear the two voices engaged in dialogue, hers soothing and syrupy, his irascible. Finally he heard Harkins grunt, then speak into the telephone.

"I better apologize. Lost my temper for a sec. Maude was a good old broad. Glad to hear she's still in circulation. She still working for the *Sun-Times* is she?"

"Uh, yes."

"Not really a bad soul. Say, you ought to see her in her skivvies! I went off to World War II, you know. She knew how to give a soldier boy a happy fare-thee-well. Say, I don't suppose she looks too much like that nowadays, does she? I know I sure don't. You should have seen me in forty-two—I was quite the dashing young blade. And Maude, well, you ought to see her in her skivvies."

Lindsey said, "Mr. Harkins, I was wondering if I might come out there. Out there to Livermore. And, uh—"

"From Chicago? You want to come out here from Chicago just to talk to me about that book? What are you, nuts?"

"No, I'm not in Chicago. I'm in Walnut Creek. About forty minutes from you."

"Oh." There was a silence as Harkins assimilated that piece of information. "Well, look, sonny, you took me away from my poker game. You better tell me quick what you want because they won't wait for me long, and I don't want 'em to go on without me."

"I'd like to see you, sir."

"When?"

"The sooner the better."

"How 'bout tomorrow, then? At my age, you know, I could cash in my chips anytime. You wouldn't want to come all the way from Chicago just to attend a stranger's funeral."

"Uh—I have a meeting in San Francisco tomorrow. A luncheon meeting. How about the next day?"

"God damn, sonny! What kind of generation are we raising? How long does it take you to eat lunch, anyhow? If you're going to be in San Francisco for lunch, you can come out here afterwards. Tell you what, you come on out here, take me out to dinner someplace. How 'bout some good Mexican? I like good Mexican. They never serve it here; everything they serve comes out the same, anyhow. Pap. Bunch of pap. You come out here seven o'clock. I'll be in the lobby; don't be late. Bring that book. You got a copy of the book?"

"Uh—yes, I—"

"Seven o'clock. Good-bye."

Lindsey heard the handset land solidly on the base. He looked at his Seiko. He didn't punch a clock or keep regular hours these days. That wasn't the way SPUDS worked. If you put in an eighty-hour week, Desmond Richelieu didn't pat you on the back; and if you disappeared for a month at a time, he didn't mind that either. Well, he liked you to report in every so often, but he'd forgive anything if you cracked the case you were working on. If you saved International Surety money.

And if Lindsey cracked this case—if he found the girl on the cover of that 1951 private-eye novel—he'd save International Surety a cool million dollars.

He left the office building and set out on foot. He bought a hot espresso from a vending cart and stood gazing up at the building housing International Surety's new area office. IS had functioned out of a run-down commercial structure for decades, its offices furnished with creaking, scratched wooden chairs and desks and file cabinets. The building was decrepit, the elevators were out of order most of the time, and a musty smell had permeated the building for so long that there was no way to eliminate it. But you could open the windows and smell the spring or summer or autumn or winter air. You could tell whether it was hot out or cold, whether the sun was shining or the day was hazy or dark.

For all its flaws, the building had history and character.

It was gone now, replaced by a multi-level parking structure, and IS had moved to a modern, glass-walled, sealed-environment building. You could sit at your temperature-controlled, humidity-controlled, light-metered, ergonomic-designed metal-and-plastic desk, in your similarly modern and efficient seating system, and December or August, noontime or midnight (if you had business in the office at midnight), it was all the same to you.

It was all exactly the same.

He finished his espresso and dropped the paper cup in a recycling bin. He decided to take a walk around the neighborhood. The town where he'd grown up, a bedroom community across the water from San Francisco, shielded by the East Bay hills, was now little more than a miniature version of San Francisco.

He wandered for an hour and wound up back where he'd started from. He retrieved his car from the garage, wondering if he was standing on the very spot where his wooden desk had once stood, and if the musty smell was the ghost of the old IS office. He smiled and drove home, humming a tune. It was the same tune, it just wouldn't leave him alone.

How much is that doggie in the window . . .

It was dark out by the time he got home. Gordon Sloane's silver-gray Oldsmobile stood in the driveway and all the lights in the house were on.

He found Sloane and Mother waiting for him in the living room. There were a few hors d'oeuvres on the low table in front of the couch, and an ice bucket with a bottle in it, draped in a white towel.

Mother gave Lindsey a kiss. She asked, "How was your day?"

He said, "Mixed. Yours? Gordon?" He shook Sloane's hand. Sloane wore a blue pinstripe suit, a white shirt and maroon tie. Mother was in a teal-blue satin dress. She wore a sparkling necklace and more makeup than he could ever remember seeing on her.

Gordon Sloane said, "We have something to tell you, Bart. Your mother and I have decided to be married."

Mother put her hand on Lindsey's sleeve. She was wearing nail polish. Another first for her, at least as far as he could remember. She said, "I hope you'll be pleased, Bart. I know we've always lived together, but sooner or later the young bird has to leave the nest and fly away."

Lindsey put his hand on hers. "This isn't quite like that, is it?"

"No." Mother laughed tentatively. "It's the mother bird flying away. Will you give us your blessing, Bart? Please? I know you must have feelings for your father, but . . . "

"I never knew my father."

"I was so young when we were married. I was really just a girl. Just a little girl. And we were married only a few months when he died. I'm entitled to—don't you think I'm entitled to—"

She left the sentence hanging.

Lindsey put his arms around her. "You are, Mother. You're entitled to some happiness. To some companionship. Love."

Sloane stood behind Mother. He held his hand toward Lindsey. Lindsey shook his hand.

Sloane said, "Your mother tells me that you and Marvia are planning to marry."

"That's the idea."

"What would you think of a double wedding?"

"Uh—I don't know. I mean, we haven't really—I mean, I'm not sure when we're going to do it. Do you—have you set a date? Have you—"

Mother said, "I thought we could talk about everything." She gestured vaguely.

"Marvia would have to be here. She's included."

"Of course." Sloane nodded. "Of course. The four of us—I think the four of us should plan, should get together and make our plans. If that's all right."

Mother said, "Bart, let's go out and celebrate. Just the three of us. Gordon has made reservations."

"I hope you don't mind," Sloane added.

Lindsey excused himself. He showered and put on a good suit. He came back into the living room quietly. Mother and Gordon were seated side by side on the couch. Sloane stood up when Lindsey came in. He said, "We've been saving this."

He unwrapped the champagne bottle and opened it skillfully. There were already glasses for three on the table. He poured champagne for them and they drank. He shot his cuff—he was wearing gold cuff links with dark red stones that matched his tie—and looked at his watch.

"I think we should be off."

* * *

DINNER WAS NORTHERN Italian. Mother ordered *petti di pollo*; Gordon Sloane, *bistecca di manzo*; Lindsey, *gamberoni alla positana*. They had wine with their meal. They talked about what they were going to do after Sloane and Mother were married.

Sloane owned a condo in Walnut Creek. He and his wife had lived there before her death. Afterward Sloane moved out and had the place completely redecorated. He'd had every hint of femininity—every reminder of his wife—removed. He'd lived a womanless life until he'd met Lindsey's mother. Once Mother moved in, Sloane hoped that she would bring back a woman's touch.

Mother glowed like a bride.

"We've already talked about selling the house," she said. "Unless you want to stay in it, Bart. Would you and Marvia want to stay in the house? Would Jamie come to live with you?"

Lindsey shook his head. "I don't know. I mean, we haven't even—"

"I know I said some things I shouldn't have." Mother looked worried. "When you first brought her to the house. I mean, I was confused for so long, Bart. You remember, don't you?"

"Of course I do."

"And that awful little man came to the house. That Mr. Zucchini or whatever his name was. And then the police came and—"

"It's all right, Mother."

"I mean, you know the world changes. It took me a while to catch up with it."

"You've done a wonderful job, Mother. I'm proud of you."

"I mean, when I was your age, you just didn't meet colored people socially. No less marry them."

"I know, Mother."

"Everything has changed."

Sloane took both of Mother's hands in his own. "Don't be upset, dear. It's all right."

She found a linen handkerchief in her purse and dabbed at her eyes.

Lindsey said, "Marvia and I have to decide what we're going to do. Her ex-husband turned up a while ago. He's remarried—there's no problem there—but he tried to interfere with Jamie. Marvia and I will probably have to talk to a lawyer before we're married, to make sure that Mr. Wilkerson doesn't come back into the picture."

"Will Marvia keep her job?" Sloane asked. "Can she move out here and still be a Berkeley police officer?"

"We haven't talked about that. We haven't worked things out." Lindsey was uncomfortable with Sloane's questions; not because he didn't have answers for Sloane, but because he didn't have answers for himself. He asked, "Have you set a date, Mother? Gordon?"

"We haven't, but we want to. That's why we both thought that you and Marvia might—well, it's a little romantic touch, I suppose. It just seemed like a nice idea."

Lindsey nodded. "I'll talk to Marvia about it." Then, "Mother, do you think you'll keep working? After you and Gordon are married, I mean."

"I don't know. I—well, I do think so. It's all been so wonderful for me, you know. All those wasted years. When I think of all those wasted years, I just don't know what was wrong with me. Now that I'm back in the world, well, I just don't think I—I mean, I couldn't just stay home again all day. When I think of all the years I did that . . . You see, I kept getting lost. Wandering off into old magazines, TV shows, dreams and memories. I did miss your father so, Hobart."

"I know, Mother."

"Well, I have a few years left. I don't want that to happen again. I want to live in the world. Have friends. Maybe travel a little. And I do want to keep working, yes. You can't imagine what it's like, after all these years, to be part of something, to do something useful."

WHEN THEY GOT home, Lindsey phoned Marvia Plum. He told her about the evening and asked when they could sit down and make serious plans.

The next day he drove into the city and parked in the garage underneath Union Square. He got to Liberté early and spent half an hour window-shopping, looking at a clothing store, then a computer-software store, then an art gallery that apparently specialized in oversized paintings of flamboyant seminudes standing in the middle of thunderstorms.

He checked his Seiko, then entered Liberté. The entrance to the restaurant was narrow and unobtrusive. You'd think you were entering your dentist's office. The restaurant was down a flight of stairs and decorated to look like the inside of a cave. Lindsey asked for Mr. Cooke's table and an Asian woman in a floor-length, drop-dead dress nodded knowingly and led him through a maze of pillars.

Roger St. John Cooke stood up as Lindsey approached. He extended a gorgeously manicured hand. He looked like a cross between Tsar Nicholas II and Warren Christopher. He wore a light brown mustache and a small beard. His suit was double-breasted, black with white pinstripes, and had clearly been made for him. His shirt caught the light of the candle on the table; his tie had tiny figures on it that Lindsey couldn't make out in the contrived cavelike illumination.

They shook hands.

Cooke said, "Hobart Lindsey, Mrs. Cooke. Cynthia."

Cynthia extended her hand. Lindsey resisted an impulse to bend over the hand and mutter something in a Bela Lugosi accent. Instead, he freed himself from Roger St. John Cooke's grasp and shook Cynthia Cooke's hand. He thought she looked like Hillary Rodham Clinton trying to look like Princess Di—or maybe the other way around.

Lindsey felt pressure on the back of his knees and let himself be seated. Even the waiter had beautifully curled hair, a slightly receding hairline, the curls graying just a touch at the temples. He wore a collarless white shirt, buttoned to the throat.

"Will the gentleman enjoy a beverage?"

Lindsey shot a quick look at the Cookes. A small blue bottle of imported mineral water stood before each of them, beside a crystal glass with sculpted ice cubes and artfully carved slices of lime. Lindsey said, "I'll have the same, please."

The waiter departed.

Roger St. John Cooke said, "So good of you to join us. I thought this would be a nicer place to get together than the office."

Lindsey thought so, too, if only because it saved him from having to lay eyes on Nathan ben Zinowicz. More likely than not, that was only a temporary reprieve. But it helped.

"This is about the Vansittart policy, of course." Lindsey's mineral water had arrived. The waiter swooped down, delivered the bottle and the glass with ice cubes and lime, opened the bottle and poured in a single graceful movement. At least he didn't ask Lindsey to sample the mineral water and approve it, lest the entire staff of Liberté be obliged to perform seppuku in penance.

Cynthia Cooke said, "Of course." Her voice was like silk. "We were heartbroken when we learned of Albert's death. He was a dear friend."

"I didn't know that."

Roger St. John Cooke said, "More of a family friend. Bertie Junior and I were roommates at Stanford. Class of—" He grinned, or at least Lindsey thought he grinned, in the candlelight, and gave a small, self-deprecating laugh. "Let's just say, a long time ago."

Lindsey was surprised. "I didn't know he had any immediate survivors. If so, I wonder if there—"

He didn't get any further. "Poor Bert. He was killed in a tragic accident. Broken neck. A football injury. Big Game of nineteen—well, a long time ago. Stanford versus Cal, of course. I was on the squad, too. But I was just a scrub; Bert was going on to great things. Not that he would have become a professional athlete. He would have stayed in the family business; I'm sure of it. I don't think his dad ever got over Bert's death. But—well, it was all so long ago."

The waiter was back. He handed Lindsey a menu. The prices were listed unobtrusively, with no dollar signs or odd cents. 17. 12. 22. One item was 7.5. Who would ever order anything that cost 7.5?

"Don't you want menus, Roger, Cynthia? May I call you—"

"Of course." Cynthia smiled. "Victor knows our preference.

I would recommend—may I?—the cold sliced duckling. On the special. The special is always good at Liberté."

Victor bowed, held the pose, awaiting Lindsey's pleasure.

"Sure. Fine."

Victor withdrew.

"What about Bert's mother?"

Roger St. John Cooke shook his head sadly. "After Bert died—well, I don't think it had been the happiest of marriages. Not like ours, dear, eh?" He took his wife's hand and pressed it to his lips. Lindsey didn't comment. "No, Albert Senior and Anna were not the ideal couple. She drank, I'm afraid, and he, well, he loved women perhaps a bit too much. If you understand me." He shot Lindsey a just-between-us-cockscombs look.

It seemed impossible that Victor could have got their orders into the kitchen and brought the food back this fast. But if both Roger and Cynthia were having their usual, and Lindsey's duck was on the special, maybe it was possible after all. Anyway, there was Roger and there was the food, on plates that looked big enough to take a walk on.

Roger waited for Victor to depart before he resumed. Roger's plate appeared to have three stalks of celery on it, trimmed and shaped to look like Mercedes-Benz ornaments. Cynthia's meal was angel hair pasta decorated with one tiny sprig of broccoli, one miniature carrot, and, apparently, a single pea. It wasn't a meal that George Bush would have cared for.

Roger reached across the linen and laid his hand gently on Lindsey's sleeve. Lindsey hoped that Roger wouldn't soil his fingers. "Not that Victor is indiscreet, you understand." He shook his head, smiling slightly. "Still, one might err on the side of caution."

Cynthia nodded her approval of the sentiment. She picked up her glass and sipped mineral water. She gazed adoringly at her husband, waiting for him to resume.

"I think that Anna just stayed with Albert Senior for Bertie's sake," Roger said. "Once Bertie was gone—well, the marriage didn't last long. And once that was over, well, Anna went for a spin one day in her hot little Ferrari that she kept in St. Tropez, and she may have had a drink or so too many, and she got dizzy, and—well, it was all a tragedy. Smashed into a tree, giant palm tree, wrecked the car of course, threw poor Anna right out. She bounced off the tree trunk, too. Right through the windshield, across the hood, against the tree trunk. Her injuries were terrible. Just terrible. Dead, of course."

Lindsey chewed the inside of his cheeks to keep himself from saying anything. Too many people were getting dizzy from the sunlight and experiencing fatal accidents. What was this, the euphemism du jour?

Cynthia put her glass back down. "You're never going to find this mythical houri of Vansittart's, you know. The old goat bedded everything in skirts. That was in the days when women wore skirts and you could tell them from men."

Lindsey blinked.

"There's no way you can track her down," she repeated. "Probably never was such a person to start with—didn't those cheapjack artists keep swipe files? Isn't that what they call them? They copied each other's pictures, they painted over movie stills, they combined models, everything."

"You know a lot about this."

"I do. You'd be surprised at some of the things I know."

Roger St. John Cooke said, "My wife holds a master's degree in commercial art." He glanced proudly at his sweetie.

"I know a lot of things," Cynthia repeated. "You'll never find that woman. The fund is entitled to that insurance policy, and the sooner your company pays up, the better."

Chapter Eight

LINDSEY GOT CAUGHT in an early rush hour. By the time he reached Livermore, the night was dark and his stomach was growling. There was nothing he could do about the darkness, and he told his stomach to be patient.

He found KDFC on the car radio and listened to some Mozart as he left San Francisco and headed for Livermore. The luncheon with the Cookes had not gone well. Clearly, they were both old San Francisco money. Albert Crocker Vansittart had also been old San Francisco money, and the girl on the cover of *Death in the Ditch*, if she existed at all, was an interloper.

Lindsey had contemplated the difficulties of finding an unnamed woman based on only a sensationalized commercial illustration more than forty years old. He'd even considered that she might well be dead by now. But the notion that she had never existed at all—Cynthia Cooke's notion—had been a stunner.

And yet it made sense. Lindsey had never worked in the world of commercial art—he wasn't an artist himself—but he'd dealt with cases involving mass culture, and he had a feel for that world. His own father had been a promising cartoonist; Lindsey had even met a onetime colleague of his father's, who claimed that the man would have had a brilliant career if he'd lived through the Korean War.

But—Lindsey snapped back to the present, abandoning his ruminations over what might have been. In the real world, in the here and now, what Cynthia Cooke theorized seemed painfully plausible.

If there was no girl on the cover of Del Marston's hard-boiled book, if there never had been, then the case ceased to exist. The money went to the World Fund, pure and simple. International Surety paid out $4 million rather than $3 million, Lindsey didn't get an oak-leaf cluster for his company hero badge, and we all went on to our next assignment.

But maybe Cynthia Cooke was wrong. Maybe there *had* been a model for the book cover, and maybe she was still alive. Maybe.

J. B. Harkins was waiting when Lindsey arrived at Shady Oaks, good as his word. Lindsey expected to see somebody like Joseph Cotten in *Citizen Kane*, and he wasn't disappointed.

Harkins was tall and cadaverously thin. He stooped slightly, but even so he was taller than Lindsey by a good three inches. His hair was white, as were his bushy eyebrows and thick mustache. He wore rimless spectacles. His clothing could have been a parody of Roger St. John Cooke's: a threadbare double-breasted suit that must date from the last time the style was fashionable—or maybe the time before. A white shirt frayed at the collar and cuffs. A tie that he must have bought when the GIs came home from Europe and the Pacific and threw their Ike jackets in the garbage.

The old man said, "Grub. Let's get the heck out of this joint and find some decent grub. If I have to shovel this pap down my gullet one more night, I think I'll just lie down and invite the angel of death to take me away."

Lindsey said, "Uh, I've got my car outside. Do you want me to bring it to the door?"

Harkins shook his head. "Let's hoof it, chum."

Lindsey didn't know anything about Livermore, certainly didn't know the restaurants, but they managed to find a Mexican place that looked pretty good. They left the Volvo in the street.

A couple of Mexican kids in flannel shirts and jeans were leaning against the restaurant wall drinking out of brown paper bags. Red Tecate beer cans stuck out of the bags. One of the kids said, "Nice short, man."

Lindsey said, "Thanks." Short. Had anybody called a car a short in thirty years?

Inside the restaurant, Lindsey and Harkins got a table and Harkins said, "I want a whiskey sour, no quarrel, right? You want something from me, you better make me happy. A whiskey sour will make me happy. You came all the way from Chicago to talk to me? I'm flattered. How's Maude doing? I should have married her in forty-nine, but I thought there was plenty of time. I guess there was. Where's my whiskey sour?"

Lindsey looked around, spotted a waitress, and signaled. The waitress swirled over to their table. She wore a peasant blouse and a colorful skirt. She had lots of blue-black curls. She must have weighed 200 pounds. She made Lindsey repeat "whiskey sour" four times. In a little while she brought Harkins's drink, a Tecate for Lindsey, a basket of chips, and two cups of salsa, one red and one green.

Lindsey asked Harkins, "Will you tell me about your book?"

Harkins tilted his head like a dog listening to a Victrola. "What's to tell? I had the hots for Maude Markham. She was giving me a little, but not all I wanted. So I figured, maybe we should get married. You know, buy a little house, they cost about three, four thousand back then. Put in a lawn. Buy a new Nash or maybe a Kaiser or one of those super-duper Tucker Torpedo cars. Don't see many of those anymore, do you?"

Lindsey admitted that was true.

"I guess they just didn't catch on, then, did they? Well, anyhow, look, I was covering the Cubs in those days." He picked up his drink, toasted Lindsey. "Here's to ya. Never let 'em screw ya. If they try to, do it to 'em before they do it to ya."

Lindsey was puzzled. It must have shown. Harkins swallowed half his drink, found a U-shaped tortilla chip and used it to dip up a dose of red salsa and popped it in his mouth. He grinned, chewed, and swallowed. "Never heard that one? We used to say it in the gyrene corps whenever we got some home brew. On Bougainville. Ever hear of Bougainville? Well, never mind. Shitty place, anyhow."

"You were covering the Cubs," Lindsey reminded Harkins.

"So I was. For the *Chicago Daily News*. Pretty good old paper. Hell of a lot better than the *Inter-Ocean*. Summer of fifty-one. Not a good year for the Cubbies. We finished seventh in fifty. Seventh out of eight teams, eight teams in each league back then, the way God intended God-damned baseball to be played. And no night games at Wrigley. Can you imagine that, big ugly electric lights at Wrigley, playing baseball at *night*. I tell you, chum, I nearly slit my wrists when I turned on the TV and they were showing a night game from Wrigley Field."

He downed the second half of his whiskey sour. "That was one lousy drink; I'll tell you that, chum. Tell me your name again."

Lindsey did.

Harkins said, "Get me another one of those, would you? It's a lousy drink, but it beats hell out anything they serve out there at the graveyard."

"Graveyard?"

"Okay, Shady Oaks, whatever. Worst mistake I made in my life, coming out here. I think I'm going to get a little place of my own and move out of there. Should never have left Chicago to start with."

Lindsey signaled the waitress. To Harkins he said, "I think we should get some food."

Shortly, Lindsey ordered a second whiskey sour for Harkins. He still had half his Tecate. He asked the waitress for a taco deluxe for Harkins and arroz con pollo for himself. He asked Harkins again about the Cubs.

Not that he cared that much about baseball, certainly not about a pennant race that took place before he was born, but he wanted to get Harkins back onto his book. Thence to the cover, the artist, the artist who did the cover for *Death in the Ditch.* . . . It was a long trail, but he was on it, and that was something, anyway.

"Fifty Cubs, best players we had were Andy Pafko and Hank Sauer. Pafko played the center field, hit .304, 36 home runs, 91 RBIs. Sauer played left, hit .274, 32 homers, 103 RBIs. Good numbers. I see your eyes glazing, sonny. Not a baseball man, are you?"

The waitress brought Harkins's second drink along with their food. Harkins lifted his glass and said, "Here's to ya. You know the rest. We didn't have much else to put on the field—only one winning pitcher on the whole damn staff, Frankie Hiller, went twelve-and-five, career season for him. Say, doesn't that smell nice. Always said, hot fresh food is the second-best smell there is. First best is hot and fresh, too. Heh!"

Harkins dug into his dinner. The taco came with rice and beans, a green salad, and a covered dish of corn tortillas. He slathered the food with extra salsa, loaded up a tortilla with rice and beans, and demolished half of it in a rush. He sat back and sighed, rubbing his belly. "Can't tell you what a difference this makes, mac. But I do appreciate it."

"The fifty Cubs," Lindsey prompted, "or the fifty-one Cubs."

"Yep. Started fifty-one full of optimism. I'd have to stand by a couple of pieces I wrote in spring training. Cubbies in the pennant race, Cubbies in the World Series, best Cubs team since Charlie Grimm's day. Heh! Started out lousy and got worse. Fired Frankie Frisch after 80 games, made Phil Cavarretta player-manager, didn't help the poor saps any. Finished dead last. Dead last. Pafko was out most of the year. Sauer still had a good year, 30 homers, 89 RBIs. Pitching stank on ice. Lefty Minner, poor sap, led the league. In losses."

He shook his head in despair.

"Team stank on ice," he concluded.

Lindsey asked, "What about your book, Mr. Harkins?"

"You got a copy, mac?"

Lindsey placed his copy of *Baseball Stars of 1952* carefully on a folded napkin. Harkins laid down his self-service burrito and picked up the book. He had a dab of refried beans and salsa on his fingers. Lindsey winced.

"Yep, this is it all right. Took me a week to write this bugger. Would have done one every year if poor old Kleinhoffer had managed to keep his company going. Tell ya what, you got a twenty to spare?"

"What for?"

"Trust me. I know what things are worth nowadays. Ain't like the old days. All different now. Rotten. Gimme a twenty."

The last thing Lindsey wanted to do was trust Harkins, but he reluctantly fished a twenty-dollar bill out of his wallet and laid it on the table. It disappeared with amazing speed.

Harkins picked up Lindsey's copy of *Baseball Stars of 1952*, opened it, held out his hand, and said, "Gimme a pen."

Lindsey complied.

Harkins scrawled something in the front of the book and handed it back to Lindsey. Lindsey demanded his pen back and got it. He read Harkins's scrawl. *Fuck night ball, Jeb Harkins.*

Lindsey said, "You knew Kleinhoffer's real name."

" 'Course I did. Everybody did. Everybody knew those names they took were just to sound like real Murricans. Nobody took that stuff seriously." He turned the book around and around, studying it. Lindsey had trouble reading the expression on his face.

"Do you know who the artist was?" Lindsey asked. "I can't find any art credit on the book. On any of them, in fact. Walter Paige's—Werner Kleinhoffer's—granddaughter gave them to me. They all look like one artist's work. I can't be sure, I'm no authority, but they look like the same artist's work. But there's no signature, no art credit on the books."

Harkins shook his head. "No signature? Look here, bub, just look here." He pointed at one of the sketches on the cover of *Baseball Stars of 1952,* one of the miniature baseball parks that surrounded the faces of the baseball stars. Lindsey used his napkin to clean the smear of refried beans off the cover and to wipe Harkins's fingertips.

Hidden in the line work and almost too small to see was a drawing of a gun with two bullets coming from its muzzle. Lindsey jumped in his seat. "I see it. Yes. But why a gun? And why those bullets?"

"No, no, young fellow. Look, bullets aren't round. Those aren't bullets, they're BBs."

"So what?"

"That's the artist's signature. BB. His name was—he called himself Bob Brown. His real name was Benjamin Bruninski. Benny Boy Bruninski. BB. Don't you get it?"

"I get it." Lindsey took the book back from Harkins. Benjamin Bruninski. "He did all the covers for Paige?"

"Far as I know. I didn't have that much to do with that Paige outfit. Werner called the *Daily News* office, asked for me. Said he read my stuff every day in the paper, really liked my writing, how would I like to do a book for his company? I had the hots for Maude Markham, you know, wanted to pick up some extra moola. If that book company hadn't gone belly-up, I'd have probably made enough in a year or two to marry her. Would have made a better wife than any I ever had."

"Did you know a model who posed for Bob Brown? She was on several of his book covers for Paige. She was on *Death in the Ditch*. Blonde girl, green eyes, very busty, very beautiful. At least, she was blonde on that book. He must have used the same model for *Buccaneer Blades*, only she had flame-red hair. And on *Cry Ruffian!*, she's sneaking up behind this thuggish-looking fellow who's making a phone call, she's got a whiskey bottle in her hand, it looks as if she's going to clout him with it. She has black hair in that one, striped shirt, and a beret."

"Sounds like hot stuff. I wouldn't know. Talked with Benny Boy only a couple of times, about the cover for *Baseball Stars*. I had to tell him who the players were that I was writing about. The clubs sent us publicity stills, and Benny used those to paint from. Stan Musial, Ralph Kiner, Preacher Roe, Sal Maglie, Ferris Fain, Don Newcombe, Ted Williams, Bob Feller, Jackie Robinson. And Minnie Minoso from the White Sox and Hank Sauer from the Cubs. We had to have a couple of hometown boys, had to sell books to the local fans. They don't make ball players like they used to."

He took the book back and pointed to one of the stadium sketches. "Old Benny Boy, you know, he was a baseball man himself. Really knew his stuff. You see these ballparks? Oh, the best ones are gone now. Tore 'em down. Parking lots and apartment houses and freeways. They build these ridiculous domes and things now. No character to 'em. They have no-character ball players and no-character ballparks. No wonder the game stinks. Call a strike and call off the season, and nobody even cares. Serves 'em right, greedy s.o.b.'s."

He picked up his fork and speared a slice of tomato in a pink creamy sauce. He ate it. Then he said, "You see this ballpark here? Now, that's really interesting."

Lindsey looked. It didn't look interesting to him. Still, Harkins was trying to tell him something. Lindsey was going to help Harkins do that. "Why is that?" he asked.

"See, all these parks are big-league parks except this one.

Takes a real baseball man to know. You're no baseball man, mac. No offense to you, but you just aren't a baseball man."

He paused for breath and a drink of whiskey sour.

"See, this here is a minor-league park," he resumed. "Don't guess you'd recognize it. This here is Pelican Stadium, New Orleans, Louisiana. Had the craziest outfield I ever saw. Deeper to left and right than it was to center. Your eyes are glazing over again, boy. You are not a baseball man, I can see that. New Orleans Pelicans played there, and the New Orleans Stars, Negro League team. Crazy ballpark. Gone now. All they build nowadays are giant spare tires with ball fields in the middle. Even put lights up in Wrigley Field. My God, like putting tits on a bull, lights in Wrigley Field. Just not right."

Lindsey put the book away, carefully. He paid for their food. On the way back to Harkins's retirement home, Lindsey asked if Harkins had any idea where Bob Brown—Benjamin Bruninski—might be today. If he was still alive.

Harkins looked at Lindsey. "You're quite the detective, aren't you, sonny?"

"I'm trying to find him."

"Now, why would that artist make that nice cover for my book, and all of the players are big-league players and all of the ballparks are big-league ballparks except for one? How stupid are you, mac?"

At the Shady Oaks Retirement Villas Lindsey walked into the lobby with Harkins. Harkins said, "You're pretty stupid, but you're better than the fools they have running this place. You come back and take me out for another good meal, will you?"

Lindsey said, "I'll try." He started for the door, then turned back. Harkins was looking after him with an expression of loss. "I'll come back," Lindsey amended.

He started for the door and turned back a second time. "How did the Cubs do in nineteen fifty-two, Mr. Harkins?"

"Cavarretta got lucky. Sauer got over his aches, led the league in home runs and RBIs. Cubs went 77-and-77, finished fifth. See, God wants them to play 154 games a year, too."

Chapter Nine

FABIA RABINOWITZ HAD moved back to the UC computer center after finishing her assignment on loan to the Pacific Film Archive. Her workplace was a combination office and computer lab. A custom-built processor stood on her desk, a printer beside it. A VCR was cabled into the processor. The walls were lined with shelves of manuals and computer magazines, and stacks of printouts. There were a few metal chairs, and a window that looked out on Sproul Plaza.

Students moved briskly between classes. There were no political speechmakers in evidence, no arm-waving evangelists, no musicians or street-theater performers.

It was raining very hard.

Fabia Rabinowitz, tall and dark-haired and elegant, sat at the computer keyboard. The others were crowded into the small room: Hobart Lindsey, Marvia Plum, Willie Fergus. Plum and Fergus were both in uniform, each exhibiting a More Copper than Thou expression.

There were a series of introductions. Willie Fergus's was the only new face to Lindsey. He was about Lindsey's height, clearly older but in good shape. He wore his Washoe County, Nevada, uniform with obvious pride. The wool was spotless; the creases were sharp; the metal glistened. Decked out as he was, and with an erect, muscular body, he might have passed for a man half his age. Only the gray in his crinkled black hair and the lines around his mouth gave him away.

After quick handshakes all around Fabia Rabinowitz took center stage. She gestured casually at her computer. "What we've got here is some fancy software that we've been working on. We tried it out a while ago on those old movies—you re-member, Mr. MacReedy from the retirement center provided them. We were trying to deconstruct the footage to determine if a certain famous actor had been replaced in mid-career by a dou-ble."

"And he had," Lindsey volunteered.

"Yes. The program established that conclusively." She rolled open a file drawer and extracted two videocassettes and held them up. "This is the tape of the UNR fiber-optic probe of the helicopter wreck. And this is Jamie Wilkerson's tape of the heli-copter crash. Actually, these are high-quality copies—no way we'd want to work with the originals if we can possibly help it."

She slid a cassette into the VCR and punched a few buttons on the device and a few more on the computer keyboard. The monitor screen came to life. "I'm going to take these in reverse sequence because the fiber-optic tape shows us what to look for in Jamie's tape. I know he wanted to be here, but Sergeant Plum says he has to be in school today."

She played Captain Kirk, and the monitor screen showed an eerie dark green scene. "This is the bottom of Lake Tahoe. The lake is far too deep for natural light to penetrate to the lake bed, and the temperature is constant. Four degrees Celsius, about 40 degrees Fahrenheit."

Suddenly the scene brightened. "There was a tracer light on the cable; that was what we saw until now. At this point the oper-ators turned on the main light. We can see the crashed and sunken helicopter. It is lying on its main rotor. The tail is broken off and lies beside the major wreckage. We can see that the Plexi-glas bubble has been crushed by the weight of the wreck. Now the probe is going to move."

The scene shifted dizzyingly. After it stabilized, Fabia Rabino-witz explained. "Here we see the downrigger cable that was at-tached by the *Tahoe Tailflipper*. The captain of the *Tailflipper* was trying to save the occupants of the helicopter, of course, but in fact it was this, we believe, that caused the helicopter to invert as it sank."

"That's all that saved John O'Farrell," Willie Fergus put in. "Once he was down there in that sinking chopper, pitch-black, broken leg . . . I've interviewed O'Farrell . . . no way he would have made it without that cable."

The monitor screen showed the inside of the helicopter bubble. The probe had crept in like a water snake, powered by fractional horsepower motors and guided from the surface of Lake Tahoe. The light glinted off a metal surface, then moved on, toward a grisly figure.

Fergus said, "Hold it there."

Fabia Rabinowitz punched a key. The image froze.

"Can you back that up?"

Rabinowitz clicked at her keyboard, its sound a staccato rhythm. Frame by frame the probe backed away from Albert Crocker Vansittart's remains.

Fergus barked, "Stop!"

The glinting metal object looked like a bit of dull mirror surrounded by green murk.

"Can you sharpen that any more?"

Fabia Rabinowitz's hands flew over the computer keyboard like Liberace's over a piano's ivories.

Miraculously, the image on the screen grew clear. The glare faded, the shape of the object was clearly defined.

Lindsey frowned. "What is that?"

Fergus had been jotting notes. He used his pen as a pointer, tapping it against the glass face of the monitor. "That's a tire iron."

Lindsey sat up straighter. "Why would they need one of those in a helicopter? It doesn't even have tires, does it?"

"Nope. Some do—God knows I've ridden in enough. But I know those old Bells. That's an old Model 47, upgraded and modified to civilian use, but it still has landing skids, not wheels."

"Well, then—?"

"Dr. Rabinowitz, can you step that forward again? Just a few seconds' worth."

Fabia Rabinowitz played with her keyboard. The monitor image moved again, not in natural time but in single-frame increments. Eventually the body of Albert Crocker Vansittart became visible, hanging upside down by its safety belt. There was some flesh left on Vansittart's face. Lindsey's stomach lurched. He could have dealt with either a complete face or a bare skull, but he was not prepared for the horror that appeared.

He felt a strong hand on the back of his neck. His world was black, with dancing points of light. From a great distance, he heard a voice: "Just put your head between your knees. Try to breathe deeply. You'll be all right."

A few minutes later, the dancing lights disappeared, and the ragged, rasping sound that he recognized as his own breathing grew steadier. Marvia Plum and Willie Fergus had got him outside the building and were walking him up and down. The rain had lightened, although it hadn't stopped yet. The cold droplets on his face helped.

When they got back inside Lindsey said, "I'm sorry. I never fainted before. I just—"

Marvia Plum held his hand.

Willie Fergus said, "You'd be surprised. I see it all the time. I remember the first time I had to attend an autopsy. It was a pregnant woman, and when the coroner opened her up and—"

Marvia Plum pulled her hand away from Lindsey and shook Willie Fergus by the shoulders. "Willie, stop that!"

"Oh. Sorry."

"You're talking to a civilian."

"I said I'm sorry. Mr. Lindsey, you think you're up to this? You don't have to watch."

Lindsey stood up. He felt a little bit light-headed but otherwise okay. His stomach had settled and the points of light had gone away.

"Sure. Sure. I'm sorry, I shouldn't have—"

When they got back to the computer lab, Fabia Rabinowitz was still sitting at her keyboard, rolling a mouse around a rubber pad, blowing up segments of the screen and working with them to turn blobs of murky brown and green and gray into discernible objects.

She turned around and said, "This is what I think you wanted to see."

She moved the mouse again, clicked at its buttons, tapped a few times at her keyboard, then stopped.

What was left of Albert Crocker Vansittart's face filled the screen. Fabia Rabinowitz hit some keys. The face rotated 180 degrees. It seemed to stare at them. Lindsey shut his eyes, breathed deeply, then opened them again. He was all right. This time he was all right.

Willie Fergus said, "That's what I wanted. That's it." He tapped the screen again with his pen. "See that hole in Vansittart's skull? That's not an impact fracture that he'd get from hitting his head when the chopper crashed. No way. It's a puncture wound. He was struck, and it was the tire iron that was used to strike him. Maybe once with the flat of the shaft to stun him, then a poking-type blow that penetrated his skull. That's what killed him. And the tire iron, I'll bet my stripes, was the murder weapon."

"Then the killer was O'Farrell."

"It could only have been O'Farrell. I think I'd better get on the horn to my boss and have him call the Placer Sheriff's office. Can I use your phone, Dr. Rabinowitz?"

"If you can hold that for five minutes, there's something else you ought to see."

"I don't want to hold it for five minutes. I don't want to hold it for any minutes."

"All right." She handed him a telephone. He placed the call and spoke briefly. There was a silence that dragged on. Then he spoke a few more words and lowered the receiver. He looked around, then he said, "What else do you have for me?"

Fabia Rabinowitz said, "Jamie Wilkerson's tape."

She popped the cassette out of the VCR and inserted another in its place. She hit *play*, and the screen came to life.

Lindsey watched the familiar footage, the pride and excitement on Hakeem White's face, the wriggling salmon, the lake surface and the fir-covered mountains in the background. He could hear the excited voices of the two boys.

Then the image panned diagonally as Jamie Wilkerson turned in place and raised the Handycam to capture the image of the oncoming helicopter. The Handycam's built-in microphone caught the sound of the helicopter's rotors. *Whup-whup-whup.* The rhythm of the sound hesitated, and the copter shuddered once, then began to whirl around its vertical axis and to drop toward the lake.

The camera followed its descent. The helicopter disappeared from the frame momentarily. Then the image caught up with it. The copter splashed into the lake and almost at once began to founder.

Jamie had caught most of the action on his Handycam, including Captain MacKenzie's heroic dive into the lake to rescue John Frederick O'Farrell. The sequence ended with O'Farrell's words, "I've got to get him out of there! It's Mr. Vansittart!"

The monitor screen went blank. The tape began to rewind; the whole process lasted only a matter of seconds.

When the whir of the rewinding tape stopped, Fabia Rabinowitz said, "Now, I'm going to run the tape again, stopping at crucial moments to show you a couple of blowups and refined images."

The tape started again. The picture of Hakeem White and his Tahoe salmon, the wobbly pan to the helicopter, the peculiar syncopation in the rotor's steady beat, the shudder of the aircraft.

As the helicopter dropped toward the lake, Rabinowitz froze the image.

Lindsey could see the helicopter and its Plexiglas bubble. The rotor blades were a frozen blur. Rabinowitz played her keyboard-and-mouse game. A frame appeared around the bubble. Then the image within the frame sprang toward Lindsey until it filled the monitor screen. Lindsey could see two shadowy figures inside the bubble.

Rabinowitz advanced the tape, frame by frame. She stopped and played with the mouse again and tapped commands into the keyboard. The image on the monitor became defined more clearly. With a grunt of satisfaction, Rabinowitz punched a few more keys. "Watch this."

The image was still far from portrait-clear, but Lindsey could clearly distinguish two figures inside the bubble. The one closer to the camera held a long, thin object in his hand. The tape advanced, frame by frame, with nightmare slowness. The hand came up. The second figure, farther from the camera, raised both its hands. The object fell across the second man's temple.

As the second man slumped, the first man drew back his arm, shifted his grip on the long object, and jabbed it, point first, into the second man's skull. Then he dropped the object and moved his hands back to the controls of the helicopter.

By now the copter was close to the surface of the lake—not more than forty or fifty feet in the air. The Handycam followed it down to the surface. As the copter splashed into the lake, Fabia Rabinowitz slowed the tape again. She played keyboard-and-mouse, and Lindsey saw the two men in the Plexiglas bubble. One was slumped in his seat, unmoving. The other was struggling frantically with the copter's controls. As the machine neared the water, he gave up on the controls and struggled frantically to undo his safety belt.

Then the copter splashed, foundered, slowly sank. There was confusion on the *Tahoe Tailflipper*, much of it caught by ace cameraman Jamie Wilkerson: Captain MacKenzie getting the downrigger cable onto the copter, then John O'Farrell climbing up the cable, and MacKenzie and Marvia Plum pulling him into the *Tailflipper*.

The tape ended and rewound again.

Willie Fergus said, "Well I'll be damned. I haven't seen anything like that since Jack Ruby shot Lee Harvey Oswald. I'd better phone Reno again. This is going to be a mess. We'll have to ask the California police to hold O'Farrell while we get a warrant in Nevada. That son of a bitch—he'll probably fight extradition."

Marvia Plum stood up. "Don't be too sure of that, Willie."

Fergus grinned. He had a gold lower tooth, Lindsey noticed. "You think he'll come willingly?"

"I don't know about that. I'm not so sure the crime took place in Nevada. The copter apparently sank in Nevada water, but it was coming from the west, from California. Jamie's tape shows the crime being committed as the copter approaches the *Tahoe Tailflipper*. The crime might have been committed in California."

Fergus let escape a burst of ironic laughter.

Marvia Plum said, "Let me get on that phone. I'm going to

alert Placer County. Let's pick him up in California, since that's where he is now. See if he can travel. If not, put a guard on him right in the hospital. Then we'll see who gets jurisdiction. And I'm sure that the Placer County Sheriff has been talking to the Coast Guard and the FBI and half a million other feds."

She took the phone and placed her call.

She'd barely put the telephone down when it rang with an incoming call for Sergeant Willie Fergus.

Fergus took the handset, listened, grunted, listened some more, then returned the handset to its cradle. He looked around at the others. His face had gone from a rich chocolate brown to a sickly gray.

"O'Farrell checked out of the hospital this morning."

There weren't many details. O'Farrell had been in a private room. His broken leg had been set, he'd recovered from the shock and exposure. X-ray and MRI examinations had shown a concussion, but that was clearing up. With the broken leg in a cast and a few visible bruises, the man had been ready to travel.

A friend had arrived with a station wagon. O'Farrell had signed himself out. The friend had not been identified, and apparently nobody on the hospital staff had particularly noticed him or bothered to note the license number of the station wagon. An orderly had helped O'Farrell and his friend to the wagon, rolling O'Farrell along in a wheelchair, helping him to make the difficult move from the wheelchair into the rear of the wagon, where he could sit with his broken leg outstretched.

The station wagon had a California license; the orderly remembered that. And the make of the wagon was a common one. It was a Ford. Or maybe a Chevy. Or a Chrysler. Oh, or a Jeep. There were lots of Jeep wagons in the Tahoe area, the ones with optional four-wheel drive, because there was so much snow. Yes, the wagon was a Jeep, or at least it *might* have been a Jeep. Oh, unless it was an import.

Willie Fergus and Marvia Plum, the two sergeants, were equally delighted.

Fergus addressed the others. "Okay, there's already an APB out for O'Farrell. Washoe has it in effect for all of Nevada, in case they headed down toward Reno and Carson City. The sooner we get out the word, the smaller the area they're likely to be in. Marvia, Placer County is putting one on the line for California, in case they headed back toward Sacramento. Or any-place else, of course. O'Farrell is going to be pretty conspicuous with his leg in a cast. And he won't be very mobile, either. That's our best bet. No way he can just mix and mingle with the public—he'll have to hole up."

He turned to Lindsey. "I guess that settles things for you, sir. Even without a body, the probe proved that Vansittart is dead, and—"

Lindsey held up his hand like a schoolboy. "How do we know that was Vansittart? We saw a body in the helicopter. We know it wasn't O'Farrell because he survived. And he told Captain MacKenzie on the fishing boat that his passenger was Vansittart. Suppose it was somebody else? Do you just take O'Farrell's word? Especially now that we know O'Farrell is a killer?"

Fergus nodded. "You're right. I should have thought of that. Would have if I'd sat down and concentrated for five minutes." He looked up, locking eyes with Lindsey. Fergus had very large, very dark eyes. "But in any case, I think you're out of this for now. The coroner will have to make a ruling on Vansittart, and since the body is in Nevada, it will be the Washoe County—not Placer County—coroner."

He pointed at Fabia Rabinowitz's computer/VCR lash-up. "Can you tape that whole thing? Everything you showed us, ma'am? And—I'm getting way ahead, I know, but just in case—when the time comes, you'll be willing to appear in court? This is going to wind up in the DA's lap sooner or later, and you will surely be called."

"Certainly," she nodded, "I can do that. Make a tape of all my blowup and refinement work. And appear in court if I have to."

"What about you, Mr. Lindsey? You and Sergeant Plum were both witnesses to the helicopter crash. You're as close to witnesses to the crime itself as there are."

Lindsey shot a look at Marvia. "I don't know what good I could do. I just saw the copter crash. Then I saw O'Farrell climb back up that cable."

"That's right," Marvia agreed. "I don't think we can add anything useful. But both boys saw the crash, and Captain MacKenzie."

"Well, just in case." Fergus nodded. "I think I'd better call in again. Then I expect they'll want me back in Tahoe. I don't see what more there is to do down here. Dr. Rabinowitz—again, this is fantastic work. We'll want to get it into evidence ASAP. How soon do you think you can have a package ready for us?"

Rabinowitz said, "I want to tweak the images a little more. I think I can still sharpen them up a little bit. Give me a week, and I'll have a package for you."

Fergus nodded and shook Rabinowitz's hand. "Marvia—you want to have a cup of coffee with me? I need to talk with you a little more. Then I think I'm out of here."

Marvia nodded. To Lindsey she said, "This is just cop stuff. Give me a call later, all right?"

The group scattered.

Lindsey reached Marvia Plum later by telephone and they planned dinner. He drove back to the IS office in Walnut Creek and caught up on paperwork. Then he went home and changed to fresh clothes and drove back to Berkeley.

Chapter Ten

LINDSEY DIDN'T HAVE much of an appetite, so Marvia suggested a sushi and robata bar on Solano Avenue. They nibbled unidentified morsels. Lindsey tried a jug of hot sake. He'd never had sake before, and the first sip tasted like rubbing alcohol. The second was better, and he wound up liking the stuff.

He told Marvia about his dinner with Mother and Gordon Sloane. He didn't know how she would react to their suggestion of a double wedding. When he sprang the idea, she shook her head. "What kind of double wedding? Bart, if we do this, I want it to be just us. I'm sorry. Your mother can be there, of course, if you want her to. But I don't want a fuss. I'm no blushing bride. I want to keep it small and quiet."

Lindsey blinked. "All right." He took a bite of sushi. His mind was not at its sharpest. He said, "How long since you saw Willie Fergus? Before today, I mean."

"We were in Germany together."

"I know. I just—I wondered, that's all."

She pressed her face against his shoulder. She was in civvies, a plain blue work shirt and jeans with a loose vest over the work shirt. Nobody would take her for a homicide detective. Nobody would ask whether she was carrying a revolver and a badge under that vest.

"You're jealous. You're jealous, aren't you?"

Lindsey felt himself flush. Maybe it was the sake. At least it was partly the sake. "I didn't mean—I mean, of course I know you—" He let his words trail away.

"We were never romantically involved, Bart, if that's what you're getting at. Willie's twenty years older than I am. He was like an uncle over in Europe. When I got involved with James Wilkerson, I was so confused, I was in so much trouble, I didn't know what to do. My parents were six thousand miles away. My friends—girlfriends—were all as young and as baffled as I was. Everybody lived in terror of getting pregnant, and when it happened to me, I didn't know what to do. Willie Fergus helped me."

Lindsey nodded. The conversation was getting away from him. The topics were swirling like snowflakes in a blizzard. Their wedding, Mother's wedding, the helicopter crash, Willie Fergus, Vansittart, the Cookes, John O'Farrell.

"Bertie Vansittart," he blurted.

"What?"

"Bertie—Albert Vansittart, Jr. Wasn't Vansittart a confirmed bachelor? Wasn't that what CNN said?"

"Sure they did."

"Cooke—Roger Cooke—told me that he was college roommates with Vansittart's son. He fed me this line about his wonderful roommate, the football hero. I guess that was before they had separate sports dorms. Then Albert Junior was killed. It was pure soap opera. Young Vansittart died of a sports injury. Broke his neck on the gridiron."

Marvia watched him with a look of intense concentration. To Lindsey, she appeared to be in sharper focus than he was. She hadn't been drinking hot sake.

"Then his mother . . . " Lindsey picked up the sake jug and tilted it over his tiny porcelain cup. There were herons on the jug and the cup, matching brown herons edged in gold. A single drop came out of the jug, tilted the cup, and splashed onto the bottom of the tiny cup. Lindsey set down the jug, tilted the cup, and swallowed the last drop of sake. He felt a little bit dizzy.

Marvia was prompting him. "What about his mother?"

"Bertie's mother—Albert Vansittart Senior's wife—she was always a drinker. Marriage was pretty unhappy. After Bertie was gone, she climbed into the bottle and pulled it in after her. She wound up in St. Tropez. She took out her Ferrari and ran it into a palm tree. End of Mama Vansittart. It was an accident."

"Presumably."

"But, Marvia—what was the story all about? I mean, if Vansittart was a confirmed bachelor, then why the whole story about a wife and a son and the football team and the car crash in St. Tropez? It was all made up. It had to be. Didn't it?"

Marvia said, "I don't know. I'll get in touch with Willie Fergus, and with Placer County. We'll see what happens. They might even ask somebody at this end to look into it. Somebody will have to go down to Belmont and check out Vansittart's situation. Check those college records, too. See if there ever was a missus and a junior. If that happens, guess who gets the call."

Lindsey tilted the sake jug over his cup once more. Maybe some sake was hiding in it, and maybe he could coax it out this time. It seemed like a good idea, but it didn't really work.

Marvia coaxed him into the Mustang and drove to Oxford Street. She helped him up the stairs and he flopped onto the bed. It was really nice to be home.

HE WASN'T SWIMMING in the warm waters of Lake Tahoe, and Tahoe Tessie wasn't licking his face with her warm, wet, rough tongue. He knew that was impossible. He opened his eyes and Marvia Plum was scrubbing his face with a rough washcloth soaked in warm water.

"You tied one on, Hobart. I've never seen you do that before. How's your head this morning?"

He sat up gingerly and put his hands to his temples. "I'm okay. Tied one on, did I?"

"Just a little. You had a whole jug of sake. You must have been running on empty to start with. It'll do that to you."

He tried a small smile, then a slightly bigger one. "I don't think I'm hung over. Still—did I disgrace myself? How did I get here?"

"You were okay. Just a little silly. In fact, you were coherent right up to the end. Some drunks are like that."

He winced.

"I don't mean you're a drunk. Just that you *were* drunk."

"A fine distinction."

"And another fine mess. Do you remember what you told me about Vansittart Junior?"

"Wait a minute. Sure. Roger Cooke handed me some cock-and-bull story about being college roommates with Vansittart's son. At Stanford. Class of he didn't want to say. And Vansittart getting killed, and Mama Vansittart running a Ferrari into a tree in St. Tropez."

"But Vansittart Senior was a bachelor. While you were snuggled in the arms of Morpheus, my sleeping beauty, I've been doing my job. Checked with the Santa Clara Sheriff's Department, Belmont Police Department, Hall of Records down there—nothing. Nothing on any missus or any junior. The late Mr. Vansittart was what CNN says he was. A lifelong bachelor. So, to quote you before you passed out last night—why the yarn?"

Lindsey said, "Do you have any coffee, Marvia?"

She clucked her tongue. "Is this what married life is going to be like with you? My Prince Charming gets tipsy, I have to carry him home and pour him into bed. Then he wakes up and demands his morning coffee. Is this the answer to a maiden's prayer?"

Lindsey said nothing.

"Sure. It's all made. I'll fix you a cup. But don't think this is the way it's going to be."

"I'm sorry, Marvia. How many times have I done this?"

"First time that I know of."

Lindsey nodded. He remembered a night in Santa Barbara, when he was tracking down a batch of stolen comic books, but he was alone then, and he'd had to deal with his condition himself. Twice in—how many years? That wasn't so bad.

She handed him a cup of Jamaican Blue Mountain. He sniffed it, then tasted it. The coffee was delicious.

Lindsey gathered his thoughts. "Mr. and Mrs. Cooke run the World Fund for Indigent Artists. The fund stands to collect four million smackers if International Surety—read, *Hobart Lindsey*—can't turn up the girl on the cover of *Death in the Ditch*."

"Have you found her?"

"No."

"Didn't think so."

"But I've made some progress. I still think there's a chance."

"But if you don't find her, the fund gets the money. What's their operation like? Are your friends the Cookes ragged-sleeve do-gooders? They operate out of a grimy walk-up in the Mission? They are in San Francisco, right?"

"San Francisco, sí, Mission, no. They're in 101 California."

Marvia's eyebrows rose.

"I haven't seen their office, but you can bet it's posh and pricey. And their sleeves are hardly ragged. We lunched—is that the right word?—at Liberté. Cooke picked up the tab, but he did it with a World Fund credit card. Showed it to me. Proud of it. They have custom cards, I guess they send 'em to their members. Every time you charge something on it, the fund gets a little rake-off."

Marvia chuckled. "Did they offer you a ride after lunch?"

"I was parked in Union Square. Walked back."

"Bet a nickel, if they'd given you a ride it would have been in a Mercedes. Mercedes or something equally spartan."

"No bet. I'm sure you're right."

"So what this sounds like is, the Cookes are both old San Francisco money."

"I think so. I don't think he worked his way through Stanford raking leaves. I didn't get as much from her, but I got a definite feeling. If she wasn't to the manor born, I'll eat my hat."

"I've never known anybody too rich for greed. Sounds to me as if they're doing well by doing good. If they're doing very much good at all. I think I'll send a telex to Sacramento and see if the fund is up on its filings. Be interesting to see what their annual revenue looks like, and what percentage of it gets used up on overhead. Want to bet that hardly any money actually gets into the hands of down-and-out ex-cartoonists or whatever?"

"No bet. No bet, no bet, no bet."

Marvia said, "You want to finish up and walk me down, or you want to lock up when you leave here? I have to get to work."

* * *

KARI FIELDING SMILED her adder's smile when Lindsey arrived at the IS office in Walnut Creek. He felt her eyes on his back as he made his way to his desk and picked up the memo slip. Just two words were scrawled on it, in Kari Fielding's favorite purple felt-marker ink. *Call Richelieu.*

He moved around his desk, slid into the chair, and picked up his phone. Kari Fielding nodded cheerily at him.

Mrs. Blomquist put him through to Richelieu without keeping him on hold for the usual five minutes. Richelieu opened the conversation with a compliment. "You've been keeping KlameNet/Plus up to date pretty well on this Vansittart thing."

Lindsey grunted an acknowledgment.

Richelieu said, "I want that girl." Ah, no more Mr. Nice Guy. "You've been running around like a chicken without a head. Chicago's a garden spot in January. You can't fool me. You must have been out there surfing on Lake Michigan. What's your game plan now?"

Lindsey said, "Is it all right if I call you back in five minutes, Mr. Richelieu?" He didn't wait for an answer. He hung up and walked out of the office, past an angry-appearing Kari Fielding.

Well, Mathilde Wilbur had kept him abreast of company scuttlebutt, he supposed it was only fair that Kari Fielding do the same for Lindsey's successor as branch manager, the loathsome Elmer Mueller. Even so, it wasn't so nice being the subject of Kari's surveillance.

He called back on a public phone and got through to SPUDS/ Denver. Richelieu was raging, but Lindsey managed to calm him down. "There was somebody in the office—I didn't want to discuss internal matters." He didn't say who the somebody was, and Richelieu didn't ask. He just waited for Lindsey to answer his last question,

"I've got a lead on the artist who painted covers for Paige Publications. If I can track him down, I think I might be able to find his model. Or at least get a lead on her."

He heard Richelieu exhale loudly. "Okay, Sherlock. Keep at

it. But watch your expenses. And remember, the clock is ticking. And don't hang up yet. What about the World Fund for Indigent Artists? You smoothing their feathers for them, or we going to have a lawsuit on our hands?"

Lindsey cleared his throat. "It doesn't look so good on that front, Mr. Richelieu. I had a meeting with Mr. and Mrs. Cooke, and they want the four million. They know about *Death in the Ditch*, and they don't think there's any way we're going to find the model, so they're demanding the money. I think they're going to sue IS."

Richelieu hissed, "Son of a bitch." Then: "Not you, Lindsey. Just try not to rile them. And see if you can find that girl. She's a million-dollar girl, Lindsey. Keep that in mind. You find her, you're a hero around here. You fail and—I don't like failure. Need I say more?"

Lindsey said no more. He knew that if he held his silence Richelieu would tell him something else. That was the way Desmond Richelieu worked. At first Lindsey had perceived the grand high panjandrum of SPUDS as an almost-supernatural being, a demigod to be placated and feared. After a couple of years in SPUDS and a series of increasingly fruitful encounters with Richelieu, Lindsey had learned how to get what he wanted from the man. Miraculous to say, he was even starting to like him.

"One other thing, Lindsey—have you seen the media coverage on the Vansittart case?"

Whoops! Lindsey's coverage in some of his earlier—and more sensational—assignments for International Surety had made him the darling of the press and the broadcasters. He'd had his fifteen minutes of fame several times over.

This public image had both its up side and its disadvantages. The good news was, it protected him from overt attacks within International Surety. The company could hardly cashier the man who had retrieved the famous stolen comic books and the 1928 Duesenberg, ridden a fifty-year-old Lockheed Lightning in a valiant attempt to save a stolen Flying Fortress, and championed the legendary ninety-year-old film director Edward George MacReedy.

On the other hand, Lindsey's moments of fame had made him the envy of certain colleagues within International Surety, and had set him up as the strange attractor for assorted covert attempts at intracorporate sabotage.

Lindsey heard Desmond Richelieu draw a hissing breath.

"We've been getting a rash of claims in the Vansittart case," Richelieu resumed.

"You mean beside the World Fund?"

"Check your KlameNet entries. The thing is more than a mailbox, Lindsey."

"Yes, sir. You don't want to tell me, yourself?"

Richelieu sighed. Maybe Lindsey was pushing the man too far. Then again, maybe he wasn't. "It's the wackiest thing since the Howard Hughes will mess. We must have had twenty women claiming to be the girl on the cover of *Death in the Ditch*. Mostly the branch offices have been sifting these things. The messier ones get bucked to SPUDS."

"Who are they from?"

Lindsey could almost see the expression on Richelieu's patrician face. "I've got the list in my hot little hand right now. Look, here's a woman in Miami Beach. Eighty-seven-year-old pensioner, Golda Mintz. Here's one in St. Louis, thirty-nine years old, or so she says, Lucille O'Doule, a nurse. Here's my favorite. Starblaze Moonflower. You want to guess?"

"I'm afraid to."

"Damn right. Age twenty-eight, or so she says. Starblaze Moonflower was formerly Joseph Lawson. When he changed his sex to she, she figured she might as well have a new name. Fair enough. There was a little problem about the dates, since Vansittart's policy was written roughly fifteen years before Lawson was born, but Ms. Moonflower says, and I quote—Lindsey, you really ought to download this file—'I died in 1967. I was a soldier in Vietnam. I was reincarnated as Joseph Lawson, but that was all just a big mistake, the cosmic computer had a virus.' You like that one?"

"I still don't follow. Does he mean he was a man, and he was killed in Vietnam? It still doesn't hang together."

Desmond Richelieu said, "Oh, dang! You're right. I guess I'll have to deny her claim after all. Too bad."

Astonishing. Richelieu was developing a sense of irony. Lindsey blinked.

"Find the rightful bennie, Lindsey, or at least find out what happened to her. Otherwise I've got a nice cozy desk for you to fly in Fargo, North Dakota."

Now that was more like the Desmond Richelieu known and feared throughout the International Surety Corporation.

LINDSEY PHONED SHADY Oaks Retirement Villas and arranged to take Jeb Harkins out for another dinner. When he got to Livermore that night, Harkins was ready for him, pacing up and down in the lobby.

"Well, if it ain't Hawkshaw the Detective. Come on, let's get a move on." Harkins took Lindsey by the elbow and steered him through the pneumatic doors and onto the gravel driveway. A huge oak stood in the middle of a grassy circle in front of the retirement home's main pavilion. Lindsey hadn't seen any villas at Shady Oaks, but he wasn't inclined to ask about that.

"Where's that blue bomb of yours, kid? Oh, there it is. By God, you know that car looks like a nineteen forty-six Ford for midgets. I used to have one of those things, did you know that? Came home from the Pacific during the All-Star break, nineteen forty-six. Shucked my khakis and bought two things with my separation pay. You want to guess what they were? A zoot suit and a brand-new Ford."

"I thought the war ended in forty-five."

"Didn't have enough points to get out. Bet you don't know about that, do you? Never mind, let's get back to that Mex joint, I'll talk to you there."

Lindsey started the Volvo and drove to the same restaurant where he and Harkins had eaten before.

The same Mexican kids were leaning on the wall, drinking Tecate beer from paper bags. Lindsey blinked his eyes. Déjà vu, all right. One of the kids nodded to Lindsey. He had thick, curly black hair and big, liquid eyes in a handsome brown face. The girls must love him.

The kid said, "Nice short."

Lindsey wondered if it was a put-on. He said, "Thanks." He and Harkins went inside.

The place was pretty quiet tonight. They found a table and the same waitress approached. She had the biggest chest Lindsey had ever seen, and she didn't try too hard to hide it. A heavy gold-colored crucifix dangled from a chain around her neck. Jesus sprawled comfortably between her breasts. He looked pretty happy there. Just like Patti Paige Hanson in Winnetka. Lindsey wondered how many Jesuses were nestled happily in how many bosoms at this very moment, all around the world.

He felt a sharp pain in his leg. Jeb Harkins had kicked him, and the old guy was by no means feeble. "Come on, young fellow, the lady wants to bring us something nice. I'll have my usual, señorita. You remember—whiskey sour?"

The waitress said, "Sí, señor, un wheeskee sour." Lindsey figured she must practice her accent in front of a tape recorder. "And what for the señor?" she asked Lindsey.

"Just mineral water, please."

"Sí, señores." She flowed away.

Harkins said, "You gotta be nice to her, son. I'll tell you something, in case you're too dumb to notice, which I suspect you are. That señorita is in love with me. I can tell. They're hot-blooded, those Latins. They don't go through the handshake and bowing stuff that our women do. They take one look at a stud and they *know*. She's in love with me."

When their drinks came they ordered dinner. Lindsey got ready to watch Harkins down a *bistec ranchero* drowned in salsa, plus rice, beans, guacamole salad, french fries, and a couple of tortillas. How did he manage to stay thin? It must be the bland diet they served at Shady Oaks.

Lindsey said, "I hope you can give me a little more information about Bob Brown."

Harkins looked up. His jaw was working and he held his fork

upright with another slice of *bistec* at the ready. He wasn't wasting any time.

"Who's Bob Brown?"

"The artist. You told me he painted the cover for your book, *Baseball Stars of 1952.*"

"Oh, yeah. You get a little forgetful at my age, Sherlock. Bob Brown, Benny Bruninski. What about him?"

"Whatever became of him?"Harkins shrugged, his jaw working steadily up and down.

"Do you know if he's still living in Chicago? Is he still living at all?"

Harkins swallowed, washed the *bistec* down with a swallow of whiskey sour. "You think we could get the señorita over here and get me another of these? The drinks are lousy in this joint, but at least they're small. That's a Marine Corps joke, Sherlock; you wouldn't remember it."

Lindsey spotted the waitress and signaled. Harkins held up his empty cocktail glass. The señorita nodded her understanding. Jesus nestled deeper.

"Did Brown ever say anything about his model? You told me you barely knew him, but I want you to try. Where did you meet? Did he come to the *Daily News* building, or did you go to his studio?'

Harkins was following the waitress with his eyes. Now he brought them back to bear on Lindsey. "Actually, he came to the paper to talk to me a couple of times; then I went over to his studio once to look at his painting. He was a bear when it came to anybody criticizing his work, but he wanted it to be accurate. Imagine if he'd put Stan Musial in a St. Louis Browns cap instead of the Cards, hey? Couldn't have that. We had some respect for accuracy in those days, not like nowadays."

"You went to his studio?"

"Old loft over on Talman Street near Douglas Park. Must have cost him fifteen dollars a month for that place. He had an army cot and a primus stove, lived there and did his painting. I saw the original for my book. He had everything right. I asked him about that weird ballpark. I told you about that, didn't I?

Pelican Stadium, in New Orleans. He told me he used to be a hobo. Back in the early thirties. During the Depression. Used to travel around the country, ride the rails, take odd jobs. He was a hobo, not a bum. Big difference."

He stopped talking long enough to sample his second whiskey sour. He made a face, sawed off another slice of *bistec*, started to chew on it, and waved his hands, knife and fork soaring, as he spoke. "Used to get odd jobs as a groundskeeper, janitor, told me he was a candy butcher in a burlesque house once in Indianapolis, sold poor-boy sandwiches in the stands at Pelican Stadium. Said that was his favorite town, New Orleans. If he ever retired, he'd like to live there and paint."

"Then he *did* know baseball. How come you said he couldn't tell the caps apart?"

Harkins snorted. "Man knew baseball *parks*, not baseball. All the difference in the world. Man oh man oh Manischewitz, they're making 'em dumb these days."

"When did Brown give up being a hobo?"

"Thirty-six, he told me. Thirty-six. Civil war in Spain. He was an idealist, Benny was. Hated Hitler. Name like Bruninski, you can understand why, can't you? I never met him 'til fifty-one, you see, but he told me he met a recruiter riding the rails in thirty-six, talked him into volunteering and off he went to Spain. Soldiered there for about a year, I think."

"Did you ever see him after nineteen fifty-two?"

"Nup."

"Ever hear from him, a postcard, anything?"

Harkins frowned. "Let me remember." He scooped up some rice and beans and guacamole, made a neat track of them in the middle of a tortilla, added green salsa this time, rolled the tortilla into a burrito, and took a large bite off one end.

He nodded. "Think I got a Christmas card one year. Might have been somewhere around—oh, yeah, I remember now, Lyndon Johnson and Barry Goldwater were running for president so it had to be, what, sixty-four, yeah, nineteen-and-aught sixty-four. I remember, it was peculiar, he must have sent that card in October because I remember, I had it even before the election.

Just a Christmas card—he must have sent it around Halloween. And he signed it; that was all. No, now I think of it, they both signed it."

"Who's both?"

"Why, Ben and Mae."

"Who's Mae?"

"His wife."

"What wife?"

"Oh, she was his model—didn't I tell you that? That time I went over to his studio to check the baseball cover for my book. He had the cover all done, it was right, had the right cap on Stan Musial and all. But he was painting a nude when I got there. He liked to do fine art—what he called fine art, anyway. And he was painting this nude."

He took another bite of burrito, washed it down with whiskey sour. "You know, Sam, I really need a refill of this thing. They make the worst damn drinks in this joint that I've ever tasted."

Lindsey signaled the waitress. Harkins was a treasure trove. That is, he was if his memories were accurate. At their first dinner, he'd denied knowing anything about Bruninski except his name. Now Harkins was revealing everything Lindsey had hoped for. Some door of memory had opened in the old man's mind. If only it stayed open!

"Her name was Mae? You say the model was his wife? Did he introduce you?"

Harkins's eyes looked far away. Lindsey could imagine. The old man might be sitting in a Mexican restaurant in Livermore, California, in the last decade of the twentieth century, but his mind was in a painter's studio on Talman Street in Chicago, and the year was 1952.

"I tell you, Sunny Jim, that was the most beautiful woman I have ever seen. And I've seen a lot of 'em, believe me, and no disrespect to a one of 'em. They're all beautiful. Best damned thing God ever did, created woman. Now you take Maude Markham—you ever meet that cookie?"

"In Chicago."

"Fine figure of a woman. Fine figure. You ought to see her in her skivvies, Sherlock. You ought to see her in her birthday suit. And some of those native girls out in the Pacific. I'll tell you, but, they sure know how to ripen 'em in the tropics. But that Mae—" He tried to whistle, and a grain of rice flew out of his mouth and landed on the hard composition tabletop.

Lindsey said, "Did she model for his book covers as well? Do you know her professional name?"

"Never saw her again but that once. Lovely, lovely girl. Long hair, sort of a dark red color. Green eyes. You'd think, naked as a jaybird, you wouldn't exactly notice the hair and eyes, but I tell you, Sunny Jim, just one sight of that woman, you never forget a thing."

"What became of Bruninski's work?" Lindsey asked. "I mean, he sold it to Paige, but that was just the publication rights, wasn't it? What became of the original paintings?"

Harkins picked up a tortilla, filled it with rice and beans, and rolled it into a burrito. He took a bite, chewed for a while, then washed the food down with a swig from his glass. "He was serious about his work, he was. Always meant to keep his originals and have an exhibition one day. Thought some gallery would give him a one-man show, or a museum would give him an exhibition."

Part of the contents of Harkins's burrito had fallen back onto his plate. He scooped up the rice and beans and ate them. "Bennie used to complain about those cheapskate publishers. Said they always wanted to keep the originals. Don't know what the hell for. Patch broken windows with 'em, all I know. He'd never let 'em do it. Demanded his originals back. Used to get into roaring battles over 'em, but he wouldn't give in. Finally got everything back. Least he told me he did. Say, you going to eat all that food on your plate, sonny? Don't want it to go to waste."

Lindsey ignored Harkins's fork when the old man took a sizable morsel from Lindsey's plate. "So you think he might still have the paintings? I mean, if he's still alive, and we could find him, he might still have the paintings?"

Harkins shook his head. "Not likely. He was always broke. He'd make a few bucks, then he'd get onto his uppers again. Whenever he got desperate, he'd sell off an original. They were good paintings, too. He could get some fair prices, but they didn't pay the kind of price for those commercial paintings that they would for abstracts. Not back then. Nobody wanted pictures that actually *looked* like anything. But he always found somebody who'd give him a few bucks for one 'cause they were so good."

He paused for another bite of burrito and another sip of whiskey sour. "That was all a long time ago." He sighed. "They were wonderful people, Ben and Mae. Wonderful people. I loved them, you know?"

For someone who hardly knew Ben Bruninski and who met his wife and model only once, Harkins seemed to fall in love easily. Still . . .

"What happened to them?" Lindsey asked. "When did they leave Chicago? Do you remember the postmark on the Christmas card they sent you in nineteen sixty-four?"

Harkins shook his head, No. "But I remember the picture. Funny subject for a Christmas card. It was a statue of Andrew Jackson rearing up on a horse in a park."

Lindsey knew the statue and knew the park. Jackson Square, New Orleans, home of Benjamin Bruninski's favorite baseball field, Pelican Stadium.

Bob Brown. Benjamin Bruninski. And Mae? Mae Bruninski? Was she still alive? Were they both still alive? In New Orleans?

"One other thing," Harkins was saying, "That Bob Brown, he was some character. Big, rangy galoot. A long drink of water, we used to say. Must have been six-five, six-six. I was no jockey, either, but he towered over me. Thin, stringy guy. Wore a little mustache and a goatee and a little blue beret. Had to prove he was an artist, see? Think he was afraid people wouldn't believe him, he had to look like an artist."

Harkins shook his head. "Bob Brown, he was easy to remember. Walked with a limp, too. At first I thought he was faking it. You know, some of those arty types, they'll do anything for a little extra attention. But the day I went to his studio—it was raining. Raining hard. And he was in pain. I could tell that, I could tell if he was a phony. He wasn't. You could see the pain in his face. I asked him what was the matter. He said he had some shrapnel in his leg; it always hurt him when it rained. He was an interesting fella."

He stopped for a minute, took a sip of his drink, then resumed. "He was a funny-looking galoot, Ben was. But that Mae, believe you me, sonny, she was the most beautiful woman in the world."

Chapter Eleven

WHEN HE GOT home, there was a message waiting from Marvia Plum. Call her at police HQ if it was early, otherwise at home. He dialed the Oxford Street number. She answered on the first ring, and she didn't sound sleepy. And she didn't waste time on any preliminaries.

"O'Farrell's dead."

Lindsey closed his eyes, shocked. He'd stood near the front window to phone Marvia, the drapes drawn a few inches to admit a shaft of light from the street lamps outside. Now he sank into an easy chair.

"What happened?"

"I had a call from Willie Fergus. He drove back up to Tahoe to join the search. They had the highway patrol alerted in both states but nobody had even a trace of them. So they sent up helicopters. Still nothing."

Lindsey opened his eyes. He waited for Marvia to continue.

"Then somebody phoned in a fire alert. Claimed they saw a plume of smoke near I-80 west of Donner Pass. Forest Service totally freaked out. This isn't fire season, couldn't figure out why there should be a plume. So they sent a truck and they found it."

She paused.

Lindsey said, "Tell me."

"That mysterious station wagon—it was a Jeep Grand Wagoneer. Stolen, of course. Ran off the freeway, over a ravine. They must have avoided the agricultural checkpoint at Truckee; that's easy enough to do. They got onto I-80 for a few miles, then off again."

"How do they know he's dead?"

"Oh, there's no question of that. Wagon crashed and burned. A real mess. Gas tank must have been full. Highway patrol wants to get into the act and the sheriff is all in favor. They think there might have been an explosive charge in the wagon. Just to make sure."

Lindsey whistled. From across the room, the glowing numerals of a digital clock caught his attention. He hadn't seen Gordon Sloane's Oldsmobile in the driveway when he pulled the Volvo in. Either the graying lovebirds were still out somewhere kicking up their middle-aged heels, or they'd decided to stay over at Sloane's condo.

"Marvia, wait a minute." Lindsey shifted the phone to a more comfortable position. "If the station wagon was that badly damaged, would the body be identifiable? I mean—wouldn't it be burned? Are they sure it's him?"

"No question. The body was thrown clear when the Wagoneer blew. They had to search for another hour to find him. It was O'Farrell, all right. Willie Fergus gave me his personal assurance that it was O'Farrell."

"He wasn't driving, was he? Somebody arrived at Doctors' Hospital, O'Farrell checked himself out and they drove off together, right? So—where's the driver? You think those forestry guys or the Highway Patrol ought to search some more?"

"Nice try. That's possible, but they don't think so. There were two sets of tire tracks leading off the freeway. Two leading off, one leading back. That makes a nice, clear scenario. The whole thing was planned. Whoever was driving the station wagon knew that a confederate was going to pick him up along the way, follow him until he went off the freeway, and then pick him up in the second car once he'd disposed of O'Farrell. Or— if that chronology doesn't work, the pickup car might have got there first and waited for the station wagon."

Lindsey let out a long, hissing breath. "What killed O'Farrell? The explosion?"

"Not sure yet but it looks like a bullet in the brain. The medical examiner up there has to let the sheriff know. They're keeping us posted."

Lindsey stood up and paced back and forth. That was the best part of a cordless phone: you could pace back and forth. "Jesus K. Wright, the guy goes from hero to suspect to corpse before you can blink your eyes. What now? Can't they take—what do you call it?—a moulage of the second set of tire tracks? Trace the car from that?"

Marvia managed a small laugh. "You've been reading too many murder mysteries, Hobart. Right—CHP is trying exactly that, but they're not likely to get anything useful out of it. I mean, there are eighty-five zillion kinds of tires out there. Suppose they find that the second car had Michelin Steel-Belted Fifties or Firestone Specials or whatever the hell, what good does that do? The car's probably in somebody's garage by now. If they thought of it and they want to be safe, they've already changed tires. And even if they haven't, how the hell are we going to track down every set of Michelin Fifties in the State of California? Won't work. Makes a nice story, but it won't work."

Lindsey stopped pacing and stared at the glowing numerals. Almost midnight.

Marvia said, "Look, if you want to stay up to date on this, why don't you just watch some TV news? They're sure to have it by now."

Lindsey said, "Okay." He picked up a remote and clicked to CNN. Somebody was selling cars; to the sound of a Mozart quintet, the commercial showed a sleek sedan whipping around the curves of a winding mountain road. How apropos. Lindsey hit the *mute* button.

Marvia asked, "You learning anything useful?"

Lindsey said he was indeed. He'd put in a good night's work with Jeb Harkins. But then the commercial ended, and the news at midnight came on. There was a still frame from Jamie Wilkerson's helicopter crash tape vignetted in a corner of the screen. The anchor was talking about John O'Farrell. Lindsey said, "Marvia, I think I'm going out of town again. I'll call you in the morning, okay?"

The video report contained the same information Marvia had given to Lindsey, only in greater detail. The grandees at the network had rented a chopper of their own and sent it over the Sierras. It hovered over the crash site and a camera with a long lens showed the CHP and CDF searchers carrying a body bag away from the smoldering wreckage of a Jeep Grand Wagoneer. You could tell the difference even from here. The Highway Patrol types went for knife-edge creases in their uniforms, a lot of neatly trimmed mustaches on the men, and short hair on both sexes. The Division of Forestry types looked as if they were trying for a rugged frontier look.

And—how did they always manage to have body bags handy, Lindsey wondered. He tried to watch the newscast carefully, but they seemed to be rehashing the same report rather than adding new facts. By what seemed like the third or fourth go-round, Lindsey couldn't concentrate any longer. He turned off the TV and watched a tree limb wave gently in front of the street lamp for a little while. Then he went to bed.

As he fell asleep his mind wandered back to the time before he'd ever heard of stolen comic books, before he'd ever met Marvia Plum. His life in those days had been a dull round of days at the office and nights keeping Mother calm and reasonably happy.

His life was better now, and Mother's surely was. But still he found himself remembering the old days fondly.

He awakened to pitch darkness. He blinked and fumbled until he located the bedside alarm. He must have flailed his arms in his sleep, because the clock radio was turned away from his bed. He turned it back and read the glowing digital numbers. He'd dozed for barely an hour; but the harder he tried to go back to sleep, the more awake he became.

Finally he pulled on a set of sweats and a pair of sneakers. Marvia had given him the sweats. There was a portrait of Rudolph Valentino on the front of the shirt, complete with eye shadow and Arab kaffiyeh.

The air outside was bracing. Lindsey had lived all his life in this house on Laurel Drive. He knew every square inch of the pale stucco walls and Spanish tile roof, every foot of hardwood floor and plaster and glass. Mother had bought the house out of her husband's GI insurance when he was killed off the coast of Korea. She had brought Lindsey to this house when she was released from the hospital after giving birth, and it had been his home ever since.

Well, not for much longer.

He decided to jog around the block. Marvia was always after him to get in shape. That was the reason for the Rudolph Valentino sweat suit. The air was cold and wet, and his breath was a white plume.

He reached Hawthorne Drive and turned toward Palmer, keeping to the side of the road. There was no traffic at this hour, but caution was a habit. Most of the houses were dark. A light shone in an occasional window. Here was a row of hedges; here were a few trees; here was a driveway leading up to a square California craftsman home.

The car approached Lindsey from behind, its headlamps low. He heard it first, then turned and saw it moving slowly toward him. He wasn't sure what it was. Certainly a recent model and not an economy car: that was for sure. A Lexus or a Volvo or a Mercedes.

There was no reason to be suspicious. This had to be some resident returning from a party or from an evening out in San Francisco. Then why the dimmed headlamps? Somebody's teenaged daughter out on a date. Her boyfriend borrowed Mom and Dad's car. Really impressive. Some necking, one thing leads to another, and then the chilling realization that she's out past her deadline. Grounding looms.

Maybe if she comes home quietly enough, sneaks into the house without making a sound or turning on a light . . .

In a world where eleven-year-olds carried machine guns to school it was all so banal, so silly.

Yet something wasn't right.

The car pulled up alongside Lindsey. The passenger-side window slid open with a soft hiss. He saw only a vague figure inside. A voice said, "Pardon me, we've been driving around for an hour, completely lost. Do you—"

Something made Lindsey dive for the hedges lining the street. He managed to force his way through the vegetation. He felt leaves and thorns scraping his face and hands but he pushed ahead and burst through onto a lush lawn. A sprinkler was going—somebody keeping the grass moist. He sprang to his feet and sprinted toward the house.

Behind him he heard the same voice: "Hey, wait a min—" Then there were shots. He turned back. He could see the street, partly through the hedges and partly over them. The driver had turned on his brights, and a second car had rolled up Hawthorne behind the first.

There was another burst of gunfire. Lindsey heard a crash of shattering glass. Then the first car roared away toward Mountain View Boulevard. Unless there was a lucky traffic stop, Lindsey knew the car would be on Mountain View Boulevard inside sixty seconds, on the freeway and gone in a couple of minutes.

Lights were springing on in houses all around him. The second car had come to a halt in the middle of Hawthorne Drive. Lindsey trotted back to the street and stood in the glare of the second car's headlights. He heard the driver get out, recognized him when he joined Lindsey in the glow of his car's lights. It was Gordon Sloane.

Sloane and Lindsey walked to the passenger side of the car. Mother had rolled down her window. "Hobart, what happened?" She was too startled and too baffled to react.

Lindsey said, "I think we'd better call the police."

The front door of the California craftsman house opened. The man who stood there wore pajamas and robe. His hair was iron-gray and tousled. He needed a shave. He held a very large revolver in his hand and was pointing it at Lindsey.

He said, "Don't move."

"Don't worry. Did you see—did you—look, somebody just took a shot at me. A lot of shots."

The man with the revolver peered at Lindsey. "I know you."

"I live right around the corner. Hobart Lindsey. Laurel Drive."

The man lowered the revolver. He ran his free hand through his hair. A woman had appeared behind him. She was peering around him as if he were her barricade against all harm.

"What happened?" The man looked down at the pistol in his

hand. He did something to it and slipped it into the pocket of his robe. Lindsey hoped that he was putting the safety on, not snapping it off. "You really Lindsey?"

"Really. Really, I'm your neighbor. Look." He gestured. "Don't you know my mother? And her friend, Mr. Sloane."

The man nodded slowly. "All right. Come on in. I'll"—he turned to his wife—"darling, call nine-one-one, would you?"

They filed into the house and waited for the police to respond.

The police were fast. There were two of them, one male and one female, decked out in shiny midnight-blue nylon jackets with fake-fur collars. They had their hands on their pistols when they got out of the black-and-white.

The civilians sat in the living room with the female officer, her radio squawking every few seconds. She took quick statements from everyone present while her partner checked outside the house.

The officer radioed in Lindsey's minimal description of the first car. She told them that the police would try and stop any car roaring out of the neighborhood, but she was afraid that the car would be gone before the police could do anything, was probably gone already. Lindsey grunted when he heard that. It was exactly what he expected to hear.

Once she had taken Lindsey's statement about the shooting, the officer took shorter ones from the others in the room. Then she started background questions. Did Lindsey recognize the car (no), did he recognize the person who spoke to him (no), did he have any enemies (in his line of work, who could tell?), was there any known drug dealing in this neighborhood (not that he was aware of), was there gang activity in the neighborhood (not that he was aware of). . . .

The officer came back to that question about enemies. What was Lindsey's line of work? He told her about International Surety and about SPUDS. Well, there were people who didn't like the results of insurance investigations. Sometimes they didn't get money they were hoping to get. Sometimes they went to jail.

He wondered—should he tell her about Nathan ben Zinowicz?

"Something bothering you, sir?"

Lindsey looked up.

The female officer was staring at him. "You look upset. I don't blame you, after what happened to you. But please don't hold back anything from me. Even if you think it may not apply, even if you think it's trivial."

Lindsey said, "Okay." Then he told her about ben Zinowicz, about Dave Jones the parole officer, about ben Zinowicz's job with the World Fund for Indigent Artists.

"Have you seen this man since his release? Spoken to him?"

Lindsey shook his head. "But I've spoken with the directors of the fund. My company may have to pay the fund a great deal of money. And . . ." He left it there.

But this officer wasn't leaving it there. "Why is that, sir?"

"Why would we have to pay the fund?"

She nodded.

He explained about the Vansittart insurance policy and the death of John Frederick O'Farrell.

She said, "I've heard of that. Sensational case. You're involved?"

Lindsey felt like a celebrity. "I work for the Special Projects Unit of International Surety. If I can locate the primary beneficiary of Vansittart's policy and we pay her the money, the fund gets nothing. Otherwise, they get four million dollars."

The officer took a deep breath and looked around the room. Now she was the center of attraction. She exhaled visibly. "And you think the directors of this fund are using this onetime professor, this" — she checked the name on her pad — "this Nathan ben Zinowicz, as a hit man. He came here tonight looking for you. He was in your house once before, years ago, so he knows the neighborhood at least a little, and he was circling the block and saw you out jogging . . ." She gave Lindsey an inquiring look. "Is that your scenario, sir?"

"Uh." Lindsey had to think about it for a minute. Then he said, "Yes. That's it."

The officer snapped her pad shut. "In the morning we'll ask you to come down to headquarters and make a formal statement. But this should do for now."

"Are you going to check with Dave Jones? With the fund office? With the Cookes?"

"We check everything, sir. Thank you."

She went outside to check on her partner. Lindsey decided that the partner was included in everything. He entered the house and the two officers stood, conferring. Then the male officer walked to the far wall of the room. He grunted and nodded. He stood staring at a black-ringed hole in the cream-painted plaster. "We'll have to get this out. One round here; there are more outside. We should get some useful information."

The male householder got to his feet. "Who's going to pay for the damage?"

The female officer put her hand on her holster again. "Just stand still, sir. Keep your hands up, please."

The man looked alarmed but he obeyed.

The officer reached for his robe. Lindsey could see that the pocket where the man had put his revolver was sagging from its weight. The officer reached into his pocket gingerly, withdrew the revolver, and stepped away from him.

"You have a permit for this, sir?"

"Yes." He sounded offended.

"Would you get it, please? My partner will go with you." She jerked her head and the male officer stood next to the gray-haired man. The man said, "It's, er, I have it—" He started to move away and the officer moved with him.

Five minutes, later they were back in the living room. The officer held a slip of paper in his hand. He radioed in the information. After a brief conversation he handed the permit back to the owner.

"All right, everyone." The female officer was obviously in charge. "Sorry for everything that's happened. Try to get some sleep; and, Mr. Lindsey, I'll see you tomorrow, all right?"

Lindsey said, "Sure."

The female householder said, "But who's going to pay for our window?"

Lindsey got a ride home from Mother and Sloane. If the householders had an International Surety umbrella policy, they had nothing to worry about.

* * *

IT WASN'T LINDSEY'S best night, but he managed to get a few ragged periods of sleep between bouts of pillow punching and water drinking. He'd got the female officer's card as the party was breaking up at Hawthorne Drive. Then he'd got a ride home—all block-and-a-half of it—with Gordon Sloane and Mother in Sloane's Olds.

Lindsey thanked Sloane. "If you hadn't come by, things could have been much worse. They might have jumped out of the car and started looking for me. What made you drive on Hawthorne? That isn't the way you come from Mountain View Boulevard."

Sloane made a wry face. "Fate. Dumb luck. An angel whispered in my ear. I don't really know. What about you, dear? Why do you think we went that way?"

Mother shrugged. "We've never done that before. Not in all the time we've known each other."

Sloane spread his hands. "I guess we just wanted to go sightseeing."

"Right." Lindsey rubbed his head. He recalled vaguely a quotation about the prospect of being hanged in the morning concentrating a man's mind wonderfully. That was the kind of thing Lindsey's friend and sometime lawyer, Eric Coffman, would know to the last syllable and comma, complete with author, source, and date. Lindsey couldn't do that, but he could add to the quotation. Nothing disturbs a man's sleep like being shot at.

All of that was before he climbed into bed.

A few hours later, he drove downtown and parked the blue Volvo near police headquarters. He found his way to the officer's desk and gave his statement again, this time into a tape recorder. He asked what came next.

"I already had a chat with Dave Jones in Oakland. He said that Dr. ben Zinowicz had been a model client since he got his walking papers from San Quentin. Jones phoned that World Fund office where Dr. ben Zinowicz works, and he was there, bright and early this morning. Didn't know anything about an incident last night. Offered to do anything he could to assist in the inquiry."

She looked at Lindsey with innocent eyes. "What do you make of that?"

Lindsey felt his jaw clench. "I make this," he managed. "They're in cahoots. That's what I make."

The officer nodded. "You really think so."

"I do."

"Well, you may be right. Dave Jones is a good man, I know him slightly. He told me that he'd called through again and talked to a Mrs. Cooke. She's a big shot over there, right? Do you know these people?"

"Yes. Cynthia Cooke is more than a big shot there. She and her husband run the place."

"Well, they had a staff meeting last night. Top executive staff. Mrs. Cooke, Mr. Cooke, Dr. ben Zinowicz. He was there with them. They started with dinner after work, they ate at"—she consulted a notepad—"Harry Denton's. You know Harry Denton's, Steuart Street, very chichi. Maître d' can verify that. Then they adjourned to the Cookes' condo on Nob Hill and continued until the wee hours. In fact, the meeting ran so late that Dr. ben Zinowicz had to put up in the Cookes' spare room. Poor baby."

Lindsey blinked. "So there's nothing."

"Nothing to go on. You think it was this fellow. He's got an alibi. We could ask Dave Jones to bring him in for a paraffin test, but if he's as smart as he seems to be you can bet he was wearing gloves. And he's surely got rid of them by now."

There wasn't much more to say. Lindsey was intrigued by this officer's dual role. Last night she was in a rolling unit, responding to a 911 call. Today she was sitting at her desk, acting like a detective.

But she seemed competent in both capacities. Maybe she'd be police chief someday.

Within hours Lindsey found himself sitting in another client chair, facing another female police officer across a battered, cluttered desk. This time the officer was Marvia Plum, and today she was decked out in her full, official midnight-blue uniform, badge reflecting the room's fluorescent lights, stripes standing out on her sleeve like Bill Shatner. Or maybe Ernie Bilko.

When Lindsey told her about the shooting on Hawthorne Drive, Marvia dropped her other work and listened to a repetition of the night's events and of this morning's meeting with the Walnut Creek Police Department.

"Trouble is, I don't know if I can take a hand in this." Marvia shifted some folders around on her desk. "This is clearly Walnut Creek's case. If you're right, and it ties in with WFIA and the Vansittart and O'Farrell killings, then I have a little hook into it. Very little. Only because I'm providing the local liaison with Fabia Rabinowitz."

"So you can't do anything?"

She didn't answer directly. "How sure are you that it was ben Zinowicz in that car?"

"What do I know or what can I prove?"

"Either."

"I can't prove a damn thing. I didn't get a good look at the guy. I heard his voice, but just a few words. And I haven't heard it for something like five years, so I can't say for sure based on that."

"And you didn't recognize the car? License number, make, anything?"

"It was dark. It was fairly big. Sedan big, not limo big. I think it was black but it could have been dark blue or dark green. I think it was a Mercedes but it could have been half a dozen makes. One of those big Buicks or Chryslers. And I didn't see the license plates at all."

Marvia grunted. "So how do you know it was ben Zinowicz and not some random event? A mugging, a local drug deal that went sour, a turf war?"

"Come on, Marvia. What's your boss's favorite saying?"

"Okay. You're right. *Coincidences really do happen, but they make me very nervous.*"

"That's right. I'm working on this case. The World Fund stands to make a lot of money if I fail. Nathan ben Zinowicz has a major grudge against me. And he's now executive director of the fund."

"Well, you cost him his academic career and several years of his life. I'd say that could produce a grudge. We get some very angry ex-cons coming around here, believe me."

"I do." Lindsey felt a wave of helplessness wash over him. "Do you need the rest of it? Ben Zinowicz gets out of San Quentin, gets a job working for the Cookes, hears about Vansittart's death and the big insurance policy—"

Marvia Plum was waving her hand in front of his face. "No, no, no, no, no."

"No?"

"No. He was working for the Cookes *before* Vansittart bit the big one. How's this for a theory? These three sweeties knew each other before Nathan went away. They were waiting for him when he got back. They knew all about Vansittart's eccentrically worded insurance policy. They knew about his gambling habit and his preference in transportation."

Lindsey made a humming noise, tilted his head.

Marvia Plum stopped talking and shot an inquisitive look at him. "No?"

"I don't know. You're the cop. Go ahead."

"They suborned O'Farrell. He was to dispose of Vansittart, which he did, very successfully. He was then to disappear, probably with a large stash of cash, provided by the Cookes. How's that?"

"Give me some more."

"Okay, I will. Everything is going fine until the helicopter comes down. Instead of ditching smoothly in Lake Tahoe, the chopper has a rough touchdown and starts to sink. Along comes Captain MacKenzie of the *Tahoe Tailflipper* and gets a line on the chopper; but he can't hang onto it, and the chopper flips over as it sinks. Instead of emerging safe and sound, O'Farrell breaks his leg in the chopper crash. He winds up in the hospital."

She paused for breath. Lindsey waited for her to go on.

"This makes the Cookes very nervous. They dispatch ben Zinowicz to break O'Farrell out of the hospital, which *he* does, very successfully. But O'Farrell is now damaged goods. Risky goods. So—maybe the Cookes and ben Zinowicz worked this

out in advance, maybe ben Zinowicz was playing it by ear—"
She wrinkled her brow.

"No," she resumed. "Scrub that. We need to account for the
second car. Incidentally, CHP up in Placer County *did* get some
nice moulage of the second set of car tracks. Must be at least a
million cars in this state could have those tires, and surely the
Cookes have changed tires since then."

She waved away an errant thought.

"Okay, here's the plan. Ben Zinowicz heads up to Truckee in
the Wagoneer, the Cookes follow in their Mercedes, ben Zinowicz busts O'Farrell out of medical durance vile—"

"Medical what?" Lindsey interrupted.

"Stay on your toes, sweetie. He busts him out of the hospital.
O'Farrell is getting antsier by the minute, the longer he stays in
there. He's afraid they're going to catch on to him, he'll hear a
knock on the door, and it'll be the sheriff with an arrest warrant.
Instead, he sees this nice friendly professor type—whom he
probably knows already; we can't be sure of that, but I'll bet you
a Popsicle it's so—and a chance to get the heck out of there. You
see?"

"Okay." Lindsey nodded. "And then?"

"Then ben Zinowicz tells O'Farrell that they're headed for
Brazil via SFO, shoots him in the head instead, and dumps the
body and the Wagoneer both off I-80. You like?"

"Go on."

"Cookes pick up ben Zinowicz, drive sedately home to their
cabin in the sky, and nobody is the wiser. If they need an alibi,
they alibi each other. All one happy little family."

"And Hawthorne Drive?"

"You know about that. You were there."

"So—how about you pick 'em up and close the case."

"Don't make me laugh. It's all speculation, Bart. If I went to
the DA's office with that, they'd offer me an insanity discharge.
There's no evidence. It's just a fairy tale."

"I can believe it."

"Sure you can. Number one: you have reason to want to believe it. Number two: it's neat and it's plausible, if I do say so

myself. Number three: it might even be true. Doesn't matter. Might be isn't good enough. No proof, no warrant. End of chapter."

"Then nothing happens?"

"Hey"—she put her hand on his sleeve—"I said end of chapter, not end of story. Not end of story by a long shot."

He managed a feeble smile. "That's better. So—what do we do now?"

She leaned forward, took his face in both her hands, put her mouth to his ear. He felt her breath, warm and moist. She whispered softly, "What you mean *we*, white man?"

Chapter Twelve

As the Delta 757 lifted off from Oakland International, Lindsey settled into his seat as best he could. He had the window and he watched the city and San Francisco Bay shrink and fall away behind the jet as it headed inland. He'd made this flight to New Orleans once before, when he was tracing the tangled roots of a tragedy-smitten family to their origins in the tiny Louisiana town of Reserve.

This time he was looking for a onetime commercial artist named Bob Brown, born Benjamin Bruninski, and his wife, Mae. Was Brown still alive? Was Mae? Were they still together? Lindsey knew next to nothing about them, save that Brown had painted covers for a paperback house in Chicago in the early 1950s, and that his wife, Mae, had also been his model.

Was there any way Lindsey would recognize them? What had Jeb Harkins told him? Lindsey closed his eyes and conjured up the face and voice of the old man as he devoured his *bistec ranchero* and his whiskey sours, and ogled the 200-pound waitress in the Mexican restaurant.

Brown was a "big, rangy galoot. A long drink of water . . . six-five, six-six. . . . Thin, stringy guy . . . mustache and a goatee and a little blue beret. Had to prove he was an artist."

And Mae . . . Harkins had said, "Never saw her again but that once. Lovely, lovely girl. Long hair, sort of a dark red color. Green eyes."

That was something to go on. Chances were that her long, dark red hair wasn't dark red after nearly half a century, but her eyes would still be green. And Lindsey had pictures of her. He had the Paige Publications paperbacks with Bob Brown's cover paintings, and Mae had been Brown's model as well as his wife.

Lindsey rummaged through his carry-on bag. Paperback collectors like Scotty Anderson or the tyrannical, almost-mythic Lovisi would have a fit if they could see Lindsey jamming the books into a flight bag, then tugging them back out to read on a transcontinental flight. But Lindsey was not a collector, he was an investigator. And these books were important clues.

There was *Death in the Ditch*, by Del Marston. Lindsey studied the cover. The artist had chosen a scene in a barroom. A gorgeous blonde was framed against the open doorway, and behind her a street scene was barely visible. An old-fashioned office building, some passing cars. Maybe that was the Paige Building at the corner of Kinzie and LaSalle.

Inside the bar a rugged-looking individual in a double-breasted suit, a fedora on the back of his head and a shot glass in his hand, gaped at the blonde. Behind the bar, a shirtsleeved individual poured whiskey from a bottle. It was hard to tell, but Lindsey thought the bartender had only one arm. And the label on the bottle—Lindsey had to turn the book sideways and strain to read the tiny lettering—said "BB Whiskey."

BB Whiskey.

Bob Brown.

Benjamin Bruninski.

Lindsey opened *Death in the Ditch*, by Del Marston, and began to read.

The sun went down, but the night was as hot as the day had been, and besides, who could tell the difference once you were inside O'Hara's saloon? The street lamps on Halsted would have given more light than the incandescents in O'Hara's, but Seamus O'Hara was like that: too cheap to put in anything brighter.

"You want another one, Marston?"

Marston pressed his belly up to the mahogany and tilted his shot glass back to get the last drop of bourbon down his gullet. "Yeah, Billy, sure. And don't use the watered bottle this time. O'Hara's not watching."

Billy smirked.

The atmosphere in the saloon was close enough to get in your ears and wet enough to wring out. The Philco in the corner was tuned to the Cubs game, covered by telegraph from St. Louis. Borowy had carried a two-run lead into the ninth. He'd been struggling all night.

The barkeep poured another shot and put the glass on the bar. When Marston reached for it Billy hung onto the glass. "Lemme see your money, Del."

Marston grumbled and threw a coin on the bar. "I ain't *that* low. Not yet."

"Didn't say you was." Billy released the glass and picked up the coin with one sweep of his hand. It was the only hand he owned. He'd left the other one with the arm it was attached to, on Tarawa. There was a picture of him and his buddies, grinning in their Marine uniforms, on the mirror behind the bar. In the picture, Billy had both hands.

Now he wore a ruptured duck on the lapel of his jacket.

Marston knew him, though. He'd even been to Billy's house up on Bellevue a couple of times. Met Billy's wife and kids. He said, "How's the family, Billy?"

Lindsey skimmed a few paragraphs. The book was amusing, a real period piece. He could almost feel the Truman era in it. The radio in the bar, no TV . . . the reference to the ruptured duck, the World War II discharge badge that millions of veterans wore . . .

Then—

The front door of the saloon swung open and a blonde shot in, running at top speed. She stumbled over a wad of Wrigley's and landed in Marston's arms. He managed to save the bourbon.

The blonde was wearing a white blouse that was pulled off both shoulders to show a chest that Howard Hughes would have paid a million to photograph. She had a little beret pinned to her hair and a skirt that would have showed her knees and then some if there'd been any more light in the joint.

Lindsey closed the book and put it back into his flight bag carefully. Del Marston seemed to be both the author of *Death in the Ditch* and its hero. He'd come across that little device before. Who was it who'd used that trick? Ellery Queen, right.

Not long ago, Lindsey had been grappling with the problem of who Del Marston was. Now he knew. Marston was—had been—Isidore Horvitz, the radical poet and Spanish war vet who had fallen to his death while sunbathing in a rainstorm.

Lindsey had solved that much of the puzzle, and now he was headed for New Orleans to work on the rest of it.

There was a time when he would have been reluctant to jump on an airplane and fly off in pursuit of a case. International Surety policy would have had him use the company's facilities, pass the problem along to someone on site, and wait for a report to come back. But SPUDS didn't operate the way the rest of IS did, and nowadays Lindsey didn't operate the way he had in earlier years. He'd taken a cursory shot at locating Brown/Bruninski via directory assistance, a few quick inquiries to the New Orleans Police Department and the Orleans Parish Hall of Records, but he felt something pricking at his mind about this case.

Something was going on. He didn't know what. He hadn't put all the pieces together, but there had already been too much mystification, there had already been too many deaths, to handle this as routine. He had to immerse himself in this case, and he had to treat it with urgency.

He leaned back in his seat and closed his eyes and tried to figure out what was really going on.

He knew—at least, he was pretty sure—that Ben and Mae Brown had both been alive and living in New Orleans in 1964. A postmark would have clinched it; but even without the postmark, Brown's inclusion of Pelican Stadium in his cover montage for *Baseball Stars of 1952* and the scene of Jackson Square on Ben and Mae's 1964 Christmas card were the best clues that Lindsey had to work with.

The 757 landed in Dallas, but Lindsey didn't bother to deplane and sample the canned air and deadening atmosphere of the airport. When the jet was airborne again he used the in-flight telephone to call Marvia.

She told him that Roger St. John Cooke and Cynthia Cooke and Nathan ben Zinowicz had all checked out for both the O'Farrell killing and the shooting in Walnut Creek. They alibied each other. Fabia Rabinowitz's work on the video images of both the helicopter crash and the wreck on the bed of Lake Tahoe had proved conclusively that O'Farrell had killed his passenger.

"And Willie Fergus tells me that they're going to try and raise the chopper," Marvia added. "The feds are insisting on it, and then the coroner can get to work on the body and find out for certain if it's Vansittart, so everybody will be happy."

Lindsey asked, "Do you think it is—Vansittart, I mean?"

"I'm pretty sure, but pretty sure isn't good enough. It will be better to get the forensic work done."

"Maybe you should call Gideon Oliver," Lindsey offered.

Marvia said, "Stay in the real world, Bart."

"I was joking."

"Sorry."

"Marvia, I wish you could have come along."

"So do I, but it just wouldn't work."

"Last time was fun."

"There will be another time. Meanwhile, I'm sure that Aurora will take good care of you."

"Sure. But it won't be the same."

"I hope not." She laughed.

As he placed the handset back in its mount, dinner arrived. He picked at the mystery meat and gray vegetables and waited for the flight attendant to take away his tray.

He retrieved the telephone from the back of the seat in front of him and dialed again.

"International Surety, Special Projects, can I help you?"

He asked for Aurora Delano.

"Hey, sure, I know you're coming. I'll meet you at the airport. Wear a white carnation and carry a copy of *I'm O.K., You're O.K.* so I'll recognize you."

He told her the landing time.

She asked, "They feed you on that airplane?"

"You could call it that."

"Think you might have a little appetite left when you get here?"

"I'm not sure."

"Think you could handle some gumbo or maybe a little *étouffé?*"

Lindsey said, "Sold."

Coming off the jetway, he spotted her in the midst of a crowd of casually dressed New Orleanians. Lindsey and Aurora Delano had been to SPUDS training school together, in Denver. Before transferring to SPUDS she'd been assigned to International Surety's tiny outpost in Grants Pass, Oregon. When he got to know her, however, he learned that she was originally from New Orleans and was eager to return there. Her chief reason: an abusive husband whose farewell present to her had been a broken arm.

Aurora Delano waved a placard in the air, but Lindsey didn't need it to recognize her. She loved to play dress-up, and New Orleans was the perfect stage for her act. Long, bright-red fingernails, blue-black hair, an olive complexion, and vivid lipstick. Somehow Aurora Delano echoed the fashions of forty years ago. but on her they seemed appropriate. It seemed almost like an omen.

They rode into town in Aurora Delano's Saab sedan. She said, "I got you a room at the Monteleone, you'll like it. On Royal Street, right on the edge of the Quarter. Where's your significant other? I liked her. Nothing bad happened, I hope."

"Nothing bad. She's stuck at her job, I'm stuck at mine."

"That's the modern way."

She flashed him a smile. In the glare of oncoming headlights her teeth were brilliant white and her dark lipstick looked as black as Sarah Kleinhoffer's. She said, "You still have that appetite? Want to stop for some food? I told the hotel you might be late; they're holding your room."

"That's some service."

"Busy time of year, too. But the power of the corporate buck, you know—International Surety commands."

Lindsey nodded. He'd been eating well lately, courtesy of IS and SPUDS. Well, that was okay. If he saved the company a million smackeroos, a few hundred in expense money wouldn't matter. And if he failed and International Surety had to pay out the full four million on Vansittart's policy instead of just three, then a few hundred more wouldn't matter either.

"Hey?"

"Oh, sorry. Sure." He checked with his inner man. "Matter of fact, I didn't eat much on the airplane. Matter of fact, the more I think about it, the hungrier I get." He grinned at Aurora.

She grinned back and punched the controls of the Saab's CD player. The music could have been straight out of the 1950s—a boy and girl singing alternate lines of a soppy love song to a walloping drumbeat and a creamy saxophone.

"You like that?" Aurora grinned. "Shirley and Lee."

"Is that new?"

"You kidding?"

"No, I'm not."

"Brought straight to you from nineteen fifty-two."

They ate at Tortorici's on Royal, not far from Lindsey's hotel. Well, you don't have to eat Cajun in New Orleans, and the food was superb. Lindsey ordered crab *fra diavolo*; Aurora chose a cold seafood salad. The night seemed warm to Lindsey, but he'd been through so many time and weather zones lately that he was starting to lose track.

Over coffee with chicory, Aurora got down to business. "Le Duc de Richelieu called me before you did, Bart. He's really got a bug up his rear end on this one. I've never seen him like this."

"Company's got a lot at stake."

"You bet."

"How much info did he give you?"

"The whole file. Sent it to me over KlameNet/Plus. You've been digging, haven't you?"

"All right, then. You know why and how the trail led me here. I figure there's a fifty-fifty chance that Mae Brown or Bruninski is still alive. Same for Bob Brown. But it's been thirty years since that last Christmas card to Jeb Harkins in Chicago."

Aurora's dark eyes flashed. "I know you've done all the obvi-

« 155 »

ous things like checking the New Orleans phone book and running a check with the local credit bureaus."

Lindsey grinned. "We went to school together, Aurora, remember? How are your connections with the local utilities and the bureaucracy?"

"Pretty good. You're not eating your bread pudding. Something wrong with it?"

Lindsey poked his spoon into the dessert. It was not very promising to the eye, but it more than paid off on the palate. "Sorry, Aurora." He washed down a mouthful of pudding with a sip of bitter coffee.

"Pretty good connections," Aurora said, "but no blips."

Lindsey chewed his lower lip. "Not good. But it doesn't prove anything. They might be using a different name or just keeping their heads down. Nobody could tell me why they dropped out of sight in Chicago back in the early fifties. But they might have taken new identities. It would have been a lot easier back then; the country wasn't all wired up yet."

Aurora said, "Okay. Anyway, you let me know what else you want by way of support on this thing. Ducky has the hots for it, and we're both positioned to make big points—or to lose big."

Lindsey put the meal on his IS credit card. Outside the restaurant, the evening air was warm and heavy. The valet pulled Aurora's Saab to the curb, hopped out, and held the door open for her. Lindsey and Aurora climbed in. Aurora said, "Nights like this, I wish I had a convertible. Maybe next time."

She drove the length of Royal Street and brought the Saab to a halt across the street from the Monteleone. "How about a nightcap? Or you too wiped out from flying all day?"

Lindsey took a rain check. He walked through the old hotel's ornate lobby, paused and admired a gigantic antique clock, then let the elevator whisk him upstairs.

When he climbed into bed, he was too jangled to sleep. He phoned Marvia Plum. She was at home and they exchanged news.

There was an important development at the California end of the investigation. Roger St. John Cooke and Cynthia Cooke continued to alibi each other and Nathan ben Zinowicz for both the

O'Farrell murder near Truckee and the abortive assassination attempt in Walnut Creek, but Nathan ben Zinowicz had turned up missing.

The Cookes had said nothing about his disappearance, but Dave Jones had decided to pull a surprise visit on the professor. The rules of the parole game permitted that. Ben Zinowicz had taken a flat in a Berkeley low-rise. Jones checked out the building himself. The landlord reported that ben Zinowicz had been an ideal tenant: paid first and last months' rent in advance, left a cleaning deposit, never gave loud parties or disrupted the building's tranquillity.

None of the other tenants could remember ever meeting him.

Jones entered ben Zinowicz's apartment. It was almost compulsively neat. Ben Zinowicz had installed floor-to ceiling bookshelves, an up-to-date sound system, and a desktop computer. The shelves were empty of books, and there was no evidence of CDs, audio tapes, or vinyl. Jones looked around for disks or documents associated with the computer, but there was nothing. He did find a file cabinet near the computer table, but it, too, was empty.

No clothing in the closet, no bedding, no toiletries, no food in the tiny kitchen.

It looked to Dave Jones as if ben Zinowicz had packed everything he could take with him and left. Maybe he had a second apartment nearby—which should have been reported to his parole officer—or maybe he had moved from the area.

Jones tried to contact ben Zinowicz at the World Fund for Indigent Artists. There he had got a runaround. Dr. ben Zinowicz was away from his desk; he was out of the office; he wasn't in today; he was expected soon, but no one knew exactly when.

Finally Jones spoke with Cynthia Cooke. She invited him into her private office, closed the door, and told him that she and her husband were desperately worried about Dr. ben Zinowicz. He had been acting more and more nervous lately, jumpy and suspicious, even paranoid. He hadn't reported for work in days, and the Cookes were beside themselves. He'd been an ideal employee, and then some—reliable, intelligent, creative.

They knew that he was a paroled convict, but they'd known

him before his first brush with the law. They had always held him in the highest esteem, and they'd been shocked at his conviction. Once he'd come up for parole, they'd jumped at the chance to bring him into their operation. His credentials were outstanding and his performance had been superb. What could have happened?

What happened was, Dave Jones revoked ben Zinowicz's parole, Marvia told Lindsey. But that was little more than a formality. Ben Zinowicz's face and information about him would go to police departments throughout the state; but unless an officer happened to come across him in the course of the day's work, ben Zinowicz might stay on the loose for years.

Once Jones had done the paperwork necessary to revoke ben Zinowicz's parole, he returned to ben Zinowicz's apartment and seized the computer. Ben Zinowicz might not have wiped the computer's hard disk before he left. Maybe a police technician could decipher the information on the disk, and something there might lead to the fugitive.

Lindsey laid the telephone down. He tried to watch television, but found it alternately irritating and simply boring. He pulled back the curtain of his window and looked across Royal Street and west toward the French Quarter. Royal was just a block from Bourbon Street, where the partying went on to all hours of the night. Lindsey considered going out again, but the prospect of colliding with noisy drunks, loud music, and strip shows did not appeal.

He removed the Paige Publications books from his flight bag and spread them carefully on a desktop. *Baseball Stars of 1952*, with its montage of ballparks and athletes. *Buccaneer Blades*, by Violet de la Yema. *Cry Ruffian!*, by Salvatore Pescara. Of course, *Death in the Ditch*, by Del Marston.

He sorted through all the books that had a female model on the cover. The hair color and the hair styling, the clothing and the poses were all different. Sometimes she was a tough gun moll, sometimes a Caribbean wench, sometimes . . . Whatever the costume or pose, she was always the same woman.

She was—she had to be—Mae Bruninski.

He picked up *I Was a Lincoln Brigadier* by Bob Walters. On

this one she was either a nurse or a female guerrilla—it was difficult to tell. She wore a uniform of sorts, stained and torn to reveal her generous bosom. But of course. A barren hill rose in the background. A wounded soldier lay across her lap; bombs burst around them and a propeller-driven fighter plane dived at them. The nurse or guerrilla fighter clutched a pistol in her free hand, pointed at the diving airplane.

Lindsey settled comfortably onto his bed. He turned the book over and read the publisher's blurb on the back cover, then turned it back and opened to the first page.

I remember exactly where I was when I signed up for the Abraham Lincoln Battalion of the International Brigades. I remember the time of night and the weather and what I was wearing. It all happened a decade and half ago, but I remember it all, and I am not ashamed. I am proud to say that I was a Lincoln Brigadier.

The headquarters of the Young Communist League in Brooklyn was on the second floor of a building at the corner of 65th and Bay Parkway in Bensonhurst. There was a pharmacy on the first floor, and there was a bowling alley in the basement. You could get everything you needed in one building: entertainment in the basement, a meal or a magazine to read in the pharmacy, and nourishment for your mind and your soul at the Young Communist League.

When Colonel Francisco Franco came back from Africa and sent his mercenary thugs into Spain, the world recoiled in horror. Every decent man and woman knew what was going on. This was a man who hated democracy. He was in the pockets of Adolf Hitler and Benito Mussolini and Pope Pius XI. What an unholy trinity! And Francisco Franco was their lickspittle and loyal henchman!

There were forty of us in the room. All young, all idealistic. We believed in democracy and social and economic justice. We weren't all Communists, let me make that clear. Some were, sure; some were dedicated, committed, disciplined Party members.

But there were Trotskyites, liberals, anarchists—everybody who recognized the growing threat. There were a lot of Jews there. Why not? They knew what Hitler meant, and they knew that if he wasn't stopped now, he'd have to be stopped later, and at even greater cost. There were Negroes there. They knew—one of them said to me—"If that man gets the Jews, the Negroes will be next. We know that. We've got to stop him *now*."

Hitler and Mussolini were helping Franco, but who was helping democracy in Spain? Juan Negrín, the Prime Minister, sent out a call for help. The world clamped an embargo on Spain. Léon Blum, a Jew himself, was afraid to provoke Hitler. Neville Chamberlain, that sniveling coward, dared not lift a finger. He learned better, later, to his regret. They all learned better, later.

What about our dear Franklin Delano Roosevelt? He put a Jew in the cabinet, and everybody thought he was so fine and noble. But he was in the pocket of the Church. Joe Kennedy, that old bootlegger and womanizer, whispered his filthy guidance into Roosevelt's ear, and Roosevelt said, "Oh, those poor Spanish Republicans," and "Oh, those nasty Nazis and Fascists helping that nasty General Franco."

That was after Franco promoted himself. Later he decided that "General" wasn't exalted enough, and started calling himself "Generalissimo." What a fine title! It sounded so grand, Chiang Kai-shek borrowed it.

As for Roosevelt, sure, he cried crocodile tears for democracy in Spain. He said some of the right things. He said a lot of the right things. But would he lift a finger to help democracy? Would he let the bullets and the airplanes and the blankets and the medicine and the food that Spanish democracy needed to survive be sent to the Loyalists?

Oh, there was an embargo. Oh, the League of Nations wouldn't permit it.

So the supplies piled up in New York and in Liverpool and in France, and the borders were closed and the ports were sealed and the Spanish people suffered and Spanish democracy died.

Spanish democracy was murdered, and Roosevelt and Chamberlain and Léon Blum and Édouard Daladier stood by and wrung their hands and did nothing.

Only the Soviet Union tried to help. Only Josef Stalin sent machine guns and tanks and airplanes and cadres to try to help.

Too little and too late, but the International Brigades fought proudly and well. We will never bow our heads and we will never forget what we tried to do.

Maybe the world will remember someday.

Somebody blew a horn outside, and Lindsey blinked. He'd been drawn into the book. It was written without grace or polish, but its obvious passion had caught him up. He laid it aside. He took a shower. It had been a long day after all. He brushed his teeth, climbed into pajamas, and crawled into bed.

He picked up the remote and tried the TV again. One channel was giving a video tour of the attractions of New Orleans. On another, a pair of women were exclaiming over junk jewelry and urging viewers to call up right now and place their orders because the supplies were limited and this offer might never be repeated.

Then there were the talk shows. They had to be taped, of course, nobody would pay a crew at this hour of the night. Oprah had a panel of females who claimed—every last one of them—to be the rightful beneficiary of the Vansittart insurance policy. Lindsey watched in horror until he could take no more. He clicked around to Geraldo—who also had a panel of Vansittart claimants. Lindsey was about to give up when the name of one of Geraldo's guests flashed across the screen. It was Starblaze Moonflower. Lindsey stared in fascination at the long-jawed, big-boned Starblaze.

Click.

On CNN a weather reporter was droning on about snowstorms in the Northeast and the Rocky Mountains. Lindsey wondered if Desmond Richelieu was going to be snowed in. When he'd had enough weather, Lindsey switched to a movie channel. Late-night movies often did the trick for him when he couldn't get to sleep any other way.

They were showing *June Bride* with Bette Davis and Robert Montgomery. It looked like a pretty good picture, but it was already half over, and Lindsey couldn't get involved.

Maybe some other time, Bette.

Maybe some other time, Bob.

He switched off the TV and went back to *I Was a Lincoln Brigadier*.

Somebody had turned on the radio. They were playing music. The tune was "Stompin' at the Savoy" by Benny Goodman and Chick Webb. A couple of the fellows were arguing about it. Ivan Smulsky said that light entertainment like swing music was a waste of energy and a distraction from social reconstruction and should be banned from the airwaves. Bobby Kosoff said that the music was a perfect example of what could be accomplished when workers set aside their differences and merged the efforts for the common good. Smulsky demanded, "How can you say that?" Kosoff said that Goodman was Jewish and Webb was Negro, and that their collaboration was the model for revolutionary collaboration.

Just about then a Party organizer arrived. The news was full of the war in Spain in those days, and he asked who wanted to go to Spain to fight the Fascists. I raised my hand and he gave me $10 and handed me a piece of paper. He said, "Go see this man in the morning. Keep this paper. Give it to him." Then he looked around. I remember, he had rust-colored hair, very curly, and freckles. He asked if anybody else wanted to go to Spain. There was a lot of stirring around and muttering, but nobody else raised his hand. Then the Party organizer left and Smulsky and Kosoff resumed their debate.

I looked at the paper. It was an address and it was signed with the Party organizer's initials.

A few of the fellows came over and patted me on the back and said they were proud of me. After a while, the place started clearing out. Some of the fellows had to go to school in the morning. A couple of us went downstairs to the pharmacy and drank chocolate malts or ate cherry frappes. Smulsky and Kosoff said they were going bowling.

The next morning I went to the address the Party organizer gave me. It was a doctor's office in Greenpoint. The doctor looked at the slip of paper. He asked me, "So, you want to fight Hitler, do you?"

I told him that I did.

He asked why.

I said, I wanted to fight Fascism. I wanted to work for democracy and social justice. And I was a Jew.

The doctor examined me and said, "You look healthy enough. Do you have any bad habits? How much do you drink? How much do you smoke? Do you run around with loose women?"

I answered truthfully, and he nodded and went to his desk. He sat down and wrote out another slip of paper and handed it to me. He told me to go there the following Monday morning. Someone would take care of me.

I left his office and looked at the slip of paper. It had an address on it in Manhattan, down in Union Square, and the doctor's initials on the bottom. I went home and started to pack a few clothes. My mother came into my room and asked where I was going. I told her I was going to Spain to help the Spanish people.

My mother started to cry. She said I would be killed. And she wouldn't let me go. So I told her I was going to work in a factory in Madrid making rifles, I would be perfectly safe, replacing a Spanish comrade so he could go to the front. Then she let me go.

Lindsey read until his eyelids drooped. He laid the book on the floor beside his bed and fell into a half-sleep. The book was on his mind, as were his experiences since the Vansittart case started. He dozed and half-dreamed, half-fantasized. The year was 1936, and he was a teenaged Jewish communist living in Brooklyn. Roosevelt was in the White House, the Depression was lingering, and radicalism was in the air. Somehow Sarah Kleinhoffer was there, in her female vampire costume, and she was sending him off to fight in the Spanish Civil War by spending the last night with him before he sailed for Europe.

He woke in a sweat. He went to the window and looked out at the still-partying celebrants in the French Quarter. He opened a window. The old hotel had that much to offer. You weren't sealed off from the outer world. You could smell the city's air and hear its sounds. You could feel its presence.

Toto, he whispered to himself, *I don't think we're in Chicago anymore.*

Chapter Thirteen

IN THE MORNING, he started his search for Ben and Mae Bruninski, aka Bob and Mae Brown. The first phase was a paper trace. With Aurora Delano's assistance he looked for them through telephone books, old city directories, back issues of the *New Orleans Times-Picayune*. Those were easy enough. Tax and voter registration roles were matters of public record. So were driver's licenses.

Bank records were harder to come by, but Aurora had been running the local SPUDS operation long enough to have her contacts.

The results were either too good or too bad to be useful. Lindsey couldn't decide which, but the effect was the same. Together, he and Aurora Delano turned up just three Bruninskis: Morris, Joseph, and Abraham.

Morris Bruninski was a retired florist in Metairie; he'd never been in Chicago, didn't know anything about painting or publishing, and had never heard of a Benjamin Bruninski.

Joseph was a lawyer. He was cagey, but interested. Lindsey made an appointment to meet him at his office on Carondelet Street. Even in their telephone conversation, something about the man raised the hackles on Lindsey's neck. He didn't like his manner. He was too eager to please, too eager to ask questions and to listen, and too reticent when it came to giving answers.

Their face-to-face encounter justified Lindsey's misgivings. Lindsey held back his own information, questioning Bruninski about his family, hoping to hear something about an uncle or cousin named Benjamin; but Bruninski played the conversation like a poker wizard playing his hand. There was no way to tell what he knew or didn't know, what he held or what he was pretending to hold.

Lindsey held him to a draw, the best he could hope to do. After a period of probing, Lindsey realized he was getting nowhere. He had to call. "Let's show our cards, Mr. Bruninski. Do you have any knowledge of a Benjamin Bruninski?"

By now Joseph Bruninski knew there was a lot of money at stake, and he knew that Lindsey was the party dispensing it. "All right, let's do exactly that. Let's show our cards. Is this Benjamin Bruninski the beneficiary of an insurance settlement? If he is, and you are involving me in the case, I have every right to be compensated. Don't try to use me, Mr. Lindsey, and then cut me out of the money."

"No," Lindsey told him, "Benjamin is not the beneficiary."

Joseph Bruninski spread his hands. "Well, then, why are you looking for him?"

"I think I might find the beneficiary through him. All right?" Lindsey was beginning to lose patience.

"You know," Joseph Bruninski stroked his chin, "I think I recall a Benny at family gatherings." He frowned, concentration lines furrowing his forehead. "Was he—huh, I'm trying to remember now, maybe I'm thinking of Cousin Billy. No, it was definitely Benny. At least I think so. Did he have, ah—" Bruninski's eyes flashed.

This one should have been a palm reader, Lindsey thought. Or a detective. Looking for leads, picking up clues, reading your voice and your face. Bruninski was leading Lindsey as well as reading him, trying to get him to fill in the blanks. Then he'd say, *Yes, that's my Cousin Ben! Yes, I'll represent him. Yes, now how much money did you say was coming?*

Lindsey stood up. He was convinced there was no Cousin Ben, but you could be sure that Joseph Bruninski would turn in a lot of billable hours looking for him. And if he could, he'd bring some kind of claim against International Surety. Lindsey said, "Thank you very much. I'm afraid I have another appointment." He got out of there.

Abraham Bruninski was the Chief Rabbi of Temple Sinai on St. Charles Avenue. He welcomed Lindsey in a book-lined study. A framed painting hung on one wall. It showed a white-bearded scholar, a blue-striped, white shawl drawn over his head, poring over what had to be a religious scroll. An oil lamp cast a golden light over the scene. Either the old man was near-sighted, or he was gradually nodding off. The only other religious symbol in the room was a large menorah on a credenza. Beyond the credenza, Lindsey could see the olive-green trolleys rolling by on St. Charles Avenue.

The rabbi leaned back in his leather swivel chair. He wore a dark blue suit and maroon tie. Except for his silk yarmulke, he could have been an investment banker or a judge ensconced in chambers, primed to plunge into a heavy research session.

When he heard what Lindsey wanted, he smiled. A green banker's lamp on his glass-topped desk glinted off his rimless spectacles. Abraham was a very different Bruninski from Joseph. Eric Coffman would have liked this man and this setting.

"It happens that family genealogy is a hobby of mine." Bruninski reached back and drew a large leather-bound volume from a shelf. "You say this Benjamin Bruninski was a painter?"

Lindsey nodded.

"Did book covers in Chicago, did he? That's interesting. I dabble a little myself." He moved his head to indicate the picture of the pious scholar. "Benjamin. Let me see." He shook his head in a mixture of sadness and bewilderment.

"Here's Benjamin, all right. But he doesn't seem to be the right Benjamin."

He laid the leather-bound book flat on the desk and turned it so Lindsey could read it. The rabbi pointed to an entry. The paper was of a creamy, almost yellowish color. The edges were gilt. Lindsey ran his finger down the page, looking for the entry the rabbi had indicated. He found it quickly.

Bruninski, Benjamin, b. 1 Adar I, 5676 to Israel Bruninski and Vera Chemsky Bruninski, Brooklyn, New York. Unmarried, no issue, d. 6 Adar II, 5698, Belchite, Spain.

"You see?" The rabbi swung the book around again, closed it carefully, and replaced it on the shelf. "You see?" The green light glinted on his glasses. "Benjamin Bruninski has been dead for more than fifty years."

"I don't see. What were those dates, 5676, 5698? Are those from *Star Trek?*"

"Oh, excuse me, those are according to the Hebrew calendar. Let me see, by our common calendar, Benjamin Bruninski was born on 5 February 1916 and died 9 March 1938."

"Are you sure?" Lindsey had found Benjamin Bruninski—at least he'd found one Benjamin Bruninski. He didn't want to give him up.

The rabbi tented his fingers. "What do you know about the Spanish Civil War, Mr. Lindsey?"

"Not much. In fact, I've just been reading a book about the war. It's part of why I'm here. It happens that the cover was painted by a Bob Brown."

"Oh?"

"Brown did a number of book covers, and I've located the author of one of the books. He knew Brown, gave him some information to help make the picture accurate."

The rabbi nodded.

Lindsey went on. "He told me that Brown's real name was Benjamin Bruninski."

"Now, that sounds like a great detective story, Mr. Lindsey. I can't say that I really understand it, and I'm afraid it's really a little out of my bailiwick. But my research"—he reached back and tapped the book with one finger—"my research is pretty conclusive. Ever since the Soviet Union collapsed, records about that war that had been sealed since nineteen thirty-eight have been coming out. I visited Moscow personally to see what I could learn. Benjamin Bruninski is dead. His grave is in the Valley of the Fallen in Spain."

Lindsey took a breath, "Could there be another Benjamin Bruninski? Maybe a Benjamin Bruninski, Junior?"

The rabbi smiled. "You won't find many Ashkenazic Jews named Junior." He caught the puzzlement on Lindsey's face. "That is, Jews of Eastern European ancestry. The Sephardim— Mediterranean Jews—have different customs. But for Ashkenazi—well, it's an old belief of ours, really a superstition." He laughed softly, self-deprecatingly. "Our tradition is that the Word is sacred. The soul is tied up with the name. If a child were given the name of a living Jew, you see, there would be two persons competing for that soul, and one would probably die."

He grinned broadly. "Of course we don't believe in that nowadays. We're modern. Scientific." He laughed again, again softly. "But old customs have value, I believe. And you won't find many Ashkenazic Jews named 'Junior.' "

Outside the synagogue, on St. Charles Avenue, a streetcar ground to a halt, and half a dozen passengers debarked.

Lindsey said, "Rabbi, could there be another Benjamin Bruninski?"

"Of course there could. But if there is, I don't have him in my book."

Lindsey thanked the rabbi. He walked to the streetcar stop and waited for the next car to carry him back to Canal Street. He tried to make sense of what Abraham Bruninski had told him. He knew that Benjamin Bruninski had been alive in the 1950s, working for Paige Publications, and at least as late as 1964 when he sent the Christmas card to Jeb Harkins. Lindsey had the Paige books that proved it and he had Jeb Harkins's personal testimony about the greeting card.

But if Bruninski had not died in Spain, who had? Had there been two Benjamin Bruninskis? Had one of them died in Spain and the other returned to America? Or had someone else died in Spain and been misidentified as Bruninski? Or had Bruninski really died, and someone else taken his identity? Lindsey had encountered a similar case a few years earlier, involving three half-brothers. When one was killed in World War II, another had taken over his identity and lived under a false name for the next fifty years.

The olive-green streetcar ground to a halt, and Lindsey climbed on board and paid his fare. No solution to the puzzle was in sight. He would have to find Bruninski himself—if that was possible—and then, in all likelihood, the mystery would unravel before his eyes.

So much for the Bruninskis, at least for the time being. The Browns were worse. Four hundred of them in New Orleans and surrounding areas. Almost sixty Robert or Bob or R. Browns. As a last resort, Lindsey might have to persuade Aurora Delano to twist the arm of the local International Surety office for help. Put a couple of office slaveys onto checking out every possible Bob Brown in southern Louisiana.

Trouble was, that kind of helper wasn't usually much help, and if Lindsey and Delano had to do it themselves it could take weeks.

Lindsey returned to the Monteleone. Just off the hotel lobby he stopped for a meal of crawfish and rice. One thing about New Orleans, you'd always eat well there. The crawfish were mild by New Orleans standards—at least his waiter assured him as much—but they lit a small fire in his mouth and he washed them down with an Abita Wheat. He amended his previous assessment of New Orleans comestibles. You'd always eat and drink well there.

He returned to his room, powered up his palmtop, and logged onto KlameNet/Plus. He updated the Vansittart file to reflect data he'd received from Marvia Plum, as well as the information earlier provided by Fabia Rabinowitz and Willie Fergus. There was nothing new in the file from Aurora Delano—not that he'd expected anything there—nor further instructions from Desmond Richelieu.

He stretched out on his bed and read a few more pages of *I Was a Lincoln Brigadier*. The book was compelling. For all its crudities of expression, the author's passion pulled Lindsey in and made him feel the commitment of the Lincoln Brigadiers. They really believed in what they were doing. And they might have been right. It was like enlisting in the Children's Crusade.

If Franco had been stopped in 1936, or '37, or '38, if Hitler's and Mussolini's so-called volunteers had been sent home bloodied and humbled instead of triumphant, would Hitler have hesitated before he attacked Poland the following year?

Eric Coffman would know that, too. Coffman was a modern and worldly man, a little bit like Rabbi Bruninski for all the difference in their physical presences. But Coffman, too, could become obsessed with the monstrous tragedies of the human condition.

The bedside telephone rang, startling Lindsey out of his reverie.

"Lindsey, that you?" The voice was Aurora Delano's.

"Yes, I—"

"Okay, here it is. I've been looking at death records, and the good news is, I can't find either Ben Bruninski or Mae Bruninski. If they've died in the past thirty years, it wasn't in Orleans Parish. Thank heaven for little disks."

"But that doesn't prove they're still alive."

"Nope. They might have left town and gone to meet their maker from some other launching pad. You know, negative evidence is still evidence."

"Did you look under Robert Brown?"

She gave a breathy laugh. "Now there's an embarrassment of riches. Not one Benjamin Bruninski, a whole army of Robert Browns. We can track those all down, look at the d-o-b's and d-o-d's, and see if any of 'em look right. Do you have a birthdate for *our* Robert Brown?"

"That I have. Wait a minute. Here it is. February 5, 1916."

"Okay. I can use that and work over the Robert Browns, see if any of them lists that as a date-of-birth, and a date-of-death later than—what's your cut-off date?"

"Nineteen sixty-four." That was the date of the greeting card Bruninski sent to Jeb Harkins.

"Okay. Don't expect anything, Lindsey. This is a long shot. But if Bruninski died in Orleans Parish and his death was recorded under the name of Robert Brown, and if the d-o-b on the death certificate matches up—"

"Got it," Lindsey muttered. "Sounds as if the chances are slim or none."

"I'd say you've got it exactly right," said Aurora Delano.

"You have any other ideas?" Lindsey asked.

"You already tried our local police force, right?"

"Just by telephone. No dice."

"Maybe I'll give them one more try. I've got some friends; a little personal contact might get more out of 'em than a phone call. You can never tell, Lindsey, there might be an arrest record or incident report somewhere in the dark recesses of a disk file or backup tape."

Lindsey yawned, "Okay." He hung up the telephone. It sounded as if Aurora Delano was giving it her best shot, but it also sounded as if she wasn't getting anything useful. On the other hand, even eliminating blind alleys was worth the effort. Maybe.

Maybe.

He undressed and stood under a cold shower until he was shivering with cold and wide awake. He dressed again, more casually this time, and left the hotel.

He walked a block on Iberville to Bourbon Street. The afternoon sun had sunk low and the air was heavy and moist. Bourbon Street seldom slept, Lindsey knew, but by late afternoon the street was getting ready to move into high gear. Gaudily dressed tourists wandered up and down, drinks in hand. Packs of college students in backwards baseball caps cruised the Quarter, looking for a night's adventure. Hookers of every sex and persuasion advertised their services. Half of the celebrants carried still cameras; the more affluent held camcorders at the ready.

Lindsey stopped into an air-conditioned shop that featured New Orleans T-shirts, funny hats, Mardi Gras posters, and china crawfish imported from China. He picked up a metal street sign that read "Pirate Alley." Jamie would like that. There was a notice above the cash register, saying that the store would ship purchases. That would save Lindsey's lugging the souvenir around New Orleans, no less packing it in his flight bag for the trip home.

He stopped at a rack of postcards. There were photographs of local sites and musicians, cartoons of drunks and grossly fat women (what was funny about that, Lindsey wondered), and sketches of the city's architecture.

Lindsey's hand leaped toward a card. He felt a bolt of ice-cold electricity streak down his back. He carried the card to a bright fluorescent fixture. It was a drawing of General Jackson on his rearing horse. It was a familiar sight in the city, prominently displayed in the park at Jackson Square in the Quarter and featured on posters and postcards available in a hundred shops.

Lindsey turned the card over and read the brief caption that went with the picture. There was no credit to the artist. He turned the card over again and scanned it, centimeter by centimeter, until he found what he was looking for. The artist's monogram, worked into the textured pattern of the statue's pedestal.

BB.

Bob Brown.

Benjamin Bruninski.

He went back to the rack and examined the cards that bore a stylistic resemblance to the one of General Jackson. He found a series—St. Louis Cathedral, the Presbytère, the Cabildo, the U.S. Customs House, the onetime Confederate Mint. There was even one with a sketch of a ballpark on it. He recognized Pelican Stadium: the drawing looked like the one on *Baseball Stars of 1952.* He carried the cards to the cash register. He asked the clerk if she knew where they came from and if she could provide any information about the artist.

The clerk was short and busty. Her hair was dyed in streaks of green and blue. Her jaw was moving up and down steadily and she exhaled the scent of spearmint chewing gum. She looked about fourteen. She gave Lindsey a blank look and told him the price of the cards.

He asked again for information about the artist.

She repeated the price.

He paid for the cards and the *Pirate Alley* sign and filled out a shipping form with Jamie's address on Bonita Street in Berkeley. He carried the cards back onto Bourbon Street. Evening was approaching and the crowds were thickening. Lindsey had the feeling that the restless party-seekers could hardly wait for full dark to arrive. They would turn into something unhuman, then, and unholy.

He fought his way through the crowd until he found the Hotel St. Marie and shoved his way inside. The cool and quiet of the hotel refreshed him. He walked to the lounge, sat alone at a table and ordered a mineral water.

He studied the cards until he found the telltale *BB* on each. He turned them over and read the brief captions. The card with the picture of Pelican Stadium explained that the ballpark had been torn down in 1957. None of the cards credited an artist, but they all listed the publishing company, Janus Novelty Press, and they all had copyright notices.

Every one was copyright 1972.

Lindsey sniffed like a lion on the trail of its dinner. Maude Markham had last seen Bruninski in Chicago in 1952. Jeb Harkins had received a Christmas card from him in 1964. Now Lindsey knew that he had still been working in New Orleans as late as 1972.

Twenty-odd years. That wasn't exactly a fresh trail, but it was getting fresher. Lindsey left his mineral water on the table and found a telephone and directory and looked up Janus Novelty Press. He tried the number, but it was after closing time and there was no answer. He jotted the information in his pocket organizer.

He started back toward his table, letting his eyes study the faces of the other patrons. A male figure leaned against the bar, his back toward the room. Lindsey could tell that his hair was gray and neatly trimmed. His clothing looked expensive.

The man turned and for an instant he made eye contact with Lindsey. Horn-rimmed glasses, gray spade-shaped beard. Lindsey blinked. The man threw a bill on the mahogany bar and scurried from the room.

Lindsey dropped his package of postcards and ran after him, but the man plunged into a crowd of milling tourists. Once Lindsey thought he spotted the man's head bobbing above the crowd; but before Lindsey could close the distance, he had disappeared.

Returning to the St. Marie, Lindsey paid for his mineral water—didn't want to cheat the management of its due—and retrieved his postcards. For the second time, he left the St. Marie. This time he had more opportunity to appreciate the ambience of Bourbon Street. Every night was a witches' Sabbath here. He'd had a wild thought that he might overtake Nathan ben Zinowicz, but he quickly realized that the pursuit was hopeless. Save by sheer chance, he would not find the man again.

He ducked around a corner and walked the short block on Toulouse Street back to Royal. Here art galleries and antique shops competed for shoppers' dollars. They offered Lindsey relief from the strip joints and trashy shops of Bourbon Street. He wandered through several stores. He was no Lovejoy, but even as a layman, he was impressed by the quality of what he saw.

He'd browsed through half a dozen shops before he froze in his tracks. He stood there until he felt a touch on his arm. The individual who stood at his elbow had a decided proprietary air about him. He had black wavy hair that glistened with pomade, a neat mustache, and a pinstriped suit.

"Magnificent, isn't it?"

Lindsey asked, "Is it for sale?"

The proprietor smiled. "But of course. This is a store, sir."

Lindsey nodded, staring at the painting.

"Do you collect fine nudes, sir?"

"No, I—"

"I understand. This is a most unusual painting. We had it in the window for a few days, but we had to move it back here. People were blocking the sidewalk. The dreamlike quality—one collector said that looking at it was like an opium dream. It's really a bargain, but I must confess, I've been tempted to buy it for myself and take it home. It is unique, don't you think?"

"Unique." That was the truth.

Lindsey would have bet everything he owned that he knew the artist and the model. He remembered what J. B. Harkins had said about Benjamin Bruninski's ambition, about how he tried to hold onto his originals but always wound up selling them off when he—how had Harkins put it?—when he got on his uppers. Lindsey asked the proprietor the artist's name.

The proprietor handed Lindsey a business card. It read,

B. D. "BUDDY" PEABODY

PROPRIETOR

Peabody Fine Art and Antiques
Royal Street
New Orleans, Louisiana

In a fine hand, in purple ink, somebody, possibly Buddy Peabody himself, had added a local telephone number

Lindsey opened his pocket organizer and handed Peabody one of his own International Surety cards. Then he asked again the artist's name.

"Robert Brown."

Lindsey didn't need to hear. He knew a Benjamin Bruninski when he saw one. And after studying those covers—*Buccaneer Blades* and *Death in the Ditch* and *I Was a Lincoln Brigadier*—Lindsey knew who the model was. There was no doubt in his mind.

The background was the same hillside as that on the cover of *I Was a Lincoln Brigadier*. Lindsey couldn't spot the BB signature, in monogram or rebus, but surely it was there. The wounded soldier was gone, as was Mae Bruninski's torn uniform. This was a portrait, sans accoutrements, of Mae Bruninski. The tiny airplane still dived, Mae still pointed her pistol defiantly skyward. And, without a doubt, Jeb Harkins had been right.

"Do you know when this was painted?"

"Approximately forty years ago."

"Are you sure? It couldn't be more recent than that? Even a new work?"

The proprietor shook his head. "No way. The artist brought it in himself. Doesn't work through an agent. I was very surprised. He'd held it off the market all these years, but I didn't doubt that it was painted much earlier in his life. And there are ways to tell—from the condition of the paint, from the condition of the canvas. No, I assure you, Mr.—" Buddy Peabody read Lindsey's card again.

"I assure you, Mr. Lindsey, this painting is no less than several decades old. It has a title, by the way. Did you notice the placard? *La Pasionaria*. It's truly magnificent."

Lindsey said he'd like to meet the artist but Peabody refused to give out any information about him. "He's a very private individual, sir. I promised him faithfully not to reveal his whereabouts to anyone. Besides, the policy of the gallery . . . I'm sure you'll understand."

Lindsey studied the painting again. How had Bruninski got that color and that *life* into Mae's green eyes? And her skin—Lindsey could almost feel her heat and the sweat and the dirt on her skin. The painting was erotic, but it was more than that, it was political; it was about freedom and courage and idealism. It was amazing.

"Suppose someone bought the painting?"

"A superb choice. A fine addition to any collection. And a fine investment as well. Yes, sir. A very wise decision."

"I meant, could the buyer meet Bob Brown?"

"Oh, I see." B.D. "Buddy" Peabody lowered his head, shielded his brow with his beautifully manicured fingers, and consulted his inner oracle. Then he looked up. "I would certainly convey your wishes to the artist. I can promise no more than that." He paused. "But I expect he would be amenable. Yes."

Lindsey didn't know what to say, so he said nothing.

Peabody resumed. "Would you like to put down a deposit, or would you care to pay the full amount now?"

"Wait. What's the price?"

Peabody held out his hand. At first Lindsey thought he wanted to shake hands; then he realized that Peabody wanted his card back. Lindsey handed it to him. Peabody took the card, turned it over, extracted a magnificent antique Waterman from his suit pocket, and wrote a number on the back of the card.

He screwed the top back on his Waterman and slipped it into his pocket again. He handed the card to Lindsey, face upward. Lindsey turned it over and read the number Peabody had written there in the same purple ink as the phone number Peabody had written earlier. Lindsey counted the number of zeroes after the number 5, looking closely to make sure he hadn't overlooked a decimal point. He hadn't.

"Is this price negotiable?"

"Alas," Peabody sighed, "the artist insisted that his price be met, and we take only the smallest markup to cover gallery overhead." He shook his head regretfully.

Lindsey put Peabody's card in his pocket and left the gallery. He walked up Royal Street, looking in windows just on the off chance that he'd spot another Ben Bruninski original. He didn't really expect to see one, and he was not disappointed.

Chapter Fourteen

EVEN THOUGH IT was two hours earlier in Denver, Lindsey didn't want to face Desmond Richelieu or encounter him by telephone, viva voce. Instead he put a message up on KlameNet/Plus. It was brief.

Need $50,000 to buy great nude painting. Wd be perfect for yr office. Might also save International Surety a cool million.

He reread the message on the screen of his laptop, counted the zeroes after the number 5, and made sure he hadn't inadvertently put a decimal point into the number, connected the laptop to the hotel room telephone jack, and zapped the message off to SPUDS headquarters.

He half expected an explosion, but nothing came back. Richelieu must be asleep, or maybe even doing something besides work for a change. Lindsey climbed into bed and picked up *I Was a Lincoln Brigadier*. He'd used a business card to mark his place, but before he opened the book he studied the cover again.

There was the hill; there was the tiny strafing fighter plane; there was Mae Bruninski in her torn uniform; there was the wounded soldier lying across her lap. The painting was a modern *Pietà*. The original might have had some of the passion, some of the soul of the gallery nude, but clearly the nude was Benjamin Bruninski's masterpiece.

Lindsey opened the book and read.

I rode into Manhattan on the BMT, but instead of going to 29th Street, I stopped at Times Square and went to the movies. They were showing Jean Renoir's *La Grande Illusion* with Stroheim, Gabin, and Fresnay. I had mixed feelings about the film. The so-called Great War started as a mere clash of empires. Not worth any decent worker's life. But it brought down the Habsburgs, it brought down the Hohenzollerns, and it brought down the rotten Romanovs. You had to admire that!

After the movie I walked the rest of the way to the address I had been given. It was an unmarked Party facility. A Comrade took me downtown to the Federal Building and helped me apply for my passport. The Comrade warned that my passport would be stamped *NOT GOOD FOR TRAVEL TO SPAIN*. When I filled out my application I would have to say that I was going somewhere else. I wrote on the application, *"Paris—student."* The clerk took my application and read what I had written and looked at me as if he didn't give a damn where I was going or why.

I was given money and sent to a war-surplus store and told to buy a World War I uniform and helmet. With my bag and my uniform carefully packed in it and my passport in hand, I was given a third-class ticket to Le Havre and told that other volunteers would be on the boat but I was not to recognize them and absolutely not to talk to them.

There must have been thirty or forty of us and it was a joke. We recognized one another at once. All around us were bourgeois families on vacation, children from middle-class homes going to Europe for their cheapjack version of the Grand Tour, and retired immigrants going back to see the old country again. And thirty or forty of us, young idealists, on our way to Spain.

Of course we talked to each other. All we talked about was the War. What was Franco up to? Could Juan Negrín and his government be trusted? Would Roosevelt lift the embargo? Could Stalin get enough help to the democratic side to stop Hitler and Mussolini from winning?

The ship received war news by radio-telegraph and a daily newspaper was published by mimeograph with a summary of world events. We crowded around it and discussed the events every day.

At Le Havre we were again met by a Party representative

and given third-class coach tickets on the train to Paris. From there we traveled by rail to the Spanish frontier. We had to get off and sneak into Spain. We carried our baggage in our hands as we walked through the Pyrenees.

It wasn't a long walk. We set out at sunset and by dawn we were in Spain. We had avoided the border guards and we realized with a rush of exhilaration that we were really in Spain! We changed from our civilian clothes into our uniforms. Once more we were met by Comrades who fed us, put us on trucks and sent us to the south.

We would stop and receive training from cadres sent by the Spanish people or their Soviet allies. We were given rifles and ammunition and taught how to use them. We were headed for our first engagement on the Aragon Front, the Battle of Belchite!

First thing upon awakening, Lindsey looked for a message on KlameNet/Plus. There was nothing. Either Richelieu hadn't received his request yet, or he was preparing his response. Next, Lindsey opened the telephone directory and looked up the publishing company that had produced the Bruninski postcards. To his relief, it was still in existence; the cards he'd bought were not just old stock. He jotted the company's address in his pocket organizer, then studied a city map until he found the location of its office.

Lindsey left the hotel and walked down Royal Street. He carried his palmtop computer in a shoulder kit. He wanted to be able to reach KlameNet/Plus by modem from any telephone, not just from his room at the Monteleone.

Peabody Fine Art and Antiques was not yet open for the day. Lindsey pressed his face to the glass, trying to get a glimpse of *La Pasionaria,* but the painting was blocked from his view.

He stopped at a food stand and purchased a po' boy. He ate it and turned back up Royal until he reached Canal Street. He finished the po' boy and climbed aboard a bus. He rode out Magazine Street to Tchoupitoulas Street and found the address he was looking for.

Janus Novelty Press apparently consisted of two elderly

brothers and a female office manager. Lindsey showed them the Bruninski cards he'd bought the previous night, and the brothers confirmed that they had indeed published them. Lindsey asked if they could give him Bruninski's address.

The office manager rolled open a drawer in a sagging file cabinet. She pulled a battered manila folder and laid it in front of the brothers.

The older brother—at least, Lindsey thought he was the older of the two, although it was pretty hard to tell—opened the folder. There wasn't much in it. He whispered a few words to his brother, then told Lindsey, "I remember this guy. Funny duck. He brought in his drawings. They were really good. Wanted to sell 'em to us."

The young brother chimed in, "That's right, that's right, I remember that guy."

"He wouldn't take any royalty deal. Wouldn't take our check. I remember that guy now, right?"

The office manager chimed in. "I remember that guy."

"Only wanted cash. Had to have cash in hand. Wouldn't take nothing but cash. I told him he'd make a lot more money off royalties, but he only wanted cash, right? You remember?" He looked at his brother, then at the office manager.

They both said, "I remember that guy."

Lindsey asked if they had any address for the artist. The older brother looked in the folder and said, "No. Nothing. Look." He shook the folder at Lindsey. A few pieces of paper fell out—a list of drawings, a statement, a receipt for cash. The signature on the receipt was an illegible scrawl. Maybe Bruninski just had bad penmanship, or maybe he didn't want anyone to read his signature.

No name, no address, no phone. Nothing. It was peculiar: the man's artistic ego still made him sign his work, there was apparently a "BB" or a rebus worked into each drawing or painting, but Bruninski himself stayed in hiding.

"Did he say anything about where he lived, how you could get in touch with him?"

"Nothing."

"You remember anything about him?"

While the two brothers exchanged looks, the office manager said, "I remember that guy. Funny geek. Tall, could have played for the Jazz. That was before they left town. Or was it before they even started? Never mind. The guy was skinny. Wore a little beard and a beret and walked with a limp. A phony. You know, a phony. Like he was afraid people wouldn't believe he was an artist; he had to ham it up like that."

"But he could draw," said one brother.

"That guy could really draw. We still use his stuff," added the second brother.

"I remember that guy," said the office manager.

Lindsey left his International Surety card with the office manager. On the back he wrote the name and address of his hotel, and the Monteleone's telephone number and his room. "If you come across anything, or if you remember anything, give me a call, please. At the hotel, or if I'm not there, call the International Surety number. Call collect, it's okay. This is important."

As Lindsey was leaving, the office manager said, "I remember that guy."

He rode a bus back to the edge of the French Quarter and walked to Jackson Square. He stood in the park, looking up at General Jackson's equestrian statue. Benjamin Bruninski had stood here more than thirty years ago, sketching the statue for a Christmas card. Where was Benjamin Bruninski today?

Lindsey stopped in a restaurant on Decatur Street and ordered a shrimp salad and a beer. A television above the bar was tuned to the weather channel. In the Northeast a monster snowfall had shut down major cities from Boston to Baltimore. Closer by, a storm was brewing over the Gulf of Mexico and it was feared that it might sweep inland and cause flooding in Louisiana and Mississippi.

Behind Lindsey the door swung open and he caught a glance of the day outside. The sun was shining and the sky was blue. He finished his food and downed the last of his beer, then located a telephone and tapped into KlameNet/Plus. There was no message for him. He tried the Monteleone switchboard, but they had nothing. Surely Richelieu had received his request by now. The Benjamin Bruninski painting would cost a lot of money, but if it led to Mae Bruninski, it would be worth the price.

He stepped back into the moist afternoon. Tourists were swarming into New Orleans, eager to escape the blizzard in the Northeast. They tramped up and down Decatur and Chartres, St. Peter and St. Ann. Mule-drawn carriages loaded up for tours of the Quarter as fast as they could pull away from the curb.

Musicians and mimes competed for coins. Sketch artists would provide instant charcoal portraits for visitors to take back home and show off. If you didn't fancy a picture of yourself, how about one of Elvis Presley or Madonna, Reggie Jackson or Michael Jackson or Jesse Jackson, Mother Teresa or Princess Di?

Lindsey joined a small group watching a sketch artist create a portrait of a young mother and her new baby. When picture had been exchanged for cash, Lindsey asked the sketch artist if he knew a Benjamin Bruninski or Bob Brown.

The artist shook his head.

"Tall man," Lindsey furnished. "And pretty old. Must be close to eighty. An artist—thought you might know him."

No luck.

Lindsey tried half a dozen sketch artists plying their trade around the square. Lindsey wished he had a picture of Bruninski himself, but neither Scotty Anderson nor Maude Markham nor Jeb Harkins had furnished one. He had only Harkins's description, and that didn't evoke any positive responses.

He phoned Aurora Delano at her office. She'd drawn a blank, as well. Lindsey looked at his watch. Discouraged, he returned to his hotel room. He'd got this far, had made a fairly good ID of the beneficiary of Vansittart's life policy, and then ran dry.

He took off his shoes and swung his feet up onto the bed. He picked up *I Was a Lincoln Brigadier* and opened to his bookmark. He found himself skimming the chapters, reading a few paragraphs here and a few pages there. The author described the diet that the volunteers ate in Spain. *Garbanzos, bacalao, conejo, carne de cabra, vino, pan, café.* Beans, codfish, rabbit, goat meat, wine, bread, coffee.

Who was the author of the book? Lindsey had a suspicion that he knew who it was.

He came to a description of an engagement at the town of Quinto, south of the Ebro River.

We were pinned down. Our boys had fought well. We'd had our baptism of fire, and we knew what it was to see our comrades blown to bits by Franco's mercenaries.

Let me be clear about one thing. Whose side were the Spanish people on? Sure, Franco had some Spanish troops on his side. The soldiers were conscripts, boys with no political awareness and no understanding of what the war was about. Some of them were good Catholics, and Franco told them that they were defending Holy Mother Church against the enemies of Christ. When we got our hands on them, we just sent them to the rear. They were disarmed and neutralized, and that was that.

The Fascist officers were another story.

And the rest of General Franco's followers were colonial mercenaries from Morocco. They knew little and cared less about the issues at stake in Spain. They took their devil's shilling and they fought their master's battles. If they'd understood the true nature of colonialism they would have turned on their masters and shown them the business end of their rifles—but they didn't understand. To them, Spain was a wonderland.

Even the Germans and Italians were divided. Hitler and Mussolini sent their legions into Spain, but there were detachments of Germans on our side as well—*real* volunteers who knew what they were fighting for, not bully boys in the pockets of their swaggering bosses!

There was the Botkin Brigade—brave Jews from Poland whose eyesight was clear enough to show them what was coming if these bullies weren't stopped. The bullies could have been stopped in Spain, but they weren't stopped— not in Spain, anyway—and the world lived to regret that mistake.

The Fascists had the upper hand over us. They had more guns, more bullets, more tanks. But they were content for a while to let us sit there in our emplacements, waiting for what we knew had to come.

Then the Condor Legion arrived. German aviators, so-called Luftwaffe "volunteers" commanded by Wolfram von Richthofen. I don't know what relative he was to the famous Red Baron of the First World War. Some bastard scion or cousin or nephew. They came in Focke-Wulfs and Messerschmitts, piloted by Hermann Goering's pets, the same pets who would destroy Coventry and blast half of London from the map a few years later.

But we had airplanes, too! If Roosevelt had let us have some Thunderbolts and Warhawks, we could have matched those Fascists, but Roosevelt was neutral. Neutral!

Stalin sent what he could. I remember once I saw a medium bomber, twin engines droning, heading out on some mission. One plane, alone. It never came back.

We had fighters. Ilyushin 15s and 16s. The 15 was an older model, a biplane that looked like something left over from the First World War. We had plenty of those. We had a few of the 16s, too. The 16 was more modern, a single-engine monoplane. The Spanish people had even built an airplane factory, with Soviet help, and they were building their own Ilyushins, right there in Iberia.

But our Ilyushins still weren't up to the Condor Legion. We had good pilots. The Soviets had sent some of their best to help the Spanish Loyalists—Yakov Smushkevich, Pavel Rychagov, brave pilots and decent men.

But the Condors outnumbered us and outgunned us, and we could see the Ilyushins falling from the sky. Then one of our boys got a Focke-Wulf in his sights. We saw the smoke pouring from the Focke-Wulf's engine, then the plane go into a dive. The pilot parachuted out. I wish we'd caught him, but he landed on the other side of the Ebro River, behind the Fascist lines.

Then, just when we thought the battle was over, the Heinkels came. They were old, slow biplanes. We were amazed. If only they'd come earlier, our boys could have knocked them down. It would have been a fair fight. But that was the whole idea, as we soon realized.

The Heinkels came in low and they started dropping bombs. Flambos! Get splattered by the flaming death that those things spewed out, and you didn't have a chance.

I was sitting behind a Maxim machine gun when one of those things landed near me. I was lucky. I wasn't burned to death. The flambo sent dirt and rocks flying and one of them hit my ammunition box. The only reason I wasn't killed was my Comrade, Mel Nance.

The Lincolns were the first American military unit where Negroes and whites fought side by side, as equals and as Comrades. Mel caught most of the explosion. He was killed on the spot. I caught a piece of shrapnel in my leg. A major artery was severed, and I would have bled to death if somebody hadn't slapped a tourniquet on me. I don't know to this day who it was, but I owe him my life.

I wound up in the hospital, and that was where I met the woman who was to become my partner for life.

Lindsey closed the book and lay staring at the ceiling.

Another piece of the puzzle had fallen into place. Harkins had thought at first that Ben Bruninski's limp was an affectation. Later he became convinced that it was the result of a real injury. Harkins had met Bruninski's wife, Mae, who had served as the model for most of the Paige book covers. And Lindsey had seen Bruninski's painting, *La Pasionaria*, clearly modeled by the same woman who had posed for the cover of *I Was a Lincoln Brigadier*.

That still didn't account for Rabbi Bruninski's family chronicle. That was something Lindsey would have to work on some more. He closed his eyes and let his subconscious struggle with it.

He awoke in a state of confusion. His room was dark, the sky outside was dark, and rain was falling in heavy sheets. The rumble of thunder and flash of lightning punctuated the storm.

Shadows danced in his room like mad revelers at an unholy Sabbath.

Chapter Fifteen

LINDSEY CLIMBED OUT of bed and padded to the window. He looked out toward the French Quarter and the Mississippi River just beyond. The predicted storm had arrived from the Gulf of Mexico, perhaps more rapidly than anticipated. The sky was almost black, what little light there was scattered by thick storm clouds. A gust of wind blew a sheet of water against Lindsey's window and he jumped back, his reflexes overriding the knowledge that he was safe and dry in his hotel room.

He looked down into Royal Street. The prospect was dark except for rows of evenly spaced street lamps. A man was standing in the rain across the street, looking up at Lindsey's hotel. A flash of lightning illuminated the street and Lindsey got a brief, clear look at the man's face.

There was no question in Lindsey's mind. The sharp features, the thin cheeks, the gray spade-shaped beard, the angry eyes behind their horn-rimmed glasses. There was no question, then: it had been Nathan ben Zinowicz at the St. Marie. Not that Lindsey had doubted it, but . . . An involuntary moan escaped from Lindsey's throat.

After the lightning flash, it took Lindsey's eyes a few seconds to readjust. When he looked down into Royal Street again, there was no one there.

He pulled on his clothes and rode down to the lobby, dashed into the street, and stood, staring after the departed figure. He knew there was no way he'd catch up with him. He knew the man would be gone. But he had to try.

He went back to his room, wondering why the desk clerk gave him such an odd look. He stood in front of the mirror and saw his hair standing up in all directions. His shirt was unbuttoned and his jacket was crooked.

He hung his jacket in the closet and ran a brush through his hair. He picked up the phone and dialed Marvia Plum's apartment in Berkeley. It was late. Even allowing for time zones, she would surely be home and in bed by now.

Willie Fergus answered the phone.

Stammering, Lindsey identified himself.

Fergus must have handed the phone to Marvia. She said, "Bart, what is it?"

"He's here. I just saw him."

"Who's here?"

"Ben Zinowicz. Nathan ben Zinowicz. There's a storm, I saw him earlier, tried to catch him but he disappeared in a crowd. But now—I don't know, he must have followed me. I was trying to follow him but I gave up. I guess he turned the tables on me. There's a storm now, I'm back in my hotel, I was looking out the window, and there was a flash of lightning, and he was standing in the street, looking at my hotel."

Marvia asked, "Are you sure?"

"I know that man. I know his face."

There was a moment of silence. Then Marvia said, "What did you do? When did this happen?"

"Just now." Lindsey was standing at the window again, telephone in hand. At first there was no one to be seen, then a couple ran by, arms around each other, sharing an umbrella. The rain pounded off it, scattering like pellets of salt. They disappeared in the direction of Canal Street.

"Just now? And what did you do when you saw him?" Marvia quizzed Lindsey.

"I tried to catch him. I tried again. I tried before, and he disappeared, and I tried again and he disappeared again."

"Bart, I don't mean to doubt your word, but are you really, really sure it was him? What floor are you on?"

"The eighth."

"And you saw him standing in the street? In the rain? How can you be certain?"

"My eyes are twenty-twenty, Marvia. I know it was him. You

told me that he skipped town. He killed John O'Farrell up in the Sierras, and he tried to kill me in Walnut Creek. He's working for the Cookes. Now he's in New Orleans."

"We don't know he killed O'Farrell or that he shot at you in Walnut Creek."

"You were the one who said he did."

"That was a theory. I was creating a scenario. He's still the prime candidate for both incidents, but I don't *know* he was responsible for either."

She paused. "Bart, there's news from Tahoe. They got the body up. It's Vansittart, all right."

Lindsey grunted.

"They haven't been able to get the helicopter, and they don't have the tire iron, but the body is his, and the hole in his skull— there's no doubt about what happened. O'Farrell would be in hot water now if he were alive. But now I guess it's moot."

"He wasn't acting on his own, Marvia."

"Oh, you're right about that. We're working on that. You're right about that."

She was almost babbling, something Lindsey had never heard her do.

Lindsey took a couple of deep breaths, trying to calm himself. He looked at the bedside clock, subtracted a couple of hours. "All right, what do I do now? Marvia, I wanted you with me. I know you couldn't come, but I need your help. What do I do now?"

"I'll call Dave Jones first thing in the morning. I'll tell him that ben Zinowicz has been sighted in New Orleans. We'll widen that APB and we'll get in touch with the police in New Orleans."

"Okay. Do you want me to call them?"

"We'll take care of it. Coming from a visitor to the city, they won't know what to make of this whole thing. Coming from another police agency, they'll take it more seriously."

"Okay." Lindsey was still agitated. "Why is he here? What does he want?"

"I don't know, Bart. Listen, have you spoken with him?"

"With ben Zinowicz? No. I—why would I do that?"

"Just checking; don't worry about that. I'm trying to put this together, just as you are. If he's there in New Orleans, and if he was really standing outside your hotel tonight—well, how did he know you're there, and what do you think he wants?"

"I don't—wait a minute. Wait a minute. Scotty Anderson said something—I remember, I was leaving his apartment; I remember he followed me out to the parking lot. He—"

"Who's Scotty Anderson?"

"Lives in Castro Valley. He collects paperback books and he was doing a research article on Paige Publications. I was sent to him by the mystery store in San Francisco, and he gave me my lead to Chicago. I'd be nowhere on this case if it wasn't for him."

"And ben Zinowicz knows this Anderson, too?"

"I don't think so. I mean, I don't know. I—but look, Anderson told me that Lovisi—he publishes a collectors' journal—Lovisi told him, Anderson, that somebody else was trying to track down information on Paige Publications. You know ben Zinowicz used to be a big-time academic; he knows how to do this research. He was working for the Cookes; he heard about *Death in the Ditch*. He knows mass culture, right? He was involved with the old comic-book case; he knows about paperbacks, too."

He paused to catch his breath.

Marvia Plum said, "Go on."

"He could have done the same work that I did. Learned the same things that I did. Maybe he followed the same trail. Maybe he found some other collector than Anderson, or turned up one of the other authors. Maybe he found Violet de la Yema or—I don't know. Maybe he got to Patti Paige Hanson or Paul Paige. I don't know how he followed my trail to New Orleans, but he must have picked me up somehow and now—I don't know what he's up to. Marvia, I just don't know."

"All right, Bart. Look, we've had more news here from the computer people. That's why Willie Fergus is back in Berkeley. He came in from Reno to talk to the silicon wizards about ben Zinowicz's computer. They got some information off his hard disk. We were going to get the info to you anyhow, so let me put him on, all right?"

Lindsey stood holding the telephone, looking out at Royal

Street, watching the sheets of rain fall past his window.

"Mr. Lindsey? Mr. Lindsey? Sergeant Fergus here. Listen, Mr. Lindsey, ben Zinowicz is a smart cookie, all right, but he could learn a thing or two about computers. You with me, Mr. Lindsey?"

"I am."

"Well, it's not that I'm a bigdome myself, Mr. Lindsey, but these folks here in Berkeley, they're pretty hot stuff. They ran some of their software on ben Zinowicz's computer. The one he left in that apartment. No wonder nobody ever saw him there. He used that place for a secret hideout, my gosh, he must have gone to the movies and seen one of those superhero movies with a master criminal and a secret hideaway. Anyhow, your good guys ran something called a directory on his disk and they didn't find anything, so they put in some kind of special programs for recovering deleted files and they turned up plenty. You want to know what they found there? Mr. Lindsey, are you there?"

Someone had walked past the Monteleone, on the opposite side of Royal Street, and Lindsey had watched, fascinated, trying to imagine who it could be.

"I'm listening, Sergeant Fergus."

"One of the things they found there was a list of books. Does this ring a bell? *Cry Ruffian!*, *Buccaneer Blades*, *By Studebaker Across America*, *Al Capone's Heirs* . . . "

"That's the Paige bibliography. Does he have *Death in the Ditch?*"

"It's here, Mr. Lindsey."

"That does it. He's following the same trail that I am."

"All right, Mr. Lindsey. I'll talk it over with Sergeant Plum, we'll talk to Dave Jones, and we'll get the NOPD on it. They'll probably want to talk to you. Maybe you should check in with them before you leave your hotel in the morning. Is that all right, sir?"

"Okay. Right. Okay."

"One more thing, then. Mr. Lindsey, did David Jones tell you how many parole violators we have out there?"

"Thousands."

"That's right. I mean, California leads the way. We have

plenty in Nevada, too, but we just don't have as many people to start with. But no judge or police force there in Louisiana is going to peep if Dave Jones tells 'em that a parolee has left town without permission. There's just too much of that stuff; there's no catching up. So you better convince those New Orleans officers that this man represents a serious danger to others. I'm sure Dave Jones will send 'em a message to that effect; but if you can't convince 'em, they're just going to shine you on. Do you understand that, Mr. Lindsey?"

"I understand."

He hung up the telephone. He paced around the room, picked up the remote control and turned on the television. He channel-surfed until he found AMC. One of AMC's wonderful hosts was describing the film that was about to start.

Lindsey paused in his tracks, listened to the spiel for a little longer, then settled into an easy chair. He couldn't have planned this anywhere near as well as sheer chance had. The film was Ernest Hemingway's *For Whom the Bell Tolls*.

The host—it was Mother's old favorite Bob Dorian, and even Lindsey had grown fond of the man's genial, unassuming manner—rambled on in his casual way, listing the Academy Award nominations the picture had racked up (apparently, it was nominated for everything), the 170-minute original length and the shorter prints that had come out in later years, the reaction that the film had received when it was released in 1943, and finally the movie itself.

It was like falling into *I Was a Lincoln Brigadier*, only with Gary Cooper and Ingrid Bergman in place of the book's anonymous narrator—almost certainly Benjamin Bruninski—and the volunteer nurse, Mae, who wound up posing for *Buccaneer Blades* as well as *La Pasionaria*.

The movie dragged, and it was a little bit hard to believe in Bergman, with her blonde hair and blue eyes and flashing, perfect teeth, and her beautiful English flavored with a slight Swedish accent, as the daughter of a Spanish burgher. And why was a band of mountain-wise Republican guerrillas taking orders from an American college professor played by Gary Cooper?

Lindsey had trouble staying awake through the film but he hung in there to the bitter end, and when the film ended and he fell into bed he dreamed of Spain and Franco and Juan Negrín making a speech at the League of Nations in Geneva, pledging unilaterally to send home the International Brigades in the naïve hope that Hitler and Mussolini would also call home their legions.

He was awakened by the telephone and by a soft female voice asking him to come down to the French Quarter police station, if that wouldn't be too much trouble, and help the New Orleans Police Department straighten out this troublesome little matter that they'd just been asked to look into. It was a short walk from his hotel. And just say that he was Mr. Lindsey; an officer would be waiting to chat with him.

He got there as fast as he could. The storm had passed over the city and the sky was blue. The air was as moist as ever and the tourists were celebrating as if nothing had happened.

But the storm had not passed without leaving damage in its wake. There was standing water in some of the streets, the surfaces of the temporary ponds broken by bits of vegetation and assorted detritus. And a number of shops and bistros had apparently had their plate glass windows blown in or smashed by flying debris. Cleanup was well under way, and signs of the storm would be eradicated in a matter of hours.

Lindsey's route took him past Peabody Fine Art and Antiques. The front window was gone, replaced by a sheet of plywood.

The police officer he talked to was polite and sympathetic. He'd heard from Sergeant Plum in California, and he was eager to do anything he could to help.

"Can you find this guy?" Lindsey demanded. "He's wanted for a parole violation at the very least."

"I know that," the officer agreed. He tapped a document with his finger. "Trouble is, if we get ahold of him, he doesn't have to go back to California if he doesn't want to."

"But he's a parole violator—at the very least."

"He doesn't have to go if he doesn't want to go. You folks

have to ask for extradition. He's entitled to a hearing and a lawyer, just like a little trial. And I'll tell you something, just between you and me."

The officer leaned forward conspiratorially.

"If I was in his boots and California tried to get me back, I'd just say it was selective prosecution. See, all of those parole violators out there, why are they going after me? You see? I think he just might beat it. Stay here and thumb his nose at you folks."

"But it's more than parole. He probably committed another murder and an attempted murder."

The officer's eyebrows moved up. He picked up the document on his desk. "Nothing about that here."

"Well, no charges were filed. Not yet."

"You know about these incidents?"

"I was the target—of the attempt. He shot at me."

"The police know about this in California?"

"Of course they do."

The officer studied the paper once more, as if he hadn't read it before. "Well, I don't know, sir. It doesn't say anything about that here." He looked at Lindsey. "But maybe we ought to check this fellow out. Just on general principles, hey? Where is he staying, sir?"

"I don't know that. How am I supposed to know that? I just looked out my window last night, and there he was."

"Looking in your window? This fellow a Peeping Tom?"

"Hardly. I was on the eighth floor. He was standing across the street. I saw him by lightning. During the storm."

"I see." The officer nodded. He didn't volunteer any further help.

"Well," Lindsey said, "what are you going to do?"

"I told you, sir. We'll keep an eye out for him, and if he gets in trouble, we'll pick up the phone and call your people in California."

"What do you mean, *if* he gets in trouble? What are you waiting for? You have to—" Lindsey stopped. They'd have to, what? This officer must think he was talking to a lunatic. He just wanted to placate Lindsey and send him on his way.

"What can we really do?" the officer asked. "Think about it, sir. There are hundreds of hotels and motels and rooming houses in greater New Orleans. And if this fellow has any brains, it's very unlikely he's using his real name. What can we do? We're not a police state; we can't just line everybody up and check their IDs. People have civil rights."

Lindsey bit his lip. The conversation went on a little longer, but he didn't get any further. The officer gave Lindsey his card and suggested that he phone him if he spotted ben Zinowicz again. "Don't approach him, sir. If the man is a dangerous fugitive, he might be armed. All right? Just phone me. If I'm not here, someone else will take the call."

That was that.

Minutes later Lindsey stood outside the police station. A few paces away, on a grassy patch, a well-groomed chestnut horse snorted. A uniformed officer sat on his back. Half a dozen children stood watching. Lindsey patted the horse as he walked past.

He headed back to the hotel. In his room he logged onto KlameNet/Plus. There was a message waiting for him, from Desmond Richelieu in Denver.

With your shield or on it.

That was the whole message. That, plus a series of digits that Lindsey recognized as an International Surety financial-control number. He was authorized to spend the $50,000 for *La Pasionaria*. He knew, now, that he had Richelieu's backing. And he knew that, if he failed, his career was on the line.

He keyed in a report on his activities and shot it off to Denver. Then he checked his wallet to make sure that he had his company charge card, left his hotel room, and started down Royal Street for the second time this morning.

Workers had already replaced the plate glass window at Peabody Fine Art and Antiques. An artisan was lettering the name of the establishment in gold and black on the new window.

Lindsey had no trouble finding Buddy Peabody. The store had taken some water damage, but altogether things were not in bad shape. Lindsey got a quick look at *La Pasionaria*. The painting was undamaged.

Peabody was dressed as elegantly as he had been at their previous meeting, but his unflappability had failed him. Lindsey told him that he wanted to discuss the Bruninski painting. Peabody's hands twitched but he managed the standard, "Of course, of course. Isn't it fortunate that it wasn't damaged in the storm?"

He led Lindsey to a private office. The room was crammed with antique furniture, statuary, graphics, vases, coat trees, lighted display cases jam-packed with chinaware and miniature paintings and flatware.

Lindsey said, "I have to set a condition. If I make this purchase—"

"Is this for yourself, sir?" Peabody interrupted.

Lindsey frowned. "No. It's part of a corporate acquisition program. For my company."

"And may I inquire as to that organization?"

Lindsey said, "You have my card."

"Ah, certainly." Peabody had placed himself behind a massive, ornate desk. "Many corporations are making such investments nowadays. A fine decision, very fine."

"If I—ah, *we*—make this purchase, it's imperative that I meet the artist. Absolutely imperative."

Peabody's manner had changed. Ever since Lindsey announced his intention to buy *La Pasionaria*, Peabody had been getting friendlier and friendlier. His smile faded. "We already discussed that, sir. I'll try, I'll definitely try to arrange a meeting, but I can't promise you . . . "

"How soon can I meet him?"

"Please, sir. I just told you that I can't promise anything."

"How soon?" Lindsey kept a poker face; inside, he wondered if it would work. If it didn't, he was stymied once again.

"I'll try right away. Still, it may take a little while. You see, the storm—well, we'll have to back up our computer files. There was a little damage last night, and—"

"The storm destroyed your files?" Lindsey had trouble believing that.

"Everything is backed up. We lock away out backups, they go into the safe every night, and to the bank vault once a week. We'll find the address."

"You mean to tell me you don't know where Bruninski is?"

"Who?"

"I'm sorry. Bob Brown. You mean to tell me you don't know where he is, but you have his address in your backup files?"

"Sir, I pride myself on attention to detail, but I cannot memorize the address of every person I do business with. Please, Mr. Lindsey, I'm afraid you're becoming agitated. There's no cause for alarm. I'll get the artist's address and contact him. I'm sure he'll be willing to meet with you, if that is a condition of the transaction. In the meanwhile, permit me to draw up a bill of sale."

He opened a drawer of his ornate desk and pulled out a book of blank forms. He started by asking Lindsey for his permanent address.

Lindsey didn't go for it. There was something the matter here. Peabody was too eager to get a signature, to close the deal. Had he already contacted Benjamin Bruninski—the man he knew as Bob Brown—and been unable to convince him to meet with Lindsey? Bruninski had been living in the shadows for forty years. He must be in desperate financial straits to part with *La Pasionaria*. It was a magnificent painting, probably the masterpiece of his career. He had kept it all his life. He would not part with it easily.

If Peabody could close the deal with Lindsey, and stall him on meeting Bob Brown, Lindsey might never get his meeting with the artist.

He stood up and started for the door.

"Mr. Lindsey! Is something the matter?"

He turned back. "You find Bob Brown. You set up a meeting for me. Then we'll see about the fifty thousand dollars."

"Please, Mr. Lindsey! It's obvious to me that you are not an experienced art buyer. That would be out of the question. Simply out of the question. It would be a violation of professional ethics. We could never permit that."

"All right. Thank you."

Peabody was around his desk and tugging at Lindsey's sleeve. "All right, I have to tell you something that happened last night. Please—won't you sit down again. This is a very difficult matter."

Lindsey didn't sit down but he waited for Peabody to make his case.

"We have a security system here, of course. We deal in expensive goods; we have to safeguard against break-ins. Last night, when the front window was smashed, the alarm went off. We contract with a private security service, and they respond when the alarm sounds. I arrived from my home, also, and the security people were already here."

He paused and mopped his brow.

"We thought it was just the storm, you see. Nothing seemed to have been taken. We have valuable goods here, paintings and furniture and—"

"I know that."

"Well, we thought it was just the storm. We would have put up the plywood beforehand but we had no inkling of how severe the storm was going to be. Well, this morning I checked the office and our locked file had been broken into. We keep routine papers in unlocked files, you see, but anything to do with sources of merchandise or with customers, why, we regard those as sensitive files and we keep them in a locked cabinet."

Lindsey watched a drop of perspiration fall from the tip of Peabody's nose. It made a dark spot on his immaculate shirt collar. Lindsey sat silently.

"Mr. Brown's file was stolen."

Lindsey felt his jaw muscles tighten. "Just one file?"

"Just the one."

Lindsey felt as if a cold hand had wrapped itself around his chest and squeezed.

"But we really do have computer backups. We'll recover the address. I can have it for you today. Really."

Peabody was starting to get expansive again.

Lindsey said, "Call me at my hotel. I'm at the Monteleone. Call me when you have the file."

He left Peabody behind, flapping his hands and gasping for air.

Chapter Sixteen

LINDSEY HAD DRESSED like an insurance man for his visit to Peabody Fine Art and Antiques. Dark suit, white shirt, conservative tie. He would have fit in perfectly in an International Surety office. On the streets of the French Quarter he stood out like a jockey on a basketball team. He went back to his hotel room, changed to a bright shirt and a pair of khaki shorts, and ventured out still again.

He had to find Benjamin Bruninski. That was the only way to find Mae Bruninski, the girl on the cover of *Death in the Ditch*. Nathan ben Zinowicz had followed the same trail that Lindsey did. Ben Zinowicz was in New Orleans, and knew that Lindsey was there. And Ben Zinowicz had to be the person who had stolen Bruninski's file from Peabody. Otherwise—there was no otherwise. This case already had too many coincidences in it for comfort. That would have been one too many for belief.

He circulated through the Quarter. Hobart Lindsey, master of disguise. If Bruninski was still in New Orleans, it made sense that he would be known by other artists in the city. It was a basic law of human conduct: people sought out others like themselves. If you were looking for an alcoholic, there was a good chance you'd find him in a bar. A movie buff would be at a movie theater, or would be hanging out with other movie buffs. And an artist would stay with other artists.

Lindsey found Benjamin Bruninski on the corner of St. Peter and Chartres. Lindsey had tramped the Quarter for hours, hoping against hope to find the man. Now it was nearly sundown. It seemed impossible that Benjamin Bruninski had been there for the past few days or Lindsey would surely have found him earlier.

It was the music that first attracted Lindsey's attention. New Orleans was full of music, most of it jazz, from the traditional to the experimental, performers from the most consummate of professionals to the most feeble of amateurs.

But this was no jazz tune, and it was coming from a boom box. It caught Lindsey's attention and he recognized the melody, then supplied the words almost involuntarily. It was "Red River Valley."

But it wasn't. The words were unfamiliar, sung by a chorus and flowing out of the speakers of the portable tape recorder.

> *There's a valley in Spain called Jarama/*
> *It's a place that we all know so well/*
> *It was there that we fought the Fascists/*
> *We saw a peaceful valley go to hell. . . .*

It didn't quite scan, and Lindsey had heard better singing, but he listened to a few more verses, until the singers put a lock on it.

> *We were men of the Lincoln Brigade/*
> *We were proud of the fight that we made/*
> *We know that you people of the valley/*
> *Will remember the Lincoln Brigade.*

The tape player belonged to an artist sitting nearby at an easel. He was just finishing a portrait of an overweight blonde in a bulging tank top. The woman accepted her picture and handed some bills to the artist looking pleased. Lindsey could understand why. There must be a trick to making that much flesh look voluptuous rather than flabby, and this artist had done it.

The woman headed for a shady restaurant a few yards away. Lindsey saw customers in shorts and T-shirts munching po' boys and sipping Dixie beers.

Lindsey turned his attention to the artist. In the bright sunlight of Jackson Square, the man had dispensed with his beret and wore a straw hat instead. He was clean shaven and he was old, but his hands and arms looked strong.

"Mr. Bruninski." Lindsey hoped the man wouldn't bolt. "Mr. Bruninski, listen to me. You have to listen to me. You have to tell me, is your wife still alive?"

The old man looked up at Lindsey. He was seated on a wooden folding chair. "What are you talking about?"

He spoke in a strong voice with the harsh edge of one who had grown up in the rough and tumble of the crowded city. He nodded slowly, studying Lindsey's face all the while. The old man's eyes were dark and intense. When Lindsey didn't respond to his question he asked another. "What did you call me?"

"Benjamin Bruninski."

"Who's that?"

"Israel and Vera's son." Lindsey consulted his notebook. "Born February 5, 1916."

"Don't remind me," the old man said. "That was a long time ago. Sometimes I see people half my age go by this corner, people a quarter my age, and I think, I'm just like them, I have a lot of years ahead of me. I start to get up and dance. Then I remember. If I forget, my knees remind me. I'm an old man, mister—"

"Lindsey. Hobart Lindsey." He started to reach for his card, then stopped. "I've been looking for you, Mr. Bruninski."

Bruninski started to get up. Lindsey could see he was stiff with his years. He offered a hand. The old man stared at it until Lindsey dropped it. Once he reached his feet, the old man stood six inches taller than Lindsey.

"What do you want?"

Lindsey said, "Is Mae still alive?"

The old man did not answer.

"If she's still alive, she's in terrible danger. There's a man named Nathan ben Zinowicz. He's in New Orleans. He wants to kill her, and he knows where you live. He stole your file from Peabody's, and he wants to kill your wife."

The old man looked concerned now, instead of hostile or merely puzzled. "You'd better explain this to me."

Lindsey squeezed his eyes shut. How could he convince this man of the danger, and do it quickly? He didn't have time to tell the whole story. He said, "Your wife is named in a life insurance

policy. She stands to collect a fortune, but this man ben Zinowicz wants to stop her and we have to get the police to stop him.
We—"

"Can you prove any of this?"

Lindsey lifted his hands in the air and revolved slowly, wondering what the swirling streams of tourists thought was going
on. "Look. No weapon. No wire. Nothing." He fished a business
card from his pocket and handed it to the old man.

Bruninski studied the card, stared at Lindsey with overt skep-
ticism, then seemed to make a decision. He barked, "No police,"
making a slashing gesture with one hand. The hand was larger
than Lindsey's, and it looked strong.

"Mr. Bruninski—this man is a killer."

"No police. I'll handle this." He folded his easel and chair and
carried them and his sketching paper and supplies and boom box
to the corner restaurant. He must have been friends with the
staff. A young woman put down her tray and took Bruninski's
belongings into a back room.

"Lindsey, is it?" Bruninski set off in front of the St. Louis Cathedral and the Cabildo, across St. Ann Street, plowing through
clusters of tourists, Lindsey in his wake. "This man of yours is
after Mae, is he? Has my address? He's in for a little surprise, I
think."

Lindsey was panting for breath. Approaching Dumaine, Lindsey was out of breath. "We'll take a cab," he panted. "If you
won't tell me your address, at least let's take a cab."

Bruninski shook his head and kept walking. Despite his stiff-
ness, his legs were longer than Lindsey's, and he was in good
shape. Lindsey had to fall into a dogtrot to keep up with the old
man.

"What can you do?" Lindsey panted. "He may be armed.
He's capable of anything. Did I tell you, he shot me? Years ago,
shot me in the foot. I still—it still gets sore—he—let's stop a
police officer and get help."

Bruninski made his cutting gesture again. "No police." They
passed St. Philip, Ursulines. They were nearing the edge of the
Quarter. Governor Nichols Street. Barracks Street. Bruninski
turned away from the river and kept striding.

Time after time, Lindsey wanted to grasp a stranger by the sleeve and beg for help. The sun had sunk beyond the river now, and the city was transforming itself. Music and revelry filled the street. Mule-drawn carriages passed, full of tourists, the drivers calling out the historic sites of the Quarter.

A police car rolled past and Lindsey made a move toward it, but Bruninski caught him by the elbow and steered him onward.

The house was on Barracks at Dauphine. It looked as if it had seen better days. The stucco had been whitewashed many times, and its coat was faded and uneven. The wooden shutters had long since lost their paint.

Bruninski stopped and looked up. Lindsey followed his lead. The second story apartment had a small wrought-iron balcony. The balcony held rows of flowerpots and planters. The windows were shut and covered with thin yellowish curtains. Light from inside the room illuminated them.

"My God."

"What's the matter?"

"The lights are on."

"It's night."

"You'll see." Bruninski faced Lindsey. He put his hands on Lindsey's shoulders. Lindsey felt as if the old man could throw him across Barracks Street. Out of the corner of Lindsey's eye he spotted a neighborhood saloon. This corner wasn't quite on the tourist track, and the saloon seemed to be filled with locals. A TV set flickered above the bar. Raucous voices echoed off the old buildings that lined the street.

"You get out of here if you want to be safe," Bruninski husked at Lindsey. "Go away. Do what you want. If you come with me, you have to stay behind me, and you have to play it by ear. It's up to you. I can't make you."

Bruninski started up the four cement steps that led to the front door. His sore knees bothered him; that was obvious. The front door was unlocked. Bruninski looked around the building's tiny front hall. There was no one there. He took a deep breath, grasped the iron banister with one hand, and began working his way up the stairs.

At the upper landing Bruninski stopped and pressed his ear

against the door. He reached into a pocket of his old khaki pants and withdrew a key silently. He fitted it into the lock and swung the door open.

Lindsey stood on the landing behind Bruninski. He heard a shout of rage and saw the old man launch himself. It was an amazing move. His joints might be stiff, but Bruninski had the strength of an athlete. He seemed to fly across the room.

Lindsey took two rapid steps and was across the threshold.

Even after his years in prison, there was no mistaking Nathan ben Zinowicz. This was the man Lindsey had known before those prison days, the man he had seen at the St. Marie and lost in the crowd of Bourbon Street, the man who had stood outside the Monteleone in the rain.

He leaned over the bed, a pillow in his hands. A heavy rectangle of wood lay nearby, and the side of ben Zinowicz's face nearer to Lindsey's view was reddened and abraded as if he had been struck by the wooden beam. An old woman lay on the old bed, staring with terrified eyes at the three men. Lindsey made a mental photograph in a single, frozen instant. Then the players snapped into action.

Bruninski crashed into ben Zinowicz. The pillow flew from ben Zinowicz's hands. Lindsey knew that ben Zinowicz was taller and more massive than he was, but Bruninski was taller yet by several inches, and he was moving like an aged demon.

Bruninski and ben Zinowicz crashed into a window. The sounds of panes smashing cut through the thud of bodies and the gasping of breath.

Lindsey crossed the room in three more strides. Ben Zinowicz had squirmed out of Bruninski's grip and crouched, facing the older man. Still half-erect, he fumbled to pull a revolver from his trousers pocket. Lindsey made a grab for ben Zinowicz's gun-hand. He grasped the wrist in both of his hands. Ben Zinowicz was cursing steadily. He pounded his free hand into the side of Lindsey's head once, twice.

Bruninski had pulled himself painfully to his feet. Ben Zinowicz occupied Lindsey's attention, but somehow Lindsey became aware that Bruninski had reappeared. He saw the old man swing something dark and deadly looking. It caught ben Zinowicz across the temple.

Ben Zinowicz's fingers closed spastically, and a shot crashed harmlessly into the ceiling. The gun tumbled from ben Zinowicz's hand and ben Zinowicz stumbled across the beam that lay crookedly near a tattered armchair, falling to the bare hardwood floor.

Lindsey craned his neck, panting. Bruninski stood over him and ben Zinowicz, a huge black revolver in his hand. It looked three times the size of the one ben Zinowicz had dropped.

"I brought this back from Spain," Bruninski panted.

Lindsey lifted the weapon that ben Zinowicz had dropped. He stared at it briefly, baffled, then looked at Bruninski. He got no help. He studied the weapon, found what must be the safety—he hoped that was what it was—and put the revolver in his own trousers pocket.

Bruninski was at the bedside where Nathan ben Zinowicz had stood when they arrived at the apartment. He was leaning solicitously over the woman, who lay in unmoving silence.

Lindsey stood watching them, the mental photograph he had made still clear and sharp. The woman was old and obviously very ill. Her wispy gray hair was disordered, her face drawn. He wondered whether she could move or speak.

But her eyes had not changed.

They were the green eyes of *La Pasionaria*. They were the green eyes of the girl on the cover of *I Was a Lincoln Brigadier*, of the buxom wench on the cover of *Buccaneer Blades*, of the gun moll on the cover of *Al Capone's Heirs*.

They were the eyes of the girl on the cover of *Death in the Ditch*.

Chapter Seventeen

SHE WAS ALIVE, and her husband, Benjamin Bruninski, tended to all her needs. Nathan ben Zinowicz was moaning and stirring while Lindsey secured his hands behind him and his ankles to each other. The only things he could use to accomplish the task were his own belt and Benjamin Bruninski's.

There wasn't a telephone in the apartment, so Lindsey pounded down the stairs and across Barracks Street to the saloon and used the pay phone there to call the police. They arrived soon after he got back to the apartment.

They took a quick report from Benjamin Bruninski and another from Lindsey. Lindsey was happy to give them the revolver he'd taken from ben Zinowicz. Bruninski's heavier weapon had disappeared while Lindsey was making his telephone call. He hadn't really seen it clearly; he'd been struggling with the intruder when Bruninski hit him. He wasn't really that sure it was a gun.

One officer called in an inquiry, listened, nodded, shut off her belt radio. She was a big woman, competent in her own way, but somehow uncomfortable looking in a police uniform. Another officer was present, but the woman seemed to be in charge. Eric Coffman would have called her "zaftig," Lindsey thought.

She had already examined Lindsey's ID. The police had removed the belts that Lindsey used to secure ben Zinowicz, but they insisted on keeping them. They wanted to keep them as possible evidence.

The gray-bearded ben Zinowicz was sitting on the floor now, his hands cuffed behind his back. The heavyset officer asked, "Are you Nathan ben Zinowicz, sir?"

He stared at the floor. "I want my rights."

"I merely asked who you are, sir. There's a fugitive warrant out for Nathan ben Zinowicz. He violated parole in the State of California. If you are Mr. ben Zinowicz—"

"Doctor. I'm a doctor of philosophy. I worked hard for that degree, and I want my rights."

The officer sighed. She pulled a card from her pocket and read the familiar Miranda warning. When she finished she asked, "Do you understand that, sir?"

"I want a lawyer."

"Do you understand your rights, sir?"

"Damned right I do, and I want a lawyer. Stop asking me questions. Get me a lawyer. Better yet, give me a telephone and I'll get my own lawyer."

The heavyset woman sighed again, straightening up. "All right, sir. You'll have to come with us, and you can contact a lawyer from the station." To the other police officer she said, "We'll put him in the car in a minute. I have to talk to these other people." She bent over the bed and asked Mae Bruninski a question.

Benjamin Bruninski said, "She can't talk. She had a stroke. Can't talk. Can't . . . " For the first time, Lindsey heard something close to tears in Benjamin Bruninski's voice.

The police officer said, "Sir, I think this woman belongs in the hospital. I can call for an ambulance."

Benjamin Bruninski said, "We've been together since nineteen thirty-seven. Through thick and thin. Since nineteen thirty-seven."

Lindsey stared at the old man. Earlier, he had looked far younger than his eighty years. Suddenly, he looked older.

"We don't have any money," Bruninski told the officer. "The landlord lets us pay what we can. When we can. I make a little money doing sketches. We can't afford a hospital."

Hobart Lindsey said, "Yes, you can, Mr. Bruninski. Don't you understand? I explained this to you. Mrs. Bruninski is the beneficiary of a large insurance policy. She has three million dollars coming to her. She's—you're millionaires. She was the model for *Death in the Ditch*, wasn't she?"

Bruninski nodded.

"She is Alfred Crocker Vansittart's beneficiary. She has three million dollars coming to her. She can afford care."

Bruninski turned tear-filled eyes on Lindsey. "This is her home. She'll die in the hospital. I know it. She used to be a nurse—that was how we met. She nursed me and Alfred both, in Spain. She knows what happens to people in hospitals."

Bruninski blinked, then went on. "Her name was Maizie then. Maizie Carcowitz. She changed it when she started to model in Chicago, years later. Alfred and I were both in love with her and she picked me, God damn it. I won't send her to a hospital to die, God damn it."

To the senior police officer, Lindsey said, "He may be right. Could you get a doctor to come out here?"

"You mean, make a house call?"

"A house call."

She scratched her head. "I guess I could. I'll call it in and see." To her associate she said, "Okay, let's get this gentleman out of here. He'll have some local charges to deal with. Then we'll see what happens about returning him to California."

To Lindsey she said, "I hope you'll be in town a little longer. We'll need your help, sir."

"I'm at the Monteleone. I'll call you before I do anything like leaving."

That was how he got another New Orleans Police Department card. He could start a collection. Maybe a bubble-gum company would issue a series of Famous Cop Cards. Melvin Purvis, Elliot Ness, Hal Lipset. But Famous Cop Card #1 would surely be J. Edgar Hoover. J. Edgar Hoover in a double-breasted suit. Or maybe J. Edgar Hoover in a frilly frock. Desmond Richelieu would have a mint set, and if anybody swiped the cards, Hobart Lindsey would be hot on the case.

Maizie Carcowitz Bruninski, the breathtaking model Mae Carter, moved her hand feebly in Lindsey's direction.

Ben Bruninski said, "She wants you, Lindsey. Understand, her mind is clear. We have ways of communicating. She can hold a pencil and write a little, and we have other ways. She wants you to come over by her."

Lindsey leaned over the old woman. The pillow was back beneath her head; at least the cops hadn't seized that as evidence. Her gray hair was spread around her face. She lifted her hand and touched the back of Lindsey's. Her fingers on the back of his hand felt like the touch of a spider. He looked into her face and detected the shadow of a smile. The eyes were the same. They were the eyes of *La Pasionaria*.

The doctor came to Barracks Street and checked Mae Bruninski. He chatted briefly with the two police officers. Nathan ben Zinowicz still sat on the floor, a yard from the beam that had earlier crashed into his head. Soon the police departed, taking ben Zinowicz with them.

The doctor stayed behind. He had a lot to say, mostly about residential care, but the gist of it was, she was stable and could live on as she was, with nourishment and attention. Eventually, nature would take its course. Maybe tomorrow, maybe in ten years. Then he departed, leaving behind a stack of prescription slips.

Bruninski brought a glass of tea to his wife's bedside and held it while she drank a little. Then he turned away. "She's sleeping," he said.

Lindsey said, "I should go, then. We have to talk. In the morning."

"Why in the morning?"

"Well . . . " Lindsey looked at the sleeping Mae Bruninski, then checked his watch. "It's late. It's late, and . . . well . . . "

Bruninski said, "Sit down. Talk. She's asleep. She likes company. She doesn't get enough. If she wakes up, she hears us talking, she'll like it. Sit. Talk."

Lindsey lowered himself into a wooden chair. He gathered his thoughts, trying to decide where to start. There was so much to tell Bruninski. Instead he asked, "Who hit him with that wooden beam?"

The old man grinned wolfishly. "Look over the door there. My little booby trap. You open the door a crack, reach in and disarm the trigger, nothing's gonna happen. When you go out, you rearm it. Somebody comes in, doesn't know about booby traps, gets conked. Mae can't protect herself these days, I can't stay with her all day, I have to work. So we set Comrade Wood up there."

He walked over and nudged the beam with a foot that was large enough to match his giant hands. "First time that thing ever had to do its job. Really should have put that skunk out of action. Looks like it just slowed him down. But that was enough, wasn't it, eh, Comrade?"

Lindsey wasn't sure whether Bruninski was addressing the beam or him.

"Okay," said the old man. He dropped into an armchair. "You talk, I'll listen. Start with Vansittart. I didn't know he was dead. And what's this about three million dollars?"

"It was on all the news. It was all over the TV."

Bruninski gestured. There was no TV in the room.

"All right," Lindsey sighed. "I'll give it to you briefly. Then we can fill in the details later. If that's satisfactory."

"Shoot."

Lindsey told him the story, starting with the helicopter crash at Lake Tahoe. By the time he came to Buddy Peabody's story of the missing files, Bruninski said, "All right. Break time."

He levered himself out of the easy chair and shuffled to the bathroom. When he came out, he walked to his wife's bedside, leaned over her, touched her gently, then turned back. He crossed to a cupboard, opened it, and lifted out a bottle of wine and two mismatched glasses. He poured a glass of wine for himself and one for Lindsey without asking, handed a glass to Lindsey, and touched his own to its rim. *"Salud y suerte."*

He emptied half his glass, then refilled it. He said, "So all you have to do is find Mae—you've found her—and she gets four million dollars? Or three million dollars? Which is it? I don't get it."

Lindsey explained the proviso in Vansittart's policy that provided International Surety with a twenty-five percent finder's fee if they were able to pay the money to Mae.

"I see." Bruninski grinned his wolfish grin again. "So you're acting out of conscience and goodwill. And to save your company a million bucks."

Lindsey said, "I can't deny it. But you still get a fortune. Your wife does." He leaned forward. "Do you have any idea why Vansittart would specify his beneficiary that way? As 'the girl on the cover' instead of by name? Did you ever know Vansittart? Did Mae?"

"Sure, I knew him. We were together in Spain. We were together in the Brigade."

"Albert Crocker Vansittart?"

"Sure. He's dead now, right? Nobody can hurt him."

"He was a Communist?"

"No, no." Bruninski shook his head, sipped his wine more slowly now, said, "Don't you know anything? I thought you read my book. There were a lot of Communists in the Brigade, sure, but a lot of us weren't. We were fighting Fascism over there. How many times do you have to hear that?"

"Even so." Lindsey got up and walked to the front window. He looked across Barracks Street. The saloon was doing a steady business. There was no sign that Nathan ben Zinowicz had been here, that a murder had been narrowly averted, that the police had arrived and departed with their prisoner. "Even so—I'd have thought—nobody ever knew, did they?"

"Half the guys in the Brigade took false names. There were Party names and there were others. Noms de guerre, right? Albert was—well, what difference does it make now? We were as different as we could be, Albert and I. He was a blueblood, an old American, filthy rich, Episcopalian. My parents came from Poland, we were dirt-poor Jews. But Albert saw something in Franco and in his pals Hitler and Mussolini that most members of his class couldn't see. That's why he volunteered. But he knew he'd have to go home sooner or later, so he gave out the story that he was on an extended European vacation. He was in my company. We were both wounded at Belchite. We both fell in love with a nurse."

Lindsey was still standing by the window. Two men came lurching out of the saloon and stood swaying on the sidewalk. One of them wore shorts and a bright yellow shirt covered with green and brown pineapples. The other wore a sweat-stained denim work shirt and jeans. The man in the pineapple shirt had a potbelly. The man in the work shirt was thin as a rail. He carried a brown paper bag wrapped around a bottle.

The two men set off toward Canal Street.

Bruninski said, "You want some more wine?"

Lindsey looked at his glass. It was mostly full. He held it up so Bruninski could see it. The old man shrugged and emptied the last of the wine from the bottle into his own glass. He said, "This is one soupy melodrama, isn't it?"

Lindsey watched the man in the pineapple shirt and the man in the denim shirt disappear around a corner. He turned away from the window and returned to his chair. He said, "What is?"

"Albert, Maizie, me. Something that fool Hemingway could have written. After the war, the three of us wound up in Chicago. Don't ask me how we got there. We were all young and crazy. Young and crazy. Maizie called herself Mae Carter. Albert and I both wanted to marry her. She picked me. Isn't that rich? She could have gone back to California with Albert, been a millionaire's wife, lived the life of Riley. But she picked me, and he never stopped carrying the torch for her, did he? That's why he never married. The poor little rich boy, carrying the torch for the beautiful little poor girl."

"She'll be a rich girl now," Lindsey put in. "A rich woman."

Bruninski jerked his head up. "You saw my painting at Peabody's gallery, did you?"

Lindsey nodded. "You want it back?"

"I sold it only because I had to. It's the best thing I ever did. Sure I want it back—for me. I want to look at it. I want *her* to look at it." He nodded toward the bed. "After we're both dead, it can go to a museum. If anybody has the brains to see how good it is."

"I'm sure they will."

"Don't be so sure. But maybe."

Lindsey grunted.

"I'll cut a deal with that s.o.b. Peabody. Five hundred dollars he pays me, and he tries to sell it for fifty thousand dollars. I'll get it back."

"It's late," Lindsey said, "I should be going."

"Sit down. I won't sleep. Stay where you are." He went to the cupboard and returned with another bottle of wine.

Lindsey said, "I don't want to intrude."

"I'll tell you if you're intruding." He refilled both their glasses. "You're not drinking much. This stuff not good enough for you?"

"No," Lindsey shook his head, "I'm just not—I just don't drink very much, that's all."

Bruninski frowned. "All right. You read my book, did you?"

"*I Was a Lincoln Brigadier.* But I haven't finished it yet."

"I kept a few copies," Bruninski said. "I keep thinking, maybe somebody will reprint it someday. I keep thinking, maybe somebody will care about the Lincolns someday. Dumb, eh?"

"I don't think it's dumb. I think people should know."

"They didn't care then, they don't care now." Bruninski shook his head. "Soon we'll all be gone, and no one will know."

"But somebody has to care. Historians, universities."

Bruninski let go a bitter laugh. "Drink up, Lindsey." He emptied his glass and refilled it from the bottle. Lindsey took a cautious sip of his own wine.

"When I think of the boys who are still there," Bruninski sighed. "You know how many boys died for democracy in Spain? Girls, too. There were all those nurses. And we had a few women in the fighting units, too. Nobody knows exactly how many. A lot of records, they wound up in Russia. Thank God they're starting to come out now. Secret files, Stalin's eyes only. What bushwah. Maybe we'll find out everything now. There must have been forty thousand volunteers in Spain, maybe three thousand Americans and boys and girls from countries all over the world. Thousands died. Half of the Americans, at least. Untrained, lousy equipment, garbage for food. But still we could have won, you know. We were in the right, we had passion, we cared. And we were learning how to fight."

He drank.

"We were getting pretty good at it."

He lowered his glass. Lindsey could see that his eyes were not trained on this little room. They were trained on a distant land and on a long-ago war.

"But the embargo, you know?" There was a kind of growl in Bruninski's voice. "Can you fight a tank with a rifle? Can you shoot down a Stuka with a revolver? I put that in my painting but that was symbolic, yes? You understand? That was my darling Mae, shooting down that Fascist plane with a revolver. Can't be done. If we'd just had the equipment, we could have won that war. God knows how different history would have been."

He smiled, but not happily.

Lindsey asked, "What happened after you came home?"

"After we came home? After we came home? Juan Negrín took a chance and sent us all back. The Loyalists still held Madrid. Negrín thought he could get Hitler and Mussolini to pull their forces out, let the Spanish people settle their own differences. The Republic would have won. But they didn't pull 'em out. No way they were going to pull 'em out. So the Spanish got Franco and the world got a great big war. That's what happened."

"But after you came home . . . "

"That was nineteen thirty-eight. Henry Ford gave me a ticket back on the Île de Paris. You didn't know that he paid the freight for us to come home, did you? Fascist anti-Semite that he was. Go figure. I went over on the Île de France, came home on the Île de Paris. Some class, hey?"

"And then what?" Lindsey pushed on. "You were still young. Nineteen thirty-eight minus nineteen sixteen, you were only twenty-two years old. What happened then? And why does Rabbi Bruninski's book say that you're dead, you died in Spain?"

"Rabbi Bruninski says I'm dead, does he? Maybe I am." He stood up painfully and crossed to bend once more over his wife. He held his face close to hers, then nodded and returned to his chair. "So she's a millionaire, is she? She should have had the money first and the stroke after, not the other way around. My poor girl." He shed tears.

"Ah, after we got back, eh?" Bruninski shook off his tears. "You want to know, after we got back. The first thing they did was take away our passports. After all, we'd violated their terms. Not valid for travel to Spain, right? And we'd fought in a foreign war, we'd violated the Neutrality Act, so I guess we were some kind of criminals. Dangerous men. We'd gone and fought for democracy while Roosevelt sat in the White House reading murder mysteries, feeding biscuits to little Fala, playing footsie with the Pope."

"Well—"

"Not 'well.' I'm telling you what happened. This is what happened, Lindsey. You asked what happened when we got back and I'm telling you what happened." He reached for the bottle, saw that his glass was still nearly full, and put the bottle down.

"When was that? When did you actually get back from Spain?"

"The farewell parade in Barcelona was October thirty-eight. Cheering crowds, big speeches. You must have heard of La Pasionaria. The real one, not the painting. I used Mae in that painting in her honor. We thought we'd won. We thought Franco would fold up. Hitler and Mussolini would pull out and the Republic would live. Hah! Were we ever wrong."

He downed a slug of wine.

"I got home in time for Christmas. Is that what they always promise, bring the boys home for Christmas? Well, I got home in time for Christmas. We had a few stragglers, but everybody was out by January, February thirty-nine. FDR was still playing both sides against the middle. Chamberlain and Daladier and the rest of them."

"Wasn't that the time of the Hitler-Stalin Pact?" Lindsey was pushing himself to his limit. He wished he knew more about this stuff, but he was learning. There was nothing like getting it from somebody who was actually there.

Bruninski shook his head. He had a thick head of salt-and-pepper hair, and it wobbled when he shook it. "Nah. That came a little later. Stalin wanted to cut a deal with France, England, America. Nobody would touch him. He remembered what happened during the Revolution, the Russian Civil War, the interventions. Bet they don't teach you about that, about Czechs and Japanese and God knows who else, tramping around Russia trying to stop Lenin and put the Whites back in the saddle. And the Americans. That wonderful idealist Woodrow Wilson, who kept us out of war until he got us into it, sent his uniformed thugs in, too."

"I didn't know that."

"Look it up. Don't take my word. Read the histories. Not the cheap ones, read the real histories."

Lindsey stood up and paced across the room. Barracks Street was empty. The saloonkeeper had apparently ousted the last of his customers, locked up for the night, and gone home. The air was warm and moist and the sky was dark with heavy clouds. It looked as if it was going to rain again.

"So there I was," Bruninski resumed.

Lindsey turned around and stood watching the old man. Bruninski seemed to have forgotten about Lindsey. He was staring into the past, telling his story.

"They took away my passport right on the dock and I got on the subway and went home to Brooklyn. My mother was surprised to see me. She'd thought I was dead. I fed her that cock-and-bull story about working in a factory, but she knew the truth. She thought I was dead. She was amazed, hysterical. She thought I was a ghost. She pinched me, she kissed me, she made me turn around so she could look at me from every side. I remember that night. I woke up in the middle of the night; I saw her standing in my doorway. She was wearing a long nightgown, and she had her hair in braids, and she was holding a candle in a candlestick. Isn't that peculiar? It was nineteen thirty-eight and I can remember it like yesterday. She always put her hair in braids to sleep."

"Yes, your mother must have thought you were dead," Lindsey agreed. "You must have been reported dead."

"I guess so. When I was wounded . . . You know, wounded soldiers, stragglers, deserters get reported as dead in every war. And then you turn up years later. It's one of life's little tricks."

"Where was Mae during all this?" Lindsey asked.

"Oh, she came down with undulant fever and amebic dysentery and influenza and a couple of other diseases. You have to understand, conditions were pretty primitive up on the lines. The cities came through the war a little better. Those Fascist bastards would bomb—never mind—anyway, out in the field, things were pretty bad. A lot of the nurses got sick. They shipped them off to France or to England. By the time Mae got back to the U.S., we were in the war and I was in the army. Mae found my mom and got my address and she wrote to me, but she was in the service, too. We didn't get together again until the war was over."

Lindsey said, 'You told me you all went to Chicago."

"We did. After the war. The Second World War. That's when we wound up in Chicago. I was an art student—you didn't know I drew cartoons for the Brigade paper over in Spain, did you? And Mae was working again. We got married. Oh, it was really something. And now—"

He walked to his wife's bedside. Lindsey watched him lean over the frail form. He arranged her gray hair and returned to sit near Lindsey. A heavy-limbed, weary giant. He refilled his glass, drank off a little, and stared at Lindsey, waiting for another question.

"You went to work for Paige then, right?"

"That's right. I went to work for Werner Kleinhoffer. He was an idealist. He'd seen what Fascism was all about. Did you know that he was in the International Brigades, too? He was a Peat Bog Soldier. An anti-Hitler German. We had some good German boys on our side. They weren't all Nazis. Not the Bog Soldiers. Not the boys in the Thaelmann Brigade. We used to drink together when we got a couple of days' leave in the cities. We'd go drinking and whoring. Erich Weinert, Ernst Busch. Good boys. I met Werner the first time in a whorehouse in Barcelona. Ran across him again a dozen years later in Chicago."

He leaned toward Lindsey pointing a long, roughened finger. He was a little drunk, or maybe a little more than a little. He poked that finger into Lindsey's shoulder. "You think I wrote that book, don't you? *I Was a Lincoln Brigadier*. I wrote only part of it. The part in America. I wrote that. The part in Brooklyn. That, too. The part in Spain, Werner wrote as much of that as I did."

He leaned away from Lindsey and struggled to his feet. "Fucking sore knees. Arthritis. Got it in those damned ice-cold foxholes in the Battle of the Bulge."

"Then you fought Hitler in Europe."

Bruninski grinned. His teeth were big, and some of them were discolored. "They didn't know what to do with us at the start of the war. They had a name for us. *Premature antifascists.* That's what they called us, premature antifascists. Stuck us in something called Branch Immaterial. You won't find anything about that in your Goddamned military histories of the glorious war. Criminals, homosexuals, and premature antifascists."

He rummaged in the drawers of a battered wooden dresser until he found his revolver. The police hadn't looked very hard for it. He brought it back and laid it on the faded arm of his easy chair.

Lindsey asked, "What's that for?"

Bruninski stared at him.

"Ben Zinowicz won't come back," Lindsey said.

"You can never tell."

Lindsey looked out the window. He wasn't sure, but he thought he detected the first signs of impending dawn. He checked his wristwatch. Had he been here that long? He'd have to speak with Aurora Delano in a few hours, have her take charge of Bruninski and his wife, Mae Carter. Maizie Carcowitz Bruninski had $3,000,000 coming to her. International Surety had an obligation to fulfill.

"After the war Mae and I were married. We decided to stay in Chicago. You know all that," Bruninski said, "I'm going in circles."

Lindsey thought, *Yes, you are. Just don't pick up that gun and start waving it around.* Aloud, he asked, "Why did Paige Publications go out of business, and why did you disappear when you did?"

"Because we were premature antifascists, that's why."

Lindsey said, "I don't get it."

"Look, back during the Spanish war, when we were in the Lincolns, we were bad guys. Then when Uncle Sam finally got around to mixing it up with Hitler and Mussolini, he didn't know what to do with us. That's why we got put in Branch Immaterial. Then, the longer the war went on, Uncle Sammy was getting close to the bottom of the barrel, so we were rehabilitated and sent to fight."

He looked at Lindsey, a ghastly grin on his face. He'd slumped in his armchair and was staring at Lindsey, looking almost bemused. Like an adult telling stories to a kid, and the kid not knowing whether to believe them or not.

"After the war, there was a little honeymoon; all the soldiers coming home, everybody loved us, everybody loved everybody. Then Truman decided that socialism was spreading too fast in Europe, and besides the war industries had wound down in the U.S. He was afraid of another depression, so he started up the Cold War."

Lindsey had heard that version of it before, on a radical radio station near his home in California. He hadn't believed it then, hearing it in the paranoid squeal of an obvious raving loony, but coming from a man who had lived through the events, it seemed to have at least a grain of plausibility. He held his tongue and reserved judgment.

Bruninski continued. "He was taking a lot of heat from the politicians, too. HUAC was riding high, Martin Dies and what's-his-name, that thug from New Jersey—yeah, I remember that one, Congressman J. Parnell Thomas. Son of a bitch wound up in jail. Where he belonged. And of course anybody that HUAC missed, Senator Joe McCarthy took care of."

"Joe McCarthy?"

"Tailgunner Joe."

"Not Eugene McCarthy?"

"No relation. Not even similar. Joseph R. McCarthy, Senator from the great state of Wisconsin, one of America's great scoundrels, and Eugene McCarthy, Senator from the great state of Minnesota, one of the last decent men in American politics."

He grunted, then went on. "Yes, they sent snoops and spooks and goons around to see us. They shut us down. Shut down Paige Publications. Oh, they didn't do it with jackboots and truncheons the way Hitler's goons would do it. They were more subtle than that. But they'd go and see people, ask questions here, plant fear there. A couple of them came around to my studio one day. I wasn't there when they arrived, I was out delivering a job, and Mae was in the studio cleaning up. My Maizie.

They scared the daylights out of her. She'd been through Spain; she was in the Pacific War; she wasn't easily frightened. But they frightened her."

He picked up the revolver and turned it toward himself. He peered down the barrel, nodded in agreement with some inner voice, then laid the revolver down.

Lindsey reached across the table, and turned the revolver so the muzzle pointed toward the wall.

Bruninski bared his teeth. "I walked in and they were asking her questions. They were playing good cop and bad cop. It was like a movie. Asking questions, wanting to know if we were getting money from the Politburo, were we members of the CPUSA, what was her opinion of Josef Stalin, where was your husband, was he at a cell meeting, and did she realize that people were spying on their own country and committing treason, and could she give them the name of the person who issued her husband's orders—"

He stood up and checked on his wife's condition. Then he went and stood by the window where Lindsey had stood earlier. Lindsey watched him. Beyond Bruninski he could see the sky growing light. The clouds were still there, and they made the early-morning sky a picture in red and orange and pink.

Bruninski stood with his back to the window. "I grabbed those sons of bitches and I told them if they didn't get out of there and leave us alone, I'd bang their heads together until their brains were scrambled." He stopped talking and held his hands up and looked at them as if seeing them for the first time. He said, "I was a strong guy in those days."

He showed his teeth again. "You want to know who those two goons were, Lindsey? Well dressed, you know, no ruffians. You want to guess who they were, those two goons working for Senator Tailgunner Joe McCarthy? I can see by your face, I've lost you. They were young Roy Cohn and young Bobby Kennedy. There's your sainted Kennedy clan in action, Lindsey. The old man practically wanted to kiss Hitler's ass when he wasn't busy kissing the Pope's ring. And young Bobby got his start working for Tailgunner Joe McCarthy."

Lindsey stood up. "Look, I think I'd better go. It's getting awfully late. Uh, or early. I think—look, I'll have our local office contact you today."

"What's the matter?" Bruninski bored in. "You getting uncomfortable?"

"No. I mean—I mean, we've been up all night. It was some night. Look, it's morning. Should you get some—"

"Sleep? I'll get all the sleep in the world, soon enough. Hell, I'll have a little breakfast, and then I'm going to work. Looks like a pretty day. Should be good for business."

Lindsey hesitated. "Are you sure?"

"Sure I'm sure. Tell you what—you walk around the block while I take care of Mae. She needs her breakfast, and I'll clean her up. Come back in half an hour."

Lindsey agreed. He left the apartment and strolled down toward the river. New Orleans was coming to life. There were no tourists on the streets. The late revelers had finally given up and gone to bed. The early risers weren't yet in evidence.

A block from Bruninski's apartment, Lindsey passed the man in the pineapple shirt who had left the saloon a few hours before. There was no sign of the man in the denim work shirt.

Lindsey reached the Mississippi River. Mist was rising slowly from its surface, evaporating into the warm air. A freighter moved past slowly, headed for the Gulf of Mexico. Lindsey missed Marvia Plum.

When he got back to Bruninski's apartment on Barracks Street, Mae was propped up in bed. Her hair was brushed and she wore a fresh nightgown. A bedside radio was murmuring. Something that might have been a smile flickered across Mae's face. Lindsey said, "Good morning, Mrs. Bruninski. It's nice to see you this morning."

He realized that those were the first words he'd spoken to her. Her green eyes were alive. They were definitely alive.

He helped Bruninski lift the wooden beam back into place. Bruninski rearmed the booby trap and they left.

They walked to the Café du Monde and ordered coffee with chicory and a platter of beignets. Bruninski said, "You're on an expense account, right, Lindsey? Your company pays?''

Lindsey laughed. "You're a millionaire, Mr. Bruninski. What does it matter?''

Bruninski growled. "It matters.''

Lindsey said, "Okay, International Surety pays.'' Maybe it was time to ease gracefully out of this situation, but his curiosity had been piqued by Bruninski's passionate story. He asked, "What happened after you threw Roy Cohn and Bobby Kennedy out?''

"They were vindictive sons of bitches.'' Bruninski resumed his narration. He'd replaced his wineglass with a coffee mug, and went on as if there'd been no break. "They shut down Paige for publishing those books and for not turning me in. And they didn't like dealing with an old Bog Soldier, either. Not with the German Democratic Republic starting to get on its feet.''

He swallowed half a beignet and washed it down with coffee. "You pay for the refills?''

Lindsey grinned. "Sure.''

"Werner could have turned his coat and gone to Washington and cried and repented like some of them did. Hell, they had him by the short hairs. They could have yanked his citizenship and sent him packing. Never did figure out why they didn't—thank God for little fuck-ups on the other side. But Werner never flinched. Even when they put him out of business. They didn't come by and padlock the place, they just saw to it that nobody would distribute his stuff. He got the message pretty quick. Not quick enough for old Izzy Horvitz, though.''

Lindsey said, "You knew Horvitz? Del Marston, Isidore Horvitz?''

"Of course I knew him. We were in Spain together. We crossed the Ebro River in the same fucking rowboat. He was a brilliant guy. A sweet guy. He wrote poetry. He was going to write great novels someday. We got back to the States, wound up in Chicago. Hell, I was the one who got his book published.''

"What? How did you do that?''

Bruninski grinned wolfishly. "Izzy wanted to write serious literature, but he wanted to cut his teeth on some kind of popular stuff first. So he wrote this goofy gangster novel. He said it was a hard-boiled, whatever that is. He gave it to me to read, but I didn't know anything about that stuff, so I just gave it to Werner. I left it on his desk. I put a note on it that said, 'Here, this might make a good book for the company.' "

Lindsey bit into a beignet, its powdered-sugar flavor twice as sweet after sipping the bitter coffee.

"So the next thing I knew," Bruninski continued, "Izzy called me up. He's all excited. He sold his book. Werner bought it, he tells me. Then the next thing I know, Werner sends the manuscript back to me and he says, 'Okay, now paint a cover for this thing.' And he jots down a few notes about what he wants me to put in the painting. We used to work that way, so I wouldn't have to spend all my time reading these books."

Outside the café, on the sidewalk of Decatur Street, a two-piece band started to play. Two ragged youngsters playing trumpet and drum. He remembered Marvia mentioning once—it had been pillow talk, late one night in her flat in the turret of an Oxford Street Victorian—that Louis Armstrong's centennial was coming up soon. Louis Armstrong, and she'd mentioned his favorite drummer, Baby Dodds. Eighty years ago, these ragged musicians might have been Louis Armstrong and Baby Dodds, playing for grocery money.

Lindsey walked over and handed them each a bill. Then he returned to the table and sat down facing Benjamin Bruninski.

"I painted the picture, Mae posed for it. I painted the thing, and it came out on the book. Izzy was so proud, Werner threw a little party for him. Izzy went around autographing everybody's copy of the book. I think I still have mine someplace. But anyway, there we were at the party. Everybody was a little bit tanked. And Werner throws one arm around me and one arm around Izzy and he says, 'Thanks to you, Ben, for reading that book and telling me how good it was.' "

"And?" Lindsey encouraged him. The musicians were playing up a storm.

"And I says, 'I didn't read that book. I never read that book. I just painted what you told me to paint.' "

"And then? What did Werner say, Ben?"

"He said, 'But you sent it to me. I never read it either. I

thought you had—that's why I bought the damned thing. I got my idea for the cover picture from Izzy, I called him up and told him we were taking the book, and he had some ideas for the cover, and I wrote them down and sent you the note with the manuscript.' "

Bruninski grinned, picked up another beignet, and swallowed half of it. He washed it down with coffee. Was that his third cup? Fourth? The man was amazing. "So Werner bought the book on my say—he thought I thought it was great—and neither of us ever read the thing. He just published it."

He looked around, seemed to notice the musicians for the first time, then looked at Lindsey. His eyes were wet, maybe with laughter.

"McCarthy's goons found out who Del Marston was. I don't know how they found out, but it must have been pretty easy. Just hang around Paige Publications and watch people coming and going. Once they got their hooks into poor Izzy, he couldn't stand it, poor guy. He was kind of a loner, you know. Funny, a sweet guy, but he never got married or anything. Just him and his mother; she brought him over from Russia when he was just a baby. She was a Trot. A Trotskyite. And they threatened to deport her back to Russia. That would have been the end of her. Poor Izzy."

"He didn't just get dizzy then, and fall off the roof?"

Bruninski snorted. "It was raining that day. Don't be a fool. He went up on the roof to jump off, and Werner ran after him, but he couldn't stop him. Over he went, poor guy. Werner never got over that. Thought he should have been faster or smarter or something. It wasn't his fault, it was those goons' fault. Poor Izzy." He rubbed his big hand across his face. "As for me, I could have done the same. I could have gone to Washington and raised my hand and turned in my Comrades and said it was all a horrible mistake—God bless Uncle Sam and Standard Oil and the Chicago First Trust Bank—and I would have been all right."

He gazed at the two musicians and smiled.

"I wouldn't do it. I said, to hell with 'em. But after that, every place I went, they found out, and I couldn't get work. I tried using other names. I tried not signing my work. They always found me. I was dead as far as painting. So I wound up sitting in Jackson Square drawing pastel portraits of fat tourists from the Corn Belt. Some fun, hey, kiddo?"

Lindsey saw a different light come into Bruninski's eyes.

"But I always kept my greatest canvas. I always kept *La Pasionaria*. Until I had to sell it to buy medicine for my wife. That son of a bitch Peabody. Five hundred bucks, and he wants to sell it for fifty thousand. And the thing is, it's worth it. I know a masterpiece when I see one, even if I painted it myself."

Lindsey said, "I'll have my colleague Aurora Delano come by and see you. She'll see about getting those prescriptions filled, medical treatment for Mrs. Bruninski. I'll—I'm really glad I found you both. I mean, there will have to be some paperwork, affidavits and all, but we'll start the wheels turning right away. I mean, International Surety is a responsible company. It's Mrs. Bruninski's money. She's entitled to it. Ms. Delano will come by today. I'll tell her where to find you. You'll take her up to Barracks Street, won't you?"

Bruninski nodded. "Sure."

The café was filling with customers and Decatur Street and Jackson Square were beginning to show the bustle of a typical bright morning. Lindsey dropped some money on the table and walked with Bruninski and waited while the old man retrieved his art equipment and set up at his favorite station.

A few minutes later Bruninski was busily sketching a honeymoon couple from Muncie, Indiana. Lindsey knew that was their hometown because they announced it loudly while they settled into a happy pose. Bruninski winked at Lindsey and started to hum. Lindsey would have bet that the honeymooners thought the old man was humming "Red River Valley."

Lindsey walked through the French Quarter until he reached the Monteleone. On Royal Street he stopped briefly at Peabody Fine Art and Antiques. The new glass was in place and the elegant storefront looked as if nothing untoward had happened. The store was locked, of course; the carriage trade preferred later hours. Lindsey craned his neck, hoping for a glimpse of *La Pasionaria*, but the painting could not be seen from the street.

The reason was obvious. Surely, Buddy Peabody would not want plebeians to crowd in front of his store, competing for a look at the magnificent nude.

Back in his room he fired up his palmtop computer and logged onto Klamenet/Plus. He had one heck of a report to modem over to Desmond Richelieu.

He climbed into bed and slept fitfully for a few hours. Maybe the coffee with chicory was bothering him. He got up and showered and dressed and walked back to the police station to give his statement on the incident at Barracks Street. He promised the New Orleans police that he would return, if necessary, to testify at Nathan ben Zinowicz's trial.

He phoned Aurora Delano, and she met him in the Monteleone lounge for a light snack. He told her of the previous night's events. She agreed to handle the Vansittart claim for Mae Bruninski rather than leave it for standard International Surety processing. They didn't do any paperwork, sitting there watching foot traffic on Royal Street.

A couple of hours later, Lindsey was sitting in the cramped cabin of a 757, picking at a nondescript airplane meal. His hands were shaking. He was surprised. The case was going well. He had found the girl on the cover of *Death in the Ditch*. Justice would be served, the express desire of the decedent would be carried out, and International Surety would save its cool million bucks, making Hobart Lindsey the hero of the day.

Best of all, Nathan ben Zinowicz was behind bars once again. How long he would remain there—in Louisiana—was imponderable. What charges the New Orleans police would bring, what chance there was of getting a conviction with Mae Bruninski almost certainly unable to testify and Benjamin Bruninski unlikely to do so, was a puzzle.

But in any case, ben Zinowicz's parole had been revoked by Dave Jones, and if he returned to California he was headed back to San Quentin. And once in, he would likely face a murder charge in the death of John Frederick O'Farrell.

Mother was about to marry Gordon Sloane. Lindsey was close to marrying Marvia Plum.

Why were his hands shaking?

Chapter Eighteen

THE 757 SETTLED onto a runway at Oakland International, and Lindsey stood up to retrieve his flight luggage from the overhead bin. He'd given up on checking bags, he was sick of having luggage go to Auckland when he was going to Oakland, or disappear altogether. He took a cab home and let himself into the house on Laurel Drive.

He checked his watch against the clock on the mantel. It was too late to do anything more, and he was weary to the bone. Mother was out, probably spending the night at Gordon Sloane's condo. He showered to rid himself of the staleness of travel, climbed into his pajamas, and made a cup of cocoa.

He pulled back the covers and climbed into bed. He felt like a six-year-old. He wanted to phone Marvia Plum, but he was barely able to finish his cocoa and place the empty cup on the night table before he fell asleep.

He was awakened by the telephone's burbling. He blinked a couple of times until he was able to read the time. It was 5:30 in the morning. He knocked the handset off its base, then picked it up to hear Mrs. Blomquist's familiar voice. "Stand by for Mr. Richelieu, please."

If it was 5:30 A.M. in California, that meant it was 6:30 in Colorado. Had Richelieu and Blomquist pulled another all-nighter, or had they both arrived at the office early?

"Lindsey, I just pulled your report off KNP. You're sure you found the bennie?"

"Absolutely."

"Tell me why."

"I tracked her, Mr. Richelieu. It's all there in my report. From the Paige family and Maude Markham in Chicago to Jeb Harkins to Bruninski in New Orleans. Mrs. Bruninski is definitely the girl on the cover of *Death in the Ditch.*"

"Fingerprints? Documentation? Witnesses?"

"Harkins knew both Bruninskis in Chicago. We can get a deposition if we have to. But *La Pasionaria* proves it. That's the same model as the book covers, the Lincoln Brigade book, and the other Paige books as well as *Death in the Ditch.* And that's the same woman. I saw her. She isn't in good shape and the years have changed her, but she is definitely the same woman."

Richelieu hummed something under his breath. It sounded to Lindsey like the suspense music from a TV game show.

Lindsey added, "She was an army nurse in World War II. There should be fingerprints on file at the Pentagon. Aurora Delano is handling the case in New Orleans, but this woman is for real—count on it."

Richelieu stopped humming. "For once it's to our advantage to pay the claim, not deny it. I've already talked to Legal. They're rolling. And don't think I don't trust you, Lindsey, but I had a little chat with Aurora Delano this morning."

"And?"

"As a great president of this country once said, trust but verify. Delano speaks well of you, too. What about the painting? You didn't spend my fifty grand, did you?"

Lindsey found himself shaking his head automatically. "No, sir." He caught a glimpse of himself in the mirror above his dresser. His hair was disheveled and he needed a shave. He couldn't pass for six—that was certain.

"I was after it only as a way to reach Bruninski. Once I found him without it, I didn't need the painting anymore. And once Dr. ben Zinowicz got the address out of the files at the gallery, nobody really needed it anymore. Besides, Bruninski's going to try and get it back from the gallery. He wants it for himself and for his wife. She was a real beauty, believe me."

As he spoke, Lindsey heard the front door of the house open and close.

"Not interested," Richelieu ground out. "Let Bruninski have it."

"You mean, you want him to buy it back from Peabody for a hundred times what Peabody paid him for it?"

"That's his problem, Lindsey. Here's yours. You'd better go get a sign-off from Mr. and Mrs. Cooke."

Lindsey said, "I'll try."

"Not good enough. Just do it."

"Yes, sir."

Lindsey took another shower. He made a mental note to have Aurora Delano help Bruninski get back his painting. Carrot-and-stick Peabody. Offer him a nice price for the painting, but nothing like fifty grand. And if he refused, threaten him with a high-profile lawsuit. *Greedy art dealer exploits starving genius.* He'd come around. Lindsey had seen it before. Peabody would come around.

When Lindsey came out he found Mother in the kitchen. She was humming a tune that he had heard from her several times since her romance with Gordon Sloane began to blossom. "Oh, what a beautiful morning. . . . " It was soppy, but Lindsey was pleased that Mother was happy.

She turned from the stove and held her face up for a good-morning kiss. She was scrambling eggs. Lindsey could smell freshly brewed coffee. The toaster was about to pop up, and there was orange marmalade on the table and a dish with a stick of butter on it.

Mother had done a remarkable job of reconnecting with the present, but she hadn't quite caught up with modern dietary practices.

Lindsey slid into his chair and buttered a slice of toast for himself. As the butter melted in, he covered it with marmalade.

No, he didn't feel six anymore. Maybe ten or so. It was nice to feel ten.

Sloane had dropped Mother at the house while Lindsey was on the telephone with Desmond Richelieu. After breakfast she dressed for her job. Lindsey changed into a fresh suit, dropped Mother at her work, then drove on to the International Surety office on North Broadway.

He telephoned the World Fund for Indigent Artists in San Francisco. A cultured female voice answered. Lindsey could see the cool, elegantly-turned-out beauty who had answered the phone. He asked to speak with Mr. or Mrs. Cooke, and the cultured voice asked if it—she—might tell them who was calling, and in what regard.

Lindsey told her. This was going to be difficult. Lindsey was morally certain that the Cookes were behind both the killing of John O'Farrell and the attempt on his own life. That being the case, they were more than likely responsible for the death of Albert Crocker Vansittart and the helicopter crash at Lake Tahoe.

Cooke claimed to have known Vansittart's son—a son who never existed. The Cookes would have known about the International Surety policy on Vansittart's life; that information would have been in WFIA's files since its early days in Chicago. And they had every reason in the world for trying to thwart Lindsey's search for the prime beneficiary. How would they react to his phone call today? How would they feel about signing a quitclaim on the Vansittart policy? How would Lindsey himself manage to talk with them?

The owner of the cultured voice put him through to Roger St. John Cooke.

Lindsey said, "Mr. Cooke, I have some very important news for you. I think we'd better discuss this face to face."

Cooke took his time with that one. Finally he yielded. "All right. My office. One hour."

Lindsey started to say that he couldn't reach Cooke's office in an hour, but Cooke had rung off. Lindsey headed downstairs and started for San Francisco. He left his car at the transit station and rode a train through the tube on the bottom of San Francisco Bay. He wondered if this was the day that the Big One would hit, if the tube would stand the shock if it did, if he would wind up along with his fellow passengers, drowned like a rat if the big quake did strike. He looked at the other passengers. Students, workers on an unscheduled holiday, messengers, tourists, children, retirees. Fellow drowners if the Big One hit and the transbay tube couldn't handle it.

This day, the Big One did not hit.

Once he reached his stop and rode the escalator to street level, Lindsey walked to 101 California.

An hour after leaving home, he was in the reception area of the World Fund for Indigent Artists. The decor was lush. The place had the cool elegance of a modern consulting firm that charged a fortune by the hour to tell other people how to run their businesses.

The owner of the cultured voice wore ice-blonde hair, a dove-gray suit, and a don't-ask expression. The only vivid color on her was her brilliant lipstick. She informed Lindsey that Mr. Cooke was tied up but would get to him as quickly as possible.

Cooke kept him waiting for more than an hour. When Lindsey finally faced Cooke in Cooke's office, he was not in a pleasant mood.

He started, "The primary beneficiary of Albert Crocker Vansittart's life policy has been located. The World Fund will receive no payment. Just for the record, International Surety would appreciate your signing an acknowledgment of that and a quitclaim on the matter."

Cooke laughed at him.

"I have a quitclaim form right here," Lindsey volunteered. "IS might even offer a modest settlement, I mean, really a very modest settlement, in exchange. Just to clear the matter."

Cooke chuckled. "You've got to be kidding."

"We don't need your sign-off, you understand," Lindsey said. "International Surety is going to pay the beneficiary. You're not going to receive anything in any case."

"We'll tie you up, Lindsey. You don't have a chance. Tell you what; you pay that money to the World Fund, and we'll just drop the matter."

"Mr. Cooke, I want you to understand that I know all about Nathan ben Zinowicz."

There was a short silence. Then Cooke asked, "Is this blackmail?"

"Nothing like. I just wondered, have you heard from Dr. ben Zinowicz? Is he supposed to report in daily? Is that how you work?"

"The relationship between the Fund and its employees is none of your business, Lindsey."

"Then you haven't heard from ben Zinowicz today?"

"I told you, that's none of your business."

Lindsey felt the way he felt when he played checkers, something he seldom did, and his opponent left him a major opening.

"He's in jail."

Cooke's eyes widened.

Lindsey waited.

Cooke blinked first.

"Where?"

Now Lindsey smiled.

"Where?" Cooke demanded again.

Lindsey rose from his seat. The chair alone must have cost more than all the furniture in his house. He wondered again how much of the Fund's funds ever reached an indigent artist.

He headed for the exit. He could hardly contain himself. Then he passed Cynthia Cooke, looking suddenly two decades older than she had over lunch at Liberté, scurrying toward her husband's office. The owner of the cultured voice stood behind her own desk, gaping at the sight.

Lindsey would have tipped his hat if he'd been wearing one. He said, "Good morning, Mrs. Cooke. Maybe I'd better stay a little longer after all."

She preceded him into her husband's office, turned back toward him, and hissed, "You wait here." He stepped backward barely in time to avoid catching a faceful of door. He didn't wait to see what happened next; he had a feeling that it would be unpleasant, and he wanted to find out what had happened to upset Cynthia Cooke to that extent.

He rode the elevator down to the lobby, surrounded by lawyers and junior executives dressed for success. He decided against using a phone in the WFIA offices, and instead dropped a coin into a pay phone in the lobby of 101 California. He wanted to be out of the Cookes' range before he got an update on the situation.

He managed to reach Marvia Plum at Berkeley Police Headquarters. As soon as she recognized his voice she said, "Hold on to your hat. This thing is getting exciting. Where are you now?"

He told her.

She said, "Get out of there."

"What?"

"Get out of there. Put some distance between yourself and the Cookes. Do it fast!"

"Why?"

"Please, Bart, just do it. You can call me back from—from wherever. If I'm not here they'll patch you through to me."

"But—"

"Please—now!"

He hung up and left the building. He walked through the city. It was a gorgeous day, an early spring was in the air, and San Francisco was laid out compactly. He wound up in North Beach, at the Washington Square Bar & Grill. He ordered a glass of mineral water from the bartender, made his way to the pay phone, and dialed Berkeley again.

When he reached Sergeant Plum he asked, "What was that all about?"

"Your old friend Dr. ben Zinowicz is under arrest in New Orleans."

"I know that."

"You do?"

"I was there when they took him away. Are you getting him back? I mean, are they sending him back to California? Does Dave Jones have to go after him, or what?"

"We'll work that out. It won't be easy, but I don't think a man like Dr. ben Zinowicz would relish doing time at Angola. He just might prefer to come back to California. Otherwise, it's up to the DAs and the state attorneys. Bart, I have to talk to you. Right away. Where are you now?"

He told her.

"Look, can you wait for me there? Get a snack or stay in the bar and watch television or something. I'll come there. I need to talk to you."

He said okay and placed the handset softly on the hook. He walked back to the bar. His mineral water stood there, a blue bottle that looked like a piece of modern sculpture, a tall glass, a couple of ice cubes, a slice of lime slitted to the rind and hung on the lip of the glass. The glass stood on an imprinted paper napkin.

It was quite remarkable. They could make a work of art out of a drink of carbonated water.

He dropped a bill on the polished mahogany, poured the mineral water into the glass, and sipped. It was a major aesthetic experience. He turned to watch the television set mounted above the bar. He was surrounded by a mix of well-dressed San Franciscans and tourists who had possessed the good sense or the good luck to find their way to one of the city's best watering holes.

There was some kind of athletic event on the television screen. Lindsey found his eyes watering and he couldn't make out exactly what was happening, except that numbers of very large men were colliding with great force, falling down, and getting up again to repeat the exercise.

He took the lime slice off the lip of his glass and popped it into his mouth. He bit down on the lime and left the bar, and went for a short walk about the hilly neighborhood. The sky was gray, and the air was chilly and wet. When he got back, he stood in front of the entrance, waiting for Marvia Plum. He didn't feel like going inside.

Across Columbus Avenue, in Washington Square Park, a group of school children were playing ball despite the cold afternoon. The change in climate from New Orleans was dramatic, but Lindsey was so caught up in the events of recent days that he hardly noticed it.

Now he blew on his hands to warm them.

Marvia must have parked at the garage around the corner on Fillmore. Either that, or lucked into a parking spot in the congested neighborhood just as someone pulled out.

Lindsey held out his hands to her and she took his. She was wearing a quilted jacket against the day's chill, and a pair of faded jeans. She looked beautiful.

Together they went back inside the bar and grill. The lunch crowd was thinning now, and they were able to get a table without waiting. They were in the main dining room, away from the bar and the TV set, but some die-hard sports fans were still bellied up to the mahogany. Lindsey couldn't hear the sound of the TV but he could imagine the hard hits every time the sophisticated drinkers let go a collective roar, cheer, or moan.

The waiter asked Lindsey and Marvia Plum if they wanted a beverage. Lindsey was surprised when Marvia ordered a whiskey, neat.

"I thought you weren't supposed to drink on duty. Is that still another cop myth shattered?"

A suggestion of a smile appeared on Marvia's face, then disappeared quickly. "I'm off duty. I clocked out after you called the second time."

Lindsey tried to read Marvia's expression, but was unable to do so. "I don't understand. Is this official, or is it personal?"

The waiter had brought Marvia's drink. He must have set his course by the atmosphere between them because he dropped two menus on the white linen cloth and disappeared without a word.

Marvia picked up her drink and downed half of it. She squeezed her eyes shut and Lindsey thought he could see a flush in her face, despite her very dark coloring.

He asked, "What is it? Something is wrong, isn't it?"

She said nothing and he waited a beat, another beat. From the adjacent bar a roar went up. Someone had delivered a hard hit; someone else had taken it.

"Bart, let's catch up on this Vansittart case. The rest can— maybe we'll take a walk afterwards and talk things over."

Something cold sent its tendrils through him. All he could think of to say was, "Okay."

Now the waiter returned, pencil and pad at the ready. Marvia looked at the menu and selected a crabmeat salad. Lindsey ordered a bowl of minestrone and half a chicken sandwich. Obviously, neither of them was in a mood to eat a heavy meal.

Marvia looked at him expectantly. "Tell me about New Orleans. Tell me about ben Zinowicz. Did you see Aurora?".

"I saw her." The waiter had brought some bread and butter and there were glasses of ice water on the table. Lindsey picked up his glass and took a swallow. He closed his eyes for a few seconds to gather his thoughts. He reached for his pocket organizer, the habit of years with International Surety, then dropped his hand again. He told her the story, from Jeb Harkins's identification of Pelican Stadium on the cover of *Baseball Stars of 1952* and Harkins's 1964 Christmas card from Bob Brown, to Lindsey's first encounter with *La Pasionaria* in Peabody Fine Art and Antiques, to the confrontation in Ben and Mae Bruninski's run-down flat on Barracks Street.

"Chump to champ to chump," he concluded. "That was Ben Bruninski's version of his autobiography. I don't think he was a chump at all. He was an idealist."

"And Bobby Kennedy and Roy Cohn personally hounded him out of the publishing world, and destroyed his career?"

"That's what he told me."

"Doesn't sound right to me." Marvia picked at her crabmeat salad. It looked to Lindsey as if she hadn't eaten any at all. He looked at his own meal, at his bowl of soup, and realized that he hadn't touched it either.

"Was he talking about HUAC or McCarthy?" Marvia asked.

Through the window behind her, Lindsey could see the children still playing in Washington Square Park. Just to the north of the park, across Filbert, was the Church of St. Peter and St. Paul. Its whitewashed facade, its twin steeples and radial stained-glass window made it one of the city's most beautiful buildings.

"Bart?" Marvia had touched his hand.

A tiny shudder passed through him. "Oh, HUAC—the House Committee, I think that's what he said."

"I didn't think Bobby Kennedy and Roy Cohn worked for those bozos. I thought they worked for Joe McCarthy."

"Yes. Bruninski mentioned McCarthy, too. Maybe he got them mixed up. I mean, he's an old man, it's been a long time. Forty years or more. And if he's telling the truth, this must have been eating at his insides all those years."

"Is he a good painter?"

Lindsey shrugged. He picked up his spoon and filled it with red, steaming soup. It smelled wonderful but he put it down untasted. A collective moan emerged from the next room. "I don't know. I'm not an art critic. We've had a few cases involving paintings—one policy holder lost a major collection in the Oakland hills fire in ninety-one. But we always rely on outside appraisers for that."

"You told me one of his pieces was priced at fifty thousand dollars. That sounds like a pretty good painter to me."

Lindsey nodded. "I saw his book covers from the Paige Publications that Sarah Kleinhoffer gave me. I thought they were good, competent commercial pieces. I saw the pastel portraits he was doing for tourists in Jackson Square in New Orleans. Nice work, I guess. The customers were happy, anyway."

"What about the fifty-thousand-dollar painting?"

"*La Pasionaria.*"

Marvia picked up her whiskey glass and finished off its contents. She waited expectantly.

"I think it's worth every penny."

"He sold it for five hundred dollars, you told me."

"His wife had a stroke. She's bedridden. He was hounded for years, his career destroyed. They were living from hand to mouth. He kept that canvas for forty years. Finally he had to part with it. I don't think he had any idea what it was worth. He needed money for groceries, Marvia. He took what he could get."

"Do you think he'll get it back from Peabody?"

Lindsey shrugged. He picked up half his sandwich again. This time he managed to chew and swallow a sizable bite. "Peabody bought it all nice and legal—at least as far as I know. He's entitled to mark it up as much he wants." He picked up a piece of bread and dropped it again. "But I think Bruninski will get it. Peabody doesn't want that kind of publicity. He'll probably set it up so he gets some good press out of it. You know, 'Humanitarian art dealer returns painting to penniless genius.' Picture in the paper, interview on TV. We'll see."

"At least the Bruninskis will have money now," Marvia said. "They should be comfortable for the rest of their lives. Maybe he can paint another."

"Not like La *Pasionaria*, Marvia. Believe me. That painting is one of a kind."

He watched her poke at her salad with her fork. She picked up a piece of lettuce and put it on top of some crabmeat, then took it back off and put the crabmeat on top of the lettuce. As far as Lindsey could see, she hadn't eaten anything.

He asked, "What about this end of things?"

She actually smiled at that. "That's why I wanted you to get away from the Cookes. That's going to blow wide open. We've got SFPD into the act, the Feds are interested, it's huge. And you get credit. If you hadn't poked into the case, and kept on poking, the whole thing might have gone unnoticed."

"I don't know about that. I mean, Jamie's video was the first sign we had that anything was the matter."

"Well—you're due a lot of credit. The way you tracked down Ben Bruninski and Mae Carter, that was fine work. And putting ben Zinowicz away again, that was first-class. Maybe they'll throw away the key this time."

The waiter appeared and asked if they wanted anything else. There was a lovely dessert tray, or coffee, or another beverage. Lindsey had a cappuccino; Marvia Plum ordered an aperitif. Lindsey was a little surprised. Marvia was no bluenose, but he'd never thought of her as a drinker.

The waiter disappeared and Lindsey asked Marvia for more specifics. "What's going on with the Cookes? What are the Feds and the local police doing?"

Marvia looked expectantly over Lindsey's shoulder. The waiter reappeared with their beverages, and with their check. He dropped it on the table, almost equidistant between Lindsey and Marvia Plum. The placement was a perfect mixture of modern attitudes and San Francisco tradition. Lindsey picked it up, then added a bill from his wallet and put it back down.

Marvia said, "Thanks."

He waited.

"The man is a fool," she said at last. She lifted her tiny glass filled with a golden liquid and sipped carefully. "You know about his two apartments, right?"

"I knew he had one that was empty. So he must have had another apartment or a hidey-hole somewhere."

Marvia nodded. "He had an apartment here in the city, but there wasn't anything very interesting in it. Just his clothes and his personal clutter."

"But there was nothing interesting in his Berkeley apartment, either. He moved out, or maybe he never really moved in. He just kept his computer there, and he wiped that clean before he disappeared. Or he tried."

"Right." She smiled. "He wiped it clean, but you have to remember that he was a very compulsive self-documenter."

"I remember that from our first encounter. And Dave Jones told me that the computer people managed to recover his files."

"That's right. He kept very careful records on his computer. Our little wizards down at headquarters went over that machine, worked some abracadabra on the hard drive, and recovered the data he'd wiped. Or thought he'd wiped. Shades of Watergate!"

"Jones didn't tell me much of what they found. What was there?"

"He kept a diary. Well, more like an appointment book, but with detailed annotations. The wizards got most of it back, and there's no doubt that he was thick as thieves with the World Fund people. The fund was legitimate at first, but after Mr. and Mrs. Cooke got control of it, they turned it into their personal cash cow. They made a few little grants here and there. But most of what they collected—and it was *lots*—went into supporting them in their posh lifestyle. That, and lining their nest, and of course, back into fund-raising efforts for the next round of dollars and condos and limos."

Lindsey stared into his cup. There was a sprinkling of cinnamon on top of the steamed milk. He tasted the cappuccino, then wiped his mouth with his napkin.

"What about the O'Farrell murder?"

"He didn't quite say, '*I killed O'Farrell*,' but his travel plans were there, and cryptic little notes about 'Docs Hosp/Truckee' and "Donner turnoff.' My God, the man was tying a noose around his own throat with every keystroke."

"And the Cookes?"

"We already had a meeting with the DA's office and the U.S. Attorney. We'll have to sort out the jurisdictional problems, but we had a chat with ben Zinowicz in New Orleans, too, and I think he'll talk about the Cookes to save his own rear end. And he's going to need a lot of saving, so I think he's going to do a lot of talking."

She finished her aperitif and excused herself to visit the ladies' room. Lindsey watched her progress. There was a slight list to her movement. When she got back, he suggested a little fresh air. She agreed.

There was no exit directly from the dining room, so they walked through the bar to reach the front door. As Lindsey pushed the street door open, somebody must have hit somebody else very hard in the game on the TV screen, and maybe that somebody hit the first somebody back, because half the drinkers in the room cheered and the other half moaned. Hobart Lindsey and Marvia Plum left the restaurant and crossed the street to Washington Square Park.

When they got there, the schoolchildren had departed, but a wino lurched up to them and asked for money.

Chapter Nineteen

THE GRASS IN the park was in good shape, and they walked slowly past the old San Francisco Firemen's Monument and stopped just across the street from St. Peter and St. Paul's.

Lindsey said, "We could go in right now and ask a priest to marry us."

Marvia Plum turned to him and put her arms around him. He was wearing a rough tweed jacket and he was worried that she would scratch her face on the cloth. He felt her shaking and saw that she was crying.

"Marvia, tell me what's the matter." He put his face close to hers, and felt her tears on his cheek.

A couple of Chinese teenagers walking past hesitated, staring at Lindsey and Marvia Plum. Then they walked on, talking animatedly.

"I can't marry you."

"That's okay. Neither of us is Catholic, I know. Besides, we don't have a license. Let's go get one."

"No. I can't."

He tightened his arm around her shoulders, feeling her shake even through the heavy quilted jacket. He led her to the edge of the park, crossed Filbert Street with his arm still around her, and pushed into the church.

It was deserted at this hour. The late-afternoon sun coming through the radial window filled the vestibule with a rainbow of rich colors. Lindsey led Marvia to a pew and they sat together. He held both her hands in his. He repeated, "Tell me what's the matter."

She said, "I'm moving up to Reno."

He was stunned.

She said, "I'm going to resign from the force. I haven't put in my papers yet, I want to see this case through and clean up the rest of my work, but I'm resigning from the force."

"Why, Marvia?"

"Willie Fergus is eligible for early retirement from the Washoe Sheriff's Department. He'll have both his pensions, and he can get a security job at a casino. He's already had some offers—they're always eager to get people with law-enforcement experience. He thinks I can get a job, too. We'll have enough to live on."

"Willie Fergus," Lindsey whispered. He pulled his fingers free of Marvia's. He hit himself on the forehead with the heel of his hand, feeling like a fool, acting like a fool. "The night I phoned you from New Orleans. I was at the Monteleone and you were at home and Willie Fergus answered the phone. And I didn't even think about it."

"I'm so sorry, Bart. I love you. I really do. And you've been so good to me, and so good to Jamie. But when I saw Willie again after all those years, I—" She leaned her head on his shoulder and shuddered.

"I should have known. I mean, I hadn't realized about Germany until he told me. And now he's back."

"It wasn't like that in Germany. You know I was involved with James Wilkerson then. Willie Fergus was like an uncle to me. He was older, and he was sympathetic. He helped me in such a terrible time, I didn't know where to turn, and he helped me."

"Were you lovers then?"

"No."

"I don't suppose it matters."

"It does. It does matter, Bart. I never lied to you. You knew there were men before you. Men besides James Wilkerson. But not since we've been together. And in Germany, Willie Fergus was my best friend, but that's all he was. He was only my friend."

Lindsey said, again, "I don't suppose it matters." He straightened his shoulders and took a deep breath. "You were so good to me, Marvia. You brought me to life, you know. Before I found you I was just—I was a kind of zombie, you know. I was just—I got up in the morning and went to work and came home at night and just waited for bedtime, just prayed for bedtime to come because I had nothing to do, I had no one. Only Mother, and she was, you know—not really there. Not really there."

An elderly priest entered the sanctuary. He stood looking down at Lindsey and at Marvia. He said, "Is there anything I can do?"

Lindsey said, "Thank you, no," and again, "Thank you, Father, no." He felt Marvia hiding her face in his shoulder.

The priest put a bony hand on Lindsey's head, and another on Marvia's. He nodded and lifted his hands and walked away.

Lindsey said to Marvia, "What about Jamie?"

She looked into his eyes. She pulled a bandanna out of her jeans pocket and wiped her face. Lindsey wanted to kiss her eyes, wanted to make her not cry.

"He'll stay with my mother. He'll be all right. Hakeem's mother will take the boys after school. His father works and his mother stays home. Just like Donna Reed."

Lindsey said, "That's my line," very softly. Then: "What about Wilkerson? Does he know about this? What does he have to say about it?"

For a moment there was a note of anger in her voice; then it faded. "He has nothing to say about it. We've settled with him and his wonderful new wife. He's happy now, he looks like a shoo-in for the House of Representatives. Imagine, a conservative Republican black Gulf War hero freshman congressman from Texas. He'll be the whitest black man in Congress. He won't want to stir up trouble again over Jamie. He'll want to keep Jamie and me out of the spotlight."

Lindsey grunted.

"I'm so sorry," Marvia said. "Maybe it *is* the race thing after all. You're so decent, Bart, and I'm hurting you. I don't want to hurt you, but I'm doing it. I know it and I can't help it. Willie just knows things; he's lived this the same as I have."

She held her hands in front of her face and ran the fingers of one over the back of the other, as if discovering something she'd never seen before. "He knows what it is. You can't know. It isn't your fault; you just can't know."

Lindsey reached for her hands again but she pulled them away. She stood up suddenly and drew a deep, shuddering breath. He stood up with her and they walked to the front door of the church. Lindsey pulled a bill out of his pocket and dropped it in the poor box on his way out.

They stood on the sidewalk facing the park. The church, behind them, cast a long shadow. The heavy clouds were breaking up and the sky overhead was a dark, dark blue, almost purple. Spring might be in the air, but the clock knew that it was still winter and night was falling.

Lindsey said, "What do you want to do now?"

"I don't know. Nothing. I feel empty. I feel sick. I'm sorry." She turned and looked up into his face. She managed a tiny smile. She touched his cheek, and he grasped his own leg to keep himself from reaching up and taking her hand. She said, "Did you drive into the city?"

"No. I left my car in Walnut Creek. I took the train in."

Marvia said, "I'll give you a ride back. I can drop you in Berkeley, or I can take you to your car."

He stood there for a minute. Darkness had arrived with amazing suddenness. The sky above Washington Square Park was black. Beyond North Beach, in San Francisco's financial district, he could see the TransAmerica Pyramid reaching for the sky. It looked like a gigantic rocket ship balanced precariously on its tail, waiting for the countdown to end so it could blast free of its foundation and travel to the distant stars.

He found himself wishing he could climb aboard the rocket ship and travel with it far, far into space and never return to earth.

"Bart?"

He walked sadly from the launching pad. "No," he said. "Thank you, no. I'll just take the train."

When he reached Walnut Creek, he called his house, hoping that Mother wouldn't answer the phone. She didn't. He heard his own voice on the answering machine, asking the caller to leave a message so he could call him back. He hung up the pay phone, climbed in his blue Volvo, and drove home.

He paused in the kitchen, but he still had no appetite. He stood in front of the meager bookshelf in the living room, but nothing there appealed to him. He went to his room and found the set of Paige books that he'd received in Chicago, and stood studying the colorful Benjamin Bruninski covers, especially the ones featuring the lush young model, Mae Carter.

He picked through his small collection of compact disks and selected one that Marvia Plum had given him. It was Miles Davis playing Gershwin's *Porgy and Bess*. He'd listened to it when Marvia gave it to him, but seldom put it on. The music was simply too sad for him. But tonight he played it. He found himself wondering if Miles Davis had been as sad when he played the Gershwin melodies as Hobart Lindsey was tonight as he listened to them.

A little later, he found himself sitting on the rug, listening to the sad music and crying for the aged, crippled, sick Mae Carter, dying slowly in her bed on Barracks Street in the French Quarter.

He didn't remember getting into bed, but the next thing he knew it was morning. He had a headache and a sour stomach, and he felt worse than he'd felt in years. At first he didn't know why. He wasn't hung over; he didn't think he had the flu.

Then he remembered his conversation with Marvia.

He sat on the edge of the bed until he had his bearings, then took a long shower and shaved and dressed. There was no sign of Mother. He wasn't worried anymore: she was a grown woman, and she knew what she was doing.

He stood in the kitchen trying to decide what, if anything, to have for breakfast. Finally he drank a glass of water. It was all he could face.

Before leaving the house he checked the telephone-answering machine. There were two messages.

One was from the United States Attorney's office in San Francisco. The other was from Desmond Richelieu in Denver. The messages were the same: return call as soon as possible. The only difference was that the message from the U.S. Attorney was polite.

Lindsey looked at his watch. They must start work early in the Federal Building. He returned that call first and was invited to come in for a brief chat about the World Fund for Indigent Artists. He made an appointment later the same morning.

When he called SPUDS/HQ, Desmond Richelieu took the call at once. Richelieu was almost friendly. "Talked to Aurora again. Got the details from her end. Good work, Lindsey. What do you have on your plate now?"

Lindsey squeezed his eyes shut. "Nothing major, Mr. Richelieu. A lot of ongoing cases—nothing very big. But I still have to follow up on the Vansittart."

"Why? What's left to do? IS is paying out the three million, saving the million-dollar finder's fee, bennie's happy, company's happy, what's left?"

"Well, there's Dr. ben Zinowicz and the O'Farrell killing."

"That belongs to the cops, Lindsey. Don't forget who you are. Don't forget who pays your salary. Your job is to do your job, not play Elliot Ness."

"Right." Lindsey had to concede that Richelieu was on the money.

"Anything else?"

"I have an appointment with the U.S. Attorney in, ah, two hours."

"What for? I don't see anything about it on KNP."

"I just got the message from them. I called them back a few minutes ago and made the appointment. It's about the WFIA—you know, Mr. and Mrs. Cooke."

"Right. Well, you do have your duty as a citizen."

In his mind's eye Lindsey saw Richelieu, sitting behind his immaculate desk, the bright Rocky Mountain sunlight glinting off his gold-framed eyeglasses, gazing adoringly at the autographed portrait of J. Edgar Hoover that hung behind his desk. In the portrait, Hoover wore a double-breasted dark brown suit, a white shirt, and a conservatively patterned tie.

Lindsey asked, "Is that all? I'll go talk to the U.S. Attorney, and then I'll update the file through KNP. Unless you want to talk to me about it."

"I want to talk to you about a couple of things. Go have your meeting and call me again." Richelieu paused. Lindsey knew that pause; it was famous throughout International Surety. "I'll see you at the conference here in Denver, right?"

"With bells on, sir." You bet. With bells on, like a court jester.

THE U.S. ATTORNEY'S office in the Federal Building in downtown San Francisco had the dull, slightly shopworn feeling of any government office below the supergrade level. Lindsey was met by a startlingly young woman who introduced herself as Marge Tillotson. She ushered him into a cramped cubicle. She asked if he'd like a cup of coffee or a glass of water and he declined.

After a minimal amount of throat clearing and paper shuffling, she said, "This is about the World Fund for Indigent Artists."

"Yes."

Tillotson opened a folder, pulled a pair of half-height glasses from a soft case, and perched them on the end of her nose. She read, "The fund was created in Chicago, Illinois, on 1 October 1951."

Lindsey wondered why government people always said things like "One October," but he didn't say anything.

"Officers of incorporation were Walter Paige, Bob Brown, and Mae Carter. Do you know any of these people, Mr. Lindsey? Do you happen to know if they're still alive?"

Lindsey happened to know a lot that Marge Tillotson was eager to find out. That Walter Paige, né Werner Kleinhoffer, had died and been buried by the Jewish Sacred Society, but that his children and grandchildren still lived in Winnetka.

Marge Tillotson jotted notes. She used a yellow pencil and a lined pad. Lindsey wondered if that was her preference, or if the Federal Government thought it was still 1953.

"In 1954 the Chicago Artists and Models Mutual Aid Society

moved to Washington, D.C., and was renamed the National Welfare League for Graphic Creators. Information on the CAMMAS is not very complete, Mr. Lindsey. The only name we've been able to turn up, connected with this period in the organization's history, is an unincorporated partnership called Kennedy and Cohn. Records are almost nonexistent. Would you happen to know anything about this? Could this possibly be the famous Kennedy family? And could Cohn be the Roy Cohn who was on Senator Joseph R. McCarthy's staff at one time? Have your investigations turned up any information in this regard?"

Lindsey smiled slightly. "No, I'm afraid not."

"Then why are you smiling?"

Marge Tillotson was not altogether the dense bureaucrat she seemed, then.

"I've come across those names in another context. Bobby Kennedy, yes, the martyred hero of later years, and Roy Cohn, yes, the late, well-known bon vivant of New York club society. I've come across the names. But nothing to do with—what was it called at that point?—the National Welfare League for Graphic Artists. No, I'm afraid not."

Tillotson turned a sheet in the manila folder and nodded to herself. "Early in 1968, Kennedy and Cohn apparently severed their relationship with the NWLGA and the organization was taken over by Roger St. John Cooke and Cynthia Cooke. They moved the organization's headquarters to San Francisco, renamed it the World Fund for Indigent Artists, and have run it ever since."

She leaned back in her seat, smiled warmly at Lindsey, and asked, "What can you add to my knowledge?"

Lindsey responded, "Is that all you have?"

"Oh, no." Tillotson pulled open a desk drawer, removed a small computer, and placed it on her desk. She tapped a few keys, and the folding monitor screen came to life. "Can you see that all right?"

"I can."

"We have some conflicting laws, Mr. Lindsey." Tillotson ran her hand down the side of the computer. It looked like a caress.

Okay, Uncle Sam had figured out that it wasn't 1953 after all. Mother had done the same; why couldn't the government?

"Income-tax returns of course are confidential, and census data, and a lot of other things. The government certainly recognizes citizens' right of privacy." Another smile. The smile of the wolf, Lindsey thought. "On the other hand, the government is supposed to operate in the open. We can't spy on our own citizens. And records that are matters of public record have to be open to the public, don't you see?"

"I've used the Freedom of Information Act a couple of times," Lindsey told her.

"Have you? Well, good for you." She blinked a couple of times. She had long eyelashes, heavy with mascara. Lindsey didn't know that women used mascara anymore. Live and learn. "You see the dilemma we face, though. I can't show you the information I've got on the World Fund and on Mr. and Mrs. Cooke. I can only look it up for my own use, as part of my job. You understand?"

"Sure."

She tapped a few more keys on the computer, and columns of figures scrolled across the screen. Lindsey pulled his pocket organizer from inside his jacket and opened it. Marge Tillotson reached across the desk and closed it again.

"Please. This isn't happening, and you mustn't peep over my shoulder when I consult a confidential file."

Lindsey put his organizer away.

The Cookes drew salaries of $1 a year, apiece. But they had unlimited expense accounts, and they lived high. In addition to their Nob Hill condo they owned another in Maui, another in Vail, and another in St. Maarten, six automobiles, a variety of valuable paintings and sculptures with which their homes were decorated, and a gilt-edged stock portfolio. Their wardrobes were not mentioned, but Cynthia Cooke's jewels were.

Lindsey wondered what the Cookes would think of Benjamin Bruninski's masterpiece, *La Pasionaria*. Maybe it wasn't rich enough for their blood. But if Buddy Peabody could avoid returning *La Pasionaria* to Benjamin Bruninski and he could get the Cookes' attention, and maybe move the decimal point another position or two on the price, their fancy would be piqued.

Lindsey said, "I thought they were old money. Maybe those belongings all came from their inheritances."

Tillotson grinned that grin. She shook her head slowly from side to side. "No, no way. We've been tracking the bills and the payments. They did a pretty good job of covering their tracks, but not good enough. World Fund is tax-exempt. That requires pretty stringent financial reporting. We've got 'em six ways to Sunday, Mr. Lindsey."

"Then why do you need me?"

"Because of the insurance scam they were trying to pull. We haven't figured out completely how it fits in, but we have a pretty good idea."

"And what's that?"

"The World Fund is not in good shape, Mr. Lindsey."

"I was up at their office. You could have fooled me."

"Exactly. Some phony charities try to look ragged and poor. It adds poignancy to their appeal. They get middle-class people—even poor people—to fork over. The unfortunate helping those even more unfortunate than themselves. A lot of them use that pitch. But others—the World Fund, for one—would rather work the carriage trade. As Willie Sutton said when a reporter asked him why he robbed banks—"

"Don't tell me. I've heard the story. 'Because that's where the money is.'"

"Precisely. So they rent fancy office suites, they furnish them like billion-dollar corporate headquarters, staff them with fashion plates—well, you've been there; you know the drill."

"And this makes people give them money?"

"Isn't that something? Like goes to like. Money goes to money. They don't look for nickel-and-dime donations from poor working stiffs. They look for major bequests, endowments, foundation grants. Why struggle for one hundred thousand dollars worth of five- and ten- and twenty-dollar donations while you ride around in a rusty old Plymouth, live in the Outer Mission, eat at McDonald's? Why not go for a one hundred thousand dollar grant, ride in a Mercedes, live on Nob Hill, take your meals at Liberté or Jack's or the Carnelian Room?"

"All on one dollar a year?"

"All on one dollar a year, *plus expenses*. The World Fund pays for everything. Mr. and Mrs. Cooke are going to take a fall, if only for income-tax evasion. We put Leona Helmsley away; we're going to get Roger St. John Cooke and Cynthia Cooke. But there's more to this than tax evasion. What can you tell me about the Vansittart insurance policy?"

Lindsey did a quick internal review of International Surety procedures. There was nothing secret about Albert Crocker Vansittart's odd policy. It had been all over the media since Vansittart's death. And Marge Tillotson would soon be getting the complete lowdown on Nathan ben Zinowicz, if she didn't already have it.

He gave her everything.

When he finished his story she picked up her telephone and speed-dialed the County DA's office. Five minutes later, she placed the handset back on its cradle and gave Lindsey a long, calculating look.

"I'm always the last to know," she complained.

"What happened?"

"The local folks have been talking to the authorities in New Orleans. Dr. ben Zinowicz is caught between a rock and a hard place. He doesn't want to come back to California and face murder charges in the death of John O'Farrell and he doesn't want to serve the rest of his old sentence. He's pretty upset with David Jones for revoking his parole, but that's a fait accompli now. But he mostly doesn't want to face attempted murder charges in Louisiana and maybe wind up doing long, hard time at Angola."

Lindsey grinned. This was what he'd hoped for. Hearing of Nathan ben Zinowicz's discomfiture could only please him. "So what happens now?"

"So he wants to cut a deal. He wants Louisiana to let him go. And their case is pretty weak, you know. Then he wants to testify against the Cookes. He knows the insides and the outsides of the World Fund; he can ice the case for us. In return, he wants Louisiana to drop everything, he wants no Federal charges over World Fund, and he wants to cop a plea on O'Farrell."

Lindsey let out a deep breath. "Are you going to go for that?"

"I don't have anything to do with the Louisiana charges, but I think they'll be just as happy to have him out of their hair and back in California's. I don't have anything to do with the O'Farrell case, either. That's up to California."

"How about Nevada?"

"I think they're out of it. They could have arm-wrestled California for the privilege of prosecuting O'Farrell for the Vansittart killing, but they're not interested in O'Farrell's death. That's strictly California."

Lindsey grunted. "What about the Cookes? I mean, regarding both the Vansittart and O'Farrell killings?"

"Those are up to California. That's where ben Zinowicz comes in with his little vocal performance. I'll bet you a good lunch that ben Zinowicz testifies that the Cookes hired O'Farrell to kill Vansittart, and that they fed him—ben Zinowicz—a mysterious potion with the power to bend his will to theirs, and they made him kill O'Farrell."

This time Lindsey snorted. "You'll go for that? Madame, I have a wonderful bridge you would love to buy."

Tillotson leaned across her desk, locking onto Lindsey's eyes with her own. "Of course I don't buy that, and I'm sure the DA in Washoe County or Placer County or San Francisco—whoever catches the case—won't buy it, either. I'm just telling you what I expect to hear."

Lindsey stood up. "Can I go now? Do you need me for anything else?"

"I might need you later on, to give me a statement and maybe to talk to a grand jury."

"Be happy to."

HE GOT OUT of San Francisco. He'd managed to concentrate on the Vansittart case and everything that had grown from it. As long as he was talking with Marge Tillotson, and as long as he could concentrate on the topic at hand, he didn't have to think about Marvia Plum. But once he was back in his car, headed for the Bay Bridge, it hit him again. There was a wound inside him, and it ached.

He pulled his car into the garage on North Broadway and took the elevator up to the International Surety office. Kari Fielding was in the inner office with Elmer Mueller, and Lindsey found his desk and logged onto KlameNet/Plus. He pulled up the Vansittart file to check on actions since he'd left New Orleans.

Aurora Delano was handling things perfectly. She'd got a quick cash advance for Mae Bruninski, and the paperwork for the full $3,000,000 was moving as fast as it ever did. She'd even had a friendly chat with Buddy Peabody, and it looked as if he was willing to settle up with Bruninski for a small profit and a big publicity break.

He called Dave Jones in Oakland and learned that Nathan ben Zinowicz was on his way back to California in the company of a U.S. marshal. He'd waived extradition and was eager to cut a deal.

He called Desmond Richelieu—or tried to—but got only as far as Mrs. Blomquist, Richelieu's secretary. The Director was in a meeting, but Mr. Lindsey was advised to pick up his messages on KNP. There was full data there on the SPUDS conference in Denver.

Lindsey thanked her and hung up. He logged onto KNP and downloaded the SPUDS conference schedule. It was time to call the travel agent and make his flight arrangements.

Chapter Twenty

LINDSEY FLEW TO Denver early Monday morning. As he left Oakland, the sun was a brilliant disk rising over the Sierras. The day looked like a beauty.

But the wedding took place the day before Lindsey flew to Denver.

And on the morning of the day before the wedding, Lindsey carefully gift-wrapped his set of Paige Publications books and drove to Scotty Anderson's home in Castro Valley.

When Anderson admitted him to the apartment, Lindsey extended the brightly wrapped parcel ceremoniously.

Anderson switched a matchstick from one corner of his mouth to the other. He looked suspiciously at the package. He was wearing a pair of wrinkled, too-tight khakis and a plaid shirt. His sleeves were rolled halfway to the elbows and his hands were stuck in his pockets.

He said, "What's that?"

"A present."

Anderson cocked his head.

Lindsey said, "Remember me? You helped me out with *Death in the Ditch*. You put me onto Paige Publications. You were working on a bibliography for some fellow named Lovisi."

"Oh, sure." Anderson nodded solemnly. "I didn't remember you, I'm sorry. Sure, come on in."

Inside the apartment he continued, "I've kind of stalled on that Paige piece for Lovisi."

"That's what I've got for you." Lindsey made a second attempt to hand the parcel to Anderson. This time, the big collector took it.

They had reached Anderson's office. He sat at his desk, waved Lindsey to an easy chair, and carefully opened the parcel. He spread the books across his desk. As he added each one, the expression on his face evolved from pleased to delighted to ecstatic.

"Look at that, will you? *Cry Ruffian!*" He moved his hand as if to caress the lurid book, but his fingers did not quite touch the cover. "*Al Capone's Heirs!*" He looked at Lindsey the way the caliph looked at the evil Jaffar in the Korda *Thief of Bagdad* when he first laid eyes on the flying horse. "*By Studebaker Across America!*" He sighed.

"Do you know what you've brought to me? These are some of the scarcest books in the whole paperback field. These are scarcer than L.A. Bantams. This is the only *By Studebaker Across America* I've ever seen. It may be the only one in existence."

There were tears in his eyes.

"Where did you get these?"

Lindsey said, "From Walter Paige's grandchildren. They were saved when the company went under and later when the Paige Building was torn down."

"And you're giving these to me?" Anderson asked.

"Token of my appreciation."

"I don't know how to thank you, Mr. Lindsey. I'll make photos of these covers to go with my article for Lovisi's magazine. We'll cop the cover—that's for sure. I know Gary Lovisi's taste, and I'll bet he puts *Teen Gangs of Chicago* on the cover of *Paperback Parade*. This is wonderful, absolutely wonderful."

A worried look came onto Anderson's face.

"Are these a gift? You want to sell them to me, or what?"

"I told you, they're a token of my appreciation. Really. I don't want anything for them. I'm not a collector myself, but I know enough about collectors to understand that things like these books should have a good home. I know you'll give them a good home."

Anderson shifted his matchstick.

"That's a promise."

After leaving Castro Valley, Lindsey drove home to Walnut Creek. Mother was busily packing for her wedding trip. "You know, your father and I never had a real honeymoon. We were both so young, we thought he'd finish his navy service and I'd finish school, and then we could have our honeymoon. And that never happened."

Lindsey took his mother's hands. "You're entitled to some happiness. Are you sure you're doing the right thing?"

She said, "Yes, I am." She freed her hands, opened a closet door, and surveyed her shoes. "I think I'm going to get rid of three-quarters of these. I never wear them."

She pulled a pair of leather pumps from the shoe rack and rolled them carefully in an old pillowcase before she put them in her suitcase. "I've always wanted to see Hawaii. Now I'll have my chance."

She turned and looked up into Lindsey's face. "You know, I have you to thank for this. You and your wonderful Marvia." She made a funny clicking sound with her tongue. "You know, at first I almost resented her. Here was this strange woman taking my little boy away from me. I know you weren't really a little boy by then, but to me you still were."

She managed a small smile, then went on. "I clung to you so, you were all that I had left after your father died. I just couldn't let you grow up. It was bad for you and it was bad for me, I know. I'm sorry, Hobart. I hope you can forgive me."

"It's all past, Mother." He hadn't told her about Marvia and Willie Fergus. "I want you and Gordon to be happy together." He knew he'd have to tell her sooner or later, but he was content to let it be later. "You're sure you want to sell the house and move into Gordon's condo?"

Mother actually laughed, a rare event. "It's too late now. I've already moved half my belongings. Hobart, my little Hobo, I'm going to miss living with you, but I'm grown up now. It's time for me to spread my wings and go out on my own."

He gave her a hug. He looked at his watch. "What about dinner, Mother? We're due at the Coffmans'."

"All right. You go away and let me finish this, and then we'll go."

On the way to the Coffmans' house in Concord, Lindsey clicked a cassette into the Volvo's tape deck. He'd picked up a matched set of oldies compilations, and he put in the tape for 1952, the last full year of his father's life and the year when Lindsey was conceived. It was a big era for vocalists: almost every track featured a solo vocal and an orchestral backing. "Cry," sung by Johnnie Ray, "Wheel of Fortune," by Kay Starr. "Auf Wiederseh'n, Sweetheart," by Vera Lynn. The Cold War had been hot in 1952, Germany had been a grim, tense, divided country. How many fräuleins had heard that song and wept for their GIs or Tommies or poilus? "You Belong to Me," by Jo Stafford, and "I Went to Your Wedding," by Patti Page.

Mother knew all the words to every song, and she sang along with Johnnie and Kay and Vera. Lindsey couldn't remember ever hearing her sing before. She had a pleasant voice. He wondered if she had sung lullabies to him when he was a baby. He couldn't remember. He hoped that she had.

Lindsey laughed when the Patti Page track came on. Mother asked if the song was that funny, and Lindsey said no, he just happened to know a Patti Paige, and the song made him think of her.

"I used to love those songs. We used to sing along with the radio—my girlfriends and I, we used to love the songs." Mother turned her head toward Lindsey. Her features stood out in the light of oncoming traffic. When Lindsey was growing up, she'd always seemed old to him, but now that she was approaching sixty, she didn't look old at all. He felt a knot in his chest and silently wished her good health and some good years with her new husband.

They arrived at the Coffmans' house, and Miriam greeted them at the door. She embraced Lindsey's mother warmly, gave Lindsey himself a peck on the cheek, and ushered them into the living room. There had to be something between women, Lindsey knew, that would never be revealed to men, or never understood by them even if it could be revealed. Something that was communicated between a married woman and a woman about to be married.

What was the message? *Men, what can we do with them? What can we do with the big, helpless, sweet things?* Maybe that was the message. Maybe that was the message that was passed between fortunate women. And what was passed between unfortunate women—Lindsey shuddered to think.

Eric Coffman stood up and embraced Mother and shook Lindsey's hand. Coffman's beard and his waistline were as thick as ever, but the beard was starting to show signs of gray. He led Mother and Lindsey to the couch and offered them a round of drinks; Miriam disappeared from the room and returned, preceded by her daughters. Sarah carried a tray of hors d'oeuvres; Rebecca, little plates and napkins. Miriam stood beaming behind the girls as they set their cargo on the table in front of the couch.

Lindsey shot a look at Eric Coffman. The two men had met in what was at first an adversarial relationship, Lindsey representing International Surety, Coffman acting as attorney for a disgruntled beneficiary. After the case was settled Lindsey and Coffman had become acquaintances, then friends, and Coffman had become Lindsey's personal attorney as well.

Coffman knew about Marvia and Willie Fergus. He was the first person—to this moment, the only person—Lindsey had told about Marvia's decision. He'd offered a sympathetic shoulder for Lindsey to cry on, had offered to take him out and get him good and drunk if that would help, but Lindsey had turned down the invitation.

The talk was mainly of Mother's impending marriage to Gordon Sloane. Sloane was spending the evening with his own, grown son and daughter. They would meet in the morning. The wedding would take place in the garden at Sloane's married daughter's house.

Coffman avoided mentioning Marvia during the meal, and he had obviously coached Miriam to do the same. But when Miriam left the table to fetch the main course from her kitchen, Rebecca asked, "Why didn't Jamie come along? We thought he was coming along. Didn't we, Sarah?"

"We were going to show him our new Nintendo cartridges," Sarah said.

Eric Coffman caught Lindsey's eye. This time it was male telepathy rather than female, telepathy augmented by an almost-subliminal shrug of Coffman's massive shoulders.

Lindsey telepathed back, *It's all right, it's nobody's fault.* Aloud he said, "Jamie is with his grandmom tonight."

"Where's his mom?" Rebecca demanded. "Where's Ms. Plum?"

Lindsey said, "She couldn't come tonight. You know, she's a police officer. They can't always make their own schedules."

Rebecca and Sarah seemed to accept that.

Eric Coffman said to Mother, "Bart tells me you're going to honeymoon in Hawaii."

Mother picked up on that and began describing her honeymoon plans. She sounded as happy as a bride.

Miriam Coffman reappeared.

The evening went on.

Driving home to Walnut Creek, Lindsey didn't play another cassette. He turned on the radio, low, to a classical station and ignored the music.

Apparently, Mother hadn't picked up on the byplay about Marvia, or maybe she knew more than she seemed to know, and chose to keep her own counsel. When they got back to Walnut Creek, Mother asked Lindsey to drive once around the block, just for a quiet look.

"You know," she said, "I've lived in this neighborhood for forty years. We moved here when you were a tiny baby. Just you and I, Hobo. I never thought of leaving Laurel Drive."

He pulled into their driveway and helped Mother from the car. She stood in front of the house, looking at it in the pale light of the night. "It's like the end of my life," she said.

"No, Mother. Don't—it isn't."

She smiled and reached up to pat his cheek, something she'd done ten thousand times in the past.

"I'm not sad. Only a little, anyway. I'm starting a new life, I know."

"Yes, you are."

They went inside the house and she made hot chocolate for them both, even though neither felt the need for it after Miriam Coffman's generous dinner. But it gave them an excuse to stay up and to stay in each other's company a while longer. When they'd finished the chocolate, Mother pressed her cheek to Lindsey's and held him before she went to bed. He stayed up and washed out their cups and saucers a few times, then turned on the TV, then turned it off again, then sat in the living room with the lights turned off for a while, then went to bed.

THE WEDDING WAS flawless. Credit Sloane for that. The groom's daughter and her husband lived in a huge new house in Danville, surrounded by millionaire athletes and successful investors. The garden was filled with early-blooming roses (or maybe they'd been imported for the day). A rose-covered arbor had been decorated for the wedding party to stand beneath during the ceremony.

The groom's best man was his son. Mother had asked Lindsey to give her away. "Isn't it a funny custom, Hobo—you'd think men owned women. How can anybody give someone else away?"

But he said he'd be happy to do it, if that was what she wanted.

The whole Coffman family was present, and Mrs. Hernandez, Mother's onetime baby-sitter from the bad days when she'd wandered the corridors of time searching forlornly for the door into the past. Joanie Schorr, no longer little Joanie Schorr but a beautiful young premed student, kissed Lindsey's mother and cried a little.

Lindsey was astonished when he met the officiating clergyman. He wore a blue suit and a solid maroon necktie and a white yarmulke. He was an old friend of Miriam and Eric Coffman's. He referred to the groom as Gershon ben Moishe, explaining that Gordon Sloane, né Slonimsky, had asked him to use his Hebrew name for the wedding ceremony.

You learn something every day. Lindsey had never been to a Jewish wedding before, and would never have dreamed that when the day came, it would be his mother's.

After the ceremony Lindsey stood chatting with Mrs. Hernandez, a glass of champagne in one hand and a finger sandwich in the other. He felt a tap on the shoulder and whirled around, slopping a little champagne on the well-tended lawn.

"Hoholindo!"

Nobody had called him Hoholindo since junior high.

The woman was as tall as he was, big-boned, with curly hair that might have been platinum blonde or premature white. She wore a picture hat straight out of an Alice Faye movie, and a flowered chiffon dress that showed off an attractively Junoesque figure. Her makeup was also done in the 1940s style—dark red lipstick, mascara, and rouge.

Lindsey blinked.

"Don't you remember me?" The woman's voice was familiar, and once he heard it he did remember her.

"Artie? Artemis Janson?"

"That's right. It's been a few other things over the years, but it's Janson again now. I'm a friend of Gordon Slonimsky's. I heard he was getting hitched again but I never imagined the blushing bride was your mama. She must have got over her— well, she looks wonderful, Lindo."

Lindsey turned back to introduce Artemis to Mrs. Hernandez, but Mrs. Hernandez had moved off into the crowd. To Artemis Janson, Lindsey said, "I can't remember the last time I saw you. It must have been—"

"I remember it." Artemis lifted the champagne glass from Lindsey's hand. "You don't mind, do you?" She drank part of the champagne, then returned the glass to him.

"I remember it very well. Golden Gate Park. Summer of 1967. Summer of Love."

Lindsey found himself blushing.

"We were both fourteen, and we hitchhiked into the city and went to a free concert in the park. The Jefferson Airplane was playing. Everybody was smoking dope and that guru type in the Mr. Natural robe offered us a joint. Don't tell me you don't remember that."

She borrowed his glass and finished the champagne.

"Don't go away." She took a half-dozen long strides, put the empty glass down on a linen-covered serving table, and returned with two full ones.

Lindsey said, "I guess I remember." In fact, he remembered very well.

"Where did you go? One minute we were turning on and the

Airplane was playing and everything was just amazing and wonderful, and when I looked around you were gone."

Lindsey looked around for someplace to dispose of the remains of his finger sandwich. The simplest thing was just to pop it in his mouth and swallow it so he did.

"I went home to Walnut Creek. The big question, Artie, was, Where did *you* go? You didn't come back to Walnut Creek then and nobody saw you for six months and when you did come back you'd never tell anybody what you'd been doing."

She tilted her head back so the sun warmed her face. She said, "I'll tell you all about it sometime. I'm just so happy that we met again. Lindo, do you still live in that little house on Laurel Drive? I haven't set foot in Walnut Creek in twenty years. I've been all over, lived in Europe for a while, then in Japan, got married two or three times. You see that beautiful creature over there?"

She indicated a slim young woman in a bright orange dress that came to the top of her thighs. Two men were competing for her attention.

"My daughter. By my second husband. What a handful she is! But what have you been up to? Are you married? What do you think of your mother tying the knot again at her age?"

Lindsey started to explain but Artemis Janson took him by the wrist and led him away from the milling crowd.

"We have so much catching up to do! Finding you after all these years—I'm not going to let go of you again."

HE SLEPT THAT night in the Laurel Drive house, the first time in his life that he had slept there alone, without at least expecting to see Mother in the morning. The house was silent. He would fall asleep, wake up, prowl around for a while, then climb back into bed.

He put on his robe and slippers and stood on the walkway, feeling like Dick York or Robert Young. He almost wished that a Mercedes would pull around the corner from Mountain View Boulevard or Hawthorne Drive and the muzzle of an assault weapon would poke from its window.

It didn't happen.

* * *

CALIFORNIA HAD BEEN having an early spring, but Colorado caught the brunt of a late-winter blizzard. As the 737 approached Denver, Lindsey wondered why the pilot had not been ordered to turn back, but somehow the jet came out of the clouds onto an icy and windblown Denver International Airport. It was Lindsey's first look at the new airport, but on a day like this it didn't look any different from the old Stapleton.

Walking through the lobby, he caught sight of Cletus Berry and waved to his onetime roommate and SPUDS colleague. They shared a cab into town and picked up their reservations at the Embassy Suites on Curtis Street. Lindsey recognized half a dozen former classmates. It looked as if his class of SPUDS trainees had fared better than most—or maybe the fabled high rate of attrition among SPUDS operatives was a legend, carefully fostered by Desmond Richelieu to keep his troops on their toes.

Lindsey and Berry shared a suite, as they had shared a room during SPUDS training. The refresher course was scheduled to start Tuesday morning and run for four days. Lindsey phoned the desk and asked if Aurora Delano or Gina Rossellini had checked in yet. Both of them had, and Lindsey invited them to join Berry and himself for dinner.

None of them knew Denver well, but Lindsey had consulted a guidebook and settled on an establishment called Morton's of Chicago. He was in a Chicago mood, he decided, after his adventures in the Vansittart case. And he loved the guidebook's description of Morton's: "a tavern for the wealthy."

The prices were not as breathtaking as they might have been, and this trip was on expenses, anyway. SPUDS agents got the toughest cases in International Surety. They were expected to save the company large sums of money, and in exchange, the company could afford to feed them well.

Rossellini, Berry, and Delano had all helped Lindsey solve the Vansittart mystery. All three stood to share in Lindsey's glory, if only in a small way, for having saved International Surety $1,000,000. All had access to KlameNet/Plus and knew what the KNP file on Vansittart contained.

Lindsey filled them in, in more detail, on the varied aspects of the case. He asked Berry about Lovisi, the publisher.

A grin spread across Berry's face. "He's one character, Bart, I'll tell you that. I went to his place out in Brooklyn, and he showed me his collection of paperbacks. You wouldn't believe what the man has."

"Yes, I would. If it's anything like Scotty Anderson's collection in California."

"Well." Berry nodded. He lifted his glass. They'd shared a couple of rounds of cocktails before ordering dinner, and two good zinfandels, a red and a white, with the meal. Everybody was eating healthier these days: chicken instead of steak, fish instead of chicken, veggies instead of fish. At this rate, *Homo sap.* was going to ease himself off the top of the food chain in a few more years.

Neither Gina Rossellini nor Aurora Delano had ever encountered a serious case of the collecting bug. They were suitably fascinated by Berry's description of Lovisi and Lindsey's description of Anderson. The two collectors were different physical types and had different personalities, but they were brothers beneath the skin. Lindsey wondered what the famous Lovisi would say when he saw Anderson's photos of the Paige paperbacks, and when he learned that Anderson now owned a complete set of the books.

Over coffee, Aurora Delano told Lindsey that she was keeping up with the Bruninskis. "It's really sad." She gazed into her cup. "That woman stayed with her husband all these years—more than forty years, closer to fifty now—living like fugitives, poor as church mice. Now she's a millionaire, and what good does it do her? She lies in bed all day." She shuddered. "I think I'd rather be dead."

She shook like a dog coming out of a stream. "Let's talk about something else. The bad guy—what's his name, ben Zinowicz—he's back in California, right?"

Lindsey was able to smile with some satisfaction. "He is indeed. And it's going to be a long time before he sees the outside of a jail cell. *If* he ever does. The only question is who gets his services: San Quentin prison or the U.S. Attorney's office. He killed O'Farrell—not much question about that. Is it worth cutting a deal with ben Zinowicz to hang the Cookes? Or will the Cookes turn on ben Zinowicz and hope to make a deal themselves?"

He picked an after-dinner mint off a silver tray and slowly unwrapped it. Something cold and sad inside him thought, Jamie would like this.

Aurora Delano read his mind.

"Are you still with Marvia, Bart? She's wonderful, I just loved her when you were down in Louisiana together. She was terrific on that trip out to Reserve, I don't think anybody could have got the info that she did."

Lindsey bit his lower lip. "We're not together anymore."

"Oh, I'm so sorry." Aurora put her hand on the back of Lindsey's wrist. "I hope nothing—I mean, did you break up? It wasn't an illness or—or, police work is dangerous, I know."

"Nothing like that." Lindsey looked at his wristwatch. "You know, there's that little welcoming ceremony in the morning, Ducky Richelieu likes people to arrive on time, with a clean pressed suit and a bright fresh grin."

Cletus Berry called for the check. The waiter was not going to like dividing it four ways, but he was going to figure it out—that was for certain.

Back at the Embassy Suites, Cletus Berry headed straight for the elevator. Gina Rossellini smiled at Lindsey. "You're right, Bart, it is late, but I'm just so jangled up, airplanes do that to me. What say to a nightcap?"

Aurora Delano was standing a few feet away. Gina said, "You're included, too, Aurora. Of course."

Aurora turned angrily and walked to the elevator.

LINDSEY DID ALL right during the days. It was the nights that were hard to get through. After Monday night's celebration at Morton's there were working dinners every evening, and informal sessions afterward. The Director was there every day and every evening, and he wanted to have a quiet one-on-one chat with each of his operatives.

Cletus Berry's turn came Tuesday night. There seemed to be no pattern to the sequence of meetings. You just went when the Director called. Richelieu had got his pre–International Surety training in the FBI during the last years of the J. Edgar Hoover regime. Sometimes he seemed to think he was Hoover Redivivus.

Lindsey was sitting at a desk in the Embassy Suites, preparing for Wednesday's seminars, when Berry returned from his meeting with Richelieu. Lindsey looked up at his roommate.

"Well?"

"The Director is one strange man—you know that, Bart?"

Lindsey grinned. "I know it."

"He wanted to know what I thought of the mayor, what I thought of the governor, whether I thought the Bronx would ever become a desirable site for a major real estate development, and what I thought of—"

Lindsey raised his eyebrows, waiting.

"—Hobart Lindsey."

Lindsey lowered his pencil and closed the loose-leaf binder holding the conference syllabus. "You want me to say pretty please, you want to tell me what you told him?"

"I told him that the mayor was doing a better job than I expected, the governor was caught between Washington, Albany, and New York City and there was no way he could win, and the Bronx would surely recover someday, but we'd all be dead and gone before that day ever arrived."

He tossed a notebook on his bed, hung his suit coat in the closet, and loosened his tie.

Lindsey said, "I think I'll watch the headlines and hit the sack."

Berry sighed. "Okay, I couldn't resist the temptation. What the hell should I tell the Director? You're one odd duck, Bart. You wander into the God-damnedest cases I've ever heard of, not just one or two of them but a whole parade of the wacko things. Every time I see your name on KNP, I know it's going to be something odd. Every time I get a message from you I know it's going to be a bizarre case."

He pulled his necktie from beneath his collar and smoothed a wrinkle from it before he hung it in the closet. "But they're always interesting, and you always manage to solve them and save the company big bucks. Ducky Richelieu calls you his private Sherlock Holmes. I guess he's right."

Lindsey rubbed the bridge of his nose between thumb and forefinger. His eyes were tired. He wondered if he was going to need glasses soon.

"I don't always save the company money. Did you see the final report on the settlement we had to make on that B-17 a few years ago? Everyone wanted money from us, even the navy. And they collected, too."

"Okay. I remember that case. I heard a lot about it. How could I help it, you made all the papers and the TV shows and the newsmags. You were the one who talked that guy into trying to land on the aircraft carrier. Otherwise the little boy would have died with him. You were a hero."

"Some hero." Lindsey nodded.

"Anyway, Ducky isn't quite sure what to make of you. I think he might offer you a job as his personal troubleshooter. You're too dangerous to have running around loose, and you're too valuable to dump. I think he wants to keep you around on a short chain."

Berry was pacing back and forth on the thick carpet. Now he halted, standing over Lindsey. "What will you tell him? If he offers that, what will you tell him?"

Lindsey stood up and faced Berry. "I don't have the remotest idea what I'll tell him." He snorted. "And you can quote me on that."

LINDSEY'S MEETING WITH Richelieu came Wednesday night after a working dinner and a short pep talk by a faceless functionary from corporate staff. Richelieu had set up a temporary office at the Embassy Suites—he didn't want people orbiting between the conference and his permanent office overlooking Cherry Creek.

Richelieu's makeshift headquarters was an ordinary hotel room, the bed removed and replaced by living-room furniture.

Room service provided coffee and brandy. Richelieu acted the expansive host.

"You're a star again," he greeted Lindsey.

"Do I get a private trailer?"

Richelieu laughed. "Very good. I don't think so. How are you doing at the conference? Three days down, one to go. Are we giving you useful stuff? Any complaints? Anything you need that you're not getting?"

Lindsey shook his head. "It's good info. The legal types had a lot to say. And the KNP enhancement program looks good. Pretty soon we'll all be able to sit at our computers and never leave the house. Sounds like a sci-fi writer's dreamworld."

Richelieu exhaled. "I don't think so." He stood up, coffee cup in hand. He added some brandy to his cup, held the bottle toward Lindsey, and poured dark amber liqueur into the coffee.

"I've been watching you, Lindsey. You're racking up quite a record. This latest save was really something. Your name has been mentioned in high places, spoken trippingly on the tongues of the high and the mighty." Richelieu rolled his eyeballs heavenward. Behind his glinting, gold-rimmed glasses they looked like shimmering marbles.

"So we have to ask, What are we going to do with you?"

Lindsey was ready for that, thanks to Cletus Berry. "What do you want to do, Mr. Richelieu?"

Richelieu had lowered the brandy bottle. Now he raised his coffee cup and sipped. "Lindsey, do you like Denver?"

"Not especially."

"How would you like to work out of my office, report directly to me and only to me?"

"I like my work now."

Richelieu put his cup down, hard. "You don't lick anybody's boots, do you, Lindsey?"

"No, I don't."

"Are you turning down my offer?"

"I haven't heard one."

Richelieu focused on Lindsey's face. "There's hardly a soul in this company who doesn't tremble at the sound of my name—did you know that? And you act as if you just don't care." He paused, but Lindsey did not reply. "That's why you scare me, Lindsey. It's also why I like you."

Lindsey conceded a small smile. "Thanks."

"All right. Meeting over. I'll see you at the seminar tomorrow."

Lindsey stood up. He hadn't touched his coffee since Richelieu added the brandy to it.

Richelieu tapped Lindsey's coffee cup with a carefully manicured fingernail. "You're not that worried, are you? That I'd doctor your coffee?"

Lindsey said, "Of course you wouldn't," shook Richelieu's hand, and returned to his room and watched headlines before going to bed.

Thursday was another day of lectures and exercises. More KNP enhancements were coming down the road. Corporate staff was counting on SPUDS to act as the vanguard for cutting-edge corporate technology. Lindsey felt as if a heavyweight was pounding rhythmically at his head, first a left to the right ear, then a right to the left ear, then a left to the right ear. . . .

That night the TV news showed a well-dressed Roger St. John Cooke and Cynthia Cooke being taken into custody by federal agents. The announcer explained that they were being charged with multiple charges of conspiracy, fraud, and tax evasion. The Cookes had nothing to say, but their lawyer, decked out in his thousand-dollar hand-tailored suit and hundred-dollar silk tie, insisted that his clients were totally innocent of any wrongdoing, save decades of service to the artistic community of America. The government had no case whatsoever, and the Cookes would be fully vindicated when the facts were known.

There was no mention of Albert Crocker Vansittart, John O'Farrell, or Nathan ben Zinowicz.

Marge Tillotson appeared briefly, told a reporter that she would present her case fully at the appropriate time, and asked to be excused.

Cletus Berry stood behind Lindsey's easy chair, watching the news broadcast. "Those friends of yours, Hobart?"

Lindsey said, "I know them. They aren't my friends."

* * *

FRIDAY WAS THE last day of the seminar. A group of SPUDS agents assembled at the Palace Arms a couple of hours after the last session. There was no graduation ceremony this time. There were no valedictory speeches or pep talks from corporate chieftains. Just an exchange of hopes and plans, a series of good-byes and perfunctory promises to keep in touch.

Leaving the restaurant, Gina Rossellini invited Lindsey to her room for a nightcap. She'd lucked out with the arrangements, or maybe she knew somebody in the assistant manager's office. At any rate, her quarters at the Embassy Suites included a fireplace and a bottle of brandy and even a CD player.

The music might have been furnished by the management but more likely, Lindsey surmised, Gina had brought it with her from Chicago. Her taste ran to lush orchestrations of familiar tunes that he could almost name. But not quite.

Her roommate, if she had one, was nowhere in evidence. He wondered for a moment where she was, then he wondered if Cletus Berry was worried about him. He decided that Berry wouldn't give a damn, and he didn't give a damn about Gina Rossellini's roommate.

The fire crackled, the brandy was splendid, and outside the Embassy Suites, a few snowflakes were drifting from sky to street.

Gina had worn something in midnight blue to dinner, with a broad V-neck that bared her generous bosom. Her raven hair swept over one shoulder and onto her chest. Lindsey realized that his first glimpse of her in Chicago, his first take on her, had been unfair. She was no young girl, and she had taken her share of life's hard knocks; that much was obvious.

But she was a survivor. She was the kind to get back up when life knocked her down, and here in a hotel room a thousand miles from either of their homes, she was an attractive woman.

"Bart?"

She touched Lindsey's hand. "Are you all right?"

He blinked. "I'm sorry. I was just—I guess I'm a little tired, that's all. Did you ask something?"

"I asked about your plans. Not the stuff everybody was bull-shitting about at the restaurant. This is just the two of us. What are you going to do?"

He raised his brandy snifter and held it before his eyes, gazing through the golden liquid at the fire. "My job," he said.

They were seated side by side on a sofa. Gina leaned toward him and brushed the side of his neck with her fingers. "Come on, Lindsey, you're too old to play coy. You've been dumped. What are you going to do?"

He looked into his brandy snifter for an answer but he couldn't see one there. Maybe he could find it in a sip of brandy. He tried, but that didn't work either.

"You're headed out of here in the morning, back to Pecan Patch, California, right?" Gina was close to Lindsey and he was finding the sensation pleasant. He blinked at the carpet in front of the couch and saw that she'd kicked off her shoes. He liked the sight of her feet.

"Walnut Creek," he corrected.

"You say po-tay-to, I say po-tah-to."

He grinned. "Sorry. That was deliberate, wasn't it?"

"And I'm headed back to Chicago. And here we are at a corporate conference. It's classic, isn't it?"

She stood up and slipped one arm out of her blouse, then the other. Lindsey watched her silhouette moving between him and the fireplace. The music could have been less corny, but what the hell, it wasn't *that* bad.

She said, "If you don't start doing something, I'm going to cry for help."

He said, "Promise you'll still respect me in the morning."

BUT IN THE morning, he made a call to Desmond Richelieu's private number. He got the Director, sounding wide awake and chipper as ever.

Lindsey said, "I'll take it."

The Director said, "Go home and start packing. Call Mrs. Blomquist for details."

Richelieu hung up.

A few hours later, Lindsey arrived at his house on Laurel Drive. Mother and Gordon Sloane were in Hawaii, and Joanie Schorr had kindly brought in a week's worth of mail and put it on the dining room table.

Before he looked at the mail, he checked the telephone answering machine. There were several messages from Marge Tillotson at the U.S. Attorney's office. He'd have to follow up on the Cookes and ben Zinowicz, but already the Vansittart case seemed like part of a life that he'd lived on another planet.

There was a message from Artie Janson, inviting him to call her and catch up on their lives. There was even a message from Mother and Gordon Sloane, having a grand time in Hawaii and hoping to see him when they got home.

Nothing that couldn't wait.

The mail consisted of an assortment of bills and ads and a single personal item. It came in a square envelope with a Reno postmark. Lindsey tried to tear it open, but his fingers were suddenly stiff and numb.

He got a kitchen knife instead, and slit the envelope. And read exactly what he expected and exactly what he feared. A printed announcement of the marriage of Willie Fergus and Marvia Plum Wilkerson. He turned the announcement over and saw a hand-written message in greenish-blue ink. It was from Marvia, and it said that she was sorry she'd hurt him, and she would love him forever, and hoped that someday they could be friends.

He climbed the stairs to his room. The hallway leading to his room was covered with heavy-napped, gray-patterned carpeting that had been there as long as Lindsey could remember. His bedroom door was open, and the three-way bedside lamp was turned to its brightest level.

A man and a woman sat on the bed, their feet stretched before them, their backs supported by the headboard. It was a single bed, and there was no room to spare.

They were both fully clothed.

For a moment Lindsey stood in shock. Briefly he wondered who they were, then recognized them, then wondered what they were doing in his bed, then realized that their clothing was soaked with blood and that they were dead.

He realized that the water was running in his bathroom.

He saw a weapon lying on the bed near the woman's feet. It was a revolver. He couldn't tell its caliber.

The water ceased running in the bathroom. Lindsey turned toward the bathroom. The door opened, and he saw Nathan ben Zinowicz.

Lindsey and ben Zinowicz dived simultaneously toward the bed, collided, and wrestled for the revolver. But ben Zinowicz had got his hand around its carved wooden grip and broke away from Lindsey's grasp. The two men clambered to their feet and stood staring at each other.

The two bodies on Lindsey's bed had fallen sideways, knocked aside by the violence of Lindsey and ben Zinowicz's struggle. Cynthia Cooke lay on the carpet, on her back, staring at the ceiling with dead eyes. Roger St. John Cooke lay facedown, half on, half off the bed, his arms stretched toward his wife as if pursuing her in an amorous mock contest.

Lindsey looked at Nathan ben Zinowicz. Ben Zinowicz's shirt was soaked with water, but the pink bloodstains were still clearly visible. His face and hands were wet as if Lindsey's arrival had interrupted him in the midst of washing, and there was even a red streak in ben Zinowicz's beard. He must have left his glasses on the kitchen sink, but he could see Lindsey well enough without them to keep the gun pointed at him.

"You killed them," Lindsey said.

Ben Zinowicz grunted.

"I'm going to call the police." Lindsey started toward the bedside telephone.

"Don't. I'll kill you."

"Why did you do it? How did you get in? The door was locked. I—"

"You're really stupid. You didn't lock the back door. Not that it matters. We could have got in, one way or another. If you'd been home, Roger and Cynthia would simply have rung the doorbell, and you'd have let them in."

"But—" Lindsey raised a hand to his forehead. Ben Zinowicz jerked the revolver upward, then relaxed.

"No sudden moves."

"What are you going to do?" Lindsey felt strange. He felt as if he'd been stretched, as if his consciousness were being pulled through the top of his head. He was afraid that he was going to pass out and that ben Zinowicz would kill him while he lay unconscious on his own bedroom floor. "Why did you come here?" he asked. "How did you get out of jail?"

"I got a card from Community Chest."

Lindsey blinked. First he didn't know what ben Zinowicz was talking about. Then he did know, but he had no idea how to respond.

"They were going to double-cross me." Ben Zinowicz gestured toward the Cokes.

"And so they're dead?"

"Dead. Dead and dead and it is time to redeem the unread vision in the higher dream while jeweled unicorns draw the gilded hearse."

"I don't understand."

"You wouldn't."

"They got you out of—you were in Santa Rita and they got out and—I don't understand."

There was something new and insane in ben Zinowicz's eyes, or maybe it had been there all along and Lindsey had never seen those eyes without lenses in front of them.

"I'm finished," ben Zinowicz said. "I thought they were my friends. I thought they were going to get me out of the country. That way I wouldn't tattle on them and I'd be safe and have a bundle of money to live on, and they could blame everything on me and get away free. They wouldn't get the insurance money—it's too late for that—but they would still have the World Fund and their collections and their houses."

"Why did you come here?"

Ben Zinowicz was becoming animated. That might be good. That might offer a break for Lindsey. But it might be bad. The man might lose control and start shooting. How many bullets did the revolver hold? How many bullets had ben Zinowicz fired into Roger and Cynthia?

"That was my idea. They didn't know I had a gun. I didn't when I came out of Santa Rita. They signed for me. They vouched for me. Somebody's going to be awfully embarrassed. They shouldn't have let me out. Davy Jones is going to be pissed. It'll be like pissing in the ocean, but he'll be pissed."

Ben Zinowicz whirled around, turned 360 degrees, and pointed the revolver at Lindsey again before Lindsey could react. He held his free hand in the air.

"See this?" A plastic bracelet circled his wrist. "One of those electronic gadgets. Officially, I'm still in custody. What a joke. If I cut this off, it sounds an alarm. If I keep it on, they can check up on me. Why are our two consuls and our praetors all got up in their embroidered scarlet robes? Why are they covered with bracelets and rings? The barbarians are coming today. And such things impress the barbarians."

Lindsey started to say something, but he got only as far as, "I don't—" before ben Ziniowicz interrupted.

"We really came here to kill you, you see. Roger didn't know that. Cynthia didn't know that. Man may escape from rope and gun; / Nay, some have outliv'd the doctor's pill; / Who takes a woman must be undone, / That basilisk is sure to kill." A drop of reddened water fell from the tip of his beard and splashed on the back of the hand holding the revolver. Ben Zinowicz stared at it, then back at Lindsey.

"They had a different plan, did my dear friends." Ben Zinowicz showed his teeth. "They weren't going to send me out of the country, they were going to kill me. That's what they did to John Frederick O'Farrell. You remember John Frederick O'Farrell. He thought he was going to Mexico, or maybe Brazil, with a pile of money. Death and sorrow were the companions on his journey, but it wasn't a long one."

"But you were the one who—" Lindsey stopped. What a blunder. That might set ben Zinowicz off. That might—

But it didn't.

Ben Zinowicz said, "You're right, of course. And a horse is a horse, of course, of course. They planned it and I did it, and they thought they could run the same scheme again with me as its victim. Not likely. Not likely. Not likely. Not likely. Not likely. Not likely."

He was nodding and chanting, rocking like a praying Jew.

"But I killed them instead. We learn, as the thread plays out, that we belong less to what flatters us than to what scars. So, freshly turning, as the turn condones, for her I killed the propitiatory bird. Kissing her down, peace to her bitter bones, who taught me the serpent's word, but not the word."

Lindsey said, "What happens then? What happens after you kill me?"

Ben Zinowicz shrugged. He swung the revolver up and pointed it at Lindsey's face, then circled. Lindsey turned slowly on his heel, keeping his face toward ben Zinowicz.

"I'm going to call nine-one-one," Lindsey said.

"I'll kill you first," ben Zinowicz said.

"I'm going to call nine-one-one."

Ben Zinowicz slammed the revolver, side-on, against Lindsey's shoulder. The gun was surprisingly massive.

Lindsey staggered, righted himself, took a step toward the telephone. "Put the gun down. Sit down. I'll get you a glass of water. I'm going to call nine-one-one."

Ben Zinowicz pointed the revolver at Lindsey.

"You're going to kill me anyway. I'm not going to take it lying down."

Ben Zinowicz shook his head sadly. "You almost got it right, didn't you? By accident, of course. Do not go gentle into that good night. Do you know the rest? Rage, rage against the dying of the light, Hobart Lindsey."

Lindsey shook his head. "I don't know what you mean. I'm going to do it now. Kill me or don't kill me, you have to decide." He picked up the telephone, punched three digits on the keypad.

"Well," ben Zinowicz said, "this is the end of a perfect day." He laughed.

Lindsey was startled. It wasn't a sane man's laugh, it was a crazed giggle, a Richard Widmark, Johnny Udo *Kiss of Death* giggle.

Ben Zinowicz said, "Squirt."

Lindsey looked at him over one shoulder as the emergency operator came onto the line.

"Near the end of a journey, too," said ben Zinowicz.

The operator started asking Lindsey questions.

Ben Zinowicz pressed the revolver's muzzle to Lindsey's head. Lindsey ignored it. Ben Zinowicz stepped back. Lindsey turned and watched him. The operator was asking questions and Lindsey was answering them like a man on autopilot. Ben Zinowicz turned the revolver and stared down its barrel very much as Benjamin Bruninski had stared down the barrel of his own revolver in the Barracks Street apartment.

Ben Zinowicz shrugged his shoulders and pulled the trigger.

Author's Note

LIKE ALL BOOKS in the Hobart Lindsey/Marvia Plum series, *The Cover Girl Killer* is a work of fiction and should not be mistaken for one of history or of journalism. However, like the earlier volumes in this series, it is based on modern American history and mass culture, and I would like to point out just which elements in this book are real and which are not.

The Spanish Civil War of 1936–1939 was one of the great tragedies of the twentieth century. Like any war it caused immense suffering, vast devastation, and many thousands of deaths. The exact number will never be known. The casualties included not only the soldiers and civilian people of Spain, but tens of thousands of "volunteers," most of them authentic, the rest forced, from nations throughout Europe, North America, and North Africa.

At the end of the war, Spain was left suffering under a military dictatorship that survived for nearly forty years. The dictator, Francisco Franco, outlived his mentors, Adolf Hitler and Benito Mussolini, as well as his bitter foe, Josef Stalin. Only with Franco's death in 1975 did Spain become a constitutional monarchy whose people enjoy the benefits of free institutions and civil liberties.

It has been suggested that the outcome of the Spanish Civil War matters little, that the resulting regime would have been a brutal dictatorship in any case. Under a Fascist regime or Communist, the people suffer equally. Not everyone agrees with this analysis; certainly my fictitious veteran of the war, Benjamin Bruninski, does not.

The Abraham Lincoln Brigade was very real. My cousin Aaron was a member. He died in Spain. I first heard of Aaron from my grandmother, and for half a century I searched for him, until Milton Wolff, the final commander of the Lincolns, told me of his friendship with Aaron. He told me stories of Aaron's life and of his death, and I am eternally grateful to him.

Esther Miriam Silverstein Blanc was a nurse who served in Spain and, after returning to the United States, in World War II. Despite illness and infirmity, she told me the inspiring story of her wonderful life, and I am equally grateful to her.

Milton Wolff and Esther Blanc provided invaluable material which I used in the creation of Benjamin Bruninski and Maizie Carcowitz, but my characters are nonetheless fictitious and should not be taken as literal representations of Milton Wolff or Esther Blanc.

Benjamin Bruninski's statements about the House Un-American Activities Committee, and about the phenomenon of McCarthyism, are of course the fictitious words of a fictitious character. They should not be mistaken for statements by the author. However, I would suggest that interested readers pursue the history of both HUAC and Senator Joseph R. McCarthy, and the youthful involvement of both Richard Nixon and Robert Kennedy with these early players in the drama of the Cold War. It was the now-forgotten Charles Dudley Warner who said, "Politics make strange bedfellows," as long ago as 1870. He was a better prophet than he knew.

It was on February 20, 1950, that the self-styled Tailgunner Joe McCarthy made his most famous statement: "I have in my hand fifty-seven cases of individuals who would appear to be either card-carrying members or certainly loyal to the Communist Party, but who nevertheless are still helping to shape our foreign policy. . . . " The decent men and women whose careers, and in some cases whose very lives, were destroyed by HUAC and McCarthy are a reproach to those who remember, and even more so to those who have forgotten.

The development of paperback publishing in the United States and other countries is a fascinating story all its own, and the collectors who track down forty- and fifty-year-old "sleaze digests" and "good girl art" are not only amusing themselves with an obscure and eccentric habit—they are helping to preserve a body of popular culture which might otherwise have been lost to history.

Paige Publications is regrettably a figment of my imagination, as are all of its staff, authors, editors, artists, and the eight (or nine) titles that Paige published in 1952 and 1953. With one exception, the excerpts that appear in *The Cover Girl Killer* are all that exist of those nine (or eight) books. The exception is *Death in the Ditch*, by Del Marston. By some miracle or manifestation of ectoplasmic materialization or automatic writing, that book *has* come into being. I have held a copy in my hands; the citations in *The Cover Girl Killer* do come from Marston's hardboiled saga; and I commend any reader whose diligent efforts lead him or her to a copy of this little literary gem.

I would like to thank those who assisted me in my research for *The Cover Girl Killer*. These include my dear friend, Howard Browne, formerly of Ziff-Davis Publications, Chicago; Captain Kevin Roach of the good ship *Tails to Tahoe*, the *real* Captain Kevin MacKenzie and the *real* craft *Tahoe Tailflipper*; Mr. Ira Steingroot for information on the Hebrew calendar and funerary customs; Ms. Phyllis Eisenstein for information about the cemetaries of Chicago; Mr. Jack Leavitt, esq., for information on criminal jurisdictions and procedure; Mr. Gary Lovisi for good sportsmanship and purely for being himself. And, last but not least, Mr. Art Scott, paperback collector and scholar *par excellence*, who is not exactly Scotty Anderson, but who lent a great deal of himself to that character.

—Richard A. Lupoff